AN EYE FOR AN EYE

Gordon Anthony

Copyright © 2012 Gordon Anthony
All rights reserved.
ISBN: 9781980215684
First published in e-book format 2012 by Gordon Anthony using Kindle Direct Publishing

Note on the use of Names

Very few Pictish names have come down to us because the Picts left no written records of their own. Most of what we know of them comes from Roman, English or Irish sources. Names are therefore rare and, when they are recorded, vary considerably depending on the source. One of the principal characters in this story is named Bridei, but that name is also variously recorded as Brude, Bruide, Breidei and Bred. Some personal names, apparently Pictish, were also recorded as being the names of people who were not Picts but were more probably Scots or Britons.

The main problems I faced were deciding which names to use for people who are known historically, and which names to use for places. For example, Colum Cille (or Colm Cille or Calum Cille) is better known to most people as St. Columba. In cases like this I had to decide which variant of the name I should use. Ultimately, the decisions regarding 'real' characters were quite arbitrary. As for the characters who are entirely fictional, the names are simply labels to identify them, so I hope that readers will not be too offended by any lack of consistency as to whether the versions I have used are Pictish, Scots Gaelic or Irish Gaelic.

As for place names, most of the names that the Picts themselves used are not known and the old names that are recorded are usually Scots or Irish Gaelic versions. I generally used the Scots Gaelic versions because I felt that these fitted better with the feel of the story. The following list is my interpretation of where the various places mentioned in the story were situated. This should help clarify the approximate geography that I had in mind but readers may wish to skip straight to the story and refer back to this list if necessary.

Alt Clud - General name for Strathclyde, the territory of the Britons (sometimes referred to as the Strathclyde Welsh). Alt

Clud also refers specifically to Dumbarton Rock, the principal fortress of Strathclyde.

Am Broch - Burghead, Moray.

Cait - Caithness and Sutherland.

Cala na Creige - Stonehaven, on the east coast of Scotland.

Circinn - The region around, and incorporating, Angus, the area north of the River Tay.

Cluaidh - River Clyde.

Dal Riata - Argyll and the west of Scotland although Dal Riata technically refers to the people, not to the territory they inhabited.

Dun Add - Dunadd hillfort, near Lochgilphead.

Dun Eidyn - Edinburgh, specifically the Castle Rock but also incorporating the settlement around it.

Dun Foither - Dunnottar, near Stonehaven.

Dun Nechtan - Dunachton, near Loch Insh.

Dundurn - Dundurn Hill, near St Fillans.

Eilginn - Elgin, Morayshire.

Eireann - River Earn.

Fib - The region around, and incorporating, Fife, the area between the rivers Forth and Tay.

Fidach- The region around, and including Strathearn.

Foirthe - River Forth.

Fortriu - The northern Pictish Kingdom, now believed to have been centred on Moray and Aberdeenshire in north-east Scotland.

Fotla - The region around, and incorporating Atholl.

Gododdin - The eastern part of modern Scotland lying south of the Forth-Clyde line, incorporating modern Lothians and the Borders.

Inbhir Nis - Inverness.

Linne Foirthe - the Firth of Forth.

Manaw – The region in central Scotland roughly equivalent to modern Clackmannanshire. Sometimes combined with Gododdin as Manaw-Gododdin, reflecting the widest extent of the influence of the rulers of Gododdin.

Mercia - An Anglo-Saxon kingdom based in central England. At its greatest extent it bordered Wales to the west, Northumbria to the north and east, and stretched south as far as the River Thames.

Monadh Feith - Monifieth, Angus.

Northumbria - The old kingdom of Northumbria fluctuated in size and influence over the years but can generally be taken to mean the east of modern England north of the Humber, stretching to the Scottish Borders. Northumbria incorporated the earlier kingdoms of Bernicia and Deira. At its greatest extent, achieved around the time of this story under the kings Oswiu and his successor Ecgfrith, it incorporated most of south-eastern Scotland, certainly as far as the Forth, and perhaps much further north. In the west of England, Northumbria's influence extended as far as the River Mersey.

Obar Chuirnidh - Abercorn, West Lothian.

Orcades - The Orkney Islands.

Peairt - Perth, central Scotland.

Sgain - Scone, Perthshire, believed to be a Pictish royal centre and, later, the place where the kings of Scotland were crowned.

Spe - River Spey.

Sruighlea - Stirling, central Scotland, specifically the Castle Rock.

Streonshal - Whitby, North Yorkshire

Tatha - River Tay.

Prologue

In the Year of Our Lord Six Hundred and Seventy One, I prayed like I had never prayed before, beseeching God to save my family and to drive away the evil Northumbrians. God did not answer me that day and the evil deeds of the Angles went unpunished, leaving me alone in my misery. I rarely prayed after that dreadful day, for I believed that my prayers would be ignored.

Of course, Brother Bleddyn disagreed. When I told him how I had lost my faith because God had not answered my prayers, he said that I should not be so swift to stop believing. He told me that the Lord had sent him to me, to be my guide and my teacher and that, in time, and with his help, I would gain my revenge on the men who had done such wrong to my friends and family. Brother Bleddyn was never one for consoling those who wept at injustice or cried out that the Lord had forsaken them. Nor was he one of those monks who preached turning the other cheek, like many I have met. Bleddyn was of the old school, taught by the Ionian Church; he believed in an eye for an eye and a tooth for a tooth. But he also believed in patience and would often tell me that I would have to wait if I was to exact vengeance properly.

"If you rush in," he said to me one day, "you will only get yourself killed. A boy like you cannot fight grown men. When you are older, the time will be right."

"I don't want to wait," I declared angrily.

Bleddyn slapped my face, his palm stinging my cheek. "If you won't listen to good advice, I will not help you," he snapped.

I rubbed my cheek. His blow had hurt me enough to bring tears to my eyes, so I decided that there would be no profit in offering him the other cheek. Bleddyn was not one for giving second chances. Did I mention that he was of the old school? Sometimes I think he was of his own school.

And I was his only pupil.

In later years, he tried to tell me that everything had come to pass as God had intended, and that what happened on that awful day was part of some great plan. He may be right. When I look back, I know that I would have become a simple farmer, just like my father and his father before him. Instead, I have led a life of danger and excitement; I have dined with Kings and nobles, I have seen great events unfold and I have become a wealthy man.

Perhaps Bleddyn is correct, but I cannot help thinking that the price was too high. For me, the events that followed changed me, and if I am honest, those changes were not always for the best. Worst of all, though, many other people paid a far higher price. Too many for the peace of my soul.

But we cannot change what has passed and, as Bleddyn has so often told me, I was not responsible for the beginning of the long war.

I was, though, responsible for its ending.

Chapter 1

The sun had been shining that morning, the day I lost my family and found Bleddyn. The harvest was in, the pigs, goats, sheep and cattle were all fat and the crops of fruit and vegetables had been as good as we could have hoped for. I remember that there was scarcely any breeze that day and the insects were buzzing through the air, swarming round the cows who stolidly ignored them, except for flicking their tails and ears to ward off the more persistent pests.

It was a wonderful morning and I wanted to go fishing in the river. I was up early, just after sunrise, hunting through the clutter for my net, line and hooks but mother said, "You must stay here, Bili. I will need your help today."

"Why?" I demanded.

She did not answer. She looked troubled and on edge, ready to scold anyone who argued, so I slipped outside to find my father, thinking to persuade him to take me fishing.

I can still remember that moment. My father was there, standing just outside our roundhouse with six other men, the farmers who lived nearby. They were all dressed for war. My father had on his thick, leather jerkin and his face was half-hidden by the old, iron helmet he wore. The helmet had been in our family since my great-grandfather's day and was a prized possession, even though it was scratched and scored like a well-used old pot.

The ancient helmet was not my father's only armour. On his left arm, he carried his small, round shield and in his right hand he held his short spear. The other men were similarly attired, although only my father possessed a helmet.

I stopped, blinking in the sunlight, imagining this was just a dream. I soon realised that it was all too real.

"What has happened?" I asked. I thought that raiders from a neighbouring village might have stolen some of our cattle and our men were going to try to bring them back. I could not have been more wrong.

My father turned back to face me. His blue eyes were dark within the frame of his helmet. "Stay inside today, Bili," he ordered. "Look after your mother."

"Why? Where are you going?"

"The King has called us to battle," he replied grimly. "The Angles are coming north again. Now do as you are told and stay here."

"I want to come with you," I pleaded, excited at the prospect of war as only a young boy can be.

Sternly, my father said, "You are not old enough yet. Stay here."

One of the other men laughed. That was Talorcan. He was a few years older than me, nearly eighteen. I did not like him. He was squat and powerfully built, and he liked to throw his weight around. He often picked on me, mocking me for my small stature. Father had mentioned to my sister, Triduana, that he wanted to arrange a marriage for her with Talorcan but Triduana disliked the arrogant brute as much as I did. The problem was that Talorcan was the only unmarried young man in the valley and unless Triduana was prepared to marry a much older man, she would have little choice.

Triduana came out of our house at that moment, alongside my mother, with little Giric trailing after them. I noticed Talorcan leering at her, but Triduana turned her back on him. Like my mother, she was anxious but determined not to show her concerns, especially not in front of the other men.

"We've packed you some food," my mother said. She handed my father a small, cloth-wrapped bundle.

Father took it with a nod of thanks. He kissed her cheek, a gesture that was awkward because of his war gear, then he gave us a short wave, told us he would return soon, and set off at the head of the other men. Talorcan waved as well, promising to return with a great deal of plunder. Both Triduana and I ignored him.

We watched the seven men until they had disappeared behind a stand of trees, then mother ushered us indoors. I went back inside feeling somehow lost and alone.

Mother gave us chores to do, then she announced that she was going to the neighbouring farms to speak to the other women. She left Triduana in charge because she was a year older than me. Triduana liked being in charge. She began ordering me about as soon as mother left, telling me to fetch this or tidy that. After a while, I became fed up of her bossiness. "I'm going to chop some firewood," I said.

"Mother said we have to stay here," Triduana said sharply.

I ignored her. I picked up the axe, which was so big and heavy that I had to use both hands just to lift it, and told her, "I'll be back soon."

"You must stay here, Bili," she told me.

"You can't stop me," I shot back.

She tried to grab me but I darted out the door, evading her lunge. Little Giric tried to follow me, which helped my escape because Triduana was forced to let me go in order to catch him. She needed both hands to hold him, so I got clean away. Carrying the heavy axe, I ran as fast as I could with Triduana's cries of "Come back!" following me across the fields.

Of course, she knew what I was going to do. I had no intentions of chopping wood. My father had said that I was too young to go to war, but I was thirteen years old, nearly fourteen in fact, and I had an axe. I knew how to move silently through the hills and woods so I was confident that I would be able to kill any Angles who dared come near me. In my mind I was Bili, a mighty warrior, a hero of the Pecht. So I ran eastwards, following my father to war.

The axe seemed to become heavier the further I walked. The sun had not climbed very far into the sky before I was tempted to leave the axe behind, but I knew I would be no use as a warrior if I had no weapon, so I scurried on, staying in the trees as much as I could so as not to be seen.

It was as well that I did. Around mid-morning I heard the sound of many horses, travelling fast. I ducked low, peering out from behind the trunk of a tall elm tree. On the plain, I saw around forty horsemen, all dressed in armour of chainmail or leather, all with helmets and large, round shields. I know now that they were just a scouting party but at the time I thought I had come across the entire Northumbrian army. I decided that there were too many of them, even for a warrior of my renown, so I lay down in the shadows of the woods, keeping out of sight. They were on the far side of the river but even so the sound of the hooves was like thunder as they rode past my hiding place, throwing up dust and earth in their wake.

The sight and sound of their passing sent a chill through my bones. For the first time, my dreams of glory faded a little and I began to think that perhaps I should have stayed at home after all.

When the horsemen had ridden beyond my sight, I recovered a little of my resolve. Thinking of the scorn Triduana would heap on me if I returned home so soon, I decided I had no option but to go on. But the Northumbrian horsemen might come back. They would catch me if I stayed too near the river. I decided to find another route to the east. Gripping the heavy axe, I turned into the trees and began climbing the hill behind me. This, I decided, was a good plan; the riders would never be able to follow me up the steep, wooded slope. With luck, I would find our army on the far side. I would be able to join my father and fight alongside him. Dreaming of glory, I clambered up the hillside.

It was a long climb and I was sweating by the time I eventually reached the top. The axe felt so heavy in my hands that I dearly wanted to throw it away. Stubbornly, I clung to it. What sort of warrior would I be if I had no weapon?

At the top of the hill, I stopped. I was tired and I was thirsty but there was no water up here. A horrible thought struck me that I had come away with no food, which meant that I would soon go hungry if the King's army was several days' away. Then I remembered the Angles who had ridden past me and I knew that our own army could not be far away. All I had to do was find them. Surely that would not be too difficult from this high vantage point?

I propped the axe against a large boulder, then clambered on top of the rock so that I could gaze down on the river valley below. My eyes opened wide. I had found an army, but it was not the one I had hoped for.

Down below me was the Eireann, winding its way through the flat lands between the hills. It twisted and turned, forming a great loop to the south, before cutting northwards to join the mighty Tatha. At any other time I would have found the view entrancing but that day my eyes were drawn to the host of horsemen who were splashing across the river, heading north. There were hundreds of them, perhaps thousands. Remembering the fear I had felt when the first group had ridden past me earlier, I wondered how anyone could dare to stand against such a mighty column of death-wielding horsemen.

To my young eyes they looked unstoppable, but even as I stood, transfixed by the sight, thousands of our own men burst from cover, surging out of the trees to charge at the leading riders. I cheered wildly, knowing my father was in that army somewhere.

"Kill the invaders!" I urged him.

Most of our army was on foot. Our few horsemen galloped ahead, seeking to drive the Angles back across the ford but the Northumbrian riders were not dismayed by the sudden appearance of our warriors. They bunched together, increased their pace and swept our cavalry aside as if they were nothing more than an inconvenience. Even from my great height above the plain, I could hear the screams of the dying horses as the Northumbrians ploughed through them. In moments, the horsemen of the Pecht seemed to vanish beneath a wave of Northumbrians. Then the Angles turned on our footmen.

I was only a boy but I knew that the battle was lost almost before it had begun. Our warriors were charging in a ragged mob. If they had stood, shoulder to shoulder with shields and spears ready, the Northumbrians would not have been able to break them, but there was no order to our army and the Angles seized the opportunity. They plunged into the mass of foot soldiers, dealing death, the speed and height of their mounts making them almost invulnerable to the spears and swords of the Pecht.

The Northumbrians at the rear of their army dismounted as soon as they crossed the river. Forming up quickly into a solid mass, they advanced on foot, wielding swords and huge axes, driving into the chaos their cavalry had created. The warriors of the Pecht, scattered and demoralised by the first charge, fell before them like corn beneath a scythe.

I cannot say how long it took but it seemed to me to be no more than the count of a hundred heartbeats before panic gripped our army and men began to flee the field. The victorious Northumbrians, eager for blood, pursued them, their own force splitting into smaller groups as they hunted their foe like men who were chasing down wild boar. Except that boar are dangerous, while our army was not. All thoughts of fighting had been abandoned as the warriors sought nothing more than to escape from the bright spears and shining swords of the Northumbrians.

Through the clouds of swirling dust and the whirling mass of men and horses, I could see that far more of our warriors died while fleeing than had been killed during the initial fight. The Northumbrians simply rode them down, hacking with their heavy swords or stabbing their long lances. Every blow took down another warrior of the Pecht. Hundreds upon hundreds fell, littering the valley with their corpses. Some of our men tried to dodge past the riders but that only took them into the path of the Northumbrian footmen. Helpless in the face of such odds, they were cut down on the very banks of the river.

I watched in horror as the majority of our men fled north, leaving a trampled swathe of bloody, corpse-strewn earth in their wake. Most of them ran for the trees and hills but some headed for the Tatha, hoping that the barrier of that wide river might slow the pursuing Angles. I suppose that a few of them must have made it that far and been able to swim for safety but many of them were caught before they could get across. I heard later that the Northumbrian King, Ecgfrith, claimed that his army had filled the two rivers with so many corpses that he was able to walk across without getting his feet wet. That was a lie, of course, but then Ecgfrith was an Angle, a Northumbrian, and I have never met a single one of them who ever told the truth when a lie would suffice. Still, the rivers ran red that day; that was true, and the army of the Pecht was utterly defeated. I can bear witness to that because I watched the whole, terrible battle from my hilltop perch.

I do not know how long I stood there with the tears streaming down my face. My whole body ached with the knowledge that my father had been in that army and I did not know whether he was dead or had escaped. Either way, I hated him. If he were dead, then he had left me to care for my mother and the others, and I knew that task was beyond me. If he were alive then he was a coward because he had run from the enemy and I would never be able to respect him again. So I hated him, and I loved him, and my heart ached for him. Coward or not, I wanted nothing more than for him to return home safely because I knew I would be lost without him.

Home.

I knew then that I must go back, to take the news of what had happened. My only other choice was to search the field of dead and wounded in an attempt to find my father, but the very thought of going down to that field of death filled me with terror. The Northumbrians had charged on in pursuit of our fleeing army but they would soon return to the scene of their victory to plunder the bodies of the fallen.

Then another dreadful thought struck me. There was nothing to prevent the Angles from plundering as far afield as they could ride.

"You must warn Mother," I told myself. "And you must be quick."

Wiping the tears that blurred my eyes, I jumped down from my rock and ran down the hill.

I was half way home before I realised that I had left the axe propped against the rock on the hill's summit. I stumbled to a breathless halt, considered going back for it, then decided it could wait. Getting home was more important. Arms pumping, I ran on.

I had never been a fast runner. Other boys of my age could all run faster than me, although I could keep going for longer than most. I needed my stamina that day. I was parched with thirst, my tongue filling my mouth and my throat dry as old leather. I briefly considered making a small detour to the river to get a drink but then I remembered that the water would be full of blood, so I ran on, ignoring my raging thirst.

It was late into the afternoon before I saw the familiar landmarks that told me my home was just beyond the next stand of trees. I slowed to a walk, gasping for breath, my muscles screaming at me in protest. I felt that I could not go another step yet somehow I trudged on, unable to run because my side was aching and my legs were as heavy as lead. Then I heard the sound of hoofbeats from some way behind me and terror brought new vigour to my limbs. I ran for the trees as fast as I had ever run before, throwing myself to the cool grass as soon as I had passed the first trunk.

I lay, panting for breath, grateful for the coolness of the earth and the shade of the tall trees. I did not want to move. I could have lain there till evening came but the sound of the horses jerked me from my rest. Squirming round, I wriggled to the edge of the trees to peer out at the horsemen.

They rode at a canter, around fifty of them, led by a big, bearded man who was wearing a coat of shining mail with a gleaming helmet on his head. Beside him, another armoured warrior held a long staff from which a banner fluttered and flapped above their heads as they passed my hiding place. The banner was blood-red, with the image of a hawk's or eagle's head etched in black. I remember that banner more than I can recall the horses and the men. The sight of the ravening beak on the blood-coloured background struck fear in my heart. I wriggled low, praying that the riders would not see me. None of them did because they had their eyes on other things.

Home.

I hauled myself to my feet. Staggering, I blundered through the trees until I came to the far edge. From here I could see our fields, barren now that the oats and barley had been gathered in. I could see the stone-walled pens where our sheep and goats were herded, and I could see our house, the thin smudge of smoke clinging lazily to the peak of the round, thatched roof.

A sob like a croak escaped my parched lips when I saw my mother at the door, rising to her feet from where she had been sitting, spinning wool. She turned to shout something through the doorway then I saw her speaking to little Giric, bending down to give him an urgent message. He ran off, away from the approaching riders, heading towards the other farms that lay further down the wide valley. My mother, still armed with her spindle, turned to face the horsemen.

The big man who led them must have given some orders because the group split up. Most carried on, chasing after Giric, but the leader and around a dozen of the others reined in their horses beside our house.

Horrified, I watched Giric as he ran ahead of the pursuing horsemen. I heard my mother's scream of warning but there was nothing she could do. Giric was caught on the tip of a Northumbrian spear as the leading horseman rode past him, casually raising his spear in triumph as he swept on. Some of the horses following after him almost stumbled as they trampled my brother's corpse.

"Giric!" I sobbed.

My brother was only six years old. Now he was dead, killed as casually as we would slaughter a sheep.

I fell to my knees, clutching at the nearest tree for support. "Giric!" I croaked. "Giric!" I could see his tiny body, lying on the ground like a bundle of old, discarded rags while his killers rode on, seeking more victims among the other farms.

My mother screamed again, the sound jerking my head back to the house. Most of the riders there had dismounted and two of them had seized her. She was trying to fight them off but they were much too strong for her. More men gathered around her. They began tossing her from one to the other, each man clawing at her. Then Triduana came out of the house, wielding a large carving knife. She sprang at one of the men, who batted her arm aside, sending the knife tumbling to the ground. He grabbed for her, imprisoning her in his huge embrace. She kicked her legs wildly but it seemed to me, even from the distant trees where I was hidden, that the man simply laughed at her struggles.

That was when I began praying. I prayed like I had never prayed before, asking that God would strike down these men, or that my father would return with a thousand warriors at his back to slay these savage Angles. I prayed for the strength to rise to my feet and challenge them, the way Triduana had done. My prayers were as heartfelt as any I have ever heard any priest offer, but they were not answered.

My mother and Triduana screamed while the men stripped them, threw them to the ground then took turns at using them to satisfy their lust.

I could not watch. I slumped against the tree, unable to move. God had ignored me but, far worse than that, I realised that I was a coward. I should have gone out to challenge the men. I should have done something to save my mother and my sister but I was afraid that the Northumbrians would kill me the way they had killed Giric, so I stayed hidden, unable to move, and I wept silent tears of despair.

The Northumbrians plundered our roundhouse, herded up our cattle, sheep and goats, then casually set light to the thatched roof. Just as casually, one of them hauled my mother to her feet and bound her wrists together. Still naked, she almost fell but the Angle slapped her and shouted at her, yanking at her arms to keep her upright.

The other riders, the ones who had murdered Giric, returned, herding more livestock from the other farmsteads. They were also herding people, mostly women and girls although I recognised a couple of boys, friends I had often played with. All of them were naked, most of them were crying as they stumbled their way under the threat of Northumbrian spears. My mother was shoved among them.

I saw the big, bearded leader wave his arms in signal, ordering his men to mount up. One of them, a tall, fair-haired, young man, hoisted Triduana onto his saddle, laying her across the horse in front of him. She barely moved but I knew she was alive because even a Northumbrian would not carry away a naked corpse.

I ducked out of sight as the men rode back towards me, not daring to look while the procession of riders prodded their newly acquired slaves and plundered livestock back along the river.

I saw Triduana lying face down across the horseman's saddle, her hair hanging low. Looking at the fair-haired rider, I committed his face to my memory. He was a young man, perhaps seventeen or eighteen years old, handsome in a brutal way. With smooth features and bright eyes. His chin was beardless, his cheeks smooth, but his youth could not conceal his arrogance. He laughed as he slapped Triduana's bare buttocks in triumph.

I wanted to rush out to attack him but I was too afraid. Then I caught a glimpse of the other slaves as they passed me. I knew it was a sin to look on their nakedness but I saw my mother and I knew that it might be the last time I would ever lay eyes on her, so I imprinted her tear-streaked face on my memory, vowing that, one day, I would find her again. Then she was gone from my sight as a Northumbrian horseman rode past, blocking my view. Before long, the column of people and beasts had passed me by. In a cloud of dust and tears, they slowly vanished into the east.

I sat there for a long time, long after they had gone. I was a coward and I knew it. The shame of it burned in me. The horror of the day assailed my senses, threatening to overwhelm me. I sat there until the sun began to sink towards the west and I cried so hard that I thought I would drown the world with my tears.

Eventually, my tears dried, my limbs stopped their shaking and I remembered my thirst and my hunger. There would be no food, but there was a well at the side of the house, so I knew that I had to go there. The thought terrified me because Giric was still there, lying where the Northumbrians had left him to rot. I knew what I must do, but I hesitated to do it.

Leadenly, I dragged myself out of the trees and walked across the meadow to the house. The fire was almost burned out now, the timbers having collapsed, turning the place into a huge, smouldering pyre. When I reached the well, I hauled up the bucket. I drank as if I had never drunk before, splashing the water all over my face and body as I gulped it down. Only when my thirst was slaked and my clothes were soaked did I dare approach Giric.

I could not look at the awful gash in his back, so I concentrated all my attention on his face. That was almost as bad, because his eyes were open, full of reproach, accusing me of abandoning him, demanding to know why I had hidden while the Angles had destroyed our family. I could not answer him, so I closed his eyelids. I looked at him, trying to wish the life back into him but he was cold and still. I knelt down, lifting his head to gently cradle it on my knees. I began crying again, my tears dropping onto his pale, lifeless face.

    That was when Bleddyn found me.

Chapter 2

The first I knew of Bleddyn's presence was when I heard his footsteps only a few paces from me. I looked up, startled and terrified, thinking that the big, bearded Northumbrian and his men had come back for me, but although the man I saw in front of me was tall and powerfully built, he was no warrior.

He was middle-aged, and dressed in a brown, travel-worn monk's robe, topped by a heavy, woollen cloak. A large, wooden crucifix hung from a crudely twisted cord around his neck. His hair was brown, worn long at the back but with the front part of his head shaved clean. I knew that peculiar style marked him as a member of the Ionian Church rather than a Roman monk. In his right hand, he held a staff, a stout piece of polished oak with a heavy, rounded knob at the top. On this orb, I could see the crude outline of a cross which had been carved into the polished wood.

He smiled at me, a gentle, warm, sad smile that told me he understood my loss.

"Hello, boy," he said. His voice was strong, his accent a strange mix of northern and southern. "I am Bleddyn. What is your name?"

"Bili," I said softly. "My name is Bili."

He regarded me thoughtfully for a moment, then he said, "Well, Bili, I think it is time for us to bury your young friend there. Who is he?"

He spoke as if Giric was still alive.

"He's my brother," I said. "His name is Giric."

Bleddyn laid down his heavy staff, then squatted on his haunches, facing me. He reached out one large hand which he placed on my shoulder. The touch was both gentle and firmly comforting. "Come, Bili. Let us give him a Christian burial, then we should leave this place."

I did not move. I could not. I could not leave Giric.

"The Northumbrians came," I said. "They took away my mother and my sister, and all the other people they could find."

"But they did not find you."

"I was hiding. Like a coward."

He squeezed my shoulder reassuringly. "What could you have done? It was sensible of you to remain hidden. What about your father?"

"He went to join the King's army," I said. "He has not come back."

"Ah. I see." Bleddyn was silent for a moment. Then he stood up. Reaching out to take my arm, he gently encouraged me to my feet. "Come. Night is drawing close. We must bury Giric before we go."

I felt numb, exhausted and utterly drained but Bleddyn took control of the situation while constantly encouraging me to help him. He found some tools among the wreckage of our house. The wooden handles had all burned away but the metal, although it was slightly warped, had survived. It was hot to the touch, so Bleddyn fetched a bucket of water which he poured over the ruined implements. They sizzled and steamed as the water struck them, but Bleddyn poured more water until he was able to hold the metal, then he used a broad shovel blade to begin digging a hole near the house. "Come and help me, Bili," he said.

It was dark by the time we had dug a hole deep enough. Under the moonlight, Bleddyn lifted Giric and carried him to the grave. He lowered the tiny body into the ground, said a prayer for Giric's soul, asking the Lord to take care of him, then began shovelling the earth back into the grave, covering Giric from sight. I half expected my brother to wake up, to shout in protest at the earth being piled on top of him, but he did not move. I watched, fascinated, until the dark earth covered him completely.

Bleddyn fashioned a crude cross from two pieces of wood. Using a flat stone, he hammered it into the soft earth of the grave. Then he said another short prayer before taking my arm.

"It is time to go," he told me.

I was too dazed to ask where he was taking me but we did not go far because it was too dark to travel easily. Thankfully, he led me past the trees where I had lain hidden during the attack on our home but he stopped when he reached the next patch of woodland. Here, he quickly fashioned a crude, lean-to shelter using rocks and branches to support a large blanket which he took from his backpack and draped over the makeshift supports. He ushered me inside, then followed to sit beside me. It was a tight fit with the two of us, but at least the rough shelter would keep us warm and dry.

Bleddyn rummaged in his pack once again, producing some stale bread and hard cheese which he shared with me. I was ravenous, devouring the food as if it were the choicest cuts of meat from a freshly slaughtered lamb. When I had eaten the bread and cheese, he handed me some small, bean-like pods. "Eat these," he said.

I looked at the beans suspiciously.

"What are they?" I asked.

"They are Heath Peas," he informed me as I cautiously chewed and swallowed them. "They will stave off hunger until we can find more appetising food."

We washed down the sparse meal with cool water which Bleddyn had taken from our well. "You should sleep now," he told me. "We have a long way to go."

"Where are we going?" I asked.

"North."

In fact, when morning came, he led me east. Our breakfast had consisted of more dried Heath Peas. They were hardly tasty but Bleddyn was right about them staving off hunger. I was surprised to discover that I did not feel the need to eat anything else as we walked along the river, re-tracing the route I had taken the previous day.

I may not have been hungry but I did feel a nervousness bordering on fear. "Why are we going this way?" I asked. "This is the way to the battlefield. The Northumbrians may still be there."

Bleddyn was not concerned. "I doubt that they will have stayed too close to where the fighting was. A battlefield is not a restful place, even when the combat is over. Besides, I need to see it."

"Why?"

"I will need to tell people what has happened," he replied rather vaguely.

I said, "But the Angles are taking slaves and plundering our farms. They might take us."

Bleddyn lifted his crucifix away from his chest, holding it out for me to see. "They will not harm a man of God," he assured me. "You can be my servant, which will keep you safe from harm."

He strode on, covering the ground easily. He was a big man, broad of shoulders, with strong, muscled arms and powerful legs. More than that, he was so self-assured and confident that he seemed to bend the very world around him as if nature herself bowed down at his passing. I was still anxious, but the terror of facing the Angles seemed foolish when I had Bleddyn beside me. His calm self-assurance instilled a sense of confidence that allowed me to approach the battle site without quaking with terror.

"We are close," I told him as we reached the edges of the hill I had climbed the previous day. I wondered whether we should go up to fetch my axe but Bleddyn had said we had a long way to walk and I did not relish the prospect of carrying the heavy weapon for day after day, so I did not mention it to him.

We saw the first bodies soon afterwards. They lay scattered on the earth, twisted into grotesque, unnatural shapes, with hordes of flies buzzing around them and crows pecking at their eyes. I gave the corpses a wide berth, but

Bleddyn paid little attention to them except to remark that they were Pecht, obviously ridden down while trying to flee.

As we approached the ford, the stench of death reached my nostrils. Bleddyn stopped, surveying the awful scene. Bodies lay everywhere, men and horses, spattered with blood and gore, some with their heads smashed open, others with their guts hanging out or their limbs severed. I was almost sick, but I swallowed back the bitter taste of vomit.

"May the Lord have mercy on their souls," Bleddyn muttered.

I could hear men moaning, feebly calling for help. These were the wounded who could not walk, who had been left to die on the field. Crows flapped around the wide plain. A fox gazed at us for a moment then went back to gnawing on a corpse's leg. All I could hear were the cries of the dying and the buzzing of the swarming flies.

I thought Bleddyn would stay there, perhaps try to help some of the badly injured, but he sighed, offered up a prayer for forgiveness and led me along the river, passing through the heaps of mutilated men and horses until we had left the awful carnage behind us.

"We should help them," I said. "My father may be among them."

Bleddyn's face was grim. "And if he is? What will you do? You cannot carry him and I do not have the strength or the skills to help so many."

I did not think that a monk would be so hard-hearted but I did not have the will to argue with him and I could see that his decision pained him. "Others will come," he explained after a while. "The Northumbrians are the victors so it is their Christian duty to see to the wounded. They will have priests with them who can tend the injured. Perhaps some will survive." He did not sound confident about that.

I thought of my father, and Talorcan, and the other men of our little community. The thought brought tears springing to my eyes once again. If they were among the wounded who were crying for help, I had abandoned them, just as I had abandoned my mother and Triduana. I felt wretched.

Bleddyn may have understood. He put his large hand on my shoulder, gently ushering me on. He said, "Whatever happens will be God's will."

I never did learn what had become of my father or the others, whether they had died in the awful battle or whether they had lain, injured and unable to move, crying for help that never came. By the time I passed the place again, the dead had been buried in several great pits. I never saw my father again so I suppose his mortal remains must be in one of those pits somewhere, along with Talorcan and all the hundreds of others who died that day. Over the years since then, I have passed that way several times and each time I have experienced a feeling of loss and guilt. Bleddyn often told me that time heals all things but, for me, some pains have never gone away.

For three days we walked at a fast pace, taking me further than I had ever travelled before. My feet grew blisters and my legs ached but Bleddyn pushed on, unwilling to rest during daylight. At night, he would have me bathe my feet in a stream then he would tend to my blisters, using salves he carried in his seemingly bottomless pack. In the morning, sustained by our diet of Heath Peas, I would hobble after him once again.

Our route took us back along the southern bank of the Tatha but we walked in a great circle to avoid the villages of Peairt and Sgain because Bleddyn suspected that the Northumbrians would have gone there. Sgain, which lay a little way north of Peairt, was an important settlement, a place where the King of the Pecht often stayed when he came south, so Bleddyn reckoned that Ecgfrith, the victorious King of Northumbria, would have spent the night there.

"Sgain will be crawling with Angles by now," he declared. "We would be better to avoid it."

We saw no sign of the Northumbrians except some tracks of horse's hoofs in the earth and some distant pillars of smoke from burning homes. Once beyond Peairt, we headed north, following wild land, avoiding pathways or well-trodden tracks and keeping to the cover of the woodlands. We never saw another living soul during those three days. It was as if we were concealed by some mystical power that hid us from the eyes of our enemies while all around us, Ecgfrith and his army wreaked devastation. To my young eyes it appeared that God was shielding us, although I learned in later years that it had as much to do with Bleddyn's woodcraft as anything else.

After we passed Peairt, Bleddyn continued to hurry on, only easing the pace a little after another four days.

"I do not think they will have come this far yet," he said. I asked him how he knew. He gave me that enigmatic smile of his. "I don't know. I am guessing. But I was not always a monk, and I have some knowledge of war. After a few days of plundering, Ecgfrith will gather his army again. I suspect that most of them will go south, but some will probably stay this time, for the Pecht cannot oppose them now. Soon, we will see Northumbrians coming north to build their own homes and to farm this land. Ecgfrith will leave some warriors to protect them."

Bleddyn seemed to me to be very wise when he said this. As things turned out, he was more or less correct. As we were to discover, the southern kingdoms of the Pecht were soon absorbed into Ecgfrith's Northumbria and there was nothing that could be done to prevent the Angles taking over.

For the moment, we walked on, heading ever northwards. There were farms here, undamaged by war, although there were few men in evidence. Most of them had gone to join the King's call to arms, leaving the women and children to tend the farms while they attempted to drive back the Northumbrians. The few men who had returned were frightened and sullen because they knew what the defeat would mean for them. Bleddyn solemnly tried to comfort them but there was little he could say to ease their fears. He prayed with them, blessed them and accepted their gifts of food and shelter before moving on.

"How much further do we have to go?" I asked one afternoon as we trudged through high, forested hills that closed in around us.

"A long way," Bleddyn said. "It will take us at least another two weeks to reach Inbhir Nis."

I groaned. "Two weeks?"

"At least," he said.

"Why are we going there?"

"Because that is where the King will be. After this defeat, there will be much to discuss, much to decide. I want to be there when the decisions are made."

If I had been older or more knowledgeable, I might have asked more questions but at the time it did not strike me as odd that a wandering monk would want to be present at the King's stronghold. After all, I knew very little about the ways of monks and nothing at all about Kings. The one thing that I did know was that the Church claimed the right to govern the lives of all men, so it seemed natural to me that a man of God like Bleddyn would go to meet the King. Added to which, I was already regarding Bleddyn as the wisest man in Christendom. I was sure he would be able to advise the King on how to defeat the Angles.

Now that we were clear of the Northumbrian army, we walked on the roads, such as they were. The route north was mostly marked by a narrow, well-trodden path that was rutted by cartwheels, pitted with holes and dotted with large patches of dark mud. Still, we made faster progress than we had when we were picking our way through the woods, so Bleddyn strode out, his long legs eating up the miles while I struggled to keep up with him.

We were passing through a narrow valley, the forested hills closing in on our right, a rocky gorge dropping away to our left, when Bleddyn reached out with his left hand and squeezed my arm. We continued walking, Bleddyn's staff rapping out the pace. He did not look at me but I sensed a tension in him.

"Remain calm, Bili," he said softly but urgently. "Whatever happens next, remember that you are my servant and that I am a servant of Christ. No harm can come to us."

"What?" I was confused, wondering what he was talking about.

"The woods have fallen silent," he said.

"What does that mean?" I tried to wriggle free of his arm but he held me tightly, his fingers digging in to my flesh.

"It means that something, or someone, is very close to us, out of sight among the trees."

I jerked my head, frantically looking around at the trees. We were hemmed in here, with no escape to left or right. Bleddyn walked on as though he was impervious to danger, half-dragging me with him.

I jumped like a startled hare when a dozen men suddenly leaped out in front of us, long-haired, bearded men holding shields and spears. A rustle from behind us alerted me to more of them, thumping down to the path we had just trodden, blocking our retreat. I stifled a yell of panic.

"Bleddyn?" I whispered, seeking some guidance.

Bleddyn had stopped. "Good day to you, my sons," he called out, apparently quite cheerful and unconcerned. "What brings you here, waylaying innocent travellers?"

A middle-aged man pushed through the warriors ahead of us. He was of average build, wearing a coat of chainmail. A long sword hung at his left hip, fastened to a broad, ornately decorated, silver-buckled belt. On his head was a helmet that gleamed. His armour spoke of a man of distinction, although his hair straggled down untidily beneath his helmet, and his beard was badly in need of trimming. At first glance there was nothing special about him and yet, like Bleddyn, he moved with an easy confidence that radiated power and authority. At the merest wave of his hand, the other men moved aside to let him pass.

He walked towards us, stopping only a few paces away. His eyes, red-rimmed and heavy from lack of sleep, regarded us with apparent distaste.

"Innocent travellers, my arse," he said. Then his craggy face broke into a broad smile. "How are you, Bleddyn? And where's your horse?"

"I am well, but footsore," Bleddyn replied. "The horse was stolen by some Northumbrian bandits."

"Bloody Northumbrians. You can't trust them," the man said with feeling. He extended his right hand. Bleddyn clasped his forearm warmly. The man's eyes turned on me. He asked, "Who's the boy?"

"This is Bili," said Bleddyn. "His home was destroyed. His family are dead or captive." Bleddyn turned to me. "Bili, I would like you to meet Bridei, one of the foremost chieftains of Fortriu."

I did not know what to say but I held out my hand, as I had seen men do when they met for the first time. Bridei clasped it. His grip was powerful but he seemed friendly.

"Bili," he said. "That's a good name. That was my father's name." He released my hand as he said to Bleddyn. "Come, let's get into the hills. We can talk over supper."

Supper was a thin, tasteless broth followed by chunks of roasted horsemeat. "One of the horses died," Bridei explained apologetically. "It's a bit tough to chew but it's better than bloody Heath Peas."

We were sitting at a small fire, Bridei, Bleddyn and me, while Bridei's warriors had their own fires lit in a small hollow high in the hills. The mood in the small camp was sombre. The men were tired and downcast by the recent defeat. Even Bridei's attempts at humour were grim and rather forced.

Bleddyn asked, "Do you have enough horses for us to ride with you?"

"There aren't enough for everyone but I'll get one for you," Bridei promised.

"Thank you. Bili and I can share one."

Bridei nodded. Then his eyes grew serious. "Any news from the south?"

Bleddyn shrugged. "Ecgfrith controls all the lands south of here by now. There is nobody left to oppose him."

Bridei nodded. "Aye, the fight was a bloody shambles. The trap was sprung too soon. Ecgfrith must have pissed himself laughing at us." He sighed, then went on, "We'll stop him at the mountains, though. He won't come that far. Not yet anyway."

"Let us hope not."

Bridei seemed distracted. He turned his attention on me. "So what is your story, Bili?" he asked.

Bleddyn nodded his encouragement, so I recounted the tale of how I had witnessed the battle and what had happened when I returned home. This time I remembered more details so I told him about the big, bearded Northumbrian and the black eagle's head on the blood-red banner, something I had forgotten to mention to Bleddyn.

"It's a hawk, not an eagle," Bridei told me. "It is the symbol of Beornhaeth, one of Ecgfrith's nobles."

"Do you know him?" I asked, forgetting in my eagerness that I was addressing a chieftain.

"I know of him," Bridei replied. "He is reputed to be a great warrior."

"I hate him," I said. Then I recalled the blond man who had taken Triduana. "Do you know one of his warriors? A tall man with fair hair?"

Bridei shrugged. "That description could match a great number of Northumbrians."

Bleddyn said, "Wulfric. It was probably Wulfric, Beornhaeth's son."

I stared at Bleddyn. "Wulfric?" I asked, struggling with the unfamiliar sound of the name.

"I have seen him once or twice," Bleddyn said. "And his father, too. They are both strong men, used to getting what they want."

"I will kill them one day," I said.

Bridei gave a soft laugh.

"Perhaps you will," Bleddyn agreed amiably. "But not for some years yet, I imagine."

I remembered the slap he had given me the last time I had been impatient to get my revenge, so I did not argue this time.

Bridei said, "I would like to see them dead, too, lad. Perhaps we will be able to help one another."

I saw the look he gave to Bleddyn and I saw the brief nod that the monk gave in response although I did not understand either of them. But the thought of vengeance against the Angles had fired my blood. "I will do anything," I promised.

Bridei regarded me thoughtfully for a long moment. "That is a dangerous promise to make, lad," he warned me. "Vows like that can lead you down paths that are plagued by blood and tears."

I wasn't sure what he meant by that, but I held his gaze and replied, "I am not afraid."

I think he saw the lie in my eyes. The truth was that I was very afraid, but something inside me told me that Bridei was not the sort of man who would give in to fear. He was a chieftain, a man to be respected. I wanted his approval, so I looked into his blue eyes and I told him I was not afraid.

After a short moment he laughed softly and I saw that he approved if my bravado. He said, "Well, perhaps the three of us together can come up with something. Bridei, Bleddyn and Bili. A triumvirate of B names. Who knows, perhaps we will rival the Holy Trinity in what we can accomplish."

Bleddyn said, "Don't be blasphemous, Bridei. it does not become you. If we achieve anything, it will be with God's help."

"Aye, you are right at that," said Bridei. "We need some sort of miracle." He sounded contrite, but he gave me a broad wink when Bleddyn was not looking.

That was how I met Bridei. I know that everything that happened after that day happened by the will of God, because that is a truth that nobody can deny, but I often think that much of it happened by the will of Bridei. I never met a man so determined, yet so patient. He was outwardly open and honest yet he was able to manipulate others to do what he wanted, often without them realising what he had done. He was ruthless and kind, friendly and implacable, honest and devious.

I know that he used me as he used others but I had pledged myself to him with my vow of vengeance and, even though no words passed to acknowledge the bond between us, he accepted my pledge. That was the day that changed the course of my life. For good or ill, I became part of Bridei's great plan because, like me, he wanted revenge on the Angles and he would use any tool at his disposal to achieve his goal.

So, although I did not know it at the time, my fate from that moment on was bound up with Bridei.

Bleddyn and I did not continue our journey north because Bridei had made other plans. He told us that he intended to patrol the mountains, to watch for any Northumbrian advance out of their newly-conquered lands of Fidach and Circinn. He had also decided to carry out some raids on any of their people who ventured too far north.

"I want to show them we can still bite," he said grimly.

Bleddyn did not disagree but he was of the opinion that the Northumbrians would be content with what they had gained that year. "Winter will be here soon," he said. "They won't want to overstretch themselves."

"All the more reason to remind them we are still here," said Bridei. "And you can help us."

I was not sure what was going on but Bridei and Bleddyn had obviously been speaking while I slept because Bleddyn was quite happy to do Bridei's bidding. As he had promised, Bridei gave us a horse, together with a few small coins. "I took these off a Northumbrian lord," he said. "They might be useful."

I had never seen coins before so I asked Bleddyn to show them to me. They were small and thick, a dull silver in colour, with strange marks etched into them.

Bleddyn informed me, "They are made of brass, with just enough silver to give them their colour. They are not worth a great deal." He buried them in his backpack, then clasped Bridei's forearm in farewell.

Bridei said, "I will see you in the Springtime. Come April, be at Inbhir Nis with whatever news you can discover."

"I will," Bleddyn promised. "Will you be ready then?"

"I am ready now," Bridei replied with a wolfish smile. "I am always ready. But I need to be sure about what Ecgfrith is doing. April will be soon enough to act."

"April, then," Bleddyn assented.

Bridei looked down at me. "You can go north with some of my men," he told me, "or, if you meant what you said about getting revenge, you can help us by going with Bleddyn to see what our enemies are up to."

"Think carefully, Bili," Bleddyn cautioned. "The road I travel will often be a dark one. You would be safer in Inbhir Nis."

I did not hesitate, I had given my word to Bridei. I wanted to rescue my mother and my sister and I wanted revenge on the men who had killed my father. I was still a boy, so I had no real conception of what would happen. Nothing mattered except vengeance.

I said to Bleddyn, "I will walk that road with you."

He nodded, perhaps a little sadly. "Then let us be off," he said.

Bridei beckoned to one of his men who led a small, shaggy-coated horse over to us. Bleddyn showed me how to fasten the saddle, bridle and reins. I was worried that the small horse would not be able to carry the two of us because Bleddyn was a big man. He assured me we would be fine.

"She is a strong beast," he said.

The saddle was of thick leather, high at the front and back. At either side, great flaps of thinner leather hung down like blankets. Beneath these protective flaps was the girth strap which he showed me how to fasten so that the saddle did not slip. He tested it, then shoved his left toe into a cut-out foothold on the lower part of the blanket-like saddle flap. With a heave, he climbed onto the horse's back, then reached down to hoist me up behind him. I wrapped my arms around his broad waist. Clutching his long staff in his right hand, he grabbed the reins and put his heels to the horse, turning south again.

Bridei waved us farewell. "Until April," he called after us. "Good luck."

I was bursting with questions which I fired at Bleddyn as soon as we had left the camp. The mysterious talk of dark roads and danger were forgotten as more immediate concerns filled my mind.

"Where are we going? Why? What is Bridei ready for? What happens in April?" The words tumbled from my lips like a torrent.

"One thing at a time, Bili," Bleddyn laughed. "We are going south, perhaps as far as Manaw." Before I could interrupt, he went on, "As for the reason, Bridei has asked me to learn what the Northumbrians are going to do. You can help me with that. It is something that is best done by travelling amongst them, by using our eyes and our ears to learn what they intend."

"We are spies?" I asked.

"That is an ugly word," he said. "I prefer to think of myself as an observer."

"So we are not going to kill Beornhaeth and Wulfric?"

"Most certainly not. I am a man of God and you are still a boy. We are not going to kill anyone. As I said, we will use our eyes and our ears. Then we will return to Inbhir Nis in the Springtime and we will inform Bridei of what we have learned."

"What about the King? Won't we have to tell him, too?"

"Oh yes, the King will need to know." He said it almost dismissively, as if the King was an afterthought. Of course, he knew what was likely to happen in April while I, in my youthful ignorance, did not.

Chapter 3

That autumn and winter saw the beginning of my education. It was not an education in Latin, nor in reading and writing, the way novice monks were taught, nor did Bleddyn particularly concentrate on scripture. Instead, he began to teach me how to live off the land and, above all, how to speak English, the language of the Angles and the Saxons.

"If you wish to fight, you must know your enemy," he told me. "You can hardly learn much from them if you cannot understand them."

That made sense to me, so we spent hours every day, going over the words and the grammar of English while I struggled to get my tongue round the coarse, heavy sounds of the southern language. I would rather have learned how to use a sword against them but Bleddyn assured me that what I was learning would be much more useful.

"Any man can use a sword," he said as we sat beside a small camp fire one evening. "Not many are capable of using their brains properly."

"Perhaps I could use both," I suggested hopefully.

Bleddyn sighed. Getting up from the fire, he found a long stick which he passed to me. "Here," he said. "Pretend this is a sword. Now come and strike at me."

I weighed the shaft of wood in my hand, feeling rather uncertain, but Bleddyn beckoned to me so I hefted the stick and swung it at him. He swayed back, easily avoiding my blow, then lashed out with his hand to grip my wrist like a vice. I yelped as he twisted, forcing me to drop my makeshift sword.

Bleddyn swung his leg, catching me just above the ankle as he twisted my arm. He shoved me over his outstretched leg to send me tumbling to the ground.

Without saying a word, he sat down by the fire, gesturing for me to get up and join him. We sat in silence for a moment, Bleddyn looking serious while I rubbed my wrist and ankle.

Eventually, he said, "Listen to me, Bili. If you practise hard for many years, you might become competent with a sword but, believe me, you are too slight of build to make a good warrior. However good you become, there will be other men who are equally skilled but who are a lot bigger than you. You would never be able to win against them."

I knew he was talking about Beornhaeth and his son, Wulfric, who were both big, brawny men. My heart sank. Everyone among the Pecht was expected to be both a farmer and a warrior, switching between the two depending on the season and the circumstance.

"What can I do, then?" I asked miserably.

"You can do as I have said; use your brain and your wits. Learn the ways of the enemy. Learn to move among them, to speak like them, to think like them. That way, you and I can achieve far more than simple warriors ever could."

I knew he was probably right but I was still hurting about being told I would never make a soldier. I wanted to hit back at him in some small way so I said, "Why are you spying for Bridei? I thought monks and priests were not supposed to take sides."

I had hoped that the taunt about being a spy would irritate him but he ignored it. Instead, his eyebrows rose in mock surprise. He asked me, "Really? How many monks have you met, then?"

"Only you," I confessed.

"Well, then," he said, as if that settled the matter.

That was Bleddyn for you. Like I said, he was in a school of his own.

We travelled all through the autumn and early winter. We took shelter with local farmers or villagers when the weather turned too bad but mostly we kept on the move. Once out of the mountains, we headed east, to the coast, where we found that the Northumbrians had seized the fort of Dun Foither.

Bleddyn was upset. He could not understand how such a strong place could have fallen, but the locals told us that a huge force of Northumbrians had ridden up from the south and the fort's garrison, knowing that our army had been destroyed and that no help would come to relieve them, had surrendered the place without a fight. Dun Foither was now home to around fifty Angles and their families.

This was a blow to Bleddyn. "Dun Foither guards the coastal approach to Fortriu," he explained to me. "I had not thought they would get this far north." He was thoughtful for a long time but eventually declared that we should visit the fort to see whether we could learn anything about the Northumbrian garrison.

Dun Foither stood on a cliff-top promontory, a massive stone wall and fortified gate barring the way across the wide peninsula. There was only one way to get inside and that was through the gate which was guarded by half a dozen armed men who stood on the high battlements. We rode up to the thick, high wall but we were quickly chased away. Churchman or not, the Northumbrians wanted nothing to do with Bleddyn and we were sent packing. I could not understand much of what the guards shouted at him, but I understood the message with no difficulty.

Having had no luck at Dun Foither, we rode south, then west, through the green, rolling hills and fertile farms of Circinn. Many of the hilltops in this region were fortified with ditches and walls of stone, although most of these settlements were large farmsteads rather than true hillforts. Every man of importance wanted to keep his home secure, so minor chieftains built their own small defences around their hilltop homes. We visited more than a few of these and learned that life had not changed too much for the people here except that the Northumbrians had already visited every chieftain to demand tribute.

One or two of the more stubborn among them had refused, a stance which had resulted in their heads being removed from their shoulders and their homes being occupied by Northumbrians. After that, most of the others had paid the tribute without argument. Bleddyn was philosophical about the situation.

"I cannot blame them," he said. "These lands are part of Ecgfrith's domain now. Until the Pecht are strong enough to take them back, the people here have little choice but to obey their new masters."

We spent several weeks in Circinn, slowly making our way westwards. We crossed the upper reaches of the Tatha then headed southwards, always watching, always asking questions of the locals. I noticed that we did not go near the battlefield, nor to my old home, but we pressed on, day after day, week after week, criss-crossing the lands of Fidach and Fib. Everywhere, the story was the same. Northumbrian warriors had come to demand tribute and had established themselves in several strongholds so that they could enforce King Ecgfrith's will. His will was that the people of the southern Pecht should pay their taxes and tithes to him.

We spent the night of the feast of Samhain in a small village somewhere in the lands of Fib. I was surprised when Bleddyn joined in the festivities because Samhain was an old, pagan festival, but he managed to persuade the people to sing some psalms and offer up Christian prayers before they celebrated the old ways, blackening their faces with ash, changing their clothes so that the men dressed as old women and the women dressed as men. These were tricks to fool the evil spirits that roamed the earth on that dark night but they also helped to disguise those who wanted to play pranks on their neighbours. These pranks were sometimes known to turn violent, especially when everyone grew more and more drunk, so I stayed close to Bleddyn, knowing that nobody would dare lay hands on a monk.

I noticed that Bleddyn did not appear to be too bothered by the wild drunkenness. "Some people find it hard to forget the old traditions," he explained. "They are just having some fun. Who am I to judge them for that?"

My fourteenth birthday came two days after Samhain. I was old enough to be counted as a man, so we celebrated with a jug of wickedly strong beer that Bleddyn bought from a farmer. I don't know what the farmer made it from but even Bleddyn struggled to stay sober after we had drained the jug.

Of course, the main purpose of our journey was to learn things, which we did by listening, by chatting to the locals and even speaking to Northumbrian soldiers or merchants. Bleddyn did all the talking because I was still learning the language but he had a way of getting people to divulge what they knew. By the time we reached Linne Foirthe, we had discovered that Ecgfrith had gone south again, called back to his home in Northumbria by the need to protect his southern borders from attack by the Mercians.

That news cheered Bleddyn greatly. "The Angles and the Saxons fight among themselves as much as they fight us," he told me. "Mercia and Northumbria are often at war with one another. If Ecgfrith is busy in the south, we only have Beornhaeth to contend with."

That was because Beornhaeth, the man who had taken my mother and sister away, was now the effective ruler not only of Manaw, but also the newly-conquered territories of Fib, Fidach and Circinn.

On a cold, blustery day towards the middle of December, Bleddyn and I stood on a windswept, rocky shore, looking southwards across Linne Foirthe, a wide estuary that had once marked the border between the lands of the Pecht and Gododdin. Off in the distance, just visible under a blanket of grey clouds, I could see the lump that was Dun Eidyn, once a stronghold of the Gododdin, now the fortress where Beornhaeth of Northumbria had made his base.

"Are we going there?" I asked, gesturing south-east with a nod of my head.

Bleddyn shook his head. "To Dun Eidyn? No. Not just now. There is no need. I think we have learned all that we can for the moment. Let us return to the north."

I was both pleased and disappointed about that decision. Linne Foirthe had a bad name amongst the Pecht and I had no desire to cross it. Beyond the raised dot on the horizon that was Dun Eidyn, I could just make out the smudge of Arthur's legendary base from where, in days long past, he had ridden out to smash our armies time after time. Everyone knew those stories and the memory of them was enough to deter me from entering Gododdin, even though Arthur was long dead and the people of the Gododdin were no more.

But although I feared to go further south, we knew that Beornhaeth was in Dun Eidyn and where he was, I thought my mother and Triduana would be. I still harboured dreams of rescuing them. For the moment, I kept those dreams to myself because I knew what Bleddyn would say if I mentioned them. He had made up his mind. He looked across the wide estuary thoughtfully but said, "It would be too dangerous just now. Beornhaeth is no lover of Ionian monks."

So we turned our backs on Linne Foirthe and travelled north again, although I cast frequent wistful glances back towards Dun Eidyn until it had vanished from our sight. One day, I promised myself, I would go there. I would find my mother and Triduana and I would bring them home.

We spent Christmas at Peairt, a small settlement that sat on the banks of the Tatha in a wide, green valley surrounded by hills and forests. There were Northumbrians there, a small detachment of around twenty men who had been left to guard the river crossing. Unlike their countrymen at Dun Foither, these men did not seem to mind Bleddyn, who preached to the villagers, sang songs of worship in a loud but dreadfully off-tune voice, then went to drink with the Northumbrians.

I was used to this by now. Bleddyn could drink as much as any man I ever knew but he was rarely drunk, even though he often acted it. He was good at acting and taught me many of his tricks, showing me how to appear sad, or happy, or stupid, which was always a good one when seeking information. Nobody bothered much about a fool, so I learned to play dumb, to listen to conversations without reacting to what I heard, as if I could not understand. After four months of travelling among the Northumbrians, added to the intensive lessons from Bleddyn, I was becoming quite adept at understanding what they said, although I still struggled to speak the language very well.

Bleddyn and I had settled into a routine. He would attract attention, preaching volubly to anyone who would listen, or drinking and chatting lustily to keep everyone focussed on him while I would casually stroll around, counting the warriors and the horses, taking note of what defences they had, where they kept their supplies, and a host of other things that Bleddyn told me to watch for.

I thought it was easy work because nobody ever bothered overmuch about a boy, especially a simpleton like I pretended to be. Bleddyn, though, was always pleased.

"You have an excellent memory," he said as I recounted what I had seen.

From his pack he would take out a small scroll, some ink and a stylus and he would jot down everything I told him adding whatever he had discovered himself.

"Isn't that dangerous?" I asked him one morning as he finished his scribbling. "What if you get caught with it?"

"You think the Angles can read?" he shot back, unable to hide his scorn for their ignorance.

"No, but their priests can."

Bleddyn nodded, smiling the way he did when I had said something that showed I was thinking. That always pleased him. I knew it was a good point because the priests and monks who travelled with the Northumbrians, though few in number, were vehemently opposed to the Ionian Church. They followed the Roman ways, calculating the religious festivals at a different time from the Ionian Church. They also cut their hair short, shaving the tops of their heads to leave a ring of hair in imitation of the crown of thorns that had been placed on our Saviour's head before the Crucifixion. Bleddyn tended to avoid these men if he could. Next to him, they seemed to me to be very pious and very miserable.

He looked at me conspiratorially. "They would not understand my writings," he informed me. "I am using symbols of my own devising that only I can understand."

"Will you teach me?" I asked. I had no real interest in reading or writing but secret codes were another matter.

He rolled up the scroll, stuffing it into his pack. "No. Not yet, at any rate. There is plenty of time for things like that."

I knew there was no point in arguing with him so I changed the subject slightly. "Why do the other monks dislike you so much?"

"Because their Church does things differently."

"I thought there was only one Church," I said as innocently as I could.

He replied, "There is, but there are different interpretations of how it should operate."

"That seems silly."

Bleddyn shrugged. "Perhaps. The Northumbrians are trying to impose the views of the Roman Church everywhere they go. Not everyone is happy about that, especially considering the reason."

"What reason is that?" I asked. I loved it when Bleddyn was in a talkative mood, so I decided to keep prompting him.

"I'll tell you when you are older," he said.

"Oh, please, Bleddyn. Tell me now."

Bleddyn thought for a moment then sighed. "Oh, very well. Like many things in life, it has to do with sex, although the Roman monks would deny it."

I frowned. I knew about sex, of course. When the whole family lived close together in one large, open house, it was impossible not to, but I had never really understood why people made such a fuss about it. Apart from my sister, I had never really come across many girls and the few I had spoken to had seemed mostly distant and very full of themselves. I had not been remotely interested in any of them. Still, I wanted Bleddyn to explain so I asked, "What do you mean?"

"Well, in the past, both Churches had influence in Northumbria. A few years back, King Oswiu, that's Ecgfrith's father, called a synod to decide which one should be the official Church and which would have to change its ways."

I was still puzzled. "That sounds sensible," I ventured cautiously.

"Maybe so, but the two Churches had operated quite happily side by side for many years. The only reason he called the synod was because he was following the Ionian traditions while his wife was a member of the Roman Church."

"So?"

"So, when he had celebrated Easter, she was still observing Lent, and after his own . . . abstinence during the Ionian Lent, he still couldn't bed her until after she had celebrated Easter."

I burst out laughing. "That's just silly!" I exclaimed.

Bleddyn did not laugh. In fact, he looked quite upset about it. "That's the way of the world, boy. Great things happen because one powerful man can't get his wife into bed when it suits him. The Ionian Church is banished from Northumbria and now Northumbria is coming north. If they win, our Church will disappear forever."

I decided not to press the issue because it was clearly something that meant a great deal to him. I had not been able to learn much about Bleddyn's past but this explained his hostility towards the Northumbrians. For myself, it made little difference which Church governed, although I could tell that our conversation had made Bleddyn uncomfortable. I let the matter drop and asked. "So where are we going next?"

Bleddyn shook off his momentary bout of gloom. "We'll wander around a little, I think. There is plenty of time before we need to be in Inbhir Nis. Besides, travelling in the north during winter can be dangerous if the snows come."

So we spent the next few weeks wandering the land, checking the locations of the Northumbrians and noting everything we saw. I suppose that it was a dangerous thing to do but it did not seem so at the time. I was young and I loved being with Bleddyn. He was so confident, I believed nothing could harm us, whatever we attempted. As I grew older, of course, I became more aware of the dangers, but that winter I can truly say that I found my role in life. I knew then that I was not destined to be a warrior, or a monk, but a spy. The only thing I was not clear about was who I would be spying for. Would it be for Bridei or for the King?

Chapter 4

Towards the end of March, just after Easter, we reached Inbhir Nis, a bustling port town on the banks of the river Nis, from which the settlement took its name. It was protected by hills on three sides, with the river widening out to join the sea to the north. On a low hill overlooking both the town and the river was the great stockade where the King had his home.

I say king but, to be more accurate, that is a word the English use. For the Pecht, the concept is different. All across our lands are local chieftains who govern their own land. In some places, every farmer thinks he is a chieftain but, of course, some are more powerful than others, and one of those influential chieftains is accepted as the leader of the people. He rules by consent, not by right, and he rules because he is deemed to be the person best suited to keeping the people safe and prosperous. That is not to say he lacks authority, for he is a leader in war, he represents the Pecht in dealings with foreign kings and must also pass judgement on any disputes that may arise among our people. When he does that, everyone must abide by those judgements. But a king of the Pecht is rarely succeeded by a son and if he fails in his duty to care for the people, he can be replaced.

At least, that was the theory as Bleddyn explained it to me. The reality, he said, was that it was only the most powerful chieftains who decided who should be king and they always chose one of their own number. Once chosen, most of them remained as king until they died, but sons did not usually succeed their fathers because none of the chieftains wanted any one family to gain too much power or prestige. I was still only fourteen years old, but I grasped the concept of self-interest quickly. I think Bleddyn's cynicism was already influencing me.

Bleddyn's explanations were all very well, but I confess that all thoughts of kings vanished when I first reached Inbhir Nis. It was the largest settlement I had ever seen, filled with people and more roundhouses than I could count. Instead of the widely spread farming villages I was used to, this place was all crammed in close together, a riot of noise and smells. Bleddyn reckoned that more than three thousand people had their homes here, not counting the king's own household. Everywhere I looked, people were making or selling everything I could imagine, some of them calling out to passers-by to come and examine their wares. Dogs and cats wandered among market stalls, trying to steal some of the food that was on display. Children shouted, babies cried and gulls screeched at us as they wheeled overhead, searching for discarded scraps to eat. Some children were throwing tiny pieces of stale bread to entice the birds. They would squeal with laughter as the gulls swooped down, trying to gobble the food before the dogs and cats charged in to scatter them.

On the river, boats bobbed. There were small skiffs and long sea-going vessels with tall masts and many rowing benches. Fishermen, too, were there, mending nets or displaying their latest catch for the townsfolk to buy or barter.

I gaped, wide-eyed and open-mouthed, as we rode through the town, trying to take it all in and knowing that I just had to find time to explore this wondrous place. Needless to say, Bleddyn had other ideas.

"We must go to the fort first," he told me in a tone that brooked no argument.

We rode straight through the town and on to the fort. This was impressive too, although not as fascinating as the town. It had a double ditch, a wooden stockade and large, imposing gates that were guarded by men holding long spears. I expected them to stop us but they recognised Bleddyn so they waved us through unchallenged.

"You've been away a long time," one of them said as we reached the gateway.

"Well, I am back now," Bleddyn replied cheerfully. "I hope there is enough beer left for me."

"There's not enough beer in the whole of Christendom for you, Bleddyn," the soldier laughed as he waved us through.

Inside the wide stockade I saw a host of buildings, some round, some rectangular, all scattered in no apparent order, like a second village contained within the wooden perimeter of the stockade. There were stables and workshops, kitchens and stores, granaries and guest houses. Bleddyn led me to the stables where we dismounted and left our horse in the care of the stablemaster. Bleddyn asked whether Bridei had arrived.

The stablemaster nodded. "Aye, he's here. Most of the chieftains are here. You'll find him in one of the guest houses."

I tagged along while Bleddyn wandered through the collection of roundhouses, asking directions of anyone he saw. At length, we found Bridei in one of the small, circular dwellings, where he was sitting on a stool beside the central hearth fire. I thought it was strange that he was indoors during the day but there were other men with him, so I guessed they were discussing something they wanted to keep private. A group of burly warriors stood outside to ensure that privacy but they, too, knew Bleddyn, so we were ushered in.

Bridei rose to greet us, clasping Bleddyn's forearm warmly and clapping him on the back. "Welcome! Welcome! Come and join us, Brother Bleddyn."

I was not specifically invited but I went in anyway, moving quietly to one side of the house where I sat cross-legged on the earthen floor.

At the fire, Bleddyn joined Bridei and two other men. From their greetings, I could tell that they had all met before. I studied the two new men closely. The younger one was named Taran, a lithe, dark-haired man with sparkling eyes and a serious look about him. His beard was neatly trimmed and he wore clothes that were immaculately tailored. He did not say much but I quickly gained the impression that he was clever because what he did say was always to the point.

The other man was called Nechtan. He was older, with greying hair and beard. He was big, bigger even than Bleddyn, with a deep chest and large belly. His arms and legs spoke of great strength but he was well past his prime and he seemed slower of thought than the others. I thought he was a little unsure of himself although he covered it with a great deal of bluster. He reminded me of some old farmers I had known, except that his clothes were much finer and he had a sword, which meant he was a man of some wealth and importance.

Bridei said, "Your timing is impeccable, Bleddyn. The Council meets in two days. So, tell us what you have learned."

Bleddyn sat and dug out his encoded notes. For the next hour, he did most of the talking, recounting what we had discovered on our travels in the south. Occasionally, one of the others, usually Bridei or Taran, would ask a question which Bleddyn would answer in great detail. The men nodded their heads or clucked their tongues depending on the answers he gave. I noticed, though, that they all tended to defer to Bridei, looking for his approval on any matter they discussed.

When Bleddyn had finished his tale, Taran and Nechtan said their farewells.

"Until Monday," Nechtan said in his deep, earthy voice. That puzzled me, because it was Saturday and they would surely see each other on Sunday. Bleddyn had told me there was a church in Inbhir Nis and nobody would miss church on Sunday.

"Monday," Bridei agreed, confirming that I had not mis-heard.

"It cannot come soon enough," said Taran as he gripped Bridei's hand in farewell.

When the two men had gone, Bridei gave Bleddyn a broad smile. "Do you have somewhere to stay?" he asked.

"Not yet," Bleddyn said.

"Then sleep here. There are plenty of mattresses and blankets."

"We should not impose," Bleddyn protested, rather half-heartedly, I thought.

"Nonsense," said Bridei. "It is the least I can do. You have done well. You and the boy." He looked over at me, waving a hand to summon me away from my place near the wall. It was the first time he had acknowledged my presence although I knew he had seen me from the moment I had entered the house. "Come and sit by the fire, Bili. You can tell me whether Bleddyn missed anything out."

I think he was joking, but I sat by the fire and earnestly told him what I had learned while food and ale were brought in by some young girls. Bridei beamed when he saw the fare. "Say what you like, Drest is a good host," he observed.

I gave Bleddyn a quizzical look. "Drest?" I mouthed.

Bleddyn said, "Drest is a chieftain of Cait and King of the Pecht. We will meet him soon."

"Monday," said Bridei. "We will all see him on Monday."

There was a sombre silence, unusual when Bridei was part of the company, but it was soon broken when another girl came into the house. She was about my age, I guessed, delicate, with long, dark hair and large, inquisitive blue eyes which fastened on me as soon as she entered. I looked away quickly, although I was not sure why.

Bridei rose to his feet. "Derelei," he said warmly. "Come and meet Bleddyn and his young friend, Bili."

Derelei bowed her head to Bleddyn. "Brother Bleddyn," she said. Her voice was like the ringing of tiny silver bells, crystal clear and delicate. "It is good to see you again."

I stole a look at her. Her skin was flawless, her every move delicate yet confident. Her face, with its high cheekbones, large, blue eyes and full lips, was the loveliest thing I had ever seen.

"I am pleased to see you, too, my child," Bleddyn replied.

"And this is Bili," said Bridei, gesturing towards me.

I looked up, feeling my face burning when she looked at me. "Hello," I mumbled. I stood up but I did not offer her my hand.

"Hello, Bili," she said. Her voice was still clear but her gaze took me in, judged me and instantly dismissed me as someone of no importance. She turned back to Bridei. "Father, how long will we be staying here? I want to go back home."

Bridei replied, "We will be here at least until Monday. Perhaps longer. It depends."

"On what?" she asked.

"On what happens on Monday," he told her. "Now, it is getting late. Brother Bleddyn will lead us in prayer and we will all get some sleep. Tomorrow is Sunday and we must all be at our best."

So we knelt while Bleddyn said a long and unusually boring prayer, then we arranged our stuffed mattresses and blankets. Bleddyn and I had beds at one side of the house while Bridei and Derelei slept at the other side. The bed was more comfortable than any I had ever slept on, but I still lay awake most of the night. I could not sleep because I was trying to figure out what significance Monday had for Bridei and the other chieftains. The way they had said it, I felt sure that something ominous was brewing. I thought about it a lot, partly because I was puzzled, but mostly because it stopped me thinking about Derelei.

Sunday's church service was a torment for me. Not because I disliked things like that. Far from it, for they were new and strange and I enjoyed the singing although some of the prayers dragged on too long for my liking. The service was taken by an elderly priest called Ronan who was, Bleddyn told me, the abbot here. Ronan intoned the Latin extracts from the holy book, then told us, at great length, what they meant. He told some good stories, although I think Bleddyn was better at bringing the tales to life when he preached.

Bleddyn, though, was in the congregation, standing beside me. I had noticed that Ronan had given him a sour look when we arrived; not the sort of hostile glare the Northumbrian monks reserved for Bleddyn, but it was less than friendly, all the same. Bleddyn affected not to notice.

We were standing near the front, a place of some honour because the church was too small to admit many people and the most important folk were at the front. I was pleased that we had been allowed in because the greater part of the townsfolk stood outside while junior monks preached the sermons to them.

Inside the tiny, wooden-walled church, the chieftains and their followers gathered. I saw Drest, the king, with his family, who were right at the front. He was a thin man, tall but stooped, as if he had grown old before his time. He was accompanied by a woman I took to be his wife, three young girls and a powerfully-built, dark-haired young man of around sixteen.

Behind Drest and his family were many other chieftains, including Bridei. Beside Bridei was Derelei, the cause of my discomfort.

She ignored me, of course, even when she walked with us on the way to the church, but I found that my eyes were constantly drawn to her. It quite distracted me from the prayers and the psalms. Once, Bleddyn had to give me a sharp kick to remind me to start singing. I don't know why he bothered because his lusty, discordant voice drowned me out anyway.

When the service was over, we all filed outside, where the chieftains exchanged pleasantries with one another and with Drest, who seemed to be rather on edge. I supposed that he had a lot on his mind, what with being the king and everything.

A sideways glance told me that Derelei had gone off with a few other girls, chatting excitedly about something or other as they headed towards the town. She had ignored me again, so I was glad to see her go. At least, I think I was glad.

"What do we do now?" I asked Bleddyn.

"It is a day of rest," he said. "We must be back at the church this evening, but until then you may do as you please." With a wave of his hand, he took in the sprawling town. "Why don't you take a look around? I have things to discuss with Bridei."

"I can go on my own?" I asked.

"Of course. You can hardly get lost, can you?"

I did not need a second invitation. Before he could change his mind I was off, darting into the town to have a proper look around.

My first stop was the river. I wandered along the bank, studying the boats. The smaller ones looked dangerous and the fishing boats smelled dreadfully but I was fascinated by the warships. I had never seen such long, sleek vessels as these. I imagined myself sitting on the benches, pulling on a long oar, helping to drive the ship across the wide sea on my way to plundering Northumbria. Then I saw three crewmen as they jumped lightly aboard the nearest craft, one of them carrying a jug of whisky. They were laughing and joking, moving confidently on the gently rocking vessel. As soon as I saw them, I realised that my dream of going to sea was about as likely as my dream of becoming a swordsman. They were all big men, with more muscles than I had ever seen on anyone before. I doubted whether I would ever grow to be that strong.

With a sigh, I headed back into the town. Because it was Sunday, none of the stalls had any goods on display which was a disappointment. I had hoped to get a closer look at some of the more expensive items. Just to see what they were like, of course. I had nothing to barter with, so even the cheapest clay pot would have been too expensive for me. Still, I enjoyed strolling through the town, dodging between the houses, scaring away the cats and generally finding my way around.

I discovered that the town was home to a wide variety of skilled craftsmen and women. There were smiths and jewellers working iron, silver and gold, there were threshing houses for separating wheat from chaff, there were people who spun wool or who worked leather, there were water troughs for retting flax which would be spun into linen, and there were potters who could turn wet clay into finely decorated pots and mugs. For a fourteen year old boy who had grown up in a small farming community, Inbhir Nis was a marvellous place.

Nobody paid much attention to me. There were lots of people around but they were mostly chatting or drinking, or preparing food. After a while, I walked round the side of one house to find a relatively open space where a group of around half a dozen girls were playing 'Catch' with a small, leather ball stuffed with rags. They were tossing it to one another, laughing and calling out as they tried to throw it faster and faster from one to the other. I watched them enviously for a few moments until I realised that Derelei was there. She saw me, but looked away, concentrating on the game. Up until then I had been half considering asking to join in, even though they were girls, but when Derelei saw me, I turned on my heel and hurried back among the houses.

"No time for games, boy?" a cracked voice asked me as I passed a doorway.

I jumped, alarmed at the unexpected intrusion. My reaction brought a laugh or, rather, a cackle from the speaker. I tried to walk on, but the voice called, "Wait a moment, boy. Come here."

I turned back. There was a woman sitting on a three-legged stool in the doorway of a small roundhouse. Her head was covered by a woollen shawl which draped over her shoulders. Her face was wrinkled, with a prominent wart on her left cheek. She gave me a grin that was more gums than teeth. "You're the monk's servant, is that right?"

I nodded. "Yes."

"Your name is Bili."

"How do you know that?" I asked. I wondered whether she was a witch. She certainly looked like one, although I had never actually seen a witch before. Still, she matched the descriptions I had heard in the stories my mother used to tell. Shawl, dark dress, wart, lost teeth, harsh voice and evil laugh. She had them all.

"It's no secret," she said. "This is not such a big place that strangers are not recognised. I make it my business to know who is coming and going."

"Why?" I asked, determined to show I was not afraid, even if she was a witch. I managed to keep my voice firm although I hoped that she would not see my knees trembling.

She cackled again. "Why not? Lots of comings and goings recently, and lots more to come soon, I think. What do you say?"

"I don't know."

Her eyebrows wrinkled in a frown. "No? Then you are not much use to Fincana, are you?"

"Who's Fincana?"

Another cackle that almost turned into a hacking cough. When she had recovered, she said. "I am Fincana. Fincana the Seer, they call me. Shall I tell your future?"

"I have nothing to pay you with," I said. I still thought she was a witch rather than a seer but although I was afraid of her evil looks, I was tempted by the thought of knowing my future.

"Well now, that is no problem," said Fincana. "You tell me something of interest that nobody else knows and I will tell you something of your future. What do you say?"

I hesitated. "What can I tell you?" I asked her.

"Come inside, boy, and we shall find out."

I looked around, realising for the first time that her house was positioned in such a way that nobody could see the door unless they were very close. Other roundhouses blocked the view in every direction but, in the traditional way, most had doors facing east, so none of them looked on to Fincana's doorway.

She laughed again. "Don't worry, boy. It is perfectly safe."

She lifted herself from her stool, ducking through the heavy, leather flap of her door which she held open for me.

I swallowed nervously. Ever since that day the Northumbrians had killed Giric, I had known I was a coward. I had spent every waking moment trying to convince myself that I was not, but this was the first time I had found an opportunity to prove it to myself.

Fincana beckoned me with a gnarled, bony hand. Taking a deep breath, I went into her home.

It was perfectly normal inside. Clean, with a low, heather-filled mattress and thick woollen blankets placed against the far wall. The floor was strewn with fresh straw and there was a small table, a large, wooden dresser and two more stools. The only unusual feature was the pungent scent of herbs which hung in bunches from the roof beams overhead. On the fire a black pot bubbled away, the delicious smell of broth combining with the herbs to fill the roundhouse with a unique and almost overpowering aroma.

She saw my face. "Are you hungry?" she asked as she stirred the contents of the pot with a long, wooden spoon.

"No," I lied. I remembered my mother's stories, so I knew better than to accept food from a witch.

"Then let us begin. Sit down." She gestured to one of the stools.

I sat down. She perched herself on the other stool, facing me from barely an arm's length away. "Now then," she said. "Why don't you tell me about Bridei."

She was staring at me but I managed to hold her gaze. I think that impressed her. I asked, "What about him?"

"What does he plan to do tomorrow?"

I shrugged. "I don't know."

She scowled at me. "I thought you were the monk's servant?"

"I am."

"Bleddyn is one of Bridei's closest friends. Have you heard nothing?"

"No."

"Think, boy. What have you heard? Tomorrow is an important day for the people of the Pecht. Who has Bridei spoken to?"

"He spoke to two men called Taran and Nechtan, but I don't really know what they discussed. Something about Monday, though."

I wasn't entirely sure I should be telling her this but she had promised to tell my future, so I had to say something.

Her frown faded a little. "Taran and Nechtan? That makes some sense. Wheels are turning. Changes are afoot. But what changes, I wonder? Is Bridei ready?"

She was speaking more to herself than to me but I recalled what Bridei had said that morning when he had sent Bleddyn and me south to be his spies.

"He said he is ready," I offered.

Her eyes shone, boring into me. "He said that?"

"Yes. I heard him. He said he was ready. I don't know what for."

"Hah! I do," she said softly. "I do indeed." Her expression softened slightly. "Thank you, boy. That is all I need to know from you."

Now it was my turn to frown. I could not imagine why this news was enough for her. Then again, a bargain is a bargain. "Will you tell me my future now?" I asked.

"What? Oh, yes. Give me your hand." She reached for my right hand, turning it palm upwards. I tensed but she did nothing more than look at it for what seemed an age.

"What is it that you wish to know?" she asked eventually.

"Will I find my mother and sister again?"

She studied my palm in silence. Then she said, "They were taken?"

"Yes. The Northumbrians came and burned our house. They were taken away as slaves."

She released my hand, sat up straight and looked me in the eye. "You will search for them, over many years and many miles. It will be long and dangerous but yes, you will find them again."

I almost leaped from the stool in excitement. "Are you sure?"

She shrugged. "I am Fincana. I am never wrong."

"Thank you," I said excitedly. I almost hugged her, but she was a witch, so I stayed where I was.

"I am glad to have helped," said Fincana. "Now, you had better run along."

I practically skipped out of her house. This was a great day indeed, the best since the Northumbrians had destroyed my family. I did not care how long it took, all I knew was that I would find my mother and sister again.

Of course, life has a way of shattering hopes and dreams. Fincana's prediction had left me feeling ten feet tall but it was not long before things began to go wrong.

Chapter 5

I wanted to share the news with someone, so I headed back up to the fort to find Bleddyn. When I got to the house, though, one of the guards told me that he and Bridei had gone out riding and were not expected back for some time. Disappointed, I went to the kitchens where I begged a chunk of bread and some salted herring which I munched happily before heading back to wait for Bleddyn to return.

I reached the house to find that, rather than Bleddyn, it was Derelei who had returned. She was sitting in the doorway, deftly using a needle and thread to repair one of her father's old tunics. I stopped, hoping to dodge away but she had seen me.

"It's you," she said, as if I was interrupting something important.

"Yes." Inside, I was cursing. Everywhere I went, she was there too.

"What are you looking so happy about?" she asked. She continued sewing, giving me no more than the occasional glance while she worked.

"Nothing."

She sniffed. "Was it something Fincana said to you?"

My face and ears began to burn. How could she have known? Then I remembered she had been playing ball with the other girls nearby. Had she followed me?

"Well?" she asked. "What did she say?"

"Nothing much," I mumbled.

"Don't be silly. She must have said something. It is written all over your face."

I shuffled my feet. My tongue felt too clumsy to get the words out. I didn't want to talk to her but I had grown up living with Triduana so I knew enough about girls to know that Derelei would not let this drop. Feeling more than a little embarrassed, I said, "She told me I would find my mother and sister again."

Derelei gave me a quick look, then returned her attention to her needlework. "Is that all? How careless of you to lose them in the first place."

That brought another flush to my face but it was one of anger this time. "Don't say things like that!" I snapped at her. "They were captured by the Angles and taken away as slaves. My brother was killed."

Derelei laid her sewing in her lap. When she looked at me, she seemed to be genuinely sympathetic. "I'm sorry," she said apologetically. "I did not know that. I know how hard it must be for you. My mother died a few years ago."

That admission brought a definite tinge of sadness to her features.

"I'm sorry to hear that," I said, feeling my own anger dissipate.

She gave me a studied look. "You are very intriguing," she said with the trace of an amused smile.

"What do you mean by that?"

"You don't act all tough and arrogant like the other boys around here."

I shrugged. I didn't think I had much to be arrogant about and I certainly wasn't big enough to be tough with anyone. "I'm just me," I said.

"Bleddyn says you are clever," she observed.

That was a surprise. I asked, "When did he tell you that?"

She gave me a soft, secretive smile. "He didn't," she admitted. "I overheard him speaking to my father. He said you have a quick mind."

"Bleddyn is a clever man," I said modestly, although I was secretly pleased at what Bleddyn had said and that Derelei had been interested enough to eavesdrop on his conversation.

Derelei said, "Not many boys would dare to go into Fincana's home on their own. Weren't you frightened?"

So she had been watching me. I replied, "A bit. But it was worth it. She said I will find my mother again one day."

Derelei cocked her head to one side, regarding me curiously. "Then I pray that comes true for you. But if you are sensible, you will keep this news to yourself."

"What do you mean?"

I thought for a moment that she would roll her eyes in exasperation but she surprised me again. Regarding me calmly, she said, "The churchmen do not like Fincana. They say she uses magic. She is not a Christian."

I thought about that for a few moments. "You don't think Bleddyn would be pleased?"

"Bleddyn is a monk. If you tell him you have been speaking to Fincana, he will not be happy at all."

"But I need to tell someone. I don't know anyone else."

"You have told me," Derelei said sweetly. Then she laughed when she saw my expression. "Don't worry. I promise that I will not tell another soul. It will be our secret." I was about to say that I would never trust any girl with a secret but she stood up, crossed herself solemnly, and repeated, "I promise, Bili. I will not tell anyone you have spoken to Fincana, nor what she said to you." Then she looked at me sharply. "What did you tell her?"

I was in too deep now to escape. "Nothing much," I said. "She wanted to know about your father."

Derelei's eyes narrowed. "What about him?"

I shrugged. "I couldn't tell her very much. I hardly know him. All I said was that he had said he was ready."

Derelei smiled. "Is that all?"

"Yes. What does it mean?"

"Don't you know anything?" she asked, managing to not quite laugh at my ignorance.

"Apparently not," I muttered. "Bleddyn doesn't tell me much."

"Obviously. Well, next time you go to bed and the men stay up talking, pretend to fall asleep and listen to what they say. You will learn a lot that way."

"Like what? What is going to happen on Monday?"

She leaned closer to me to whisper, "By Monday evening, Drest will no longer be king."

I gaped at her. "You mean . . . ?"

She nodded happily. "My father is ready." Then she reached out, grabbing my hands, suddenly earnest. "You must not tell anyone that I told you. I am not supposed to know. Promise me."

"I promise." I crossed myself to prove I would keep my word.

"Good. It is supposed to be a secret. The chieftains are all meeting, as they do every year, but this year will be different."

A sudden, worrying thought struck me. "What is going to happen to Drest? Are they going to kill him?"

She shook her head. "No. At least, not unless he refuses to step down. If he does that, there may be war. My father is hoping for the support of the chieftains so that there will be no need to fight."

I was relieved to hear that. I was also delighted to find that I was now speaking to Derelei as if she were a friend. My tongue no longer stuck in my mouth although I felt my skin tingling when she touched my hand. It was a strange, disquieting, yet somehow exciting sensation. I thought she was the most beautiful girl I had ever seen. I could hardly take my eyes from the loveliness of her perfect face and the slight swelling of her chest. I wanted to do or say something to encourage her to hold my hand again but at that moment we heard the sound of men's voices. Derelei immediately sat down, picked up her sewing and ignored me. I wasn't sure what to do, so I turned away from her, just in time to see Bridei and Bleddyn striding towards us.

Derelei jumped up again, running to embrace Bridei warmly. He returned the hug, then kissed her cheek. "Making friends, I see," he said.

Derelei gave me a scornful look. "I was just giving Bili some advice," she said. "He doesn't seem to know much about anything."

Bridei laughed at that. He gave me a wink. "Don't feel too bad about it, lad. There's not a woman on this earth who thinks men know very much at all."

Bridei called for some food, so Derelei went off to the kitchens. I offered to go with her but she declared rather haughtily that she did not need my help. I felt confused and a little hurt by her sudden change of attitude, but I put on a brave face and said, "Suit yourself."

When she returned, she made a great show of ignoring me. That annoyed me, so I did the same to her. We ate and we drank while Bleddyn regaled us with some tales from the Bible. I had heard most of them before, so I sat quietly, thinking to myself about Fincana's prophecy, about Bridei claiming to be ready to be king, and about Derelei and her strange attitude towards me. I ended up more confused than ever.

Early in the afternoon, Nechtan arrived, bringing his son, Guret. He was a little older than me, I think. He was certainly taller, although pretty much everyone my age was taller than me. At Bridei's invitation, Guret took some of the food that was left and sat near to me, although he did not speak. I expect he had seen my old, ragged clothes and thought that I was beneath him. I noticed that he kept looking at Derelei, which made me feel a little jealous, but she paid no attention to him, ignoring him just as much as she ignored me.

It was Nechtan who did the talking. The burly chieftain was agitated about something.

"It's that seer Fincana," he said animatedly. "She's made a prophecy that Drest will no longer be king. The rumour is spreading all over town."

"Damn!" Bridei said. Then he gave Bleddyn a sheepish look, knowing it was wrong to swear on the Sabbath. "Sorry, Brother, but this is the last thing we need." He sounded sincere, but something in his manner suggested that he was actually rather pleased.

Nechtan asked, "What do we do?"

Bleddyn said, "She is an interfering, heathen witch and her words are not to be believed. People must be told that."

Bridei nodded sagely. "Will you tell them, Brother Bleddyn?"

Bleddyn gripped his oak staff. "I will indeed. The people must be steered away from pagan prophecies."

"Good," said Bridei. "Thank you, Brother."

"It is my Christian duty," Bleddyn said solemnly. He made for the door, full of purpose, ducking outside on his way to stamp out Fincana's rumour.

Bridei turned to Nechtan. "Thank you for warning me," he said. "I will not forget this."

"What about tomorrow?" Nechtan asked anxiously. "If Drest learns what we are planning . . ." His voice trailed off as he gave a worried shrug.

"Who will tell him?" Bridei asked innocently. "You heard Brother Bleddyn. I cannot be held responsible for the ravings of a mad woman. Even if Drest hears of it, he cannot claim I started the story." He placed a hand on Nechtan's beefy shoulder. "We proceed as planned. Nothing has changed." In a low voice he added, "Do not mention it to Brother Bleddyn, but in some ways this might be a good thing. Others may heed the prophecy."

"I suppose so," Nechtan said uncertainly.

"Then we should go about our usual business," Bridei said cheerfully.

Nechtan left, taking the sullen Guret with him. When they were gone, Bridei sat down, unable to keep a broad smile from his face.

By the time we returned to the church for the evening sermon and prayers, it seemed that everyone had heard the rumour. Bleddyn assured us that he had spoken to everyone he could find, insisting that they should not heed Fincana's words because she was a heathen. He was very pleased with himself although it seemed to me that he had done more to spread the prophecy than anyone. I mentioned that to him after the service as we were walking back to the roundhouse.

He gave me a look of pure innocence. "Do you think so? That never occurred to me. Ah, well, it is too late now. People will believe what they want to believe, I suppose."

"You did it on purpose," I accused.

He grinned. "We must use whatever resources the good Lord sends to us," he said. "I don't know where that wretched woman gets her information, but I must admit that she has come in useful today."

"Perhaps she really can tell the future," I suggested.

Bleddyn shrugged. "Perhaps. But you stay away from her, Bili. Do you hear me? Rather than tell your future, she is more likely to simply tell you what you want to hear in exchange for you divulging secrets."

"I don't know any secrets," I lied.

"Keep away from her anyway."

"Yes, Bleddyn."

That was one promise I vowed to keep. I was happy to stay away from Fincana, even though I was convinced that her prediction that I would find my family again would come true one day.

I followed Derelei's advice and stayed awake that night while Bridei and Bleddyn sat talking quietly. I could hear Derelei, breathing slowly and evenly on the other side of the house. I guessed she was pretending, so I copied the slow, regular rhythm of her breathing, hoping the men would think I was sleeping too.

"Drest has heard about it," Bridei said. "I could tell from the look he gave me."

"Good," said Bleddyn. "I wish I had thought of dropping a quiet word in Fincana's ear."

"Aye, it has helped. But it means that someone has talked."

It was all I could do not to squirm when I heard that. I realised that I was holding my breath and I had to force myself to begin breathing again.

Bleddyn said, "Still, it should work to our advantage. Tomorrow, God willing, you will be king."

"Let us not tempt fate," Bridei said.

"If you succeed, you know that you will need to act quickly to secure your hold."

"I know. I will have need of you, Bleddyn."

Not 'Brother Bleddyn', I noticed.

"Where first?" Bleddyn asked. "To Dal Riata?"

"Bloody Scots," Bridei grumbled. "I don't trust them."

"I will go there first, then. What about the Britons of Alt Clud?"

"Bloody Britons. I don't trust them either."

"King Elfin is your nephew."

Bridei snorted. "Great-nephew. I've only met him once, when he was a boy. I have no reason to trust him."

"Then I suppose he has no reason to trust you," Bleddyn observed. "But he trusts me. I presume you wish to maintain friendly relations?"

"With Elfin of Alt Clud? Yes. The Britons may aid us later."

"Against Ecgfrith of Northumbria?"

"Bloody Northumbrians," Bridei growled. "I really don't trust them."

"Ecgfrith is too strong for you to oppose just now."

"I know that, Bleddyn. But Ecgfrith will not be a problem. Not for the moment, anyway. He has other things to worry about. The Mercians are threatening war against him."

"I'll go to Dal Riata, then," Bleddyn said. "How do you want things done?"

"Stir things up," Bridei answered immediately. "Get them fighting among themselves." He chuckled. "That shouldn't be too difficult and it will keep them too busy to bother us for a while."

"It will be a pleasure."

"Just be careful, Bleddyn."

"I am always careful,." Bleddyn replied.

"What about the boy? Will you take him with you?"

I held my breath again as I waited for Bleddyn's reply. After what seemed an age, he said, "Yes, he will go with me."

"Be careful," Bridei warned. "He is young. There is still time for him to step aside from this path. If he goes with you, who knows what he might become?"

"I hear you," sighed Bleddyn, "but if he stays here, he will not be happy. He has a fire in him. I can see it."

Bridei said softly, "Do you think he could become the sort of man we need?"

"Hard and ruthless, you mean?" Bleddyn asked.

"Just like us," agreed Bridei. "These are dark times for the Pecht, Bleddyn. We will have need of clever, ruthless men in the years to come."

"Bili has the will for it," said Bleddyn.

"But do we have the right to use him?" asked Bridei.

"It will not be against his will," replied Bleddyn. "I believe he was destined to play this part. The Lord led me to him."

Bridei said, "Then take him with you and teach him."

"I will," promised Bleddyn.

I lay there, not daring to move, scarcely able to breathe. I did not really understand a great deal about what they had said but I knew that great things were being set in motion and that I would be a part of them. That was all I wanted. I was too young to understand their concerns over what those events might do to me, and by the time I was old enough, it was too late to turn back.

Chapter 6

Monday morning dawned bright and clear, with only a few high clouds decorating the serene sky.

"A good day for it," was Bridei's only comment. Considering what he was planning to do, I thought he was remarkably composed. It was as if he was merely intending to go for a day's hunting. In a way, he was, although his quarry was no stag or boar.

I wanted to say something, to wish him luck or to ask why he was about to challenge the King, but I dared not let him know I had overheard his conversation with Bleddyn, so I held my tongue and tried to act as if this sunny morning was just the beginning of another ordinary day.

Of course, it was far from ordinary. Bleddyn was unusually on edge, fussing around needlessly and constantly poking his head out of the door as if looking for something.

"Sit down, Bleddyn," growled Bridei. "This is just another Council meeting."

"Not quite," Bleddyn muttered as he seated himself beside the hearth.

"That's how we should treat it," Bridei told him.

While Bleddyn fretted, Derelei combed Bridei's hair and helped him dress in his finest clothes. She selected a brooch of gold to fasten his thick cloak, pinning it at his shoulder.

"You look wonderful," she told him.

Bridei stood up, regarding his reflection in a small mirror. He nodded approvingly, then turned to Bleddyn. "Time to go," he announced.

Bleddyn rose, picking up his staff. Then he followed Bridei to the door. Outside, half a dozen warriors fell into step behind Bridei as he set off for the great hall where the chieftains were to meet.

As soon as they had left, Derelei turned to me, her eyes bright with excitement. "Are you coming?" she asked.

"To the meeting?"

"Of course, silly. Come on."

She took my hand, sending another tingle running up my arm and through my whole body. I could not understand her at all, but I knew that I liked it when she held my hand, so I followed her willingly.

"Did you hear what they said last night?" she asked as she led me through the fort.

"Yes."

"You'll be going with Bleddyn, to Dal Riata and Alt Clud?"

"I suppose so."

"And I'll be stuck here. You'd better come back and tell me all about it."

"Of course I will." I would promise her anything as long as she kept hold of my hand.

We reached the King's Hall. It was a massive building, built to a rectangular design, with high, wooden walls of wattle and daub. The roof was of thatch, rising to a high ridge that was supported by enormous timber rafters. This was where the King of the Pecht met his people, where he gave his judgements and where he provided entertainment on feast days. I had learned that there were other buildings at the rear of the hall, housing the servants of the King's household and containing a score of private chambers for the King and his family. Compared to the simple roundhouses that most of our people lived in, the King's Hall was a wonder of construction.

It was crowded that day, with many people thronging around outside the main doors. Bleddyn had told me that the hall was large enough to hold more than three hundred people but it was full to bursting point that day. Derelei squeezed and pushed her way through, somehow evading the attention of the guards at the doors, and leading me inside.

Dozens of rushlights lit the interior but it took a while for my eyes to adjust to the gloom. The main thing I was aware of was the excited buzz of conversation all around us, heightening the sense of expectation. I heard several people discussing Fincana's prophecy. Then I heard a thumping sound, demanding attention, followed by Abbot Ronan's old voice calling for silence.

The noise settled down. Derelei and I squeezed our way to one side, edging close to the far end where we could see Drest, King of the Pecht, sitting on a high-backed chair, the other major chieftains sitting around three sides of a small square so that they could all see him. Behind the chieftains, to the sides of the hall and stretching all the way back to the doors, other men and women stood, patiently now, waiting to see what would happen.

We caught sight of Bridei, sitting at the right hand side of the square, with Bleddyn standing behind his chair. Derelei wormed her way round until we were only a couple of paces behind them. Bleddyn turned, saw us and frowned slightly before turning his attention back to the Abbot.

We began with a prayer, delivered by Abbot Ronan, who then passed proceedings over to Drest.

The King spoke in a surprisingly calm and clear voice, full of authority and sincerity.

"My friends," he said. "I thank you for coming. I know many of you are anxious for our future. I share that anxiety. I have heard the whispers and I know that some people believe I have failed you. It is true that we lost too many of our best menfolk last year when the Northumbrians came against us. It is also true that many of our people are now subject to Northumbrian rule. The lands of Circinn, Fib and Fidach are lost to us and the men of Dal Riata press on our western borders. I have been forced to offer tribute to Ecgfrith of Northumbria, binding us to his overlordship for years to come."

He was silent for a while, then he went on, his voice rising almost to a shout. "But I will not heed the whispers. I have led the people for many years and I defy anyone to say I have not ruled wisely. This last year has been a setback, but the lands of Fotla, Fortriu and Cait are still ours. These are our heartlands. From here, our ancestors drove back the armies of Rome many generations past. We can do the same to Northumbria. Not this year. Perhaps not even the next year, or the year after that. But we should gather our strength, drive back the Scots of Dal Riata and then, when the time is right, when we are ready, we will regain what we have lost."

He looked around the hall, studying the faces of the chieftains, trying to gauge the mood. Calmly, he said, "I ask for your pledges of loyalty. What do you say?"

The only sounds were the shuffling of feet on the floor rushes and an occasional cough from somewhere among the crowd.

Most eyes turned to Bridei. Almost reluctantly, he rose to his feet. He bowed his head to Drest before turning to address the assembled chieftains and warriors in a loud, confident voice.

"Drest is correct," he said. "The Lord has seen fit to send trials to test us and we have suffered greatly at the hands of my cousin, Ecgfrith. That is a fact, and cannot be altered. We have no choice for the moment, so I say that Drest should remain as our leader and should guide us through these difficult times."

Giving Drest another bow, he sat down on his chair.

I could not believe it. From what I had heard the previous evening, I had expected him to challenge Drest. It seemed that most others had thought the same because a murmur of conversation filled the hall until Abbot Ronan banged his staff to silence the crowd.

Then I saw dark-eyed Taran stand up. He turned in a circle, his arms wide, taking in the whole of the audience like a bard about to recite an epic tale.

"My friends," he said. "I understand what has been said and it is hard to disagree, but in these difficult times I say that we need a new, strong, leader; a man who can ensure that we do indeed regain our strength.

"We are pressed by three peoples; the Angles of Northumbria, the Scots of Dal Riata and the Britons of Alt Clud. In our present, weakened state, we must make peace with as many of them as possible and we must ensure that they keep the peace. There is one man here who has connections to the rulers of two of those other people, a man who is uncle to the king of Alt Clud, and who is a first cousin to Ecgfrith of Northumbria. This man can ensure peace through his blood ties." He turned to face Bridei. He pointed his hand, exclaiming, "I say that Bridei of Fortriu should be our leader!"

Nechtan immediately leaped to his feet, speaking before Taran had sat down. He pumped a fist into the air. "Aye!" he cried. "Bridei is the man to lead us. Did he not advise against the decision to refuse paying the tribute when Oswiu of Northumbria died? Look what happened when we withheld that payment. Oswiu's son, Ecgfrith, came north and has taken half our lands from us. That would not have happened if Bridei had led us."

Nechtan sat down, his face flushed, as if he had just delivered a rehearsed speech, but Taran was better at manipulating the crowd. "What do you say?" he called out. "I proclaim Bridei!"

A chant began at the back of the hall. "Bridei! Bridei!"

Bleddyn began thumping his staff on the floor in time to the chant. Soon the entire hall was echoing to the stamping of feet, the clapping of hands and the sound of Bridei's name. Abbot Ronan banged his staff in vain, his face growing ever more purple in frustration. I looked at Drest, who sat quite still on his chair, his face pale but resigned.

Then Bridei stood once more, raising his hands to call for calm. The clamour slowly subsided. When all was quiet, he looked at Drest.

"This would be a heavy burden for me, but I have heard the will of the people. You may step down with honour, for you have served the people well these past years. What do you say, Drest?"

Drest slowly raised himself from his chair. He surveyed the hall, then bowed his head to Bridei. "I will heed the word of the people," he said in a dignified tone. "The leadership is yours."

The hall erupted once more. At least, I think it did because Derelei hugged me, planting a joyful kiss on my cheek. For me, everything else faded into the background until Bleddyn found me. Derelei ran off to hug her father, leaving me rubbing my cheek and staring forlornly after her.

Bleddyn leaned down to place his mouth close to my ear. "Forget her, Bili. She is a king's daughter now. She is far beyond you."

"What do you mean?" I asked.

He gave me a smile that was tinged with regret. "You will know in time, lad. You are young enough yet. But push Derelei from your dreams."

I looked over to where Derelei was standing beside Bridei. She was smiling happily while he was fending off congratulations from a host of chieftains. All around us, people were jostling to approach him. Derelei was hidden from my view as a crowd of people shoved past us but I think she had forgotten me already.

I looked up at Bleddyn. "Can we go now?" I asked.

He nodded. Without another word, he led me from the hall.

Chapter 7

There was a great celebration that afternoon which continued late into the evening. Bridei mab Bili was King of the Pecht and he was generous in dispensing food, ale and whisky. I even saw Abbot Ronan sipping at a tankard of beer. I tried some myself. I didn't particularly like it but everyone was expected to drink, so I sipped away until my mind began to feel detached from my body and my bladder felt uncomfortably full.

There was music and dancing and it was all a bit too much for me. Derelei was there, of course, vivacious and beautiful, dancing alongside the other young girls, but I stayed away from her. She obviously had no time for me now that she was a king's daughter.

To my surprise, I saw Drest among the crowd. He was not exactly celebrating but he spoke with Bridei and seemed somehow to have had a weight lifted from his shoulders. He was no longer the king but he appeared to have accepted the change with grace and dignity. I was glad about that. He seemed an honourable man and I would not have liked to see him being forced out by an armed revolt. From what I could see, there was no animosity between Drest and Bridei, simply an acceptance of the change in their positions.

Bleddyn told me, "That is the way it should be. A man who is too proud to know when to relinquish power will only harm himself and his people. The Pecht are a civilised race, so we do these things without rancour. Drest is a good man but the present dangers are too much for him. It is Bridei's turn now."

"What can he do that Drest could not?" I asked.

"You will see," was Bleddyn's enigmatic reply. "But not today. Today is for celebrating. Eat as much as you like, but do not drink too much. Tomorrow, you and I have a long journey ahead of us."

"Where are we going?" I asked, pretending I did not know.

"Wait until tomorrow," he told me. "Today you should fill your belly at the King's expense."

I did as he suggested. The beer may not have been to my taste but the food was plentiful. I don't think I had ever eaten quite as much in a single afternoon.

As the long day wore on, I sat watching the party but I did not feel part of the celebration. Instead, I felt deflated and rather miserable. After drinking another mug of beer, I realised that my bladder was most definitely full, so I wandered out of the hall, into the cool dark of the late evening. The weather had taken a turn for the worse and the wind was now blustering in from the sea, driving the odd droplet of rain. I did not mind; after the heat inside the hall, the breeze felt refreshingly cool on my face.

I decided that the weather suited my mood. I was fourteen years old and I felt as if I had the weight of the world on my shoulders. I was sure it was all Derelei's fault. I decided that Bleddyn was right. I should forget her. In the morning we would be leaving and I would not see her again for several months at least. That thought should have cheered me up but it only made me feel more depressed. I could not forget the tingle on my skin when she held my hand nor the soft touch of her kiss on my cheek.

I left the privy feeling slightly better, or at least less physically uncomfortable. I decided I did not want to return to the hall so I headed back to Bridei's roundhouse. It would not be his home much longer, I knew. Soon he would move into the King's Hall when Drest moved out. Still, the roundhouse would do for me this night.

"There he is," a voice said from just ahead of me.

I stopped. Four boys stepped out from the shadows. I recognised Guret, Nechtan's son, and the big, dark-haired lad who had been with Drest in the church. I had seen the other two around but I had no idea who they were. Slightly drunk as I was, I still recognised their intentions. The threat of violence was unmistakeable.

The sensible thing would have been to turn and run back to the hall, but I knew that would be the action of a coward, and I still needed to prove that I was not afraid, so I stood my ground.

"What do you want?" I asked.

That brought a snigger from one of them. The tallest boy, Drest's son, confident and well-built, stood in front of me, his fists planted on his hips.

"You're the monk's new catamite, aren't you?" he sneered.

I had no idea what a catamite was. "I'm Bleddyn's servant," I replied.

More sniggers. "I bet you are," said Guret.

"Who are you?" I asked the tall boy. I knew who he was, but I was stalling for time. The longer he talked, the more my fuddled head would clear. It was clearing pretty quickly already thanks to the fear pumping through my veins.

"I am Medraut, son of Drest." He gestured to his companions. "These are my friends, Guret, Donnell and Uerb."

"Pleased to meet you," I said, affecting a calm I did not feel inside. Bleddyn had taught me how to conceal my true feelings and those lessons, designed to fool the Angles, came in useful now.

Uerb, short but fat, sniggered again. "Ooh, he's pleased to meet us," he mocked.

"Bastard," said Guret.

"What?"

"You heard."

I turned back to Medraut. "What is it that you want?" I asked. I was really frightened now but I managed to conceal it. Medraut was obviously the leader of this gang, so he was the one I needed to concentrate on.

He said, "My father is no longer King, thanks to Bleddyn and his meddling."

"Bastard priest," Guret muttered. I flicked my gaze to him. I could not understand why he was so hostile.

"I had nothing to do with it," I said to Medraut. "Anyway, your father has accepted it. And other people have gained from it." I nodded towards Guret.

Guret snarled, "If Drest cannot be king, my father should have the place. He is the senior chieftain."

"There's no such thing," I said. "Anyway, like I said, it was nothing to do with me." I was praying that Derelei had kept her word and told nobody about my encounter with Fincana the seer. I wondered whether that was why these boys had come after me. Did they know that I had given her the clue to her prophecy?

Medraut said, "Maybe not, but you are a stranger here and everyone knows about the meddling of Bleddyn Grim-Hand. It's strange how things happened as soon as he got here."

I almost laughed. "Bleddyn Who?"

Medraut ignored me. "You will fight me now," he said. "A fair fight so there can be no excuses for telling tales."

"I don't want to fight you," I said. That was true. Not only was he a couple of years older than me, he was more than a head taller and far stronger.

"Then run away like a coward," he said. "But be sure that we will tell everyone."

That settled it, of course. I swallowed hard. "All right," I said. "Where?"

"Right here." His fist flashed out so fast that I did not have time to react. It caught me in the belly, doubling me over. More blows followed, raining down on my shoulders and back. He grabbed me, hauled me upright and began pummelling my chest and face with blows so rapid that it was like a dozen boys were hitting me. Behind him, Guret and the others were urging him to hit me harder.

I staggered back, then lashed out, trying to hit him back. He easily blocked my first wild swing but then I caught him on the upper arm with a jab from my left fist. He didn't seem to notice. I swung again and somehow got past his guard to clip his chin. Again he ignored it but my fist felt as if my fingers had been broken. He hit me again, hard, one punch to the chest, another to my stomach.

I fell down. I knew I was beaten and I hoped that he would stop if I pretended to pass out. A kick to my face proved that theory wrong almost immediately. But then I heard him shout, "Enough, Guret. I said it would be a fair fight."

"We should beat him up some more," I heard one of the others say. It sounded like Uerb, the fat one.

"No," Medraut said. "That's enough. He won't forget that in a hurry." He leaned down to say to me, "Keep out of my way in future, monk-boy."

I heard them walk away but I did not move. Not for a long time. Eventually, I dragged myself upright, swaying and staggering, aching all over. I made my unsteady way to the roundhouse, found my bed and covered myself with blankets, holding my arms tight around my battered chest. It was all I could do not to cry. I hated this place.

"What happened to you?" Bleddyn asked when he saw me the next morning.

"I tripped and fell," I said. My left eye was almost closed, my ribs ached and my arms were a mass of yellow and purple bruises.

"It must have been some fall," Bridei commented.

"I drank too much beer," I explained.

Bridei groaned, "You're not the only one."

Derelei hurried over to me. "You are a mess," she said.

I shrugged. What did she care?

Bleddyn came to examine me. He took off my jerkin, which hurt, then he pressed and touched my ribcage. "Nothing broken," he said with some relief. "You'll live, which is just as well because we are leaving this morning."

"He can't travel in that state!" Derelei protested.

"I'm fine," I said. Bruised or not, I wanted nothing more than to get away from Inbhir Nis. What with Medraut and his cronies on the one hand and Derelei's constantly changing moods, there was nothing for me here.

"Best thing for him," Bleddyn announced breezily. "Get some food inside you, lad. I'm off to get a couple of horses and some supplies." He left, apparently satisfied that there was not much wrong with me. I remembered what Medraut had called him. Bleddyn Grim-Hand. Maybe that was right, after all.

Gently rubbing his forehead, Bridei said, "And I have plenty to do this morning." He came over to me, bending to look into my eyes. "Life has a way of giving us hard knocks, Bili," he said to me. "But I think you are strong enough to come back from this."

"I don't feel very strong," I said. I was feeling sorry for myself and struggling to hold back tears, but I was determined not to cry in front of Derelei. "If I was strong, this wouldn't have happened."

Bridei shook his head. "Not strong in the body, lad. Strong in here." He tapped a finger to his head. "That's where it counts. From what Bleddyn tells me, you've got what it takes. Now, I must be off, but I will see you when you return. Use your eyes and your ears, like Bleddyn taught you. Above all, use your wits."

Then he was gone, leaving me alone with Derelei. Her whole demeanour changed immediately. "Who was it?" she asked, her fists bunching angrily. "Was it Medraut?"

I nodded. "There were others, but he was the one who hit me." I dabbed a finger close to my bruised eye. "I think it was Guret who gave me this, though."

"Those two are so full of themselves. I never liked them," she said. "The other two are all right, but they follow Medraut's lead in everything."

She fetched a bowl, pouring cold water into it from a jug. Then she took a cloth which she soaked in the water.

"What are you doing?" I asked.

"I am going to bathe your wounds," she said. "Now stand still and don't be a baby."

The water was icy cold. I flinched, which made her laugh. "It's sore," I said.

"I can see that. You should have put cold water on the bruises last night."

She spent a long time gently bathing the bruises. Longer than she needed to, I think. I didn't mind, but I was more confused than ever. Bleddyn had said I should forget her, but how could I? Sore as it was when she touched me, I did not want her to stop.

"They are bullies," she told me as she worked. "If they had been so brave against the Northumbrians, perhaps we might not have been defeated."

"They were at the battle?" I asked.

"I don't think they did any real fighting," she replied. "They were too busy running away."

"I can't blame them for that," I said. "It was awful."

"Were you there?"

"I saw it from a distance," I informed her. "It was terrible."

"My father says a lot of good men died," she said. "It's a pity thugs like Guret survived."

I was surprised by the vehemence in her voice but, bearing in mind what Medraut and Guret had done to me, I couldn't disagree with her.

She finished tending my bruises, then fetched me some porridge and some honeyed bread. By the time Bleddyn returned, I was feeling a lot better.

He gave us a curious look, then asked, "Are you ready? We have a long way to go."

"We always do," I muttered. "Yes, I am ready."

Bleddyn gave a slight bow to Derelei. "Goodbye, my lady."

She was all prim and formal again. "Goodbye, Brother Bleddyn."

"Come on, Bili," he said. He went outside.

I turned to Derelei who suddenly reached out, grabbed my face and pulled me towards her. She kissed me full on the lips. I was so surprised that I almost yelped with fright.

She released me, smiled and said, "That is another thing to be kept secret. Promise?"

"Promise." What else could I say?

"Then you had better go. Make sure you come back. I want to hear all about the places you have been."

More confused than ever, I left her. That felt worse than the pain of my injuries.

Outside, Bleddyn had a horse for himself and a smaller pony for me. He helped me up into the saddle before mounting his own horse. I tucked my toes into the footholes, gripped the reins as if I was an expert and set off after him. Slowly, we headed for the gate. I twisted in the saddle, wincing with the pain of turning. Derelei was standing at the door of the house. She waved to me and blew me a kiss.

"Forget her," Bleddyn said without turning round.

I think we both knew there was no chance of that.

Chapter 8

We rode south, following the shores of the great Loch Nis. We could have taken a boat, which would have been faster, but Bleddyn liked riding and I knew that, sooner or later, he would use tracks and trails that led where no boat could possibly go.

"Your horse has an appropriate name," he told me.

"What's that?"

"Triduana."

"Really?"

"As God is my witness."

"That is a good sign," I declared. "One day, she will help me find my sister."

"Perhaps. For the moment, though, we are going west."

"To Dal Riata?"

"That's right."

"To spy on them? Or to cause trouble among them?"

Bleddyn's eyes narrowed as he looked at me sharply. I gave him my innocent face and he said, "A bit of both, probably. But you concentrate on watching and listening. If there is any trouble to be stirred, I will do the stirring. Understand?"

"Yes, Bleddyn."

"And for goodness' sake don't have anything to do with any of their girls. The Scots are very touchy about that sort of thing. They're likely to send you home without your . . ." He paused, looking for an appropriate euphemism.

"Hands?" I suggested, trying to help him out.

"Those too," he agreed. "Just act the simpleton and you'll be fine."

"Yes, Bleddyn."

"And stop saying that. It's very irritating."

"Yes, Bleddyn."

He took a swipe at me, but I nudged Triduana away and he missed me. He laughed. "Well, these few days in Inbhir Nis have taught you a lot, I think. You'll be a man soon, even if you do still look no more than twelve years old. Now, if you pay attention to what I tell you, you'll learn a lot more over the next few months."

"Yes, Bleddyn."

As things turned out, that summer was not nearly as dangerous as it might have been, at least not for me or Bleddyn. He was in a good humour and continued to instruct me in various things, including some short lessons on the language of Dal Riata. The Scots spoke in a tongue that was similar to ours, but more akin to the Irish who lived across the sea. Naturally, Bleddyn could speak it fluently.

I had heard so many stories about the fierce Scots that I was apprehensive about entering their territory but the missionaries from Iona had been among them for many years, so Bleddyn was accepted without question wherever we went. His reputation was initially enhanced because many of them thought that he had given me my bruises and black eye. They congratulated him on knowing how to keep a servant in his place. Bleddyn expressed some disappointment when my bruises faded.

"Perhaps I should hit you a few times," he suggested.

"No thanks, but you could teach me how to fight so I don't get beaten up again."

He nodded thoughtfully. I had told him the truth of what had happened but he had guessed it already. At first, he was wary of giving me any lessons in how to fight but I think he understood my fears. I was safe enough if I was with him, but if I was ever on my own, I was likely to be an easy target.

"I am a man of peace, these days," he said, "but the world can be a violent place, so I suppose you should learn a thing or two."

Reluctant or not, he knew more than a thing or two. He not only coached me in how to defend myself, he was able to give me some lessons in how to fight dirty. After one session on the best way to gouge a man's eyes out, I asked him, "How come you know so much about this sort of thing, Bleddyn?"

"I wasn't always a monk," he told me.

"You told me that before. What were you?"

"A sinner."

"Come on, Bleddyn. You were a warrior, weren't you?"

"It was a long time ago, lad."

"I bet you were good."

He shrugged. "I'm still alive."

"Did you kill many men?"

His face clouded a little at that. "I don't like to think about that," he said.

"Why do they call you Bleddyn Grim-Hand?"

"Where did you hear that?" he snapped, rounding on me.

I shrugged. "I don't know. Someone must have mentioned it."

"Bleddyn Grim-Hand is dead," he said firmly. "He died a long time ago. I am a servant of Christ now."

Our lessons stopped for a while after that, until I begged him to buy me a proper knife of my own. I only had a small, child's blade to eat my food with and it was embarrassing, even if everyone did still think I looked much younger than my years. After a few days of pestering, he traded some scraps of silver for a beautiful dagger with a double-edged blade, complete with its own scabbard. The smith he purchased it from assured us it was one of the best he had ever made, which pleased me immensely until Bleddyn pointed out that the smith probably said that about every tool he ever produced.

Still, I was very proud of my new knife. It felt satisfyingly heavy, the leather-bound handle gave a good grip and the blade was so polished that it gleamed in the sun. Of course, it could be used for things other than eating, so

Bleddyn gave me some instructions in how to use it if need be.

"Just remember, it is not your place to take away a man's life," he told me gravely.

"Men kill other men all the time," I pointed out. "And you've told me the story about taking an eye for an eye."

I thought I had him on that one, but he always had an answer. "The Lord Jesus told us to turn the other cheek, Bili. You should remember that story as well."

It seemed to me that Bleddyn could produce a story to suit whatever point he wanted to make. Sometimes he was more of a contradiction than Derelei.

I managed to surprise him one evening when we were camped out in a woodland. I had been bored and had been throwing stones at the nearby trees, trying to hit small knots in the wood and doing pretty well. On a whim, I took out my new knife and threw it, aiming for a dark spot on the trunk of a nearby birch. I hit it, but it was the handle of the dagger that struck the tree. The knife bounced back and fell to the ground. I retrieved it and returned to the fire rather sheepishly but Bleddyn came over to show me how to hold the knife properly for throwing.

"It's all about the spin," he said. "You have to judge it properly or the handle will hit the target first, so you have to gauge the distance and the strength of your throw. It depends on the weight of the knife, too, so it takes a fair bit of practice. Have another try."

On my first attempt, I hit the dark spot full on. The dagger thudded home, point first.

"That was a fluke," Bleddyn said.

I retrieved the knife and threw again. It struck in almost exactly the same place.

"Do it again," Bleddyn said. "From five paces further back."

Grinning now, I tried again. This time, it caught the edge of the trunk, a hand's width from my aiming point. Worse, it was the handle that struck first. I fetched the knife and tried again, adjusting the throw to compensate for the extra distance. This time, I hit my target dead centre.

"You have a good eye," Bleddyn said approvingly.

"I can't see what use it would be," I said. "If I throw my knife away, I have nothing left to defend myself with."

He laughed at that.

Improving my prowess with my new knife was not the main purpose of our journey, though. We had work to do and, for this, I usually reverted to acting the simpleton while Bleddyn did the talking. Things proved to be much easier than we had anticipated because we soon discovered that there was no need to stir the Scots into fighting amongst themselves.

Bleddyn told me that there were three main family groups, or clans as they called them, among the men of Dal Riata. These three clans were often in states of open hostility with one another although one group would usually be powerful enough to claim overlordship. The head of that clan would claim the title of King, although that seemed to me to be a precarious title to hold among such an unpredictable race.

Bleddyn told me, "There are often two or three men who all claim to be King of the Scots at the same time. It makes life interesting, although not very peaceful."

Once again he was correct, because we arrived in Dal Riata to find that there were two brothers, known as Domnall Donn and Mael Duin, who both insisted that they were the rightful king. We very quickly learned that they hated each other and that their tribe, the Cenel nGabrain, was in some turmoil as a result of their rivalry. Moreover, there was a third claimant to the kingship, also a member of the Cenel nGabrain. He was called Domangall and was the son of a former king of Dal Riata. Between them, these three were doing a splendid job of tearing their clan apart. They were gathering men to their respective causes and were on the verge of open warfare with one another.

Bleddyn, of course, insisted that we visit all three of them, journeys which often involved leaving our horses and taking to boats to cross rivers, lochs or even the open sea. As always, Bleddyn handled the talking while my task was to wander around to see if I could learn anything of interest. I rarely did, for the Scots were a straightforward people who hardly ever bothered to conceal anything. If Bleddyn asked a question, they were only too happy to boast of what they had done, or were about to do, or were contemplating doing. The main thing that we got out of these trips was a sense of adventure and some amusement for Bleddyn, who used to shake his head in bewilderment at the way the Scots argued and fought with one another.

This chaotic state of affairs suited us perfectly, so we visited the leaders of the other clans, the Cenel Loairn and the Cenel Comgaill, just to make sure that they were informed of what was happening elsewhere in case they wanted to take advantage of Cenel nGabrain's preoccupation with internal strife.

These visits do not take long to recount but they occupied us for most of the long, and often wet, summer. I enjoyed the travelling, seeing new places and encountering new people. Dal Riata is an impressive land, with high, steep, heather-clad mountains, deep, blue lochs and many fine pastures. The Scots themselves were a strange mix of the familiar and the foreign but I sometimes found it hard not to laugh at the way Bleddyn was playing them off against each other. I am sure they were not as simple as he made out, but he certainly had no trouble convincing them to fight one another rather than try to oppose Bridei of Fortriu. By the time we had travelled the length of Dal Riata, I think there were at least two more chieftains who had declared themselves King. Bleddyn laughed until he was sore.

Towards the beginning of September, we were at Dun Add, often regarded as the seat of power in Dal Riata. It is a high, strong fortress with massively thick walls of stone. It stands on the coast, with marshy ground surrounding most of the landward side, making it virtually impregnable. Bleddyn had been speaking to Mael Duin who had seized the place at the start of his quarrel with his brother. We did not stay long because Bleddyn felt that we had done all we could in Dal Riata. It was time for us to head for Alt Clud but he told me that there was one last place we should visit before heading south.

"It would be a shame for you not to see Iona," he said.

This involved a fairly lengthy sea voyage, so we left our horses at Dun Add and arranged passage on a small fishing boat. I was used to boats by now although the stench of fish was something I could have done without. Still, the sea breeze and the salty splash of the waves was always invigorating, so I made myself as comfortable as I could for the journey.

To reach Iona we had to sail round another, much larger island but the fishermen knew the winds and the tides and they got us there without difficulty. With so many islands sprinkled along the coast, the sea is a highway for the Irish and the Scots, presenting fewer difficulties for travellers than the land routes that Bleddyn and I usually followed.

It was raining when we arrived, the wind driving heavy, grey clouds from the west, bringing a downpour that sent most people scurrying for shelter. Bleddyn led me to the monastery, a complex of stone and wooden buildings where he asked permission to see the abbot.

"The abbot is away in Ireland," the monk who welcomed us at the main door informed us. "Would you care to speak to Brother Adomnan? He is in charge while the abbot is away."

"Adomnan?" Bleddyn responded with some surprise. "Very well, I shall speak to him."

The monk led us across the rain-lashed compound, dodging puddles as he took us to a long, low building.

"Do you know this fellow, Adomnan?" I asked Bleddyn.

"We've met," he replied without enthusiasm.

A short time later, we were admitted to a small office where we were greeted by the senior Brother.

I have heard a lot about Adomnan since that day. When I first saw him, he had only been at Iona for a short time, although he eventually became abbot there and is famous nowadays. Perhaps I do him an injustice, but I disliked him from the start. My main impression of him was one of thinness. Everything about him was thin. His tall frame, his face, his bony hands, his sense of humour and, above all, his hospitality.

While the rain lashed against the small, glass-paned window of his study, he allowed us to drip onto his bare, stone floor and made no offer of food or drink except to grudgingly say that he was sure we would find something in the refectory before we left. The way he said it suggested that he hoped we would leave very soon.

Bleddyn seemed strangely deferential, which was unusual for him, even with abbots. He made a valiant attempt to break through Adomnan's wall of condescension but I could tell that it was hard going. As for me, Adomnan turned his watery eyes on me only long enough to give me a look of utter contempt before pointedly ignoring me. Perhaps we had interrupted something important and that was why he was annoyed. Perhaps, but I suspected that his aloof manner had something to do with his previous encounters with Bleddyn. He certainly did little to mask his animosity.

Adomnan insisted on speaking in Latin. That was not a problem for Bleddyn, of course, but it meant that I was wasting my time standing there. After the two men had exchanged a few words, I piped up, "Brother Bleddyn, I am hungry. May I go in search of some food?"

"Of course," Bleddyn agreed. I know that he had not meant for me to do any prying on Iona but I wanted to look around and he obviously realised that there was no point in me staying to listen to what promised to be a long conversation that I would not be able to understand.

Adomnan's face flickered in a smile as I left. A thin one, anyway.

The rain rather curtailed my wandering. It was coming down in sheets now, so heavy that stepping outside was like standing under a waterfall. I darted from one building to the next, seeking the refectory, intending to stay there with some hot food and drink until Bleddyn found me. With my cloak draped over my head and the driving rain beating on my face, I did not spend much time looking around but I saw a long, low building that I guessed could be the refectory. I found a small doorway which I hurried through.

I closed the door behind me, glad to be out of the rain. Shaking myself dry, I looked around. I had obviously made a mistake; whatever this building was, it was clearly not the refectory. A corridor stretched in front of me with rooms leading off on either side. Standing in the doorway of the first room to my left was a man in a long, dripping wet cloak. He was facing into the room, obviously speaking to the occupant. He turned to give me a curious look when he heard me come in, but he quickly turned back and began speaking to whoever was in the room. To my astonishment, he spoke in English.

"Yes, my Lord," I heard him say.

I decided that the refectory could wait for a moment. I had no great desire to venture out into the rain anyway, so I made a show of rubbing my hair and shaking my cloak, stamping my feet to get the mud and water off my boots. While I played out this charade, I listened to what the man was saying. It wasn't very interesting, but I hadn't heard any English for a few months, so I thought it was a good opportunity to practise my eavesdropping skills.

"Can I get you anything else, my lord?" the man asked.

From within the room, I heard a rather high-pitched, querulous voice asking, "Is there anything warming to drink?"

"I could fetch some warm milk," the dripping man suggested.

That surprised me. I knew this was a monastery but most of the monks I had come across in my recent travels were happy to consume beer, wine or mead. The unseen occupant, though, replied, "Excellent. And perhaps some more bread."

"Of course, my lord." He withdrew, closing the door, then turned and walked towards me. "Can I help you?" he asked in English.

I gave him my puzzled expression. I replied in the Pictish tongue. "What did you say? I don't speak Latin."

It was his turn to look puzzled. Then he gave me a weak smile. Still speaking English, he said, "Well, we will not have much to say to each other, will we, boy?"

He mimed putting food to his lips. I nodded, giving him my idiot's smile. "Come on, then," he said wearily. "Lord Aldfrith wants some warm milk, so I had better fetch it for him. We can't have him getting wet himself, can we?"

I grinned inanely. My new, English-speaking friend took me to the refectory, a stone-built, single-storey hall set to one side of the monastery complex. By the time we got there we were both soaked again, even though it was only thirty paces away. I was happy, though, because once we were inside I was able to sit by the fire with a plate of bread, honey and fish, accompanied by a pot of mead, while Aldfrith's servant had to brave the deluge again to take the mysterious lord his milk.

Bleddyn was not in a good mood when he eventually found me. Of course, he was not able to discuss his meeting while other ears could overhear but once the rain had stopped, we returned to the shore and took another boat back to Dun Add.

We stayed that evening as guests of Mael Duin. He was a young man, perhaps in his late twenties, with a hawk-like nose and eyes that burned with a manic fervour. I was rather afraid of him because he seemed permanently on the point of exploding into a rage. I sat quietly all night, watching and listening while Bleddyn chatted away with Mael Duin and his warriors. They were all fierce men; proud, loud, boastful and aggressive, so I was pleased when we eventually found our way to our beds. Even then, Bleddyn remained silent about what had passed between him and Adomnan.

It was only the following morning, while we trotted along a narrow path which skirted the great boggy morass surrounding Dun Add that I was able to ask, "What happened with Adomnan?"

Bleddyn snorted. "Well, I think I got his agreement to help persuade the men of Dal Riata not to attack Bridei."

"I didn't think they were going to anyway."

"Not just now, but you saw what Mael Duin is like. Sooner or later he and his kin will stop their bickering and turn their minds to Fortriu. If Adomnan can persuade them to keep the peace, it will make life easier for us."

"You don't sound convinced," I said. "I got the impression he didn't like you very much."

"Adomnan doesn't like anyone very much," Bleddyn said sourly. "But you are right. He particularly disapproves of me. We fell out a while back."

"He did seem a bit austere."

"That's a good word for him," Bleddyn agreed. "He's only really interested in scripture and instructive books. In fact, he's writing one himself. He showed it to me. A life of the blessed Columba."

"You don't approve?"

"Pah!" exclaimed Bleddyn. "I would if it were remotely accurate. The bit I read told how the blessed saint saved one of his companions from being devoured by some monstrous creature that lives in Loch Nis. What nonsense! A tale for the gullible and weak-minded."

I laughed. "But Bleddyn, you tell stories like that all the time."

"That's different," he said quickly, although he did not explain how, exactly. I suspected that the cause of his irritation was that he had not thought of that particular story first. I wondered how long it would be before it featured in one of his sermons.

He looked across at me. "What about you? Did you learn anything apart from how to feed your belly and mock your teacher?"

"I learned that there's an English lord staying there."

"Well, many people travel to Iona. It is a holy place. As I told you, the Ionian church was once popular in Northumbria."

I had been feeling pleased with myself, thinking I had discovered some great secret but Bleddyn had neatly deflated me once again. Wanting to impress him a little with my diligence, I said, "His name is Aldfrith."

That shocked him. He gave me a searching look.

"Are you sure?"

"Positive. Lord Aldfrith. I heard his servant say his name."

Bleddyn beamed at me. "That, my boy, is something to remember. Aldfrith? Well, well."

"Why?" I asked. "Who is he?"

Bleddyn said, "As for the who, he is the older brother of King Ecgfrith of Northumbria. A very holy man, by all accounts, not at all suited to kingship."

"If he is Ecgfrith's older brother, why is he not the king?" I asked. "You told me the oldest son usually inherits among the Angles."

"Usually," Bleddyn agreed. "But Aldfrith's mother was an Irish princess. Oswiu met her when he was in exile during the reign of his predecessor. When he returned to Northumbria and became king, the Church did not regard the relationship as a lawful marriage, so when Oswiu died, Aldfrith was passed over and Ecgfrith succeeded their father as king."

"I didn't know all that," I said. "But why does it matter that he is on Iona?"

"It may not matter at all, Bili. It may be of no importance, but you never know when information like that will come in useful. Adomnan claimed that he had had no contact with Northumbria all year. That was patently a lie, although I cannot fathom the reason for it. Then again, he does like his secrets."

"So do you," I pointed out, perhaps a little too bluntly.

"That's different."

I laughed. This time Bleddyn had the good grace to join in.

I said, "I thought it was a sin to lie."

"So it is, Bili, but we are all poor sinners, aren't we? I am sure Adomnan is not the only one with secrets." He gave me a pointed look, suggesting that he knew more about my own private affairs than was good for me.

I took the hint and closed my mouth.

After our brief visit to Iona, we travelled south, to the kingdom of the Britons and their mighty fortress on the massive rock of Alt Clud. Dominating the land around it, Alt Clud stood beside the broad River Cluaidh which flowed serenely past the foot of the rock on its stately way to the western sea.

Here, in his hilltop stronghold, we met Elfin, King of Alt Clud, great-nephew to our own Bridei. He was a young man, quite serious but very friendly. He welcomed us warmly, greeting Bleddyn like an old friend. He asked after Bridei and assured us that he had nothing but friendly intentions towards us. His main concern was the growing power of Northumbria, whose territory now virtually barred the way between Alt Clud and Fortriu.

"If Ecgfrith turns his attention on us, we will not be able to stop him," he said gloomily. "For the moment, we must pay tribute so that we may concentrate on holding back the raiders from Dal Riata."

"The Scots are fighting among themselves," Bleddyn said.

Elfin shook his head. "That does not stop them raiding us," he said. "Every year they come seeking cattle and women. They come by sea, so it is difficult to stop them because we cannot watch the entire coast." He sighed. "And if it is not the Scots, it is the Irish."

Despite his grim pessimism, I liked Elfin. He also revealed a little more of Bleddyn's past when he said, "Have you no thoughts of returning here to live among your own people, Bleddyn?"

My ears pricked up at that. Bleddyn did not squirm, for he was never a squirming sort of person, but he was definitely uncomfortable. He said, "Not for the present. I promised to serve Bridei and I will hold to that, for he is a good man."

"Of course he is," said Elfin, as if there could be no argument about it.

Later on, when we were alone, Bleddyn forestalled my inevitable questions by explaining, "I was born near here. I was a warrior of Alt Clud for many years, before I took holy orders."

"So how did you end up serving Bridei?" I asked.

"It's a long and complicated story," he said.

"I have plenty of time. Anyway, if you don't tell me, I'll go and ask Elfin."

Bleddyn sighed. He knew I had him this time. "I knew it was a mistake to come here," he muttered. Then he said, "Bridei was born here, too. His father was Bili, king of Alt Clud. He died just before Bridei was born. Bridei's mother, who was a Northumbrian, died giving birth to him, leaving him an orphan and with his older step-brother as king of Alt Clud, so Bridei was sent to Fortriu to be brought up by his grandfather who was the King of the Pecht at the time."

My head was spinning already. I knew that marriages between important people were used to cement treaties, but Bridei's ancestry seemed unusually complex. In an effort to unravel some of the mystery, I asked, "If Bridei's father was from Fortriu, how did he get to be King of Alt Clud?"

"He married the daughter of the previous king. There were no sons, so Bili took the kingship. When his wife died, he married one of Oswiu's sisters. That was Bridei's mother."

"But what about you?" I asked, suspecting that Bleddyn had outlined Bridei's parentage to divert my attention from his own past. "How did you end up serving Bridei?"

He shrugged. "There is nothing to tell, really. I decided I wanted to travel the land, to spread the word of God. After a couple of years, I met Bridei. We were both born here, so we had something in common. We became friends and I stayed in Fortriu." He gave me a hard look. "That is all there is to it."

I was sure there was more he was not telling me and what he had said did not explain how he had become Bridei's spy, but I could tell from the look on his face that he would not divulge any more, so I let the matter drop. The next morning, obviously concerned that remaining in Alt Clud would allow me to discover more than he wanted, Bleddyn declared that we were leaving.

Elfin tried to persuade him to stay until winter had passed, but Bleddyn was adamant that we must return to Bridei, so we left Alt Clud and headed north-east. We made our way back to Fortriu by a convoluted route because Bleddyn wanted to check on the latest situation in Fidach.

The first place we stopped was the hillfort at Dundurn, near the eastern end of Loch Eireann. This stronghold occupied a steep, rocky knoll guarding the glen and watching over one of the main routes between the lands of the Pecht and Dal Riata. It was an important place, for it lay on the fringes of our territory. The men who held it were nervous, as they confided to Bleddyn.

"We are isolated here," their leader said glumly. "The Northumbrians have not reached us yet but if they do, what help can we expect from Bridei?"

"Bridei is arranging peace terms with Ecgfrith of Northumbria," Bleddyn assured the man. "Anyway, you can hold out here for a long time. The hill is steep, the walls are thick and strong, and you have water cisterns and storage houses enough to keep you for many weeks. Nobody could storm this place."

The warriors were still unhappy but they could not argue with him. Dundurn was not large but it was as impregnable a fortress as I had ever seen. I could not imagine anyone taking it, not even the Northumbrians, and certainly not the Scots who lived just beyond the far end of the loch.

We left Dundurn satisfied that this outpost of Bridei's kingdom was as secure as it could be, although Bleddyn told me that he would suggest to Bridei to send a strong captain to command the fort. It was a good idea but it was doomed to fail because we soon heard that the garrison abandoned the place only a few days after we had left, allowing Mael Duin of Dal Riata to send a host of warriors to occupy the fort.

That news was bad, but not nearly as bad as what awaited me in Inbhir Nis. What we heard there was like a knife wound to my heart because we returned late in October, just a few days before my fifteenth birthday, to learn that Derelei was to be married to old Nechtan.

Chapter 9

"Why has she agreed to that?" I demanded to know. "He's an old man."

Bleddyn tried to soothe my anger. "She has agreed because she knows that Bridei needs Nechtan's support. His domain guards the southern approaches. His wife died two years ago, so this makes sense."

"But he's an old man!" I repeated.

"He's not that old," Bleddyn said smoothly. "Not as old as me, for one." His lips twitched slightly before he went on, "I understand that there was some suggestion she should marry his son, Guret, but she refused. Perhaps she sees Nechtan as the lesser of two evils."

"I'll ask her myself."

"No!" Bleddyn said sharply. Then, more calmly, "I think it would be wise for you to stay away from her for a while, don't you?"

"Why?"

"Don't be a fool, Bili. You know why. I am not blind, and nor is Bridei. Young infatuation is one thing, but Derelei is to be married very soon, so you must mind what you do and say."

I went to see her anyway.

I was annoyed that Bleddyn thought my feelings for Derelei were nothing more than infatuation and I was hurt that she had agreed to marry Nechtan without warning me beforehand. Of course, I had been away, but it hurt none the less.

She had a room of her own now, in the large, reed-thatched building that stood behind the great hall. It was the first time I had been inside the king's private home and the unfamiliar design left me feeling unsettled. A long corridor, paved with flag-stones, stretched the entire length of one side of the rectangular building, with a door at either end. The rear door led out to the kitchen building and was reserved for the servants, while the door at the front, larger and decorated with ornate carvings of mystic symbols, was for visitors. I was let through this entrance by a bearded warrior who scowled at me disapprovingly as I passed him.

Once inside, I saw more doors leading off to my right. One of them opened onto a short corridor that led through to the rear of the great hall itself, the others gave admittance to the chambers reserved for the king and his household.

Derelei was in a large room half way along the corridor. I was admitted without question but any thoughts I had of speaking to her in private were dashed because she had a gaggle of other girls in attendance. They made me uncomfortable with their sly giggles and mocking glances and I felt my cheeks burning as soon as I entered the room.

The chamber was richly furnished with soft, padded chairs and thick rugs on the floor. I hardly noticed because my eyes saw only Derelei. My breath caught in my throat when I saw her, I had forgotten how beautiful she was. But the other girls were there, watching me closely, so I pretended that I had only come to give her the news of my travels, as I had promised to do.

"Thank you for coming to see me," Derelei said coolly. She was polite, formal and distant. She asked about my health, made me recount where I had been and what I had seen, but she showed no sign of anything other than mild interest in my adventures, so I gave her a much condensed tale of where we had been.

Eventually, I plucked up enough courage to ask, "When are you to be married?"

For an instant, I thought I might have detected a flicker of emotion in her eyes, but she replied in a matter of fact manner, "Next week. On Tuesday."

"I hope you will be happy," I said, although I think it came out sounding less than sincere.

She looked at me quite calmly. "My father needs this to happen. It is a good marriage."

"You didn't have to agree to it," I said, knowing that I was stepping beyond the bounds of polite conversation and that her maids were listening attentively. Still, it was true. However much families tried to arrange suitable matches, no woman could be forced to marry if she did not want to. Among the Pecht, women were as free as men.

"You still don't know very much, do you, Bili?" she asked in reply. "Some things are necessary and, as I say, it is a good marriage. I am sure I will be very happy."

I stared at her for a long moment but she held my gaze without revealing anything other than a serene acceptance of her fate. It was more than I could bear, so I made my goodbyes and left. The sound of the other girls' laughter followed me outside.

I did not want to go to the wedding but I could hardly avoid it. Bleddyn acquired some new clothes for me, leggings and a soft, linen shirt topped by a leather jerkin. They were very fine but they did not cheer me up at all.

Abbot Ronan conducted the service which seemed to go on forever. Derelei stood there, frail and delicate, with a garland of flowers in her hair, beside the hulking form of Nechtan, whose face wore a grin that was almost a leer. I hated him.

Guret was there too. He watched the service with almost as much anger as I did. I guessed that he had hoped to be the man standing in front of the altar, accepting Derelei as his bride. In some small way I felt better that he had been thwarted.

After the ceremony came the music and dancing, with the celebration spilling out of the great hall into the open air where great awnings had been erected in case of rain. I certainly did not feel like dancing but Bleddyn was downing the beer, as usual, and talking volubly to anyone who would listen, so I stayed near him, slowly growing more and more drunk. I could have wandered off but I had spotted Medraut, Guret, Donnell and fat Uerb at the far side of the hall.

Medraut had seen me, too, and given me a look that left me in no doubt that I should stay well away from him. Keeping close to Bleddyn seemed the safest thing to do.

Of course, I had to empty my bladder from time to time but the privies were being well used that day, so there were always plenty of people around. I made sure that I always stayed near a crowd of other men just in case Medraut decided to start anything. The worst I got were a few catcalls once or twice when he and his gang passed near me. I ignored them.

All in all, it was a miserable afternoon and evening. I ate the food, I drank the beer and I sat in a corner, wanting nothing more than for the day to be over. Quite late on, I was surprised when Donnell approached me on his own.

Brown-haired, handsome and open-faced, Donnell was the least offensive of Medraut's gang. He seemed to follow them in a disinterested sort of way, as if he was merely an observer to their loutish behaviour. For me, though, the very fact that he followed them at all did nothing to endear him to me.

As he approached me, he looked around, as if checking to see that nobody was watching, then crept to my side.

"What do you want?" I asked in an unfriendly tone.

In a low, urgent voice, he said, "You should leave Inbhir Nis. Medraut and Guret plan to beat you up again. Or worse."

The beer had relaxed my sense of danger so I asked, "Won't they be going home after this?"

Donnell shook his head. "They will be staying as part of Bridei's household."

"Hostages?" I asked.

Donnell seemed genuinely surprised at this, as if he had never considered the idea. He said, "No. Like me, they will join the King's warriors."

I gave him a knowing smile. "You are all hostages," I said with an assurance born of several mugs of beer. "Bridei wants your fathers to know he has you in his grasp. That will help ensure their loyalty."

Donnell seemed amused at that thought. "Even if you are right, it doesn't bother me," he said lightly. "I like it here. But as for the others, whatever you call them, they intend to do you some real harm. I just thought I should warn you."

"Why?" I asked him bluntly.

He shrugged. "Because they have no real reason to do it. It just doesn't seem right."

"You could stop them," I suggested.

"Don't be daft," he told me. "Well, you can't say I didn't warn you." Quickly, he ducked away to the centre of the hall, mingling with the dancers.

I gulped another mouthful of beer. Donnell's warning only reinforced my own thoughts but it had been good of him, all the same. Perhaps it was unfair to judge him alongside the others. Still, I did not expect it meant he would actively help me. Donnell was most definitely a follower, not a leader, and he followed Medraut.

I tried to take another gulp but my mug was empty. With a sigh, I took one last look at Derelei. She was dancing happily in the midst of a crowd of revellers, looking as if she was thoroughly enjoying herself. My guts churned just looking at her. Then, as the dance ended, our eyes met and her face grew suddenly sad. She gave me a look that was almost a plea for help, but then the musicians started up again and she was swept into the dance once more.

I could not stand the hurt any longer, so I went to find Bleddyn and persuaded him it was time to leave. He was reluctant, but he understood, so we quietly slipped away. I did not look back in search of Derelei. I could not bear the thought of seeing her and knowing she was lost to me.

After that day, it was to be two years before I saw her again.

I felt as if a whole part of my life had come to a close. I heard that Nechtan took Derelei away to his home in the southern glens and I knew that there was nothing to keep me in Inbhir Nis, especially if Medraut and his cronies were going to be hanging around. I told Bleddyn that I was old enough to make my own decisions now and that it was time for me to go in search of my mother and sister.

He considered that for a moment or two then gave me what I had come to recognise as his serious look.

"You are not yet fully grown, Bili. I know you think you are, but you still look like a boy and you need more experience of life. You could not travel among the Northumbrians on your own and I would not be welcome there, as you know. Their own monks are spreading north, establishing their Roman churches. They are driving out priests of the Ionian church."

"You could go in disguise," I said. "We could travel as merchants, or potters."

"Do you know how to make pots?" he asked me.

"No, but there must be some disguise we could use."

"Let me think about it," he said. "In the meantime, we should travel around Fortriu for a while. You have seen much of the rest of the land, but you have never seen your own home."

"I don't have a home," I said miserably.

"You know what I mean," he scolded.

We left the following day, fortunately without me having encountered Medraut or Guret. I had no particular desire to see any more of Fortriu but it got me away from Inbhir Nis, so that was a positive thing. It was, I know now, a good thing too, because I quickly fell in love with the heartland of the Pecht.

There were wide, green plains, rolling hills, deep, dark pine forests, bright woodlands of broad-leafed trees, long, sandy beaches and swift-flowing rivers. Villages and farms dotted the land. It was impossible to travel far before coming across a place where people lived and yet there were parts of Fortriu that seemed as remote and lonely as anywhere I had seen in the wilds of Dal Riata.

Bleddyn loved travelling anyway, but he made it his mission to spread the word about the good things Bridei would do for the people and to tell them that the day would come when the Pecht would reclaim the lands that had been lost to Northumbria. Personally, I could not see how that was possible, because I had witnessed the strength of the Angles and I knew how weak the Pecht were. But Bleddyn was Bleddyn and the truth of our precarious position did not prevent him talking about the power of Bridei almost as much as he preached the power of God.

One of the places he took me to see was the mighty fortress of Am Broch, once the principal home of the lords of Fortriu. This was an immense place, situated on a peninsula that jutted into the sea. Its walls were massive, the huge, earth ramparts topped by walls of stone, the gate decorated by great slabs which bore carved images of mighty bulls. I noticed that Bleddyn crossed himself when we passed under them and went into the fort.

"Bridei used to stay here," he told me. "Before he was elected king. Now he has appointed Taran in his place."

"Why did he not stay here?" I asked. "It is a much stronger place than Inbhir Nis."

"Aye, lad, but it was built for defence. Inbhir Nis is built to command."

I frowned. "What do you mean?"

"I mean that a king living in Inbhir Nis can easily reach Fortriu, or Cait, or Fotla. It sits at a crossroad. Am Broch, strong as it is, is a refuge, a place of last resort. If Bridei ever has to bring his people here, it means the Pecht are in dire need."

I understood what Bleddyn meant, but I was still fascinated by Am Broch. We learned that Taran was still at Inbhir Nis with Bridei, so we did not stay long. Bleddyn did show me the steps that led down to a vast underground chamber where there was a well and a great tank of water. The echoes of our footsteps vied with the constant sound of dripping water as we entered the chamber.

"This is where the kings of old used to be ceremonially washed before taking up their kingship," Bleddyn said. His face twitched in a grimace of distaste. "It is a heathen place, which is another reason it is better for a Christian king to reside in Inbhir Nis. The Church does not approve of Am Broch."

I looked around the dark, dank chamber. It must have been hewn out of the rock in ages past. It was an impressive feat but I could well understand the Church's abhorrence. The vault had an ancient, almost supernatural feel to it. Yet, despite the pagan associations, Bridei had held this place and now Taran was lord here. I suspected it was too strong a fortress to abandon, whatever the holy men might say.

I wondered briefly whether Derelei had ever come down to this place. If Am Broch had been Bridei's home, I supposed she must have done. Thinking about her made me feel even more gloomy. I glanced at Bleddyn, whose own face betrayed his unease at being here.

I said, "This is not a nice place."

"There are worse places than this around Am Broch," Bleddyn replied. He saw the question on my face and added, "There is a cave near the shore. It is large and deep. It is where the kings of the Pecht used to have criminals and enemies sent for execution." He made a chopping motion with his hand, moving it towards his neck. I nodded. Decapitation was the usual punishment for serious crimes.

"I don't think I want to see that," I said.

"Good. I think we have been here long enough, don't you?"

So we left Am Broch, with its high walls and deep caverns, and we continued on our slow journey through Fortriu. I enjoyed that winter more than I had expected, but I took every opportunity to remind Bleddyn that I really wanted to go south, to find my mother and sister so that I could bring them home again. He kept putting me off and I knew why. Bleddyn's problem was that he knew that if he donned a disguise to travel among the Northumbrians, he would be taking an irrevocable step that would mark him as a spy, not as a monk. Instead of a man of the church, he would become a man of Bridei.

When he eventually admitted his dilemma, I said, "Then come as my friend. We will not be spying, we will be looking for my family. It will be a temporary thing. You were a warrior before you became a monk. You can be a monk again when we get back."

He scratched his head. "Out of the mouths of babes and sucklings," he quoted softly. "I never thought I'd see the day when I'd be taking advice from you, lad, but the holy scripture has counsel for us all."

"Is that a yes?" I asked.

He nodded, smiling broadly. "I've never been a merchant before. Perhaps I should try it for a while. Just temporarily, of course."

Chapter 10

Bridei generously supplied us with a mule and a host of things we could sell, mostly small or lightweight items that were easily transported. Brooches, rings, small clay pots, knives, animal hides and wool made up most of our stock. None of it was particularly valuable because we did not want to attract too much attention. The poor mule was, though, heavily laden with piles of cloth-wrapped bundles, leather sacks and small, wooden boxes.

It was then that I found the flaw in my plan. We would have to travel on foot.

"Only rich merchants ride horses," Bridei pointed out with a laugh. "You have a long walk ahead of you."

"Exercise is good for the soul," said Bleddyn cheerfully.

It meant I would have to say farewell to my pony Triduana and go on foot to find her namesake, my sister. I did not mind that.

Bleddyn was less amused by the need for him to cut off his hair and shave his entire head in order to disguise his tonsure. He grumbled a great deal until Bridei pointed out that he was losing most of his hair anyway.

"Just look on it as giving nature a helping hand," Bridei chuckled as Bleddyn reluctantly took a razor to his scalp.

It was early Spring, and time for us to leave. Bridei called me aside just as we were setting off. He clasped my forearm, as if I was a grown man, and said, "Good luck to you, Bili. I pray that you find what you are looking for. Be sure to return, for I will have need of good men soon enough."

I promised that I would return, although inside my head, I recalled the words of Fincana the seer who had told me I would search for many years before I found my family.

I had not told Bleddyn or Bridei but I expected that we would be away for a long time. It did not matter to me. Now that Derelei was lost to me, the longer I was gone, the better.

So we walked south, climbing the steep hills that guarded Bridei's home, and on to the rugged valleys beyond. Our route took us close to Nechtan's home which guarded several mountain passes that opened onto a small, uneven plain. Bleddyn had taught me enough for me to realise that this was indeed an important strategic place and one that Bridei needed to know was securely held. I suppose he thought the price he had paid was worth it. Bleddyn asked me if I wanted to visit Nechtan and Derelei but I said no.

After that, we traversed Fidach and Fib, wandering all the while, putting on a show of bartering our goods. Sometimes we stayed with locals but we tried to concentrate on the places where Northumbrian soldiers or settlers had made their homes because these were the people who would know about my family. That had been my hope, at least, but none of them were able to give us any news.

Once or twice, Bleddyn received a few strange looks and one old woman even asked him if he was a monk. Bleddyn, ever quick, replied that he had a twin brother who was a monk and that must be who she had seen before. The two of us had a good chuckle about that later.

We spent many long days tramping around from place to place but we never heard so much as a whisper about my mother or sister. So we continued south, skirting the great marsh that barred the way between the northern and southern parts of what had once been the lands of the Pecht, past the high rock of Sruighlea and crossing the Foirthe into Gododdin. Inevitably, we eventually made our way to Dun Eidyn.

This mighty fortress had been in Northumbrian hands for many years, since long before I had been born. It stood on a huge, rocky crag, high above a marshy plain on the one side and low, sloping fields on the other. Clustered all around the foot of the great rock and edging up to the fort's solitary entrance, were scores of houses. Many of these were built in the rectangular, Anglian style, some with their floors dug deep into the earth so that the occupants had to climb down steps to get inside. The roofs of these houses were so low that the eaves were just above ground level. Bleddyn explained that this helped keep the homes warm as the earth itself provided the walls.

"They look strange," I observed.

"I expect our roundhouses look strange to the Angles," Bleddyn replied.

There were a few roundhouses in Dun Eidyn, but the town had a foreign feel to it. I was in no doubt that we were in Northumbria. It was an important centre, too. The town was as big as Inbhir Nis, if not larger. Merchants flocked here from all over Northumbria and some enterprising men had set up ramshackle shelters which they hired out to visitors. These places were damp and unsavoury but they were good for chatting to other travellers, so we stayed a few days while we made a show of visiting the market.

We continued to ask as many questions as we dared, but still we learned nothing about my mother or sister. We learned a great deal of other things, though. The town was buzzing with news from all over Britain, so much so that I suggested to Bleddyn that the best way to gather information for Bridei would be simply to come here rather than wander around the country.

"If you can believe what you hear," he said gruffly. "Better to see it for yourself."

He was right, of course, but some of what we heard turned out to be true. The main gossip was that King Ecgfrith's wife had divorced him and gone to live in a nunnery. That was the cause of much crude hilarity among the Northumbrian merchants who also claimed that it was the cause of the friction between Ecgfrith and a priest they called Archbishop Wilfrid, whom Ecgfrith apparently blamed for his wife's decision to take holy orders.

"The King hates Wilfrid," one garrulous trader informed us. "The two of them are always feuding."

"More problems for Ecgfrith," Bleddyn confided to me. "That can only be good for us."

Other kings had their problems, too.

"Domangall of Dal Riata has been killed," a merchant who had recently travelled to the west assured us. "And Domnall Donn, one of the two brothers who now rules the Scots, has devastated the Hebrides because of the support the men there gave to Domangall."

"That will change the balance of power," Bleddyn observed with some concern. "There might be consequences for Fortriu."

"There is not a lot we can do about it," I said. "Besides, if the men of Dun Eidyn have heard the news, Bridei has probably heard it, too."

"Aye, you are right, lad," agreed Bleddyn. "Bridei can handle any problems with Dal Riata. At least he has no need to worry about Northumbria. From the sound of things, Ecgfrith is more concerned about his troublesome Archbishop and his border disputes with Mercia."

The border disputes were another topic of much discussion among the merchants. None of them liked a major war because, although there were profits to be made, travel and trade were difficult when armed men prowled the land. A merchant could lose everything if he ventured too close to a battle. If the rumours were to be believed, it seemed likely that war was on the way. The traders all agreed that the conflict would be bad for business, which was why many of them had come north in the hope of exploiting the newly conquered and relatively peaceful lands that they called southern Pictavia.

This was all very well, but I was growing impatient for news of my family. I wandered the town every day, looking at the faces of every woman I came across. None of them was my mother or sister.

Bleddyn asked around in likely places but nobody knew of any girl called Triduana or a woman named Lindoca. I was growing ever more frustrated because Dun Eidyn was the home of Beornhaeth and I was positive that this was where his captives would have been brought. Bleddyn tried to explain that they had probably been sold and could be anywhere, but I needed to be sure they were not here before we moved on. After five days, the only place we had not been able to investigate was the fortress itself.

We tried, of course, but only the wealthiest merchants were ever allowed inside the fort and the burly warriors at the gates made sure that rule was enforced. So we joined many other traders who laid out their goods at the side of the path that led down from the fort's gates. We had nothing special to sell, but a few men stopped to have a look at our meagre wares while Bleddyn half-heartedly tried to persuade them to buy something so that he and his son - he gestured towards me when he said that - would not starve. Most of the men wandered off but one or two laughed in his face.

We had more success with the women who lived in the hillfort. Not in selling anything to them, but they were more willing to talk. Bleddyn asked one young woman whether she knew of anyone named Lindoca or Triduana who lived in the fort.

She gave him a suspicious look. "Why do you want to know?" she asked.

Bleddyn was all charm. "I was given a message by Lindoca's sister. She thought she might be here."

The woman relaxed slightly. "I don't know any Lindoca," she said. "But Lord Wulfric has a woman called Triduana."

I was on my feet as soon as I heard that. "Is she tall, with dark hair? A woman of the Pecht?" I asked.

"Forgive him," Bleddyn said smoothly while giving me a dark look as a warning. "You know what young lads are like about girls."

The woman laughed but said, "Well she matches that description, but so do a lot of other girls."

All smiles, Bleddyn said, "Perhaps you could ask her to come to speak to us? So that we can give her the message from her aunt."

"Oh, no," the woman replied. "Lord Wulfric has gone south. They say the king called him back for something or other. Triduana went with him."

Bleddyn was not keen on going deeper into Northumbria but I insisted that we go after Wulfric. Bleddyn eventually agreed but we never did catch up with Beornhaeth's son. We went a long way south, into the heartlands of Ecgfrith's realm, but the whole kingdom was ablaze with talk of war and Ecgfrith was gathering troops for his inevitable conflict with Mercia. A Pictish merchant and his son would have been objects of suspicion at the best of times, but even though Bleddyn usually passed himself off as a Briton from Alt Clud, the threat of war increased the people's fear of all foreigners. As a result, we often met with open hostility.

"This is foolishness," Bleddyn said more than once.

Despite the danger, we pressed on. We got as far as Streonshal, a small settlement on the east coast, nestled at the mouth of a deep river. Old King Oswiu, Ecgfrith's father, had built a monastery here. Despite the unfriendly reception from the locals, Bleddyn was delighted that he at last had a chance to see this famous place. "This is where Oswiu held his synod," he told me.

To me, it looked like any other monastery, although Bleddyn was deeply moved by the historic events that had taken place here. He stood staring at it for a long time. So long, that I almost had to drag him away.

The other thing that Streonshal is famous for is the black gemstone known as jet, which is dug from the moors that lie inland, then brought to Streonshal where skilled craftsmen carve and polish it into jewellery. Flakes or small pieces of jet are highly prized and were often used in barter, for Streonshal is the only place in the whole of Britain where this rare, black stone is found. We saw more than a few craftsmen working with this precious material but what we did not find was any news of Wulfric.

    Undeterred, we decided to try to find Ecgfrith himself, guessing that Wulfric and the warriors he led would be with the king. Like most kings, though, Ecgfrith was more or less constantly on the move around his kingdom. Still, I think we would have caught up with him in time but Fincana's prophecy continued to prove accurate because fate was not on our side.

    We had arrived at a small settlement, a scattering of thatched houses beside an old Roman bridge which spanned a wide river. Our misfortune was that the bridge was being guarded by a band of Northumbrian soldiers who were both bored and suspicious. As soon as they spotted us, they began to gather, looking for trouble.

    "What's your business here?" one of them demanded.

    "We are simple merchants," Bleddyn explained calmly.

    "You're bloody foreigners," another warrior spat.

    "Spies," declared another.

    "You can't pass this way," the first man told us.

    Bleddyn paused. I could see some of the men fingering their swords and I felt the same fear I had experienced when Medraut had confronted me, except that, this time, the men facing us were armed.

    Bleddyn inclined his head in a slight bow. "Then we will go back the way we came," he said.

    "You do that," the Northumbrian said.

    We turned round and hurried away as fast as we could, ducking to avoid the stones that some of them hurled after us.

    They did not chase us far, but our mistake was to make camp only a few miles from the village. We were tired and still feeling annoyed about being chased out, so perhaps we were careless. The place we picked was ideal for spending the night, though. There was a small stream, a wooded copse to provide shelter and firewood, and a patch of flat, grassy ground. We built a lean-to shelter at the edge of the trees, unpacked our goods to allow the mule to crop the grass, lit a fire and sat down to eat a frugal supper.

"We will need to find another route south," Bleddyn said. He looked at me gravely. "There will probably be more trouble like that the further south we go."

"We cannot turn back now," I said.

He nodded, giving me a sad smile. "I know," he said softly.

The evening was calm and still, the last rays of the sun still warming the land. Somewhere among the trees a bird chirped constantly. We both agreed that it was a good place to spend the night. After the confrontation at the bridge, we were glad of some restful peace.

It was almost dusk when they came. There were six of them, the meanest and biggest of the men who had chased us away from the village. They must have seen our fire, because we were well back from the old Roman road we had been following. The first we knew of their approach was when one of them stepped on a twig and snapped it. By that time, they were almost upon us.

Bleddyn rose to his feet, picking up his long staff. "Get behind me, Bili," he said quietly. "If there is trouble, run."

There was no doubt that there would be trouble. I was all too aware of just how small I was and how big these men were. My throat was dry as I watched the leading Northumbrian step forwards. It was the man who had told us we could not cross the bridge. He held a long-handled battleaxe, resting it on both hands, holding it across his chest.

"Well, well," he sneered. "What have we found?"

"Good evening, brothers," said Bleddyn cheerfully. "We do not have much food, but you are welcome to share it."

"We don't want your sodding food," a second man snarled.

The leader let out an unpleasant laugh. "I'd say you are raiders from Alt Clud or Pictland."

"We are simple merchants," Bleddyn said. "Do we look like raiders?"

"Yes, you bloody well do," the man said. "And even if you are not, nobody will argue when you're dead."

Bleddyn stepped to his right, moving to one side of the fire. He swung his long staff, letting the top half drop into his left palm. The sound of the wood as it slapped into his hand was the sound of his defiance.

I reached for my knife. It would not be much use against an axeman and five spears, but it was all I had. Bleddyn had told me to run, but he obviously had no intentions of fleeing, so I knew I could not abandon him.

The axeman let out a roar, swinging his weapon high over his left shoulder. He leaped at Bleddyn, bringing the axe down in a powerful sweep, aiming for Bleddyn's head. Bleddyn's staff came up, fast as a striking snake, catching the haft of the axe just below the blade. Bleddyn twisted, knocking the axe aside. In one smooth movement, with his right hand gripping the staff to guide the axe past him, his left hand lashed out to crash his fist into the axeman's face, pulping his nose.

The Northumbrian staggered back, blood spurting from his shattered nose. He dropped his axe as he fell to his knees but still managed to wave a feeble hand to his comrades before crumpling to the ground with his hands held to his ruined face.

The other men let out yells of fury as they rushed at us. Four of them went for Bleddyn but one came for me. He darted to his right, trying to dodge round the fire to get to me. He was gripping his spear in both hands, holding it low. When he had reached to within six paces, I threw my dagger.

It took him in the eye, burying itself deep into his skull. It had been a risky throw, for a man's head is a small target and moves quickly, but he was wearing a thick surcoat of padded wool and I had not wanted to risk the knife not penetrating deep enough. Besides, by the time the dagger hit him, he was barely two paces from me, so close that the tip of his spear had almost reached my chest. I could hardly miss at that range. He went down without making a sound.

I grabbed his spear and turned, ready to face another opponent.

Bleddyn had already downed two more men, cracking one on the skull with the heavy, rounded knob on the end of his staff and felling the other by driving the staff into the man's groin. Now he faced the remaining two men with a feral grin on his face.

"Come on then, boys. Let's see what you are made of," he growled.

I ran behind the two men, spear ready. One of them turned to face me, giving Bleddyn an opening. Swinging his staff like a giant mace, he clubbed both men down before either of them could react.

I gaped at him in amazement. He looked at the spear I was holding.

"What were you intending to do with that?" he asked.

"I was coming to help you."

"Well, thank you for that. I see you got your man."

The warrior at Bleddyn's feet groaned. Bleddyn looked down, swung his staff and smashed the side of the man's skull. Blood and brains oozed out on to the grass and the Angle's legs twitched for a few moments before he lay still.

My mouth was hanging open. Then a movement caught my eye and I tried to yell a warning as the first warrior, the man with the axe, clambered to his knees. He grabbed for his axe and swung it in a vicious, low arc. Seeing my alarm, Bleddyn turned, ramming his staff down to block the blow.

He almost succeeded. His staff broke the brunt of the strike but the curved axe head caught him on his right calf, digging deep and hacking into flesh, muscle and tendons.

Bleddyn let out a scream of pain as he fell but even then he did not stop fighting. He whirled his staff again, bringing it down on the back of the kneeling axeman's neck. I heard the bones shatter as it struck home.

Appalled, I dropped the spear and ran to Bleddyn. His face was pale, his breathing rasping. Blood was pouring from his wound.

"Get my pack," he hissed.

I fetched it from the fireside. He grabbed it then said. "Now get your knife and make sure they are all dead. Cut their throats if you are in any doubt. Do it quickly. Do it now."

"What?" I was horrified.

"Do it, Bili, or we are dead men."

So while Bleddyn applied a tourniquet to his leg, I hauled my knife from the dead man's eye socket, then slit the throats of the other men. I had thought that most of them were dead already, but two of them were definitely still breathing when I set my dagger to their necks.

My hands were shaking by the time I had finished. Bleddyn gave me a weak smile. "Now you know why they called me Bleddyn Grim-Hand," he said.

Chapter 11

Bleddyn had found a curved needle and some thread in his pack. He handed them to me then placed a stick between his teeth while I inexpertly sewed up the awful wound in his leg. There was so much blood that my hands were sticky with it by the time I was done.

Under Bleddyn's instruction, I mixed a poultice from some of the medicinal ingredients he always carried. Then I tore the tunic from one of the dead Northumbrians, ripped it into strips and bound Bleddyn's leg as best I could.

"We must leave here, Bili," he said. He was dreadfully weak by now and his voice was a mere whisper. Only the agonising pain was keeping him conscious. "Put out the fire and drag all the bodies into the trees. Do the same with their weapons and with most of our gear. I will have to ride the mule for a while, so we will take only what is essential."

I did as he said. It was hard work because a man's body is heavy and I was barely strong enough to heave the blood-soaked corpses into the trees. It was dark by the time I had dragged them all out of sight. The ground was trampled and smeared with blood but there was nothing I could do about that. I wanted to keep one spear for myself but Bleddyn insisted that our safety rested in flight rather than fighting.

"Their friends will come looking for them in the morning," he said. "We have a head start but that is all, We are hunted men now."

"Where can we go?"

"Alt Clud is the nearest safe place but even that is many days walk from here. Still, we must try."

I helped him to the mule. Using his staff for support, he scrambled onto its back. The beast protested loudly at his weight but I quieted it with a slap. Then we set off under the pale moonlight, using the old road because we could travel more quickly on that and there would be nobody else using it at night. I was not keen on travelling in the dark either; I had killed a man and finished off two others. I felt no regret over their deaths; they had attacked us and we had no choice but to defend ourselves. No, I would shed no tears for them. What worried me was the thought that the dead men's ghosts might hunt us in the night, so I hurried on as quickly as I could.

The road ran dead straight for mile after mile, taking us further away from the scene of our battle with every passing hour. I had often wondered at the ingenuity of the Romans, whose roads, though crumbling in places, were still in use many generations after they had sailed away. I was grateful for their engineering skill that night because we were able to travel a long way without any difficulty. Before dawn, though, I knew we must take a less obvious route, so I led the mule westwards, away from the road and into the hills.

I think the weeks that followed were among the worst of my life. I was sure that Bleddyn would die, for his wound was dreadful and I knew that many such injuries turned foul, bringing slow, agonising death. He had some herbs which he said would help with the pain and he insisted that the dressing should be changed every day, but we soon ran out of salves and I was worried that the best I could do with the bandages was wash them in cold streams.

With forced good humour, Bleddyn insisted he had been lucky.

"The axe caught the fleshy part of the back of my leg," he said. "It did not reach the bone. Flesh and muscle will heal in time."

I know he only said that to try to allay my fears because he was in dreadful pain, as well as being weak from having lost so much blood.

Food quickly became a problem. I pulled up bitter vetch plants whenever I found them, cutting off the tubers we called Heath Peas from the roots and drying them out by the fire each night. They kept us going but I knew that Bleddyn needed proper nourishment. I often suggested approaching farmsteads but he insisted that we needed to stay clear of other people until we were sure we were safe from pursuit.

After several days, it was obvious that he was growing weaker, often drifting into unconsciousness. Even the lurching gait of the mule failed to keep him awake. so I was forced to walk alongside to hold him in place on the mule's back. I was growing frantic by this time. I was confident that we had travelled far enough to be safe but I did not know what to do. I decided that I had no option but to find some place where there might be someone to help him. When I came across the next small river, I followed it because I knew that, sooner or later, most rivers had a settlement of sorts near their banks.

I confess that I was near exhaustion when I stumbled across a tiny, stone-built church perched on the side of a low hill overlooking the river. I blinked several times, not trusting my eyes, but it was a church right enough. The large wooden cross above the doorway confirmed it. Offering up a heartfelt prayer of thanks, I trudged up the slope towards it.

A solitary priest came to meet us. He was a small, chubby man in his forties, whose mousy hair was cut short and shaved on the crown in what I recognised as the tonsure used by monks who followed the Roman church.

"My name is Brother Guthred," he told me as he ushered us into his church. "What has happened?"

"We were attacked by bandits," I lied. "My uncle was wounded. Can you help us?"

"I can try," he said as he fussed over Bleddyn. "Come inside."

"Is there anyone here who has healing skills?" I asked.

"There is only me," said Brother Guthred. "I will do what I can."

He helped me carry Bleddyn into a tiny room at the rear of the church where we laid him on a bracken-filled mattress. Brother Guthred examined Bleddyn's leg, clucked his tongue and muttered to himself but set about cleaning and dressing the wound.

"The stitching is poor work," he chided. "But it is too late to do it again. The wound is clean, at least."

He applied a fresh poultice and clean bandages, then produced some foul-smelling medicine which he forced down Bleddyn's throat. After that, he had me assist him boil up some broth. I gulped down my bowl, then managed to wake Bleddyn long enough to feed him. He looked up at me with hollow eyes.

"Where are we?" he asked.

"In a church," I said. I had no idea where it was.

"That is a sign," he whispered. "I have been vain and foolish, denying my true calling. That is why the Lord has inflicted this punishment on me. Now we are in a house of God and I know what I must do."

"What you must do is rest," I told him.

He closed his eyes, falling into his first restful sleep in days. I held his hand, praying that he would live, blaming myself for having persuaded him to come south.

We stayed with Brother Guthred for five weeks. His church was not as isolated as I had first thought, for there were several farms nearby and people came most days to seek his blessing. On Sundays the little church was full. I was worried that word of our presence might somehow reach the friends of the men we had killed but I knew there was nothing I could do about that. Still, the thought of being discovered made our stay a nervous one for me.

During those weeks I earned my keep by chopping wood, sweeping the floor and replacing the rushes. Most of the time, I sat with Bleddyn.

Thanks to Brother Guthred, Bleddyn recovered his colour and vitality although his leg refused to heal properly. It gave him constant pain and would barely support his weight.

"It's good enough to ride a mule," he assured me.

"Brother Guthred says we should stay until you can walk properly," I informed him.

Bleddyn shook his head. "The longer we stay, the more chance there is that I will betray myself as a monk of the Ionian church. I suspect the good Brother's hospitality might not be so warm if he learns who I really am."

I said, "I don't think it would make any difference. I am more worried about the Northumbrian warriors tracking us down."

"Then we should move on as soon as possible," said Bleddyn.

Despite Brother Guthred's protests, we left the following day. Using his staff to help him walk, Bleddyn made it to the mule and we set off again. I think Brother Guthred believed we were rather rude and ungrateful. That was a shame because I rather liked him, even if he was a Northumbrian. I left him a few coins, which was, I suppose, a poor reward for his kindness.

Five long but uneventful weeks later, we reached Alt Clud where Elfin greeted us like long-lost family. He was full of concern for Bleddyn's injury and immediately summoned his best healers. They suggested many remedies, all of which were tried and none of which worked. What helped Bleddyn most was obtaining a monk's habit and being able to wear his crucifix over it rather than having it hidden under his tunic. Dressed as a monk once more, he spent a lot of time praying in Elfin's chapel.

I was relieved that we were safe but I was at a loose end for much of the time during our long stay in Alt Clud. My mission to find my mother and sister had failed miserably and now I felt as if I had lost Bleddyn as well. Aside from his injured leg, something in him had changed. He still spoke to me like a friend and a father, but I sensed that the joy of life had left him. To my mind, he spent far too long in penitence for what he saw as his sins. I knew he needed something to revitalise him, but I had no idea what that might be.

I shared my concerns with King Elfin. He was very approachable and always happy to talk to me. He was sympathetic but could offer no real solution.

"I think the best thing for Bleddyn would be for him to stay here in Alt Clud," he suggested. "This is his home, after all."

"You seem very keen for him to stay with you," I observed.

"I want him to stay because he is my kin," he told me.

"I didn't know that," I said.

Elfin's handsome young face crinkled in a frown. "Perhaps I should not have mentioned it. I know Bleddyn does not like to talk about his parents."

My curiosity was aroused now. I asked, "Why? Who were they?"

"Perhaps you should ask him," Elfin suggested.

"He won't tell me," I said. "Why is it such a big secret?"

"It is not a secret," Elfin said. "It is just that Bleddyn prefers not to discuss it."

"Then if it is not a secret, why don't you tell me?"

Elfin scratched his head. "I suppose there is no harm. But you had better not let him discover that it was me who told you."

"I know how to keep a secret," I assured him.

He sighed. "Very well. Bleddyn's mother was a slave girl. I'm not sure where she was from, but she was a maid to the king's wife here in Alt Clud. She was very pretty, from all accounts. So much so, in fact, that she caught the eye of the king himself."

"Which king was that?" I asked.

"Your namesake. King Bili."

My eyes were wide with astonishment. "Bleddyn is Bili's son?"

"He was never recognised as such," Elfin said. "Bili's wife, that was his first wife, was not happy when she discovered her maid was pregnant. She had her sent away.

The poor girl was sold to a minor chieftain who lived some distance away. I think she died when Bleddyn was quite young. It was before I was born, anyway."

"But Bleddyn is King Bili's son?"

""Almost certainly."

"Which makes him Bridei's older half-brother," I said.

"And my great-uncle," Elfin said. "But I don't think anyone among the Pecht knows. Except Bridei himself, I suppose."

I smiled to myself. Elfin's story explained a great deal. Of course, he made me swear never to let Bleddyn know that I had heard the tale from him.

He said, "Bleddyn was a mighty warrior but the sad circumstances of his birth have haunted him for many years. I think that is partly why he became a monk; to find some peace for his spirit."

A peace that had been disturbed by our encounter with the Northumbrian thugs. That was my fault, so I knew that, however much I wanted to leave Alt Clud, I must allow Bleddyn time to find himself again.

Apart from that revelation, Alt Clud had few attractions for me. It was a strange place. I never felt quite at home there, even though we stayed for many months. The Britons spoke more or less the same language as the Pecht but still I felt like an outsider among them. Even my first real encounters with women, thanks to the willingness of some of the serving girls, were not enough to make me want to stay. I could not fault Elfin's hospitality but somehow the place did not feel right for me.

I did not feel able to mention my unease to Bleddyn because he was immersed in re-discovering his old home. I think he might have stayed there forever had events in Northumbria not come to our attention.

As so often, it was a travelling merchant who brought the news. He told us that Ecgfrith had once again proven his military prowess by defeating King Wulfhere of Mercia and seizing the kingdom of Lindsey, adding it to his own, already substantial, realm. Ecgfrith had then arranged a marriage between his sister and a Mercian lord named Aethelred, who had been installed as a puppet king of Mercia. Directly or indirectly, Ecgfrith now ruled around half of Britain. Only the Saxons of the south refused to acknowledge him as the pre-eminent king in the land.

More importantly for us, the merchant confirmed that Wulfric had been permitted to return north to Dun Eidyn, bringing his army with him. That was significant for me because it meant that Triduana was probably with him. There were, though, other implications. Wulfric's return meant that his father, Beornhaeth, now had the strength to threaten Alt Clud and Fortriu.

Elfin was worried. "No doubt we will soon receive demands for increased tribute," he said glumly. "Beornhaeth sees himself almost as a king in his own right."

Then Bleddyn spoke. For the first time in many months, I saw a glimpse of fire in his eyes. "Bridei must be warned," he announced. "Bili, we must go north."

I could not hide my delight. The real Bleddyn was back.

Chapter 12

I suggested that we take a boat, sailing up the west coast, past Dal Riata and on to the mountainous lands of Cait from where we could ride to Inbhir Nis. I put that idea forward because I was worried that Bleddyn might not be able to manage a long journey on horseback but he insisted that he would be able to ride without difficulty.

"It's walking that's my problem," he said."Besides, there is too much risk of meeting up with Scots or Irish pirates if we go by sea. No, we will ride."

Elfin, generous as ever, provided us with horses and as much food as we could carry. He also presented me with some new clothes to replace my travel-worn outfit which was, in any case, far too small for me. I was seventeen years old now, only a couple of months short of my eighteenth birthday, and even though I was still smaller and slighter of build than most men of my age, I had grown a fair bit since we had left Fortriu. I had even begun shaving, although that was mostly because the fine layer of downy hairs that slowly grew on my chin were too embarrassing to be called a beard and it was easier to scrape them off every few days than suffer ridicule for not being able to grow a proper beard.

Freshly kitted out thanks to Elfin's generosity, we rode north, taking a much more direct route than we usually followed. We headed east, crossing the Foirthe near Sruighlea, then cutting northwards. It was as well that we did because we learned that Bridei was not in Inbhir Nis. As usual, he had spent much of the year travelling around Fortriu, Cait and Fotla, taking his household and his warriors with him. By harvest time, he had arrived at Dun Nechtan, taking the opportunity to visit his daughter and also placing himself conveniently should any raiders from Dal Riata attempt to relieve the local farmers of their cattle. Autumn was the traditional time of year for such raids and Nechtan's home lay on the fringes of Fortriu, so was especially vulnerable.

Despite Bleddyn's confidence, even riding proved painful for him, so he was delighted that we were able to find Bridei a day earlier than we had expected, but he was also concerned about me.

"You will see Derelei again," he said.

I shrugged. "She will have forgotten me by now. Anyway, she is married and probably has a child."

I tried to sound as if the thought of seeing her again meant nothing to me but my stomach was fluttering just at the mention of her name. I could not understand it. During the months at Alt Clud I had tasted my first experiences with girls because Elfin had many female servants and slaves who were willing enough to sleep with his guests, even if those guests were as youthful as I was. Bored as I had been among the Britons, I had enjoyed what those girls could offer but I never felt any real attachment to any of them. Yet Bleddyn merely had to mention Derelei to set my skin tingling and my heart racing.

"Just remember who she is," Bleddyn cautioned.

"I will."

What choice did I have? I vowed to remain calm when I met her but the beating of my heart told me that would be no easy task.

We reached Dun Nechtan around mid-morning. It was little more than a large, fortified farmstead which sat on a low hummock of raised ground near a broad loch, from which the River Spe began its long journey northwards. Despite the Dun's modest size, Nechtan had recently built himself a large, rectangular, single-storey house which sat in the centre of the walled perimeter. The ditch and wooden wall enclosed a few other outbuildings but the place was much smaller than I had imagined. Bleddyn explained that, in spite of its apparent insignificance, this was the home of a major chieftain. Many of Nechtan's people lived in farms or small villages that were dotted around the side of the loch or among the surrounding hills. Nechtan controlled a large territory and in time of war he could call on several hundred men to join his war band.

Perhaps it was the enclosing mountains that made Nechtan's home seem small, for it was, in truth, a lovely setting. Or it would have been had it been anyone else's home.

Bridei himself hurried to meet us, his face revealing undisguised pleasure.

"I thought you might be dead!" he exclaimed. "Welcome back. Welcome indeed." He hesitated slightly when he saw Bleddyn limp away from his horse. "What happened?" he asked.

Bleddyn dismissed his concerns, saying, "Oh, we ran into a spot of bother with some Northumbrians. It's left me with a bad leg. I'm sure it will heal in time." He sounded confident, although I knew that he was convinced the Lord had sent the injury as a punishment and that he feared it might never heal.

For the moment, Bridei took his words at face value, clapping him on the back and insisting that he tell the whole story over a mug of heather ale. Now that I knew their secret, the easy familiarity of their relationship made a bit more sense to me.

The king turned to me and smiled. "You have grown a fair bit, young man," he observed. "Did you find your family?"

"No," I replied. "Not this time. But we had some word of my sister. I will find her soon."

"Well, that is good news. Now, you'd better come and meet Nechtan."

Nechtan greeted us in the main room of his house. I don't think he was too pleased to see us but he was cordial enough as he invited us to sit at his table. He ordered food and drink to be brought and sent one of the slave girls to find his wife.

His wife.

Derelei.

She walked serenely into the room, looking even more radiant than I remembered, with her smooth, pale skin and her large eyes. Her long hair fell in glorious cascades around her shoulders. She was wearing a long dress of many-coloured cloth, trimmed with fox fur, and had a jewelled crucifix at her throat. The dress did nothing to hide her figure which, although she was still slim, had filled out since I had last seen her. She had been little more than a girl then, but now she was a woman, and proud of it. I tried hard not to stare at her.

She greeted us very formally before taking her place at table beside Nechtan. He dwarfed her, both physically and in his manner, making it plain that he was the chieftain here. I wanted to hit him.

We sat together for the remainder of the morning and into the afternoon while Bleddyn recounted what had happened to us and the news we had heard.

Bridei was concerned when he heard about Wulfric's return. Chewing on a hunk of dark bread, he said, "We are not ready to face Beornhaeth yet. I have men constructing ships and I am slowly building the core of an army but if Beornhaeth decides to march against us, we will be hard pressed to stop him."

"Do you think he will?" Nechtan asked. He sounded a little nervous but I suppose he had every right. He knew that if the Northumbrians advanced up the central glens, his home would be in their path.

Bridei shrugged. "We have agreed to remain at peace but Beornhaeth is an ambitious man. I am hoping that he will be kept busy controlling the lands he already has, but it is hard to be certain what he will do." He looked meaningfully at Bleddyn. "I may need your help discovering his intentions, Brother Bleddyn."

"I will do what I can," said Bleddyn. I wondered whether I was the only one to detect a hint of uncertainty in his voice when he said that. I knew how painful his leg was. It was difficult to imagine him roaming the country when he was in such pain.

Bridei nodded thoughtfully. "Bloody Northumbrians," he grumbled. "I don't trust them."

"What about Dal Riata?" Bleddyn asked.

Bridei grinned. Mocking himself, he said, "Bloody Scots. you can't trust them either. But there has been nothing serious. Only a few minor raids. Fighting them off is helping our young men gain experience of war, so Mael Duin's folk are doing us a favour. Most of the time, he and Domnall Donn are too busy fighting one another."

The conversation turned to more mundane matters like the harvest and the health of the cattle, both of which were apparently good. I had no interest in any of that, so I glanced over at Derelei, only to see that she was looking at me intently. Our eyes met briefly before she looked away. It was hard for me to say what her gaze was telling me.

In an attempt to hide my confused feelings, I turned back to listening to the men. Bridei was saying that he intended to return to Inbhir Nis soon because he had already stayed with Nechtan for a few weeks.

"I've got more than fifty warriors with me," he explained. "They have been living in temporary huts they have built near the loch shore. It's time I took them home."

"Why so many?" asked Bleddyn.

"They've been patrolling the hills to watch for raiding parties from Dal Riata," Bridei said, adding with a laugh, "The strange thing is that some of those patrols have returned leading cattle that must have accidentally strayed away from Dal Riatan farms."

Bleddyn laughed. Life on the frontier was often like that.

Nechtan said that Bleddyn and I were welcome to stay as long as we wished. I don't think he really meant it, but he knew that Bleddyn was a friend of Bridei and Nechtan was a chieftain, so he observed the rules of hospitality.

"Thank you for the offer," said Bleddyn, "but I think we will travel to Inbhir Nis with Bridei."

"Then you will be my guests tonight," Nechtan declared. " I'm afraid there is no room in the main house, but I will have one of the outbuildings cleared and have some mattresses filled for you."

"Thank you," said Bleddyn. "That is very kind."

I was pretty sure we could have bedded down in the main room, but I think Nechtan may have wanted to keep me away from the house.

Bridei stood up. "I need to visit my men," he announced. He looked at Nechtan. "Will you accompany me?"

Nechtan nodded his agreement and Bleddyn said he would manage to keep up as long as he had his staff to support him. For a brief moment I thought I would be left with Derelei but Bleddyn said, "Come along, Bili."

I glanced at Derelei but her expression was unreadable, so I tagged along after the three men as they made their way through the door.

Outside the walls of the dun, we wandered for a while. Nechtan proudly pointed out how many cattle he had, a sign of his wealth and status. I could also see the white specks of his sheep dotting the hillsides around us. Sheep are important, for their meat, and especially for their wool, but it is still cattle that denote a man's standing. Nechtan had plenty of both.

We were approaching the collection of huts where Bridei's warriors were housed when I had a sudden thought that Medraut and his gang might be there. Even with Bridei and Bleddyn around, I did not want to meet them. Guret would almost certainly be there.

Using the first excuse I could think of, I announced that I wanted to climb one of the hills, to get a better view of the place. The men did not seem bothered, so I turned away from the loch, heading for the nearest hill.

Dun Nechtan lies on a broad expanse of rough, wooded lowland, well watered by the river, the loch and countless tiny streams that trickle down the hillsides. As Bleddyn had pointed out before, no fewer than five mountain passes opened out around the lower ground, providing access to Dal Riata to the west and Fortriu to the north and east. It was a place of vital importance to Bridei and to the safety of Fortriu. Climbing one of the hills would allow me to see more of the land. It would also mean I would avoid meeting Medraut and would be able to keep my promise to stay away from Derelei.

I had no specific direction in mind, but I tramped across an expanse of marshy ground, then negotiated some tree-covered hummocks until I reached the lower slopes of one of the hills. It took me the rest of the afternoon to climb to a point where I could look back over the valley below. The wind ruffled my hair, bringing with it the faint cries of a lone curlew. Some distance away to my right a few sheep cropped the grass and heather. One of them looked up, stared at me blankly for a while, then calmly resumed eating.

From further up the slope, hidden by another ridge in the hillside, I heard an angry shout, the call of a stag. I sat on a rock and enjoyed the splendour of the isolation. Down below were dozens of people, a few hundred if you included all the farmers and their families whose homes fell under Nechtan's protection, yet up here, even though I was nowhere near the highest reaches of the hills, I was alone with the wind, the sheep and the deer, as if I were the only person in the entire world. I felt remarkably at peace up there on that windswept slope. The thought of returning to sit under Nechtan's doleful gaze and to have Derelei close but apparently oblivious to my feelings for her, was almost enough to make me stay there all evening, but I knew that even the long summer days come to an end, so I reluctantly pushed myself up and began the long walk back down the hill.

By the time I had reached the foot of the slope, the sun was edging lower in the sky, turning slightly red, bringing the promise of a glorious sunset and another fine morning to follow. I had judged my time just about perfectly, I thought. Once I rounded the next small, wooded hillock I should be able to see the walls of Nechtan's home.

I stopped abruptly when a man jumped out from behind the trees to face me from around ten paces ahead. He was followed by three more figures, all of them wearing swords. I recognised Medraut instantly, noticing that he was even bigger and more muscular than he had been when I had last seen him. His dark hair was now complemented by an equally dark beard, trimmed to a neat point so that it gave him a piratical appearance. Inevitably, the three men with him were Guret, Uerb and Donnell.

Medraut cocked his head slightly as he regarded me.

"I saw you arrive earlier, monk-boy," he said. "I thought you'd stay close to your protector."

"What do you want this time, Medraut?" I asked, trying to quell the mounting apprehension I could feel growing inside me.

"I want you to grovel and weep like the child you are," he replied. "I'm going to teach you a lesson. You think you are high and mighty because your monk is close to Bridei? You think you can look down on us?"

"That's not true," I protested. Remembering the warning Donnell had given me at Derelei's wedding, I said, "You just want to rough me up because you can. You know you can beat me because I'm smaller than you. Why don't you grow up, Medraut? Or are you afraid to fight someone your own size?"

If I had expected my taunt to give him second thoughts, I failed. He laughed at me.

"Earlier this year, I killed two men of Dal Riata in single combat," he informed me proudly.

"Then you have proved yourself already," I said. "Hitting me won't do any good for your reputation."

"It will make me feel better, monk-boy," he retorted.

"You should kill him," Guret said. "Stick him through the belly and listen to him squeal."

Donnell butted in then, saying, "You'd better not kill him. The king would not be pleased."

"The false king," Medraut growled. Then he said, "Still, you are right. A beating will suffice." He unbuckled his sword belt, passing the weapon to Uerb to hold.

I exchanged a brief look with Donnell who shrugged as if to say he had done all that he could for me. Next to him, Uerb was licking his lips, his piggy eyes shining with anticipation, while Guret stood gripping the hilt of his sword, his expression full of venom.

I thought of the way I had hidden while the Northumbrians raped my mother and sister. I had been a coward that day and even though I had faced up to the Northumbrians who had attacked me and Bleddyn, I knew that my cowardice was still a part of me. It told me to run. I remembered the beating Medraut had dealt out to me before and I knew I was likely to receive another one. Every fibre in me wanted to run but I stood my ground because I knew that running would be the action of a faintheart and that I would never be able to bear the shame if my fear was revealed to the world.

The fact remained that Medraut was much too strong for me. My only chance was to use my brain but it was plain that my attempts to talk my way out of the fight had failed so far. In desperation, I put on an air of confidence.

"A fair fight?" I asked. "If I beat you, the others will let me go?"

They all laughed at that. Medraut said, "You won't beat me, monk-boy."

"But if I do? Make them swear to allow me to pass."

"All right. If you win, they will let you go."

"I want to hear them swear it."

"Want all you like. You have my word. That should be good enough."

It wasn't nearly good enough, but there was no point in arguing. Still stalling, I asked him, "You say you killed two men earlier this year?"

"Stone dead," he said with an arrogant smile.

"Not bad. I managed three myself. Northumbrians who came after me and Bleddyn."

Strictly speaking, that was not a lie. I had killed one and at least two of Bleddyn's victims had still been alive when I had slit their throats.

"Lying little sod," Guret said.

"Ask Bleddyn if you like," I told him. "There were six of them. He killed three and I got the others. You do know why he's called Bleddyn Grim-Hand, don't you?"

I could tell from their faces that they didn't. I said, "He knows how to kill. He's been teaching me."

A flicker of what might have been uncertainty appeared in Medraut's eyes. I had gained a very slight advantage but I needed to press it home. I held up a hand, gesturing to Medraut to wait.

"I still have my knife," I said. "If this is to be a fair fight, I'd better put it aside."

I looked around as if wondering where to put it. I pointed to the nearest tree, a small silver birch that was only around ten paces from me.

"That tree will do," I said. Quickly, I drew out my dagger, reversed it and threw. The endless practice paid off. The blade thudded neatly into the centre of the trunk, quivering slightly.

I turned back to face Medraut. "Ready when you are," I said.

He was surprised. I could see it in his face. I knew he would still beat me, but at least I had the satisfaction of knowing that he was capable of doubt. I bunched my fists, waiting for him.

He did not run at me. I had been hoping he would, because Bleddyn had shown me how to use a man's speed and weight to knock him off balance. Medraut, though, stalked up to me, his fists ready to strike. He would go for the chest and belly, I reckoned, because hitting someone's chin is likely to break your knuckles. I raised my fists in front of my chest, guarding my body.

Snarling, he swung a right hook at my head. I ducked, then dived at him. His left arm came across to block me but I drove the top of my head into his belly. It hurt me almost as much as it hurt him because he had a metal buckle on his trouser belt which caught my scalp. I ignored the pain and drove into him as hard as I could.

He grabbed for me. If the fight turned into a wrestling contest I had even less chance against him but my head-butt had winded him and he was unable to get a proper hold on me. I lifted myself, my face scraping up his leather jerkin. Pushing with my arms, I pretended that I was trying to scramble away from him. I had only a brief instant before his arms would clamp around me but that was enough time. Remembering Bleddyn's lessons on how to fight dirty, I jerked my knee up as hard as I could, ramming it into Medraut's crotch.

His mouth opened in a horrified gasp and his eyes went wide. He staggered back a step, his hands clutching at his groin. I swung at him, smashing my forearm to the side of his head. He went down in a heap, curling up on the ground at my feet. I was tempted to kick him in the head but I left him and darted to the trees to retrieve my dagger.

I was only just in time because when I turned back, Guret was advancing towards me with his sword drawn. Behind him, Uerb and Donnell were trying, without much success, to help Medraut to his feet. I knew those two were no real threat. It was Guret who was the problem.

I raised the knife to let him see it. "I can put this in your eye before you get anywhere near me," I told him. "I've killed men that way before."

"You fight dirty, you yellow bastard," he hissed.

"I fight to win. Do you expect me to stand still and let you do what you want to me? Now put down your sword and step aside."

He hesitated but I waggled the knife gently. Slowly, he stooped to place his sword on the ground. Glaring at me, he took a few steps back.

Still holding my dagger, I circled round Guret, passing the other three. Uerb looked horrified but Donnell's lips twisted in a faint smile. Medraut was lurching to his feet, still doubled over.

I said to him, "Now we are even. An eye for an eye. Let it stop at that."

"I'll kill you," he gasped.

There was no point in staying. I walked away as quickly as I could. As soon as I turned the corner, moving out of sight behind the trees, I ran for Dun Nechtan.

I reached the gates out of breath but exhilarated. I knew that I would need to be careful in future but for the first time, I began to believe that perhaps I was not a coward after all. I would simply have to avoid being alone any place where Medraut or Guret could get to me. That might not be easy, but I would just have to stay close to Bleddyn. As soon as his leg healed, Bridei would have a mission for us and the problem would be solved.

I felt good as I strolled across the yard towards the house. Then I saw a girl approaching me, obviously intent on speaking to me. She was one of the servants, or perhaps a slave. I guessed she was around fourteen years old, just beginning to show the first signs of growing into a woman. Her face was pretty, her long hair tied back under a headscarf. I gave her an admiring look as she approached me. She blushed and lowered her eyes.

"You are Bili?" she asked me.

"Yes."

"Lord Nechtan has prepared a place for you and for Brother Bleddyn. I am to show you."

I followed her around the back of the house. Here I saw several storehouses and a barn, along with a couple of old, rather worn-looking roundhouses. She led me to one of these. It was a high building, of the two-storey type where people brought their cattle in overnight during winter so that the heat from the animals would keep the house warm. I guessed it might have been where Nechtan had lived before he had built his new house. The sleeping quarters were on the upper level, on a wide ledge that ran around the circular interior. The place smelled as if Nechtan still used it to keep his cattle but the floor had been covered with fresh straw and it seemed clean enough.

The girl pointed to a wooden ladder that allowed access to the upper level.

I took a quick look around. I had slept in worse places.

"Thank you," I said.

The girl looked around too, a furtive glance to make sure that we could not be overheard. Urgently, she said, "I have a message from my lady."

"From Derelei?"

She nodded. "She says two things. First, you must not betray yourself at supper. Nobody must know that she has sent me to speak to you."

"All right. What is the other thing?"

"Be at the barn just after midnight. She will meet you there."

Chapter 13

Trying to behave naturally during supper was one of the worst torments I have ever endured. Derelei was so close, sitting just across the table, yet she was so far away as to seem unreachable. As usual when we were with company, she barely paid attention to me, which made things even worse.

The food was plain but wholesome, although I hardly noticed what it was and did not eat much. Virtually the only time Derelei spoke to me during the meal was to enquire whether the food was not to my liking.

"I have a bit of an upset stomach," I explained. Which was true. It felt like a thousand butterflies were whirring around inside me.

When night fell, everyone retired. Bleddyn and I took a candle to light our way, moving carefully once we reached our designated house because fire is deadly and everything around us would burn easily. Bleddyn struggled to climb the ladder but made it eventually, grimacing with pain as he hauled himself onto the upper level.

We found our mattresses, undressed quickly, piled the blankets high and blew out the candle.

I lay in the darkness, listening to the scrabbling of mice and trying to judge the time. Bleddyn was soon snoring, as I knew he would be. I had no fears of waking him when I left, nor of finding the barn. My main worries were Derelei's reasons for this secret assignation. I had my hopes, of course, and I could not think of any other reason, but I tried not to dwell on my dreams. Apart from the message she had sent, she had given no signs that she had any feelings for me at all. Perhaps she wanted to meet only to tell me to leave her in peace.

I waited until I judged that midnight was near. Slipping from the bed, I pulled on my shirt, trousers and boots, then quietly felt my way to the ladder. Bleddyn's snores continued undisturbed. I reached the ground, eased outside the door's leather cover and crossed quickly to the barn.

The wide doors were barred, of course, but I lifted the locking beam and slipped inside. The barn was piled high with bales of hay and straw, fodder stored for feeding Nechtan's livestock over the winter months. Quietly, I closed the door, took a couple of steps to the side and listened. I was alone, so I sat down and waited.

I don't know how long I sat there but I knew it was until well after midnight. I began to suspect that someone was playing a cruel joke on me. Guret? No, I had beaten him back to the farmstead so he could not have primed the slave girl. Derelei? Could she be that cruel? I doubted it. I decided that something must have happened to prevent her from coming.

Then I heard footsteps outside the door. Soft, cautious movements. The door opened a fraction. I sensed someone sticking their head inside. A girl's voice whispered, "Bili?"

That was not Derelei. Was this a trap? No, it was a girl, not Medraut or Guret.

"I'm here," I whispered.

She jumped. I could hear her fright. I caught the briefest glimpse of her silhouette framed in the moonlit doorway. I was fairly sure it was the girl who had brought me the message. My heart sank. I had been dreaming of Derelei. If this girl, young as she was, wanted a tumble in the hay I would be happy enough to oblige. She was very pretty, but I felt cheated none the less.

There were whispers from outside. She was not alone. Then another figure slipped through the door which was quickly pushed shut, leaving the two of us in almost total darkness.

"Bili?"

"Derelei!"

"Shhh!" she hissed. She came to me, hands reaching to embrace me. Her arms encircled me and she clung to me, kissing me, hard. Amazed and delighted, I put my arms around her slim waist, holding her close to me, scarcely believing that it was truly her.

She stopped kissing me at last. I touched her cheek, felt it damp with tears.

"What is wrong?" I asked.

"Nothing is wrong. Everything is right now. But we do not have long."

"Nechtan?"

"Snoring like a pig." Her voice sounded full of disgust and contempt.

I said, "I cannot bear it when I think of you with him."

"It is a price I must pay for my father's sake. But I don't want to talk about Nechtan. We have little enough time as it is. Sorcha will keep watch for us. We can trust her."

I almost asked her why she had come here but she took a step back and I heard the soft rustle of clothes as she pulled her long shift over her head. Then she was clinging to me again, kissing me, pressing her naked skin against me.

I don't think I have undressed so quickly in all my life. She let out a giggle as I struggled out of my trousers but soon we were both naked, touching and caressing each other, hungry for one another. Clinging together, we turned so that I could ease her back to lie against the bales of straw. Then she pulled me close, encouraging me with urgent whispers, telling me that she was mine. Guiding me with her gentle touch, Derelei made my world complete.

She shed more tears when we were done. I held her until she was quiet, then we lay side by side. I ran my hands over the smooth firmness of her belly and the softness of her breasts.

"You must keep this a secret," she said. "Promise?"

"Promise."

She rolled towards me, leaning over to kiss me again. "I have to go now. Before anyone wakes."

"I thought we both made enough noise to wake the whole house," I said.

"You did, anyway," she laughed.

"When can I see you again?"

"You haven't seen me tonight, Bili. It is too dark. But if you mean when can we do this again, I don't know. Sorcha will send you word when I think it is safe."

"Tomorrow?" I asked eagerly.

She stood up, fumbling around for her shift. She tossed items of my clothing at me from where I had discarded them. "I don't know, my love. We must be careful. We cannot afford for anyone to find out."

"I think Nechtan suspects me already," I said.

"No he doesn't. He just knows that Guret dislikes you. Also, he thinks he should have been king so he is jealous of anyone who is close to my father."

"I thought he supported Bridei? He made that speech to the chieftains."

"You still don't know much, do you, my love? He didn't have enough support to become king himself, so he agreed to support my father in exchange for a position of honour and for . . . " she hesitated, " . . . for me."

She pulled her shift on, then pushed me back on the straw, clambering on top of me to give me another passionate kiss. It did not last nearly long enough for my liking. In far too short a time, she had rolled away and made for the door.

"Get back to your bed before dawn," she whispered. "And if anyone ever challenges you, tell them you were bedding Sorcha. She'll back you up."

I heard the door open, then she was gone, leaving me naked, clutching my clothes and covered in straw.

"You've got straw in your hair," Bleddyn informed me the next morning. "And you look dreadful."

"I didn't sleep well. Bellyache. I had to get up during the night."

"I hope you didn't shit in Nechtan's barn," he said, lifting a strand of crumpled straw from my shoulder.

I brushed my hand through my hair, dislodging several more stalks. "My mattress must have a hole in it," I said. I did not dare look at him. That comment about the barn was too close to the mark.

I wanted to go down to the loch for a swim but the chances of meeting Medraut were too great so I contented myself with fetching a small pail of cold water from the well and washing myself all over. I felt better for it, but Bleddyn said he still thought I looked exhausted.

"Perhaps you should rest today," he suggested.

"I'll manage."

We crossed to the house, where Bridei met us at the door. He dragged Bleddyn away for what he said would be a few words in private. I left them to it and went inside, anxious to see Derelei. She was there, but so were Nechtan and Guret. Both of them glared at me, giving me greetings that were barely civil. Feeling like Daniel in the lion's den, I sat opposite them, keeping the width of the table between us.

Fortunately, Bridei and Bleddyn came in after only a few moments. Nechtan continued to brood over his breakfast, sending several dark looks in my direction. I thought he had discovered my night with Derelei but I soon realised that Guret must have told his father about what I had done to Medraut the previous day. I did not really care. I felt invulnerable and my main worry was trying not to look at Derelei too often. Once more, she had reverted to being polite and very formal towards me. I supposed I would get used to that in time, although it was hard. Whenever I looked at her, I found myself imagining what her body looked like under her dress.

Bridei broke the awkward silence by asking Guret, "How is Medraut this morning?"

I tore my attention away from Derelei.

In a surly voice, Guret said, "Sore. He will be fine."

Bridei looked at me. "I hear you and he had a disagreement yesterday."

How did he know that, I wondered? I shrugged. "He started it," I said casually.

"That's not what I was told," Nechtan growled darkly. "I don't approve of men who fight dirty."

I felt my cheeks burning. I wished they would not do that. I coughed, trying to cover the unwanted reaction.

Bleddyn came to my rescue. "You would rather a boy like Bili should stand still to be beaten up by a gang of four bigger lads? Would that make him a man?"

"You know what I mean," Nechtan said. "A warrior should not have to stoop to such things."

Guret was grinning at me now. Derelei's eyes were wide. She had obviously not heard about the fight. "What happened?" she asked.

Bridei took charge before Nechtan or Guret could speak. He said, "I have not heard Bili's version of events but it seems that while he was out yesterday evening he attacked Medraut, Guret and two other lads single-handedly. He felled Medraut with a kick to where it hurts most and threatened to put a knife in Guret's eye. Is that right, Bili?"

"More or less," I said. "Except that they came looking for me. I was only defending myself."

Bridei's eyes were hard. He stared at me, then at Guret. I stared back but I noticed that Guret could not hold the king's gaze.

Bridei said, "Let this be known to everyone involved. I will not have my men fighting among themselves. We are Pecht. We must stand together. Medraut has the potential to be a great warrior. Bili is useful to me as a gatherer of information. If there is any repeat of this or if anyone suffers an accident of any kind, I will know where to look for the culprits. I am trying to make our people strong and I will need you all in the years ahead. Do I make myself clear?"

My sense of invulnerability had evaporated under the intensity of his anger. I nodded my head, "I understand," I said.

Guret mumbled some agreement.

Bridei sat back on his chair. "Good. Now, to business. It seems, Bili, that Bleddyn's leg will hamper his efforts to gather information for me. I need someone to go to Dun Eidyn to discover what Beornhaeth is planning. Can you do that for me?"

I expected Bleddyn to protest that I was too young, but he said nothing. I supposed that must have been what Bridei had spoken to him about. Feigning a confidence I did not feel, I said, "Yes, I can do that."

He jabbed a finger at me. "To gather information for me," he repeated. "Not to try any foolish rescues of captive women. Do you hear me?"

I flinched at that. I was about to argue but I caught the warning look in Bleddyn's eye. "I understand," I said.

"Good. Bleddyn tells me that you are feeling a little unwell. I will grant you a few days to rest here before you go. Nechtan will provide for you." Nechtan scowled but nodded his head, so Bridei went on, "I am going back to Inbhir Nis. I want to see how my ships are coming along."

"Will you be leaving any of your men here?" Nechtan asked.

"No. The raiding season is almost over. Your men can handle anything that Dal Riata sends now. My warriors will return with me." He turned to Bleddyn. "I need you with me, too, old friend."

I could hardly believe it. I was to be left close to Derelei while all my enemies were to be taken away. Only old Nechtan would be there and I already knew that Derelei could slip away from his bed at night. I felt my legs trembling. I did not dare look at her for fear I would betray my excitement.

Bridei rose to his feet, scraping back the chair. He looked directly at me. "Walk with me a while, Bili. I have some instructions for you."

I followed him to the door. Bleddyn waved a hand, indicating that he would not accompany me. As soon as we were outside, Bridei set off for the gates at a brisk pace. I hurried to catch up with him.

He was silent until we had passed beyond the dun then he slowed and said, "Those things had to be said, Bili. I know you did not start it, but I also know that I need men like Medraut and the others. Not least because each of those four is the son of an important chieftain."

"I understand."

"Good lad." He grinned. "As it happens, I need men who know how to fight dirty, too."

"I'd rather not fight at all," I said.

"Sometimes it is necessary," he said. "And if you must fight, then fight to win."

"I will."

"I know you will. Now, it seems that Bleddyn will be out of action for some time. I don't blame you for that but it means you must take on his role. He says you can do it."

"I will do my best."

"I am counting on you. And I meant what I said about not doing anything stupid. Get me what I need to know and then you can go off to find your sister. The future of Fortriu is at stake here, Bili. The future of the Pecht is at stake. That future is more important than any personal considerations. Perhaps you are too young to understand how hard it is to make some decisions, where the people come before yourself and your family. Men who aspire to lead must sometimes make those decisions. Do you understand?"

"Yes." I knew he was speaking of Derelei and the sacrifice he had asked her to make. I could hear the undercurrent of emotion in his voice.

He stopped, turning to face me. Reaching up to place his hands on my shoulders, he gazed into my eyes. "Bleddyn speaks very highly of you, lad. I think you are capable of great things. You are young to be taking on a task such as this, but you speak their language and you have had the best of teachers. Just be careful."

"I will be careful," I assured him.

"Good. I will save this land, Bili. Nothing is more important to me. The only thing that comes close is my daughter. I do not want to see her hurt."

I almost blurted out that he should not have married her to Nechtan but I held my tongue. I looked into his eyes and I realised that he knew, or at least suspected, something of what had passed between me and Derelei. I could not guess how he had found out, but I was convinced that he knew. I supposed that, for all Derelei's precautions, he could read her better than anyone else.

He smiled, clapped me on the shoulders and said, "Now be off with you. You have a few days, that is all."

"Thank you," I said.

He knew, he understood and he was leaving me alone at Nechtan's home.

With Derelei.

A few days was all I had been allowed. There was room in the main house for me once Bridei had gone, but I stayed in the old roundhouse, sleeping alone on the wide upper level. Nechtan was pleased about that. So was I, because it meant I could leave whenever I wanted to meet Derelei.

I knew it was a sin. Bleddyn had told me the Ten Commandments often enough but then, one of those was Thou Shalt Not Kill and, to me, that injunction, which I knew Bleddyn had broken himself, seemed more serious than taking another man's wife, especially when he had more or less forced the marriage on her.

And take her I did. Repeatedly.

Three times we met in the barn at dead of night, once during the day when she went out riding with only young Sorcha for company and we met in a small corrie high in the hills, and once in her own bed when Nechtan was called away because there had been another cattle raid.

We did more than make love. We talked, holding back no secrets at all. I could tell her anything and know that she would love me, no matter what. I had never felt closer to anyone.

We agreed that her father knew what we were doing and that Bleddyn probably did, too. I told her what I had learned about Bleddyn's parents. That made her smile. "My uncle Bleddyn," she laughed.

She also talked, quite openly, about her distaste for Nechtan but she told me that she would be compelled to make love to him very soon.

"He doesn't bother me often," she said. "And I can make sure it is over quickly. I don't want to do it, but I cannot risk having a child without him thinking he is the father."

That shocked me. "A child?"

"Don't panic," she laughed. "It is much too soon to tell yet." Then she ran her hand down my thigh, teasing me. "But we could try again if you like."

After ten days, Nechtan pointedly asked me whether I felt well enough to go on my mission for Bridei. "You look fit to travel," he said sourly.

"I will leave tomorrow," I told him.

He grunted, which I took to be a sign that he was pleased.

Derelei and I met for one final time, in my house where she climbed the ladder to join me. If anything, she was more passionate than usual, clinging to me tightly all through the night.

"I don't want you to go," she said as we lay, exhausted, in each other's arms in the dark hours before dawn.

"I don't want to go either but at least it means we will both get some sleep at nights."

"I'm serious!" she said.

"So am I. I don't want to leave. I want nothing more than to stay here forever, with you. But I have no choice. Your father needs me to go. He said the future of the Pecht is more important than what we want ourselves."

"He said the same thing to me when he asked me to marry Nechtan."

I sighed. "The problem is that he is right. I have seen what the Northumbrians can do. I watched them slaughter our army and I saw them kill my brother, destroy my home and steal away my mother and sister. We cannot allow them to do the same to the rest of our people."

She laid her hand on my chest. "I worry about you, Bili. I know you are clever but you are not a warrior. I worry that something will happen to you."

"Nothing will happen," I assured her. "Bleddyn has taught me well. I am sure I can pass as an Angle, Nobody will suspect me. I'll be back by next summer."

"Promise?"

"Promise."

Chapter 14

Bridei had presented me with a purse containing small silver rings and a handful of Northumbrian coins, enough wealth to ensure I would not starve. Bleddyn's parting gift had been a great deal of advice.

"You are too young to travel as a monk or a trader," he had said. "So you would be best to try to stay invisible. Become a wandering beggar."

It was sound advice which I accepted gladly. Bleddyn had embraced me before he had gone north with Bridei.

"I wish I could come with you, lad," he had said. "Maybe next year when this leg has had a chance to heal properly."

I had been sad to see him go, yet at the same time I had been eager because his departure, along with that of Bridei and the warriors, had given me my few days with Derelei. When those days were over and Nechtan had pointedly reminded me that I was expected to leave, I slung my pack over my shoulder, waved farewell to Nechtan and Derelei, and set off for the south.

I was wearing old, rather grubby clothes, a pair of sturdy boots and, of course, I was on foot because wandering beggars did not ride horses.

I walked the long miles in all weathers. Autumn had turned to winter by the time I reached the Foirthe at Sruighlea. I hung around the base of the towering rock for some time, hoping to overhear some careless word from one of the Northumbrian soldiers who manned the high hillfort but I learned nothing of any note, so I moved on, aware that some of the locals had been eyeing me with suspicion. It would have been a simple end to my task if I had learned anything important at Sruighlea, but I knew that there was really only one place I could go if I wanted to have any chance of learning what Beornhaeth intended to do. That place was his home in Dun Eidyn.

I wasn't entirely sure how I would be able to get close enough to learn his plans but I knew that rumours and gossip were no strangers to the homes of great lords, and I remembered how the travelling merchants who visited Dun Eidyn had always been free and easy with their stories, so I set off towards the east, following the south bank of the ever-widening Foirthe.

Rain, sleet and buffeting winds accompanied me all the way from Sruighlea, making the journey cold, wet and miserable. I reached Beornhaeth's home with my head burning, my throat dry and painful, and my nose blocked.

Feeling dreadful, I made my unsteady way to the merchant's ramshackle quarter where one of the men who rented out beds threatened to have me beaten if I hung around his premises. I produced a couple of brass coins which softened his mood considerably. He told me that his name was Thingfrith and that the coins were sufficient to allow me to stay for a week in what he grandiosely named his inn, but which was little more than a large, rat-infested, wooden shed. Inside, half of the space was given over to what Thingfrith called his common room, where he had set out some wooden tables and benches, with the other half of the building divided into tiny cubicles, each of which was just large enough to hold a straw-filled mattress. The way I was feeling, the place seemed like a palace.

I lay in the flea-ridden bed for several days, only venturing out to barter for some of the thin gruel or even thinner broth that Thingfrith's wife produced in seemingly endless quantities, or to sit shivering by the fire that burned constantly in the common room. The rest of the time, I lay wrapped in as many blankets as I could find.

By the time I was feeling well enough to get up and about, it was almost Christmas. Preparations for a feast were under way in the fort and in the surrounding town. Best of all, Beornhaeth had returned from a tour of his kingdom to be at home during the Christmas celebrations. Now that I had recovered from my fever, all I needed to do was find a way to learn his plans.

First, I needed a reason to stay and I was worried that Thingfrith might become suspicious if I kept producing coins or silver rings, so I asked him whether I could work for my keep. The idea intrigued him.

"Do you know anything about horses?" he asked.

"Enough to get by."

"Then you can help look after the guests' horses. I've got a stable out back."

Like his description of his lopsided hut as an inn, the flimsy construction he termed a stable was everything that I had expected. It was little more than a leaking wooden roof supported by one wall of planks and a few heavy poles that had been sunk into the ground, leaving it open on three sides. Still, as Thingfrith said, it provided some shelter for the horses, and travelling merchants always prefer cheap lodgings, so none of them were likely to complain.

Even in midwinter, Thingfrith usually had a few merchants staying at the inn. I was not overworked, but I had enough to keep me occupied and staying with Thingfrith gave me plenty of opportunity to eavesdrop on the merchants' gossip.

Thingfrith, always seeking value, very quickly increased the tasks he asked me to do. I don't think he entirely trusted me at first, but I put on my vacant, simpleton's act for him so he probably thought I was harmless enough. He sometimes sent me on simple errands or had me accompany him to fetch supplies of meat and fish from the market or to carry some kegs of ale from Toki the brewer.

Christmas Day passed with little celebration in Thingfrith's home. Business was business as far as he was concerned, and holidays would mean a loss of income. This attitude was shared by the majority of his customers, so even Christmas made little difference to our daily routine. In the evening, though, Thingfrith drank rather more than he normally did and spent some time sitting with me in the common room, sharing his views on life.

"It's all very well for the lords and their warriors sitting in their fancy halls," he declared, "but they'd soon be in trouble if it wasn't for the likes of me. I sometimes wonder if they know where their clothes, their weapons and their food come from. Someone has to tend the horses, someone has to bring leather and metal and wood to keep things going. And if it wasn't for me providing beds and food for the traders, well, Beornhaeth and his like would be in a sorry state."

I nodded, letting him know that if it was not for him, the whole kingdom would probably collapse. "Have you ever met Beornhaeth?" I asked.

He peered at me, his eyes slightly glazed by the effects of the ale. "Me? No. I've seen him once or twice, though. He's a big fellow. Very fierce, so they say."

I pursed my lips. It had been a long shot. Thingfrith was hardly likely to move in the same social circles as a lord like Beornhaeth. "I'd like to see him," I ventured cautiously.

"Hah! You? You'd never get near him, lad. Even if you got hired by one of the men who supply goods to the fort, you'd still not get further than the kitchens or the stables."

"I suppose so," I said.

Thingfrith changed the subject but I was barely listening to him because he had unwittingly told me how I could get into the fort.

A few days later, I went to see Toki the brewer. He was a small, squat man, fussy and industrious but with few interests outside of brewing ale and making himself as wealthy as possible in the process. I asked him whether he would let me help with his next delivery to Beornhaeth's hall.

"There's a girl up there I'd like to see," I explained. "But she doesn't get allowed out very often."

Toki scratched his head. "I'll not pay you," he informed me once he had considered my request, "and if you get caught, I'll have nothing to do with you."

"Fine."

"And you'll help out with other deliveries too. With no wages."

"Agreed." It was no wonder Thingfrith and Toki got on so well, I thought to myself. At least Toki had asked no questions but he had got himself an extra pair of hands at no cost.

"I'll have a cart going up tomorrow. Be here by midday," he told me.

"I'll be here."

The cart was a small, two-wheeled thing, piled with half a dozen kegs and pulled by a donkey that had more intelligence than the handler, whose name was Berht. His pale, slack-jawed face was lop-sided, topped by a mop of unruly hair, and his eyes had a vacant look about them. He was Toki's son, which explained why he had the job. Even my simpleton's act was nothing compared to Berht. He did not speak to me at all during our trek up the steep slope to the fort's main gates, he simply stared ahead, tugging the donkey's halter rope.

Idiot or not, the guards obviously recognised him because we were waved through without question.

The summit of the great rock contained a large number of buildings, most of them built of wood, with thatched roofs. There was a hall, dominating the centre, surrounded by stores, a smithy, stables and, of course, homes for the many people who lived up here. It was a different world to the teeming settlement outside. The atmosphere of affluent superiority made me wonder whether Thingfrith might have a point. The people up here lived off the labours of the ordinary folk who were never allowed to pass through the gates.

We led the donkey round to one of the buildings at the back of the hall. This turned out to be the kitchens and stores. A large woman with arms that were thicker than mine, big-bosomed and with a belly to match, showed us where to put the kegs. Her appearance and her permanent expression of harassed impatience with the world told me she was probably one of the cooks.

"Hello, Aeldgyth," Berht mumbled.

"Good afternoon, Berht," she replied. "Who is this you have brought with you?"

"My name is Bili," I told her, treating her to my best smile. "I'm just helping out."

She returned my smile with a cautious one of her own. "Pleased to meet you," she said.

I took a chance. "Do you know where Triduana is?" I asked.

She frowned. "Triduana? Lord Wulfric's woman?"

"Yes."

"In her rooms, I expect."

"Do you think I could see her?"

She barked out a mocking laugh. "You?" What for?"

I slipped a silver ring from my purse and handed it to her. "It's personal. But I need to see her. Can you get a message to her?"

The cook looked from me to the shiny ring in her palm. "What message?" she asked uncertainly.

"Just ask her to come and meet me. Here, When we come back with the next delivery."

"And who should I say wants to meet her?"

"Tell her it's Bili. I'll bring you a silver penny if you can get her to meet me."

"Make it two," she said instantly.

"All right. Two." I smiled at her. "Thank you."

By this time, Berht had unloaded all the kegs and stacked the waiting pile of empty ones onto the cart. Fortunately, he was too dull-witted to wonder why I had come to help him and then left him to do all the work. If all went well, I would probably do the same when the next delivery was made.

Toki's next delivery was not to be for two days. I returned to Thingfrith's inn, went to the stable and tried to keep myself occupied. Unfortunately, grooming and feeding horses was the sort of task that allowed me to think while I worked, so I was in a state of more or less permanent agitation. Bridei had warned me to get his information before looking for my sister but I reckoned I had found a way to do both. Despite my apprehension, I was feeling particularly pleased with myself and impatient to return to the hilltop fort.

    The two days slowly dragged past until, at last, it was time to take Toki's next cartload of kegs to the fort. I helped load the ale barrels onto the cart then accompanied Berht up the long, steep climb. I struggled to remain calm as we trundled through the gates. The fat cook obviously knew that I was up to something and she could quite easily betray me. I was worried in case I arrived at the kitchens to find a horde of Beornhaeth's warriors waiting for me. I could only hope that the promise of more silver would overcome any such thoughts Aeldgyth might have.

    Berht and I reached the rear of the kitchens without incident. I gave the cook an expectant look as she came out to meet us, but she held out her hand, palm upwards. "Two pennies," she said.

    I gave her the last of my coins. "Where is she?"

    "I am here, Bili," said a voice from inside the storeroom.

    I pushed past the cook to get inside. It was her. She was taller, fuller of figure and her features had matured from those of a young girl into the face of a woman, but it was her. I had found Triduana.

I had found her but I did not know what to say to her. I stared at her for a long time, taking in the sight of her, matching her features to my memory and noticing the finely woven dress and gold rings that she wore. The Triduana I had known had been transformed into a noblewoman.

She gestured to the cook. "Give the other lad something to eat while we talk. We will not be long." She spoke like someone who was used to giving orders to her servants.

Aeldgyth closed the door, leaving us in the gloom of the storeroom. There was an awkward silence, then Triduana said, "I thought you were dead."

"No. I hid. I am sorry. I saw what they did to Giric."

"And to me?" she asked softly.

"Yes."

"It was a long time ago, Bili."

"Only four years."

"Long enough."

"What about mother?" I asked. "Is she here?"

Triduana shook her head. "She died. Not long after we were taken. A fever." She paused, then added, "Why are you here, Bili?"

Her question gave me no time to grieve for my mother. I said, "I have come to take you away. To take you home."

Her expression was one of infinite sadness. "This is my home now, Bili. I have a son. I cannot leave."

"You must! You are not one of them."

"I belong to one of them. Even if I wanted to go, Wulfric would come after me. Can you stop him?"

"We could steal horses, be away before you were missed."

"I have a son, Bili!" she said insistently. "He has a good life here, better than the one we had when we were young. I cannot take him away from that and I will not leave him." Her hand dropped to gently rub her belly. "Besides, I am pregnant again."

"Wulfric?" I asked.

She nodded. "He is not a bad man, really," she said.

153

I snorted at that. "He is a Northumbrian. You know what he did. By God, Triduana, you, better than anyone, know what he did."

"Men do evil things in war, Bili. It has always been so. Wulfric is a mighty lord and a great warrior. He takes what he wants. I am lucky. As long as I have my looks, and as long as I please him, he will want me. But if he found you here, he would kill you." She grasped my hands, folding them in hers. "You must go, Bili. There is nothing for you here."

"I must stay for a while," I told her.

"Why?"

"Bridei of Fortriu has asked me to discover what Beornhaeth intends to do."

She stared at me. In a whisper tinged with fear, she said, "You are a spy?"

"Will you help me?" I asked. "You can learn things. Things I cannot discover on my own. I can come here every few days so that we can see each other. Please, Triduana. For the sake of our mother and father. If you won't come away with me, then at least help me."

She was silent for a long time. Eventually she took a deep breath and said, "I will not do anything to harm Wulfric. He is the father of my child. I want you to promise that you will never harm him, or have someone else harm him."

"You cannot love him," I said.

She shook her head. "No, but I love my son. Wulfric can give us a good life here. I need him for that, Bili. So I want you to swear that you will never harm him. For the sake of my son and my unborn child."

I had never met Wulfric, but I hated him all the same, just as I hated his father. Still, I had no choice. Reluctantly, I said, "I swear it. I am no warrior, Triduana."

"I don't know why I am agreeing to this," she muttered.

"Because you are not a Northumbrian," I said.

She shook her head. "It is not that. Things beyond the walls of this place have little impact on my life." She gave me a gentle smile and I saw a spark of the Triduana who had faced a dozen warriors armed with only a carving knife. She said, "I think it is because the way they talk about our people makes me so angry. They think we are savages. Even Wulfric says hateful things when he thinks I cannot hear him."

"You are bored here," I guessed. I almost accused her of being content to live the life of a concubine but I needed her help, so I kept that thought to myself.

She shrugged. "I am the woman of a powerful lord. I have servants to do everything for me. I have fine clothes and plenty to eat. It is a far better life than I would have had if I had married that pig, Talorcan."

"Talorcan died trying to protect us," I said. "He died fighting alongside our father."

"That does not make him a good man," she retorted. "He was a pig. Wulfric is a far better man than Talorcan would ever have been. Do you not understand, Bili? For all that has happened, I have far more here than I could ever have hoped for at home."

I said, "I know Bridei, the king of the Pecht. You could have a good life if you came with me. Bridei would see to that."

She shook her head. "I told you, Bili. I will not leave my son. Wulfric would never let him leave here, so I must stay."

"But you will help me?"

"Only because you are my brother," she said. "I don't think I will hear much but if I learn anything, I will meet you here. I will not see you every time you come. That would arouse suspicion, but if I have anything to tell you, I will be here. Now go."

I kissed her hands, then left, dragging Berht away from the sweetmeats the cook had been feeding him. I returned to the town feeling more bewildered than happy. Triduana and I had never been very close but, even so, speaking to her had been almost like talking to a stranger. Four years as a captive, even a favoured one, had changed her more than I would have thought possible. Yet there were blood ties there, obligations that bound us together. Whatever her reasons, she had agreed to help me. I was sure that, in time, I would be able to persuade her to return north with me.

Chapter 15

Dun Eidyn became my home. I stayed there for much longer than I had intended because helping deliver Toki's ale to Beornhaeth's hall allowed me to see Triduana. I had been searching for her for so long that I simply could not leave her. Yet however often I asked, she would not change her mind about leaving, especially when her belly started to swell as the child grew within her.

Her refusals annoyed me but as for providing me with information, I could not have had a better source than if Beornhaeth himself had told me what he intended.

In truth, I could have returned to Fortriu by Easter because it was plain from what Triduana had gleaned from Wulfric that Beornhaeth was content to hold what he had. Ambitious as he was, he knew that attempting to enlarge his sub-kingdom without Ecgfrith's approval would bring the king's displeasure down on him. And Ecgfrith, it seemed, was preoccupied with Mercia and with his new, young wife. For the time being, Beornhaeth would keep the peace.

I should have hurried back to Bridei with that news but I reasoned that if Beornhaeth was not going to attack him, then there was no need to rush north. I was still intent on persuading Triduana to come with me and I knew she would have to wait until after her baby was born, so I stayed all through the summer, working for Thingfrith and for Toki and becoming just another Northumbrian.

My English was good enough now that I could easily pass for an Angle and I was forced to admit to myself that I quite enjoyed the work, however dull and mundane it might be. Sometimes I almost forgot my main reason for being there.

Triduana was very circumspect. Toki delivered ale to the fort at least twice a week but if I saw her one time out of five or six, I was lucky. On those rare occasions, Aeldgyth, the fat cook, would feed Berht while my sister and I held a hurried conversation in the storeroom. We always spoke in our native tongue, just in case anyone overheard. For safety's sake, we never lingered for long even though Triduana was sure that nobody else knew about our secret conversations.

Apart from those irregular meetings with Triduana, that summer was largely uneventful. I saw Beornhaeth once as I was walking alongside the cart on our way out. He was standing near the gate, chatting to some workmen who were repairing a section of the thick, perimeter wall. He did not even glance my way but I marked him, recognised the bushy beard and his powerful build. He must have been in his fifties, I reckoned, but he looked as fit and strong as a man half his age. Seeing him reminded me of my home and my dead family. I could not understand how Triduana could bear to be near him or his son. My skin crawled at the very sight of him.

As for Wulfric, I only saw him once and that was from a distance, which was probably just as well because I was not certain I would have been able to keep my promise to Triduana. It would have been a simple thing to walk up to him and to stick my dagger in his belly before he knew I was coming for him. I pictured the scene in my mind but I did nothing about it, consoling myself with the thought that, one day, I would get my revenge on the two of them. Beornhaeth and Wulfric had destroyed my home and my family. Whatever changes had come over Triduana, I wanted the two of them dead. An eye for an eye, the Bible said. One day.

By late summer, Triduana's time of confinement arrived. I heard from Aeldgyth that she had given birth to a daughter, a girl she called Eormenburg in honour of King Ecgfrith's new bride. I never saw the babe, just as I had never seen Triduana's son, Eowa. I think she wanted to keep them away from me. I did not even see Triduana herself for three weeks after the birth. Then, while I was unloading the ale as usual one afternoon, she came to the kitchen, all full-breasted and looking tired from lack of sleep.

I gave her a gentle hug. "How are you? And the baby?"

"I am well," she said. "Just tired. Eormenburg is sleeping. She is a good baby."

"I am very pleased for you." I hesitated. I wanted to say something about her daughter having an English name, but I held my tongue. Instead, I asked, "Do you think you will be able to travel soon?"

She seemed more sad than angry as she said, "Bili, I have told you before. I cannot leave. I will not leave." She shook her head. Wiping a small tear from her eye, she said, "I only came here to tell you that I will not be coming to see you again. I have had enough of this secrecy and spying, so I don't want you to come here any more. There is nothing here for you. You should leave. Go back home."

I did not know what to say. I had waited four years to find her, then I had managed only a dozen brief meetings with her over a period of several months. Now she was telling me to go.

I reached for her hands but she shrank back.

"Goodbye, Bili. You must go and live your own life now. Leave me to mine."

She turned and walked away, leaving me staring after her like a fool.

I said my farewells to Thingfrith and Toki. I was surprised to find that they were sorry to see me go. I think Toki was upset at losing a labourer who worked for nothing, but Thingfrith was genuinely upset and even tried to offer me a small weekly allowance if I would agree to work on.

"I must go," I said.

"Why? What's so urgent that you must go now?"

"Girl trouble," I said. "If an angry father comes looking for me, tell him I have gone south."

"So you're going north?" he asked with a knowing grin.

I nodded. "Plenty of opportunity up there," I told him. "Goodbye, Thingfrith, and thank you."

Heaving my pack over my shoulder, I turned my back on Dun Eidyn and set off for the north.

I was tempted to steal a horse but the weather was generally fine, so I walked, travelling the length of the country on my way back to Bridei. I had done all he had asked of me, even if I had taken far longer than he would have wished. I did not really care. He would get what he wanted, which was more than I could say for myself.

The problem with the endless walking was that it gave me plenty of time to think and the things that dominated my thoughts were my complex relationships with the two most important women in my life. There was Triduana, who had been stolen away more completely than I could ever have imagined. I knew she was alive, I knew she was well, but I also knew that she was more Northumbrian than Pecht now. My entire family was gone.

Bitterly, I tried to remember what Fincana the seer had told me. Had she said I would find my mother and sister? Had she prophesied that I would bring them home? Or had she merely said that I would discover where they were? I could not recall her exact words. I had certainly believed that I would find them both and return north with them.

I began to suspect that Bleddyn had been correct about the old witch. She had simply used me and told me what I had wanted to hear. In my mind's eye, I imagined confronting her about it but the picture of her confessing in terror under the force of my anger was not one I could believe. She would probably claim that she had predicted exactly what had happened, and I knew that I had no way of proving she was wrong.

Then there was Derelei. I had been away from her for so long that I was desperate to see her again. Yet when I did, what would I do? I might be able to rest at Dun Nechtan for one night on my way north, but that would be all. After that, she, too, would be lost to me. I could hardly imagine Nechtan welcoming me to stay with him on a permanent basis. Still, thoughts of being with Derelei again, even if it was for only a single night, sustained me on the long walk. I knew I would have a perfect excuse to visit her because Dun Nechtan lay on the most direct land route to Inbhir Nis and it would have been impolite not to visit such an important chieftain if I was passing his home.

 After several weeks of walking, I was footsore but smiling when I approached the familiar farmstead. One of the farmhands went to the house to announce my arrival and I was admitted to the main room where Nechtan welcomed me to his table as graciously as he could. My heart skipped a beat when I saw that Derelei was there, radiant as a moonbeam. Something about her was different but for a moment I could not place it until I recognised that she had gained a little weight around her bust and her belly. That thought vanished as she clasped my hands warmly, genuinely overjoyed to see me.

 "We thought you would have returned long before now," she said. "I was so worried about you."

 I could feel her hands trembling with emotion and saw her blink away a tear.

 "It took me longer than I had hoped," I explained weakly.

 I wanted nothing more than to take her in my arms and kiss her. I knew she felt the same but Nechtan was there, so we were compelled to restrain ourselves to mere expressions of polite happiness at seeing one another again. Even then, Nechtan seemed less than pleased at Derelei's open display of affection.

 A baby's cry came from one of the rooms at the back of the house. Derelei jumped to her feet instantly.

 "He's awake and he'll be hungry," she said. She looked at me, gazing into my eyes with an expression that was clearly intended to tell me something important. "Of course, you would not know, Bili. We have a son."

"A son?" I felt my ears burning. She had said "we". Did that mean what I thought it meant? Somehow, I managed to mumble some congratulations. The news had stunned me. She had borne a child while I was away? That explained the change in her figure, but had it really been that long since I had seen her?

Derelei said, "We have named him Bridei, in honour of my father." Then she apologised because the cries were more insistent now. She hurried away to the rear of the house.

I looked at Nechtan hoping he could not see through my confusion. "You must be very proud," I said.

"Aye, a son is always welcome," he growled. "But what of your mission? Have you learned what Beornhaeth intends? Nothing has happened so far, but the harvest is being gathered and if he is planning war, he will come soon."

"He will not come," I assured him.

"Are you certain?"

"As certain as I can be. I heard it from someone close to him."

Nechtan relaxed slightly. I had not realised just how tense he had been. He must have been genuinely concerned at the thought of the Northumbrians coming north but my news cheered him so much that he sent one of the kitchen girls to fetch a jug of whisky, the water of life, which he shared with me.

Derelei joined us later, accompanied by Sorcha who was carrying a baby wrapped in soft blankets. She cradled him in her arms while Derelei said to me, "This is our son. He is only two weeks old but I already know that he will grow up to be a fine man, just like his father." She smiled at Nechtan but her eyes held mine for just a moment longer than necessary.

I grinned stupidly. I knew what she meant but Nechtan was nodding proudly so I toasted his health, then the baby's health, and all the while I hoped that Nechtan would not see through what Derelei had said.

Derelei and I managed only a few short words in private when Nechtan staggered drunkenly outside to visit the privy. Sorcha hurriedly took little Bridei away, saying she would put him to bed.

As soon as we were alone, Derelei hurried to me. She took my hands, kissed me and said, "He is your son, Bili. He is our son."

I put my arms around her, holding her. "But I cannot tell anyone."

"No. Sorcha knows, of course, but nobody else can ever know. Not ever. Not even little Bridei."

"That is a terrible secret for us to keep."

"But you must keep it, Bili. Promise me. Nobody must ever know." She kissed me again. "Promise?"

"Promise."

Nechtan's heavy footsteps sounded from outside the door. By the time he came in, Derelei was sitting across the table from me. I poured myself another small measure of the whisky and drained it in one throat-burning gulp.

I only stayed one night at Dun Nechtan. This time I was given a room in the main house but Derelei did not come to me. I heard little Bridei crying during the night so I supposed that she was too busy with him and that Nechtan must have been kept awake too. My own sleep was troubled enough by the conflicting emotions of my desire for Derelei and the need to keep the secret of young Bridei's birth. My troubles over Triduana's refusal to leave her home among the Angles suddenly seemed trivial.

In the morning, my head thumping from the effects of too much whisky, I waved them farewell and continued on my way. Nechtan generously provided me with a horse, although he asked that I return it the next time I saw him.

I reached Inbhir Nis that same evening. Bridei did not greet me in the great hall where there were too many ears to overhear us. Instead, I was fed and allowed to wash in warm water before being taken to his private chamber at the rear of the hall.

Bleddyn was there. He grabbed me in a bear hug of an embrace, lifting my feet from the floor and squeezing the breath from my body.

"Put me down!" I gasped.

He lowered me and released his crushing hold but then proceeded to slap me on the back so hard that I almost stumbled.

Bridei laughed. "Leave the lad alone, Bleddyn. He has a story to tell us, I think."

So I told them what I had heard in Dun Eidyn, adding that the information had come from Triduana and could therefore be trusted.

Bleddyn said to Bridei, "I told you he was smart."

Bridei nodded. "Aye, you've done well, lad. Very well. In a bad year, it's almost the best news I've heard."

"A bad year?" I asked.

Bridei explained, "Raiders from the Orcades plundered several of our villages. I sent my new ships to carry out reprisals. They burned a few settlements and took some slaves but they were caught by a storm on their way back. The survivors say it blew up out of nowhere. We lost five ships. A lot of good men went down with them, too. Now I am going to have to build some more and find men to crew them. A bad business. Still, at least we have time now, if Beornhaeth is going to rest where he is." He looked at me keenly. "Did you stop at Dun Nechtan on your way here?"

"Yes. I thought I should tell Nechtan the news. He seemed relieved."

"Aye, he would be. He'll be among the first to know if the Angles come north." He sucked in his cheeks, thinking, then he asked, "So you saw Derelei?"

"Yes."

His blue eyes held mine. "And the babe?"

"Yes."

It was a while before he released me from his stare. He knew. I was certain of it, although I also knew that he would never acknowledge it aloud.

He said, "I've not seen him myself, yet. I will travel down there soon. Is she happy?"

"Yes, she was happy when I saw her."

Bridei understood what I was telling him. He sat back, raising his eyes to gaze up at the roof timbers. When he looked back at me, he said, "So you found your sister?"

I nodded glumly. "Yes, but she is not my sister any longer. I will not see her again, nor will I speak of her."

Bridei said, "Aye, losing someone close to you can be hard."

We exchanged a look of mutual sympathy. Then Bridei shook off his gloom. Brightly, he said, "Well, lad you've been wandering the lands for five years now. Perhaps it is time we gave you a rest."

"I don't need a rest," I declared.

"You'll have one anyway. I'll not have it said that men who do me a service are not rewarded."

"I want no reward," I told him.

"You'll have one anyway," he repeated with a hint of a grin. "Bleddyn will show you in the morning."

I looked at Bleddyn but he just said, "Wait and see."

Chapter 16

My reward lay some miles to the east of Inbhir Nis, out along the coast. It was a farmstead, complete with a house, newly built of stone, with a turfed roof and two spacious rooms. Behind it stood a small, wooden barn and to one side was a storehouse and a granary.

There were pens containing some sheep and goats, and chickens wandered the yard. In a wide field bordered by dry-stone walls were four cows. A river, deep and fast-flowing, ran past the rear of the barn. All around were other fields, ripe for ploughing.

Bleddyn grinned. "What do you think?"

"This is all mine?"

"All of it."

"I'll never manage this on my own."

"You won't have to." He gestured to a stand of trees that lay some two hundred paces to my right. For the first time, I noticed a group of three roundhouses.

"You've got people to do the work for you," Bleddyn grinned.

"Slaves?"

"No. It's some people who were forced off their land by the Northumbrians. They came to Bridei, seeking help, so he sent them here."

"I cannot believe this!"

Bleddyn laughed. "Come on, have a look at the house. I'll show you the rest of the place tomorrow."

"You've been here before?"

"Who do you think has been looking after it for you?" he asked. "Mind you, there is still a lot of work to be done. I thought we should build a church, just beyond the woods there."

"You want to settle down, Bleddyn?"

He tapped his leg. It still gave him pain and made him walk with a pronounced limp.

"I don't think I have much choice, lad. Riding's not too bad but walking is difficult. Anyway, I am getting on in years and perhaps it is time for me to stay in one place for a change." He pointed across the fields to a low hill. "Maybe over there would be better. What do you think?"

"Better for what?"

"For my church, idiot."

I laughed. "Build it where you like, Bleddyn. This is as much your home as mine."

That, at least, was more or less true. Bleddyn and I shared the house although he insisted on sleeping in a low cot in the main room while I had a room all to myself. I had expected to find two beds but instead there was a large wooden bedframe complete with a wide mattress stuffed with fresh straw. It did not take long before I realised what was behind this arrangement.

Over breakfast the next morning, Bleddyn said, "You need a woman."

"No I don't."

He wagged a piece of toasted bread at me. "Yes you do. And soon."

"I don't know any women," I said. "I can't imagine that any of the chieftains will be lining up their daughters for me."

"You don't need to aim so high," said Bleddyn. "The important thing is that you get a woman of your own. The sooner the better."

"What's the rush?" I asked.

He gave me his serious look. I hadn't seen it for many months but I recognised it instantly. He leaned his elbows on the table, still holding his bread.

He said, "Look. Bili. Some secrets can be kept and some can't. You must have a woman here to keep your mind from . . . from other men's wives. Before any stories start to reach ears they shouldn't."

I stared at him. "This is part of the price for my new home?" I asked.

He nodded, obviously pleased that I had grasped the situation quickly. "That's right," he agreed. "What's done is done but it can't continue. You know that."

With a sigh, I sat back on my chair. As usual, he was right. I did know it. I hated it, but I could not deny it.

"So where do you suggest I find myself a wife?" I asked him.

He popped the last piece of toasted bread into his mouth. "It's all taken care of," he said between chewing. "Bridei's men brought a few slaves back from the Orcades. I brought three of them out here. All you have to do is choose which one you want. The other two will be sent back to Inbhir Nis."

The air was still and bitingly cold. An early frost had covered the ground although the sun was slowly melting it away by the time we went outside. Still, it was a reminder that winter was not far off. Wrapped in a new cloak, I accompanied Bleddyn as he took me round the farm.

My tenants were a middle-aged man called Entifidich and his family. As Bleddyn had said, they had come north after some Northumbrians had evicted them from their own farm in Circinn. There were seven of them; Entifidich himself, stocky and strong but with tanned skin and calloused hands from a lifetime working the fields, along with his wife, two teenage sons, two younger girls and a little boy of around three or four.

I was uncertain about their status. Entifidich was old enough to be my father, yet he clearly regarded me as his chieftain.

Bleddyn said, "That's more or less it, Bili. These are your people. They will work the land and you must look after them."

Entifidich and his family seemed to accept the situation happily enough but I felt bewildered and out of my depth. I struggled to grasp the concept that I was a chieftain. Even if my new family was only seven strong, it was still an unexpected responsibility.

Then we came to the slaves.

There were three of them, young women who had been taken from their island homes in the reprisal raid that Bridei had sent across the northern sea. Bleddyn presented them to me as trophies, telling me I should choose one of them.

I looked at them, all shivering in the chill morning air. They each had their hair combed and brushed, and their skin looked freshly washed. I was sure they were all pretty, but all I could think of was Triduana, who had been stolen away by Wulfric. I wondered whether these girls had been raped before being hauled, screaming and struggling, onto the long warships. I suspected they probably had.

Triduana had said that men do evil things in war and I realised at that moment that she was right. Did this mean that we were no different from the Northumbrians? I felt almost physically sick at that thought.

Among the people of the north, raiding their neighbours is a way of life, of course. The Pecht pride themselves on it, as do the Scots of Dal Riata. The rewards for successful raiders are excitement, honour, booty, cattle and women. It has been going on for generations and I expect it will go on forever. Yet for me, the memory of what I had lost to raiders still hurt.

Bleddyn nudged my elbow, prompting me to make a decision. I scowled at him. I had seen him walk past wounded men who were calling out for help, I had seen him kill men who were already wounded, but I never thought he deserved the name of Grim-Hand more than on that morning. I still loved and respected him but I understood then why others hated him. He would do what had to be done, regardless of the cost.

"You must choose," he told me. "Speak to them if you wish. Strip them naked and inspect them if you must, but make a decision."

I did not talk to any of them, nor did I order them to strip. I made my choice quickly, selecting the one who looked least like Derelei. That was my only consideration, the sole basis for the decision.

I pointed at a short, fair-haired girl and said, "That one." Then I walked back to the house, feeling utterly disgusted with myself.

Her name was Mayota. She had strong, well-shaped legs, broad hips and a more than ample bust. Her blonde, shoulder-length hair was naturally wavy, and her eyes were a green-brown colour that I had rarely seen before. She was very pretty, beautiful even, but she was not Derelei.

I quickly learned that she was also strong-willed. This came as something of a shock but I decided that it would not make much difference to me. I had been forced into taking a wife and even though we would be living in the same house and sharing a bed, it did not mean that we had to be close to one another.

She came into the house, stood facing me and asked, "Am I still a slave?"

I glanced at Bleddyn, who said, "You were a captive, not a slave. Now you will be married to Bili."

"Do I have a choice?" she asked, not masking her defiance or her contempt for me.

"Yes," said Bleddyn. "You can let one of the other girls become Bili's wife and you can return to Inbhir Nis. I am sure the king has need of house slaves to do the drudgery."

Mayota looked at him coldly, glanced at me, then said to Bleddyn. "I'll stay."

Bleddyn performed the marriage ceremony right there in the house, calling Entifidich and his wife, Niamh, as witnesses. Before the sun had reached halfway to its zenith, I was married with God's blessing and, I reflected bitterly, at Bridei's insistence.

There was no feast, no special celebration. Entifidich and his wife went off to resume their work, no doubt discussing the strange event they had been called upon to witness, while Bleddyn took the other girls away, driving a four-wheeled wagon which apparently belonged to me, with the two girls sitting miserably behind him. I was left alone with Mayota.

She gave me a defiant look, placing her hands on her well-rounded hips.

"Well?" she asked. "Are you going to bed me now or wait until later?"

Even a year before, I would have blushed at a direct comment like that, but I knew what she was doing. This was a test, to see who would be in charge of our relationship. I may have just turned nineteen years old and perhaps I did not have to shave more than once or twice a week, but I was a chieftain and until that morning she had been a captive slave. I stared back at her.

"Now," I said, in as gruff a voice as I could manage.

She pursed her lips as she thought about her next move. Then she made for the bedroom door, saying, "Come on then. Let's see what you are made of."

I felt a momentary panic, realising that I was about to undergo another test, one that, if I failed, would no doubt result in her proclaiming my inadequacy to the world. But I could not back down now, so I followed her through the door.

She untied the fastening of her dress, letting it fall to the floor, then quickly removed her undergarments. She was on the bed before I had time to pull my shirt over my head. She lay there, watching me, trying to intimidate me, but I took one look at the glorious curves of her naked body and desire took over. There was no denying her beauty.

I was stripped and lying beside her in moments. "Let's see what you are made of," I said in an attempt to show her that I was the one in charge.

It turned out that neither of us was entirely in charge but, equally, neither of us could complain, for we spent the afternoon satisfying one another. Our couplings were energetic and certainly passionate but there was no love or tenderness between us. When we were utterly spent and I lay on my back, exhausted, with Mayota cuddling into me, half-asleep, her arm across my chest, I stared up at the ceiling, thinking of Derelei and how we had both paid the price Bridei had asked of us.

I wondered how I would react if Mayota had a child. If it was a boy, would I feel like a father? I already had a son, a son I could never acknowledge and who would grow up never knowing me. How would I treat another son? I did not know. It would be better if she had a daughter, I decided. Mayota, though had no intentions of falling pregnant if it could be avoided, as I learned when we travelled to Inbhir Nis for Christmas.

I had been reluctant to go, but a king's invitation is not refused lightly, so Mayota, Bleddyn and I joined the king, along with dozens of other guests. Medraut was there, naturally, together with the other members of his gang. I paid no attention to them, although I saw Guret looking enviously at Mayota. She certainly knew how to display her charms and I admit that, despite our strained relationship, I was pleased to have her at my side that Christmas, although that may have been because Derelei was not there. She and Nechtan had not come to Inbhir Nis that year.

As always, Bridei was a generous host. Nobody could complain that there was any lack of food or drink. Of course, Abbot Ronan ensured that prayers and singing of psalms were equally prominent although I knew that many people still preferred the wilder festivities of the old mid-winter feasts. Bridei knew that too, so he had arranged for musicians to cater for the dancing, which ensured that everyone was satisfied.

We had been at Inbhir Nis for only two days when Mayota said to me, "I need to go into the town this morning."

"I'll come with you," I said. I did not really want to, but I had seen the way Guret had been looking at her and I thought it would be best if she did not go alone. Not that I felt particularly confident of my ability to fight off Guret, but he knew that I was under Bridei's protection so I reckoned he would not try anything.

I asked her, "What is it you want down there?"

She replied, "I need to find a woman named Fincana."

I sat up straight. "Fincana? She's a witch. You should not go near her."

She looked at me, quite calm and unperturbed by my sudden outburst. "The other women say she has things that I need."

"What sort of things?"

She gave me a half-smile, "Things that will prevent me falling pregnant," she said. "You don't want a child, do you?"

"I hadn't thought about it," I lied.

"Really?" Her eyebrows arched and she looked at me as if I was some sort of idiot. Then she asked, "Who is Derelei?"

The change of subject caught me off guard but there was no secret about who Derelei was, so I said, "She's Bridei's daughter. She's married to Nechtan, one of his chieftains."

I thought I had said it quite coolly, betraying nothing, but Mayota immediately shot another question at me.

"So why do you mention her name in your sleep?" she asked, her eyes studying my face to see my reaction.

"I don't!" I protested.

"Yes, you do. Why?"

I replied with the first answer I could think of. "Well, if I do, it's probably when I'm having nightmares. I used to know her when she was a girl. She was always tormenting me."

"She still is, I think," Mayota observed drily.

"Only in my dreams," I said. Which was true enough. "Forget her. I try to." Which was also true.

So we headed down to the town, arm in arm as befitted man and wife. It was a fine day, bright and sunny, much milder than usual for December, so we were able to walk without the need to wrap ourselves in heavy cloaks. Mayota was pleased about that because she was able to show off a new dress she had made.

I was worried that we would meet Medraut or Guret but there was no sign of either of them. Instead, we saw Donnell and Uerb.

There was no way to avoid them because they were coming back up the path from the town, heading towards the king's hall. I was going to pass them with nothing more than a curt nod of acknowledgement, but Donnell stopped us.

Smiling, he said, "Good to see you again, Bili. I hear you are doing well."

"Well enough," I agreed, trying to sound non-committal.

"And this must be your wife? We heard you were married." He was smiling pleasantly, looking Mayota in the face, although I noticed that fat Uerb's eyes were firmly fixed on her breasts. She must have noticed, too, because she deliberately thrust them out slightly. Uerb gulped.

I said, "This is Mayota."

Mayota said hello and Donnell, turning on his charm, complimented her on her dress, something I had only done when she had asked me what I thought of it. She smiled, thanking him for noticing. Showing off, she smoothed the dress down so that Uerb's eyes almost popped out of his head.

Donnell pretended not to notice. Turning to me, he said, "Medraut and Guret went out hunting with Bridei and some of the others."

"You mean I am safe for a while?" I asked. I wasn't entirely sure about Donnell but he was obviously making an effort to be friendly and the truth was that the more I met him, the more I liked him. His biggest fault was being in thrall to Medraut.

He laughed, "Oh, you are safe enough, Bili. After that last little bout you had with Medraut, the king made it perfectly clear that he was to leave you alone."

"I know, but I'm not sure I can trust Medraut to remember. Or Guret either, for that matter."

"Don't worry," Donnell said reassuringly. "As long as you do your best to keep out of their way, they'll do the same to you. After all, we are grown men now, not boys."

I said, "Well, when you see them, tell them that, as far as I am concerned, matters are settled between us."

"I'll do that," he promised. "As far as I am concerned, it is good to see you back. You were away for a long time."

"Yes."

He grinned when he heard my surly response. "I see you still don't trust me."

"Should I?"

"Of course you should. Everyone else does. Isn't that right, Uerb?"

Uerb reluctantly tore his eyes away from Mayota's bosom. "What? Oh, yes. Donnell is everyone's friend."

"You see?" Donnell smiled. "So where have you been for the past year?"

It was none of his business but he was being friendly, so I said, "I was looking for my sister."

"Ah, the one who was taken by the Northumbrians."

"Yes." I wondered how he knew that. I had not kept it a secret, but I had not told many people either.

"Did you find her?"

I shook my head. "No." I had decided that it would be better for everyone if I kept quiet about Triduana. Despite the way we had parted, I did not know whether I would ever need to secretly visit her again. The fewer people who knew of our relationship, the better."

"I am sorry to hear that," he said. He looked genuinely sympathetic. "Well, we will not detain you any longer," he said. He turned to his chubby companion. "Come on, Uerb. There are a couple of pretty girls up at the hall who might be willing to spend some time with us. I'm sure Bili and Mayota have things to do."

Uerb nodded weakly. The fat fool's eyes were still studying Mayota's ample curves. He managed to say farewell before Donnell, giving me an apologetic shrug, dragged him away.

When they were gone, Mayota crinkled her nose in disgust. "The fat one is a pig," she said.

"You shouldn't have teased him like that," I told her. "He has a nasty streak in him."

"Men like that are such fools," she commented. Somehow she made it sound as if she considered me to fall into the same category as Uerb.

Fool or not, at least I knew we could spend some time without worrying about bumping into Medraut or Guret. Feeling more relaxed than I had done earlier, I took Mayota towards Fincana's roundhouse.

We passed the open ground which was being used by a gang of young boys who were kicking a heavy, rag-filled leather ball around, chasing one another energetically in their attempts to gain possession of it. It was an old game, although the Church had spoiled it for some people by insisting that the heads of defeated enemies should not be used as a ball. Most people observed that rule but the game continued none the less. The main object was to kick the ball so that it reached the opposing team's designated home base, but the game also provided an opportunity to punch, kick or gouge your rivals. Judging by the way these boys were yelling and flailing around, a few scores were being settled. There was a fair amount of blood in evidence and one lad had dropped out to nurse his twisted arm.

Skirting round the edges of the near-riot, we managed to avoid being caught up in the rough and tumble. Once we had passed the open ground, I led Mayota through the houses to Fincana's home.

The old witch was sitting just inside the door where she could get the benefit of the daylight while still gaining some shelter. She had a small, wooden tray on her lap and was chopping some herbs into fine strands. She lifted her sharp knife in salute when she saw me.

"Lord Bili! All grown up now, and quite a hero, I hear." Her eyes took in Mayota. "And this rare beauty you have brought to see me must be Mayota."

I could sense Mayota stiffening slightly when she heard that, but I said, "That would not be hard for you to guess, Fincana. Mayota is my wife."

"Is she indeed? Well, if you say so, I am sure that must be correct. As for me, I never guess. I know."

She gave us a wide grin. I thought she must have lost a couple more teeth since I had seen her last. Putting aside her tray of herbs, she said, "Well, come in and tell Fincana what it is you want."

Mayota had suddenly lost her brash self-confidence and was as nervous as I had ever seen her. She looked genuinely frightened but I took her elbow, ushering her inside.

I said, "Don't listen to what Fincana says. She claims that she knows the future but she doesn't."

That earned me a dark look from the old seer. "Who says I don't?" she snapped. "I am never wrong."

"You were wrong when you said I would find my mother and sister. My mother is dead."

Fincana wagged a bony finger at me. "Foolish boy! I never said they would be alive when you found them." She gave me a hard stare. "I told you, I am never wrong." Then she relaxed, "But enough of this. Is that why you came to see me, bringing your lovely . . wife? To bandy words about the past?"

I gave up. I had known I would not be able to best her in an argument. I said, "Mayota wants some things from you."

Fincana's eyes fixed on Mayota. "Does she indeed? What sort of things, my dear? A love spell or potion perhaps? I would have thought that you have more than enough charms of your own not to need that. But perhaps your husband does not fully appreciate what you can offer him?"

Brusquely, I said, "Enough of that, Fincana!"

Fincana cackled at me. "Well, do you need something to help with morning sickness?" she asked. Then, fixing her eyes on Mayota, she added, "Or something to prevent it?"

I had the feeling that there had been some unspoken communication between the two women, as if they had somehow recognised each other, or as if a challenge had been made. It was a strange sensation, but I had never done anything like this before, so I thought that perhaps Fincana was like that with every woman who went to her.

Whatever had silently passed between them, Mayota had recovered her poise enough to say, "To prevent it."

Fincana paused, looking at us with a calculating stare, then she scurried to her dresser, gathering up a small clay jar that was sealed by a piece of cloth tied round the top of the jar.

Passing it to Mayota, Fincana said, "Take one pinch after each time he lies with you. You can put it in a drink of water. It is not infallible, mind, but it works quite well."

Mayota said nothing. I asked, "What do we owe you?"

"Perhaps you could give me some information," Fincana leered.

I shook my head. "No. Not this time."

"No? Then a pretty brooch, or a silver ring. What can you offer?"

I gave her some twisted strands of silver from an old brooch I had cut up. Then I took Mayota's arm and turned for the door.

Fincana called, "Wait! Do you not wish to hear your future?"

"No," I said emphatically. "I do not."

"You should listen, Bili. What I have to tell you is important."

I should have gone outside. I should not have stopped. But I did.

"I have nothing to offer in exchange," I said, hoping that would keep her quiet.

"Consider this a favour," she said. "You should beware, Bili. There are dark forces moving against you. Plots and treachery will dog your footsteps."

I shook my head. "In my experience, life is full of plots and treachery," I said. "That is nothing new."

"Well, you are a man of great experience, of course," she said mockingly. "Just remember, I am never wrong."

I felt a shiver of fear run down my spine. Grabbing Mayota, I hurried from the house as quickly as I could.

Chapter 17

As I'd expected, Fincana's dire prophecy came to nothing and, once we returned home, Mayota and I soon settled into a routine of sorts. There was never any love between us, although there was a physical attraction; or at least there was as far as I was concerned. But outside the bedroom we tended to have as little to do with one another as we could.

It was not easy in the winter months, of course, when the long nights meant that we were in the house together for much of the time, but Bleddyn often spent the evenings with us, re-living stories of our adventures and telling Mayota how proud he was of what I had achieved for Bridei.

"Walked right in to Beornhaeth's hall," he told her.

"You're exaggerating," I scolded. "I only ever got as far as the kitchens."

"That's further than anyone else could have got," Bleddyn replied.

I protested as modestly as I could, but I was secretly pleased that Mayota learned something of my past. I thought it might make her respect me a little more. Perhaps it did, although it was difficult to tell with Mayota. Most of the time, she tended to regard me with an expression of scorn or mild disappointment. Except when she was arguing with me, which she did on a fairly regular basis.

If Bleddyn was not around, Mayota and I tended to go to bed early because, apart from sitting right beside the fire, it was the warmest place in the house, and also because we did not need to say much to one another once we were under the blankets. It was the one place she did not mock me.

When the weather was fine, I helped Bleddyn with his church. We had built a small roundhouse for him, beyond the woods on a patch of level ground near the river. He was delighted with it.

"I can become a hermit here," he joked, "and still be close enough to visit friends when I want company."

He called us "friends," but I know he was not overly fond of Mayota, even though he enjoyed her cooking. Still, Bleddyn was well practised at getting on with people he did not particularly like, so there was never any real tension between them. In any event, Bleddyn was too wrapped up in his plans for his new church to worry overmuch about Mayota's fiery temper.

He had decided to build the church next to his home, near the river, choosing a spot a little way up a gentle grassy slope so that it would not be flooded if the river ever burst its banks as it sometimes did after heavy rain or when the snow-melt from the mountains swelled its water. Once he had selected the site, we marked out the area with wooden pegs and ropes of twisted sinew. Then we began digging the foundation trenches and levelling the land. This was hard, back-breaking work but Bleddyn was determined to build the church in stone, despite my objections.

"It will take years," I said.

"What else do we have to do?" he asked with an irritating cheerfulness.

So we dug, sometimes joined by Gartnait, Entifidich's oldest son, but more often just the two of us. It was slow, laborious work, but it kept me out of the house and meant that I did not need to speak to Mayota too often.

I had no idea how to build anything out of stone but Bleddyn, as usual, had a solution. He had spoken to Abbot Ronan during the Christmas feast, outlining his plans for a new church. The abbot had been so pleased that he had arranged for a dozen men to travel out from Inbhir Nis to help us. As well as doing the heavy work, some of them were carpenters while others were skilled stonemasons. The master mason, a middle-aged man named Cinead, claimed that he had once helped build a Northumbrian monastery, so he was familiar with the techniques required for building a stone church.

"Got to get the foundations right," he told us. "And use good quality stone."

The stone was quarried from a nearby hillside. Under Cinead's supervision, the masons hammered and chiselled, turning rough lumps of rock into more regular blocks which were heaved onto our cart and hauled to the riverside site. It remained slow work, even with a dozen men to help, but Bleddyn was happy and the foundations were soon laid. As the year advanced, the walls gradually began to rise.

I frequently felt useless among such skilled artisans. I was acutely aware that I did not have the muscles that they all seemed to possess, a fact which meant I was often relegated to driving the cart, transporting blocks of stone from the quarry. When I did try to help out at the quarry, I was usually allocated the most menial tasks.

Still, it was a pleasure to watch craftsmen at work. One thing that particularly intrigued me was a carving that Cinead had undertaken. He had found a large stone, cut thinner and longer than the normal building blocks, which he had laid out on a raised, wooden platform. He had sketched some designs on one side and spent hours each day chipping away with a mallet and chisel.

"What is that you are doing?" I asked him one day.

"We need a stone beside the river," he replied.

"We do?"

He nodded, still concentrating on his work. "The monk says he wants Moses and the Ten Commandments," he said as he tapped another small sliver of stone from the block.

"How long will that take?" I asked.

He shrugged. "It will take as long as it takes. You can't rush these things. One mistake and it is ruined."

Each day, I saw him working away at the carving but he was jealous of the design, refusing to let anyone see it. He would cover the block with animal hides whenever he left it or if someone else came too close.

As the months passed, Bleddyn's church slowly took shape, the walls rising ever higher, while Cinead's carving continued. Eventually, he declared that it was ready, so he had the men lift his block onto the wagon, still wrapped in its protective covers. He sat in the back of the cart, like a broody mother hen while I drove slowly down to the church.

We dug a hole near the river bank so that the carved stone could be set upright in the earth. I wasn't sure why we needed to do this, but Cinead was most particular about the precise spot where the stone was to be erected. Once he was satisfied that the hole was deep enough, several workers hauled the stone using ropes and levers, dropping one end into the hole. The earth was then packed tightly around it, planting it upright like a stone sapling.

With a flourish, Cinead removed the furs that he had tied around the block, revealing his carvings.

Bleddyn nodded approvingly. "Excellent work," he told Cinead. "Truly excellent."

I studied the carvings that Cinead had laboured over for so long. On the side that faced the church he had made a wondrous representation of Moses holding two tablets, presenting them to a multitude of tiny, stone people who clustered at the foot of the stone. I was amazed at the detail he had managed to carve, shaping the solid rock as if it had been soft clay.

"It is very good," I said.

I walked round to the other side, nearest the river. Here, the designs he had carved were entirely different. At the top were abstract symbols, then a man on horseback, spear in hand. Below the rider were hunting dogs pursuing a stag. Again, the detail was incredible. I looked at the carvings with undisguised admiration. As I gazed up and down, a peculiar design at the foot of the stone caught my eye. It looked like some strange beast, although I could not make out what it was. I pointed to it.

"What is that?"

Cinead frowned, giving me a look of disbelief. "It's a kelpie," he said. "Got to have a kelpie when there's a river nearby."

Now it was my turn to frown. I knew that kelpies, or water-horses, lived in many rivers. They were secretive, dangerous beasts, often snatching away unsuspecting travellers who tried to cross their rivers. Very few people ever claimed to have seen one because, as a rule, if you saw a kelpie, you would soon become its victim. I knew the tales but I did not know why Cinead had carved one on the stone. It was as far from a Christian symbol as I could imagine.

I glanced at Bleddyn but he merely shrugged. He turned away, heading towards the church as if to say that he did not approve of the pagan symbols on the reverse of the stone, although he was clearly prepared to accept that they were, in some mysterious way, necessary.

I looked at Cinead. "Why do we need a kelpie?" I asked him.

He shook his head, as if disappointed at my ignorance. "They are solitary beasts and they each have their own stretch of water. If we make one here, then it will keep the river clear because no other kelpie will move into his territory. That way, it will be safe to cross the river."

I glanced over to where Bleddyn was busy chatting to some of the other workers. "Did you tell Bleddyn you were going to carve this?" I asked Cinead.

"The monk?" He shrugged. "Got to have a kelpie, whatever he says. He knows that. Everyone knows that."

Everyone except me, it seemed. Once again, I had been shown the extent of my ignorance. I was a chieftain but I still felt like a small boy around these men.

I could not spend all of my time helping build the church. I was the chieftain, the head of my small community, so I knew I had to take an interest in what my people were doing, not least because my own livelihood depended on it. Not that they needed any help from me because Entifidich knew everything necessary to manage the farm.

Sometimes, though, I accompanied him to the market in Inbhir Nis. It was a long trek even on the cart, taking all day to get there and back, but we were able to barter our surplus eggs, milk and wool for other goods like pots and pans, leather hides or metal tools. Entifidich, dour though he was, was good at haggling, so I usually left him to it.

Several times, Mayota accompanied us on those trips. She enjoyed wandering round the market in Inbhir Nis and often disappeared for hours at a time, returning with an armful of goods so late in the day that it was dark by the time we reached home. Entifidich never complained when she did that, but I think he was pleased whenever she decided to stay at home on market days.

Back on the farm, we were usually up at cock-crow. We ploughed the fields, sowed the corn, milked the cows and sheared the sheep. We chopped wood for fuel and for making tools or repairing the houses, and we cut and stacked peat for the fires.

Lambs were born, the weakest of them providing fresh meat for the table. Some were sent to Bridei as part of the taxes we owed him, but the rest were nurtured so that they could provide more wool and yet more healthy lambs in future years. Entifidich also arranged for a neighbouring farmer to have his bull service our cows so that our tiny herd would increase.

Watching Entifidich work reminded me of my father who had tried to scrape a living on a farm much smaller than the one I now owned. I think he would have been proud of what I had achieved. I also recalled old Thingfrith, who had claimed that it was the ordinary people who made the world go around. Having experienced life among kings and life with ordinary folk, I began to think he had been right. Across the whole of Fortriu, people were working, like us, to provide the food or raw materials while others, like the stonemasons or the smiths in Inbhir Nis, made carvings, jewellery, weapons and tools. In the eyes of a man like Thingfrith, chieftains like me or kings like Bridei lived on the benefits produced by other people's hard work. That year, I came to appreciate Thingfrith's point of view, and yet I also knew that when it came to keeping the land safe, the ordinary folk would always look to someone like Bridei for protection.

Fortunately, we were left in peace to get on with our lives. That year leading up to my twentieth birthday was one of hard work and great reward. I still thought of Derelei from time to time, but she was far away and she had her own life to live. We had both paid the price that Bridei had asked of us. Far to the south, Triduana had her own life too, and had told me to live mine. That was hard, because there was an emptiness inside me that I knew Mayota would never fill, but during that year I felt that, at last, I was making something of myself. The dark road that Bridei had warned me about had not been so dangerous after all.

Only one thing happened to disturb my contentment. It was when I returned to the house on a fine, late summer's evening. I was hot and sweating from the effort of lifting heavy blocks of stone to build Bleddyn's church walls ever higher. The sun was sinking over the western horizon, the heat of the day fading as dusk gathered and insects buzzed around my head. I was hungry after the day's strenuous work and looking forward to filling my belly with some hot food.

I opened the door to find Mayota stirring a pot of lamb stew. She looked over her shoulder as I came in, her expression more of a smirk than a smile.

"You had a visitor today," she informed me.

"Who?"

"That man called Guret. He said he was passing and thought he'd come to see you."

I froze. "Guret? Where is he?"

She continued stirring the pot, not looking at me. Casually, she said, "He went away when he heard you were working. Said he didn't want to disturb you."

"What in Hell's name did he come here for?" I wondered aloud.

Mayota said, "He wanted to apologise to you. He said there had been misunderstandings between you." She shrugged. "He seemed very nice."

"Guret said that?" I could not believe it. I said, "Trust me, he is far from nice."

"You can say that without even speaking to him?" Mayota challenged.

"You don't know him," I said.

The smirk briefly crossed her face again. "You didn't even speak to him," she said. "I asked him to wait but he said he had to get back to Inbhir Nis."

"I don't trust him. Tell me everything that happened."

She dished up a plate of steaming stew, putting it down on the table with a thump that told me she was growing angry with my suspicion.

"Sit down and eat your supper," she ordered.

I knew it did not take much for me to make Mayota angry. She was already simmering more than the pot of stew, but I persisted.

"I want to know what he was up to."

She turned to face me across the table, hands on hips the way she always did when she was going to argue or provoke me. Her green eyes were shining angrily.

"What do you think happened, Bili? He came to the door and asked for you. I let him in, I gave him some food and drink, then I took him to bed and spread my legs for him."

"What?"

She threw up her hands in exasperation. "By all the gods, you are such an idiot! I told you what happened. He wanted to speak to you but you weren't here, so he went away. There is nothing else to tell."

She served up her own meal, then sat down, grabbing at her spoon and starting on her supper. After a few moments, I sat on the chair opposite. The stew was good but we both ate in an angry silence that was almost tangible. When Mayota had cleaned away the plates, banging and clattering so much it was a wonder she did not break them, we retired to the bedroom.

    We both knew what would happen because we always made love after an argument. With Mayota, anger was an emotion that quickly aroused other passions in her, but that night she was even more energetic and demanding than usual. It made me wonder just what Guret had said to her.

At harvest time, when I was spending most days in the fields helping Entifidich and his family gather in the crops, a worrying omen brought Fincana's prediction back to haunt me.

    A new star appeared in the sky, shining more brightly than any other, and seemingly bearing a fiery tail. Nobody knew how, or precisely when, it had first appeared; it was just there when we looked up to the heavens one night. It stayed there, night after night, dominating the sky and slowly, almost imperceptibly, seeming to have grown slightly larger each time it appeared. Each morning, people hoped that it would have gone, but when the sun set, it was still there, sparkling more brilliantly than ever.

    Many people were terrified, fearing that it heralded some calamity. Bleddyn insisted that it was probably a sign of some miracle.

    "Did the Lord not set a bright star in the sky to show the Magi where to find the newborn Christ?" he said. "Something great and wonderful will happen soon."

    I hoped that he was right.

    After two weeks, the star began to fade and soon it had vanished altogether. No calamity struck us, except a storm damaging the roof of one of the storehouses. We heard no news of other disasters that were out of the ordinary, nor was there any sign of Bleddyn's predicted miracle, so people went back to living their lives and ensuring that supplies of food and animal fodder were stored away for the winter months.

Entifidich, though, took some extra precautions. We stored most of our cereal crop in the small granary but he also dug some pits, into which he placed some large. clay jars that he filled with grain. Then he re-filled the holes, covering the pots.

"The grain will go rotten," I said when I discovered what he was doing.

"Only the stuff at the top," he replied. "The rest will stay fresh for months."

"Are you sure?"

He gave me a look that once again told me I was ignorant.

"It's an old custom," he said. "It will keep a safe reserve for us."

"Let's hope we don't need to rely on it," I said.

No great disasters befell us and things soon returned to normal. Four weeks later, my birthday came and went, its passing marking the arrival of winter. Two months after that, we were again invited to Inbhir Nis to celebrate Christmas with Bridei.

"It will be a good end to a good year," Bleddyn announced.

We travelled to Inbhir Nis in our cart, with Bleddyn beside me and Mayota sitting in the back, eagerly anticipating the festivities. She was in a particularly good mood, which made a pleasant change. As we trundled along the worn trackway towards the king's home, her enthusiasm made me begin to look forward to it myself. Bleddyn, of course, did not need encouragement to enjoy a celebration.

On arrival, we were shown to a guest house which we were told we would be obliged to share with several other visiting families. Even that did not bother us very greatly. There was an infectious air of carefree happiness all around, and everyone seemed to have caught the spirit of the occasion. The fact that the blazing star had not brought disasters in its wake had cheered everyone. This, Bleddyn pronounced, would be a Christmas to remember.

As a chieftain, even a minor one, I was expected to meet the king formally, so I walked over to the great hall wearing my finest clothes. Bleddyn, dressed in his habitual monk's robe, accompanied me. There were a great many other people there, mostly chieftains waiting patiently to meet with Bridei for a few, short words. When it came to my turn, I stepped forwards and stopped, my breath catching in my throat.

Bridei sat there, in the place of honour at the head of the hall. To the sides, seated at long tables, were his principal advisers; Abbot Ronan with a gaggle of churchmen sitting alongside lords like Taran and, as I could not fail to notice, grey-haired Nechtan.

Sitting beside Nechtan was Derelei.

Chapter 18

The shock of seeing her was almost too much for me. I felt suddenly weak and flustered in a way that had never happened to me before.

Bleddyn nudged me.

"The King is waiting for you," he whispered urgently.

Somehow, I managed to get through the formal greeting. Bridei enquired about my farm and asked whether I was enjoying my new position as one of his chieftains. I replied briefly, my mind seeming to have frozen, leaving me incapable of clear thought. I left as quickly as I could, unable to look at Derelei for fear of giving myself away.

When we had passed back through the doors, Bleddyn said, "You are a married man, Bili. Remember that."

"I'm not likely to forget it," I retorted.

"Then act like one," he warned me.

I did my best. For the next three days I stayed close to Mayota, walking with arms linked or hand in hand, doing my best to be an attentive husband and to keep well clear of Derelei. Mayota was delighted, smiling and always cheerful. Her mood was so uncharacteristic that I almost enjoyed being with her.

On the fourth morning, Mayota said that she needed to visit Fincana again.

"Do you want me to come with you?" I asked.

"There is no need for that," she replied. "You can stay here. I will be fine. I have visited her on my own before now, you know. I am used to her ways now."

I remembered her trips to Inbhir Nis on market days and how she had often wandered off on her own. She was perfectly capable of going alone but Bleddyn had told me to act like a married man.

"I'll come with you anyway," I offered.

"Stay here," she insisted. "I am meeting up with some of the other women. You would be out of place."

So she went off, returning some time later with another of Fincana's little clay jars. She was very pleased with herself. In fact, I had rarely seen her so happy as during that holiday.

"I am just enjoying seeing so many other people," she said when I remarked on her good mood. "We never see anyone when we are stuck out on that wretched farm."

I was glad to see her happy for a change, but it was not all fun. Christmas is a time of celebration but it is also a time to remember the birth of Christ. Bleddyn had told me that the churchmen knew that the traditions of a midwinter feast were so old that they were lost in the mists of past generations, but Abbot Ronan once again did his best to ensure that the proper religious ceremonies were observed with due solemnity and that people knew why we were celebrating. So we attended the church, joining the throng to pray and sing and to listen to the Abbot drone his way through his interminable sermons.

I managed to exchange a brief glance with Derelei only once, when she was leaving the church alongside Nechtan. It was over in a heartbeat, yet it was a look that told me she still loved me. I was sure of it.

"Was that her?" Mayota asked later as we walked back to our guest house.

"Who?"

"Derelei. The king's daughter."

"Yes, that was her."

Mayota's nose wrinkled in the way that always indicated her disapproval of something or somebody. "I suppose she's quite pretty," she said. "But she's much too skinny."

"Not my type at all," I agreed.

"Not like me," she said happily. She waggled her chest at me to prove her point, laughing as she did so.

"She's not like you at all." I assured her.

When the religious ceremonies were over, the feasting began in earnest. The celebrations lasted for two days, with Bridei providing food and drink during the day, then having the hall cleared to allow dancing during the evenings. It was wild, joyous, enthusiastic and as noisy as anything I had ever witnessed.

Mayota insisted I join in with some of the dances. I was not a great one for dancing but on the second evening of the feast, I had managed to get fairly drunk, so I followed her into the melee that was swirling around the floor in time to the wild music. In some of the dances, we changed partners, swinging one another around, then moving on to meet the next dancer. It was chaotic, laughter-filled and very tiring. Caught up in it all, I whirled, releasing one woman's arm to find myself suddenly linked with Derelei.

I almost stumbled, but somehow I managed to keep my feet. She laughed. We spun round the floor, our hold on one another all too brief before the music demanded that we separate and move on to other partners. In the short time our arms were linked, the way she held me and the way she looked at me told me all I needed to know. Then she was gone and the dance moved on.

Later, I sat at the side of the hall, taking a break to recover my breath and consume some more heather ale. Mayota was still dancing, lost in the leaping shadows of the darkened hall. I was looking for Derelei but could not see her. I noticed Donnell, standing alone against the far wall with a mug in hand. He raised it in silent salute, giving me a friendly smile. Then he pointed with his chin and I saw fat Uerb, staggering drunkenly after Mayota who was walking hurriedly towards me, clearly annoyed at his unwanted attentions.

I stood up, taking her arm as she reached me.

"What's wrong?" I asked. I had to shout over the noise of the music and dancing.

"This fat slob keeps pestering me," she said. "Tell him to leave me alone."

I stepped past her, placing myself in Uerb's way. I was nervous, not because I feared him but because I knew who his friends were. There was no sign of Medraut or Guret nearby and Donnell appeared to have moved off somewhere, but I knew they would not be far away.

Uerb stopped, swaying drunkenly. He peered at me. "It's you," he said. "You little shit."

I stood my ground. "My wife wants you to leave her alone. Why don't you go and have another drink?"

"I only asked to see her tits," he said, the words slurring. "Nothing wrong with that, is there? I heard she does more than that for other men."

I wanted to hit him but I confined myself to stabbing a finger to his chest and hissing at him, "You heard wrong, Uerb. Now piss off and leave us alone."

"Or what?"

"Or I'll do to you what I did to Medraut."

He blinked, his eyes heavy with the drink. He glanced at Mayota. "Bitch!" he said. Then he turned, weaving his way back across the hall, disrupting a group of revellers as he staggered through their dance.

I turned back to Mayota. "Are you all right?" I asked.

She nodded. "He's disgusting. Thank you."

"Perhaps we should leave. Go back to the house? We could be alone for a while."

She considered it, but then nodded her head towards the door where Uerb was lurching his way outside.

"I want to stay," she said. "If he's gone, I'll be fine." She looked at me. "You're almost as drunk as he is," she said. "You should get some fresh air yourself."

"That's a good idea," I agreed.

I was a little disappointed that she had refused the offer of being alone, but she had been in such good humour recently that I could put up with that. She took my arm, walking with me as far as the great doors, then she kissed my cheek before heading back to join in the dancing. I watched her go, smiling to myself in anticipation when I saw the seductive sway of her hips. She may have declined the chance to be alone for a while but I guessed that there would be plenty of time later on. When she had disappeared into the shadowy crowd of dancers, I stepped out into the chilly darkness.

There were people all around, some talking, some lying sprawled in a drunken stupor. There was no sign of Uerb, which was probably just as well. I have never been violent by nature but he deserved a burst nose for what he had said.

I took several deep, invigorating breaths. It was cold outside but the riotous noise from within the hall was less appealing than the calm out here. I looked around, then felt suddenly sober as I saw Medraut and Guret walking towards the hall.

I had managed to avoid them all night but unless I moved now, they would pass right by me. They were deep in conversation, so I didn't think they had noticed me. I considered going back inside but I felt a hand touch my elbow. Turning, I saw Donnell standing beside me.

"Why don't you go for a walk?" he suggested. "I'll keep them occupied for a while."

I nodded. "Thanks," I said.

Hurriedly, I walked away from the hall, moving deeper into the clutter of buildings, away from Medraut and Guret.

I left the crowd, heading into the shadowy night. When I felt that I was far enough away, I turned to look back. Medraut and Guret had stopped at the entrance to the hall and were chatting to some men I did not know. Donnell had vanished again.

I decided to wait. They would not stand there all night. Once they had moved, I would slip back into the hall and find Mayota or Bleddyn. That way there would be no trouble.

"Bili?"

The unexpected voice startled me, making me jump. I turned to see Sorcha emerge from the shadows. She was around sixteen now, growing into a fine-looking young woman, although she still had her auburn hair tied back in a severe fashion and hidden beneath a headscarf so that she looked more stern than I knew she was. I peered at her drunkenly.

"Sorcha?"

"Follow me," she said. "Please."

I followed her without question, There could only be one reason why she wanted me to go with her.

"I have been waiting for you to come outside," she explained. "My lady asked me to watch for you."

She led me to the rear of the hall, where the private rooms were located. Slipping in through the servants' entrance at the rear, she took me to a chamber where she gave a soft, elaborate knock on the door which swung open almost immediately. There, illuminated by the room's solitary candle, was Derelei.

Sorcha hurriedly ushered me inside, then pulled the door shut behind me. By that time, Derelei and I were already in each other's arms.

"Oh, my love," she whispered. "You don't know how much I have missed you. I thought we would never have a chance to be together."

I bent to kiss her neck, finding the spot where I knew she loved to feel my lips. She shivered under the touch.

"I missed you, too," I said between kisses.

"We don't have much time," she said. Her voice was urgent and hoarse with desire. "Nechtan thinks I am with little Bridei."

"Where is our son?" I asked.

"Sleeping in the next room, Sorcha is with him now." She was tugging at the ties on my shirt as she spoke.

It was mad, desperate, reckless and foolish but it was also passion and love unlike anything I had ever experienced with Mayota. We fell on the bed, entwined together and made love with an urgency and need born of the agonisingly long time we had spent apart. She clung to me, crying out in pleasure, while I repeated her name over and over again until, at last, I fell to the bed beside her, exhausted.

I don't know how long we lay there, holding one another. It seemed such a short time, far too short to say everything that we needed to say. After what felt like little more than a few minutes, Derelei pulled herself away from me and began to dress.

"I must get back," she said. "Sorcha will show you out the back way. Wait a while before you go back into the hall."

"I cannot live my life like this," I said to her. "I need to be with you."

"You have a wife," she said.

"I don't love her."

"I have a husband."

"You don't love him."

"There is nothing we can do about it, Bili," she said.

"But I need you."

She fastened the ties at the front of her dress. "I need you, too," she said. "But it cannot be. Not just now."

"When?"

She grabbed a brush, running it through her long hair. Her expression was full of longing and sadness.

"I don't know. Nechtan will not live forever. Perhaps then, if your wife is prepared to look the other way . . ."

"That could be years yet," I said. "I don't think I can bear that."

"You must bear it, Bili. We both must." She leaned over to kiss me gently. "Promise?"

It was the hardest word I have ever had to say but I loved her more than anything, so I said it. "Promise."

Another kiss and she was gone.

I dressed, blew out the candle and went out into the narrow corridor. Sorcha was already there. Wordlessly, she showed me out, then barred the rear door behind me.

I walked slowly round the wide perimeter of the hall, the faint sound of the music barely registering through the whirl of my emotions. Was my life with Derelei to be nothing more than a few hurried, secretive couplings? I wanted to be with her, to talk to her, to watch her at night when we sat beside a hearth fire. I wanted to lie beside her, as we had lain for such a brief time that evening. I wanted to touch her, to feel her next to me and to love her.

Yet that would never be, not while Nechtan and Mayota lived. At that moment, I wished them dead. It was a wish, a desire; nothing more than that. I knew there was no way I could harm people whose only crime was that they stood between me and Derelei. I had thought that the past year would have diminished my love for her, but I knew now that an eternity would not be long enough for that. In vain, I tried to think of a way for us to be together.

I thought of Mayota, remembering her happiness, the gentle kiss she had given me and the promise in the way she walked, but now, desire had gone, driven out by guilt. She was a victim of my tangled life as much as anyone. I wondered how she would react if she learned that I had been with Derelei. I knew it was unfair to conceal it from her, but Derelei had extracted my promise and I could not break my word. There was nothing I could do. I was trapped.

When I reached the front of the hall, I found that the crowd at the door had gone. I wandered inside, suddenly aware that the music had stopped. People were clustering round the centre of the hall, their voices angry and shocked. I stopped, wondering what had happened.

Someone in the press of people must have seen me because I heard a woman shout, "There he is!"

As one, the crowd turned to face me. My heart thumped in my chest, my immediate reaction one of fear that Derelei and I had been discovered. Then Medraut pushed through, all muscle and repressed fury, his eyes blazing. He jabbed a finger at me.

"You murdering bastard!" he yelled.

I ignored him. The crowd had moved aside and I saw, lying on the floor the bulky shape of Uerb. He was on his back with a knife buried to the hilt in his chest.

It was my knife.

Chapter 19

I was lucky. Bridei took command of the situation, preventing the mob from doing anything more than bruising my ribs and my face. For a short time, everything was a blur of pain as people punched, kicked and scratched at me but, fortunately, it did not last long.

Battered and bleeding, I think I caught sight of Derelei, frantically screaming at her father to stop them beating me, but I may have imagined it. I think I also saw Mayota, her expression one of smug satisfaction. I may have been wrong about that too, because I also vaguely recalled an image of her standing next to Guret, the two of them smiling in triumph. I knew that must be wrong, so perhaps the other memories I had were also only in my imagination.

Once Bridei had stopped the beating, he had me taken to a small room somewhere beyond the hall, probably quite close to where I had been with Derelei only a short time before. This room had been hastily emptied, leaving nothing except a bucket and the bare floor for me to lie on. The door was barred, a guard placed outside and I was left there to shiver in the dark.

I could scarcely comprehend what had happened. Uerb was dead. With my dagger in his chest. It was like a bad dream.

Bitterly, I recalled Fincana's warnings from the year before, and the bright star that had blazed in the sky like a herald of doom. I almost sank into self-pity but Bleddyn had told me often enough that such feelings achieved nothing, so I tried to think rationally about what had happened.

The fiery star may have been set in the heavens as a portent of some great disaster, but the truth was that neither Uerb nor I were great men. Our deaths would hardly warrant a divine warning.

As for Fincana, I had my doubts about her abilities to foretell the future. Her warning had probably been genuine enough but I suspected she had heard whispers of some plot against me. If that was true, then I had no doubt about who the plotters were.

My mind raced, trying to work out why and how this had been done. I could not find any answers. Eventually, I lay on the hard floor and fell into a fitful sleep.

In the morning I was given a breakfast of lumpy porridge, then left alone for several hours. I thumped on the door, calling for some water to wash and shave but a surly voice from the other side told me to be quiet. Disconsolately, I sat down until mid-afternoon, when four warriors, armed with spears, came to fetch me.

Unshaven, bruised and with my clothes ripped in several places, I was led back to the hall which had been cleared of the debris from the previous evening. Bridei sat behind a long table at the head of the chamber, several of his chieftains around him. Taran was there, I noticed, and so, too, was Nechtan. He scowled at me with a sullen expression clouding his features, but that was usual for Nechtan.

Standing at either side of the hall were dozens of men and women, spectators come to witness the king's justice. I looked for Derelei but could not see her. Mayota was there, standing beside Bleddyn. Both of them looked miserable and anxious.

Medraut, Guret and Donnell all glared at me as I was dragged to face the king. Beyond them, standing near the back, I caught a glimpse of Sorcha. She was chewing her lip nervously, her young face radiating concern.

Bridei thumped his fist on the table, killing the murmur of conversation that had greeted my entrance. He looked directly at me, his face stern. On the table in front of him lay my dagger, the blade still dark with the stain of Uerb's blood.

At a nod from Bridei, Abbot Ronan pushed himself to his feet. He announced that everyone there was under an obligation to tell the truth if called upon to speak, and to bear witness that anyone who uttered a lie would suffer eternal damnation at the hands of Satan and all his devils. He gazed myopically around the silent hall to make sure that everyone understood, then sat down, his duty done.

Bridei spoke. He did not stand up. He simply sat there, his hands resting on the table, his deep voice filling the hall.

"Bili, you are accused of murdering Uerb, son of Eurgain. Before this assembly and in the eyes of God, I ask you, did you kill him?"

I spoke as confidently and clearly as I could. "No, I did not."

"Liar!" boomed Medraut from the side of the hall. Others joined in until Bridei hammered his fist on the table again. Then he signalled for someone to step forwards from the crowd on my right.

It was Mayota.

Bridei looked at her, his eyes hard. "You are Bili's wife?"

She nodded. "Yes." Her voice was strangely muted, not at all what I was used to.

"You were with him when he argued with Uerb last night?"

"Yes."

"Tell me what they were arguing about."

Mayota did not look at me. She held her hands together in front of her, nervously twisting her fingers. Eyes lowered to gaze at the straw-covered floor, she replied, "I was dancing with Uerb. Bili objected to the way he was looking at me. He threatened to kill Uerb if he did not leave me alone."

The hall filled with the roar of angry voices. I gaped at her.

"That's not true!" I exclaimed but my voice was lost in the clamour.

Again Bridei thumped his hand. Mayota, her face pale, stepped back beside Bleddyn who looked utterly distraught. I shook my head, letting him know that Mayota had lied.

Next it was Medraut's turn to speak. He said, "Guret and I went looking for Uerb when we heard he had gone outside. He was very drunk and we were worried about him. It took us a while to find him but when we went round to the guest houses, we saw someone crouching over a figure on the ground. Whoever it was, he ran away when he heard us coming. He ran, but he left his knife buried in Uerb's heart."

"Did you see who the killer was?" Bridei asked.

"No. It was very dark. Guret chased after him but lost him. I stayed with Uerb."

Then Guret stepped up. In a clear, confident voice, he confirmed everything Medraut had said, except that he added, "Whoever the killer was, he was not a large man. His build was slim." He looked directly at me as he said, "Just like Bili."

Bridei stared at me. "This is your dagger?" he asked.

"Yes, but I left it in the guest house when we came to the hall."

"You argued with Uerb over your wife?"

"Yes, but not the way she told it."

"Why would she lie?" he asked.

"I don't know," I admitted weakly. It sounded pathetic, even to me. Why would anyone risk eternal hellfire by lying about such a thing?

"Where were you when Uerb was killed?" Bridei asked.

I said, "Outside."

"Where?" he demanded.

"I was drunk. I sat at the side of the hall."

Then he asked the question I knew was coming and that I knew I could not answer truthfully.

"Was anyone with you? Did anyone see you?"

I closed my eyes. Eternal damnation loomed in front of me. I briefly considered claiming that I had been with Sorcha but I knew she would never be able to withstand Bridei's questioning. Abbot Ronan had said we were on oath here, and I could not ask Sorcha to risk her soul by lying. I certainly had no wish to put her, or Bridei, in a situation where the truth would come out. I opened my eyes again to look Bridei in the face.

I told him, "No, I was alone the whole time."

I said it quickly, I said it firmly, daring him to disbelieve me.

Bridei looked around the hall. "Does anyone else have anything to say on this matter?"

Bleddyn stepped forwards immediately. "My King," he said, "Bili would not have done this. I know him. He would not have done such an evil thing. I beg you to spare him."

Angry voices tried to shout him down. Bridei banged the table again. When calm had been restored, he asked Bleddyn, "Can you prove he is innocent?"

Bleddyn looked at me. I know he considered lying but he was a good man, a man of God. He would not risk his soul, so he shook his head. Helplessly, he replied, "No."

Bridei nodded. He still showed no emotion. Everyone waited in silence for his verdict. After what seemed an age, he said, "Some of those who have spoken here today are known to have lied in the past about what happened between them and Bili. I know this, but the evidence in this case is clear enough and I cannot dispute what they have said on oath. I cannot conclude anything other than that Bili murdered Uerb following a drunken argument. The only thing I need to decide is the just punishment."

"Death!" came a shout from the crowd. Medraut or Guret, I guessed. My knees felt weak. I knew the penalty well enough.

Bridei held my gaze. "Bili, you have done me great services in the past. You have always shown yourself to be loyal to me and to my friends. Because of that, I will allow you to live." He held up a hand to stifle the protests from the hall. Still looking into my eyes, he went on, "But you are banished from Fortriu. You must leave within thirty days and never return. If you are found anywhere within my kingdom after that time, any man may slay you without fear of retribution." He signalled to the guards. "Take him away and let him gather his things."

  The last person I saw before the four warriors dragged me away was Sorcha. She mouthed the words, "Thank you." Then she hurried off to tell Derelei that I had kept my promise.

Bleddyn brought my dagger. Bridei had handed it over to him without question when he asked for it. I noticed that he had cleaned the blood from it. Wordlessly, I put it in my pack with my torn clothes. I had changed into my everyday leggings, shirt and jerkin, gathered up my cloak and my few other belongings and was ready to go.

  There was a tense silence. The house was empty apart from the two of us because the other guests who stayed there had no wish to be seen in the company of a murderer.

  Bleddyn cleared his throat then said, "I have the cart outside."

  "I didn't do it, Bleddyn," I told him.

  "I believe you, Bili."

  "She lied. Mayota lied. Why would she do that?"

  He shrugged. "I don't know."

  "Where is she?"

  Shaking his head, he said, "I haven't seen her for a while."

  We went outside. I hefted my pack onto the back of the cart then clambered up to sit on the driving board. Bleddyn climbed up beside me. He flicked the reins, urging the horse into motion.

People stared at us as we passed on our way to the gates, some of them crossing themselves, others spitting at us. I looked straight ahead, trying to ignore them.

Then I saw Derelei standing in the crowd, holding her son, my son, in her arms. I could hardly bear to look at her. She was so beautiful. I thought she might have cried, but her face was set in a determined expression.

She mouthed the words, "I love you."

I responded with the slightest nod of my head, letting her know I had understood. Beside her, young Sorcha's cheeks were wet with tears as we passed. I turned so that I could watch Derelei for as long as possible. I felt as if my heart was breaking.

As we approached the gate, I saw Mayota standing there, with Guret beside her. She wore a new cloak wrapped around her shoulders, fastened by a golden brooch. She was looking at me with a malicious smirk one her lips. I signalled to Bleddyn to stop as we reached them. I stared at her.

"You lied," I said accusingly.

"No I didn't," she said haughtily. "I told the truth."

I thought she was not far from laughing at me. I glanced at Guret. "And what are you doing with him?" I asked her.

Guret put his arm around Mayota's waist, drawing her close to him.

"Mayota and I have had an understanding for some time," he gloated, his triumphant grin mirroring hers.

"An understanding?" I asked.

His eyes narrowed. In a low whisper so that only the four of us could hear, he said, "I just did to her what you were doing to my father's wife. An eye for an eye, Bili."

Mayota gave me a scornful look. "Guret can offer me much more than you ever could, Bili. You would have been content to live on that little farm for the rest of your life. Soon, I will be the wife of a real chieftain."

"You are still my wife," I told her. "You may live with him but you cannot marry him."

Mayota laughed. "You have been banished, Bili. Any man who abandons his wife for a year and a day is considered dead. After that, I will be free to do whatever I choose."

Guret grinned evilly. He said, "You should have been executed, Bili, but perhaps this is better. Now you can spend your life thinking about the two of us, the things we will do together."

I spat in his face. "You are welcome to the bitch," I said.

I signalled to Bleddyn who snapped the reins, taking us out of the fortress of Inbhir Nis for what I knew would be the last time. As we left, I heard Guret calling angry insults after me but I did not turn round.

On the journey home I gave Bleddyn my version of what had happened, only missing out my meeting with Sorcha and the time I had spent with Derelei.

"They were in it together," I said bitterly.

"Guret and Mayota?"

"Yes. Medraut as well."

"You think they killed Uerb? He was their friend."

"Guret would sacrifice anyone to get what he wants, and Medraut's a vicious bastard. Anyway, Uerb wasn't a true friend, he just followed them around."

Bleddyn pondered that for a while. "It sounds rather extreme," he said cautiously.

"You heard what Guret said. He has always hated me."

"Enough to kill his own friend? Or follower, if you prefer."

I jabbed my elbow into his side. "Bleddyn! If you don't believe he would do that, then you must think it was me who killed Uerb."

Bleddyn shook his head. "Not at all. I am just trying to think of a reason why they would take such elaborate measures. Revenge is one thing, but Guret could have gained revenge for your, ah, relationship with Derelei by simply continuing his own affair with Mayota. Revealing that would have hurt you enough." He paused. "When did they see one another anyway?"

"She said he came to the farm once," I explained. "She claimed he didn't stay long but I am not so sure now." I remembered the way she had taunted me that day. Perhaps her boast of bedding Guret had been true, after all. I added, "And she often came to Inbhir Nis on market days. Maybe they met then."

"So why did she not simply run off with him?" Bleddyn asked. "That would have been just as effective if their intent was to hurt you."

"Because they're an evil-minded pair," I said.

"I think there may be more to it than that," Bleddyn mused. "Perhaps Mayota has something that Guret wants. Some skill or other. Aside from the obvious, of course."

I could not help laughing at that. "Like what?"

"I don't know," he admitted.

"You are seeing too much in it, Bleddyn," I said. "Guret wanted to get at me and Mayota offered herself to him. She's a good-looking woman, so he jumped at the chance. Literally. Then they got thinking and came up with this plan to get rid of me so that they could be together. Mayota wants to marry him, so they needed me dead. It's simple. As for Uerb, perhaps he annoyed Guret or Medraut in some way. God knows, that's easy enough to do. They probably decided to deal with both of us at the same time."

"I suppose so," Bleddyn conceded. "I just don't understand why a man like Guret, who will be a very influential chieftain when his father dies, would agree to marry someone like Mayota."

"Two very big reasons," I said, curving my hands out in front of my chest.

He gave a weak smile, shaking his head. Then his serious face appeared. He said, "Whatever happened, you are banished, Bili. Where shall we go?"

"You'll stay right here," I said instantly. "Finish building your church and terrorise the congregation with your tales of hellfire and damnation."

"You can't go on your own," he protested.

"And you can't travel the world with that leg of yours."

"It's getting better," he said. "And I miss the travelling."

I squeezed his arm, saying, "Stay here, Bleddyn. I have been on my own before. I can do it again. Besides, if you stay here, perhaps we can keep in touch. Maybe, once your leg is better, you can come and find me, let me know what is happening up here. You might even be able to convince Bridei I am innocent."

He sucked in his cheeks, pondering the suggestion. "Well, I know Bridei is a fair man. If he finds evidence of the truth, he will release you from banishment. But how would I find you?"

"I'll go to Dun Eidyn. Not to spy, this time. But I can get a job working with Thingfrith or Toki. It won't be exciting but after what happened yesterday, I think it would be nice to become one of the ordinary people who help make the world turn."

After a while, Bleddyn said, "All right. Bad leg or not, I'll come looking for you in the summer."

With that agreed, events moved quickly. I spoke to Entifidich and Niamh, explaining what had happened.

"The farm is yours," I told them, "Unless the king decides otherwise, but I have asked Brother Bleddyn to speak to him about it."

I don't think they understood because Entifidich said, "We will take care of it until your return."

"I will not be returning," I told him, but he just smiled and bobbed his head.

I took most of the few scraps of silver I had in my strongbox, leaving some for Entifidich. Then I scooped up some jewellery that Mayota had left behind and stuffed it into my pack. It was not worth much but I took it anyway.

Bleddyn insisted on riding with me until I passed beyond the borders of Fortriu. At his insistence, we travelled round the coast, avoiding the shorter, inland route past Dun Nechtan. I think that was probably a wise choice, though my heart ached to speak to Derelei one more time. I often thought of her, wondering what torment she was going through, knowing that I had been banished and that she could have proven me innocent of murder. I wanted to hold her, to tell her that I understood. If she had spoken up, we would both have been admitting adultery, a mortal sin in the eyes of the church. More importantly, her father's fragile alliance with Nechtan would have been shattered, leaving Fortriu weak and divided.

"When you see Derelei," I said to Bleddyn, "tell her I understand."

"I will," he promised.

When we reached the tiny fishing village of Cala na Creige, at the southernmost extent of Fortriu on the east coast, I dismounted, resuming my disguise as a poor, wandering beggar. Bleddyn embraced me, wishing me luck, then he took both horses and rode north while I set off to the south, leaving Fortriu, and Derelei, behind me forever.

Chapter 20

"Woden's balls, lad, you've got some nerve!"

It was not quite the greeting I had expected after such a long, foot-wearying journey in the middle of winter.

"Hello, Thingfrith," I said. "How are you?"

He had been standing at the door of his inn, saying farewell to one of his guests who was obviously an important man to judge by the string of servants, ponies and pack mules that followed him. Now the burly innkeeper looked at me with an expression of alarm, as if I had returned from the dead. He grabbed my arm, ushering me round the side of the inn to the yard at the back.

"What's wrong?" I asked as he hurried me out of sight.

"What's wrong?" Thingfrith echoed. "I'll tell you what's bloody wrong, lad. Beornhaeth's men have been here looking for you. Turned the place inside out, they did. Scared my customers half to death. So you'd bloody well better tell me what's going on."

A cold finger of icy dread ran down my spine. "When was this?" I asked.

"Three days ago. They stormed in, six of the biggest and meanest thugs I've ever seen. Said they were looking for a man called Bili. They weren't wanting to play with you, either." He eyed me suspiciously. "What have you done?"

"Nothing, Thingfrith. Honestly. I've been up in the north for the past two years."

I could tell he did not believe me. I could hardly blame him.

He said, "Lord Beornhaeth does not send his toughest warriors out to find someone who has done nothing. I heard they turned over Toki's place as well. He's not happy at all."

"I don't understand," I said. "I've never even met Beornhaeth."

"No, but last time you stayed here, you were up at his hall a lot." A look of startled realisation crossed his face. "Thor's hammer!" he exclaimed, once again forgetting that he was supposed to be a Christian. "You said you had girl trouble. It wasn't one of his daughters, was it? That would explain why he wants you so badly."

"No, it wasn't," I said firmly. "Even if it was, why would he wait two years before trying to find me?"

Something else was bothering me. I asked, "How would he know I was here? I've only just arrived and I came straight to you. Nobody else knows I am back in Dun Eidyn."

"I wish I bloody didn't know either," Thingfrith muttered gloomily. His eyes narrowed. "You can't stay here," he told me. "And what do I tell them if they come back?"

"Tell them nothing. I'm just a wandering beggar, You sent me packing and you don't even know my name. You haven't seen Bili for two years."

He grumbled at that but I pressed a decorated, silver brooch into his hand which mollified him slightly. I gripped his hand, said farewell and turned to leave.

"Where are you going?" he asked me.

"Best you don't know," I called back over my shoulder.

He looked relieved at that.

I went to see Toki. His reaction when I walked into the tiny room where he tallied his accounts was even less welcoming than Thingfrith's. The little brewer leaped up from his table, barking obscenities and threatening to have some of his heavies drag me up the hill to Beornhaeth.

"Give me a chance to explain!" I begged.

"Why in God's name should I?"

"Because I haven't done anything."

He gave me a grudging stare, folding his arms across his chest. "Well?" he demanded testily.

He watched me while I dug out some pieces of Mayota's silver and bronze jewellery. I laid them on the table in front of him. He eyed the trinkets hungrily.

"What's that for?" he asked.

"I need you to do me one last favour, then I will leave and never come back."

"I've done you a big enough favour already by not calling Beornhaeth's guards down here," he growled.

"Suit yourself," I said, scooping up the brooches, necklaces and rings. "I'll find someone else to do it."

"Wait!" he snapped, his little eyes still on the trinkets in my hand.

I knew I had him. Outside of brewing ale, the hoarding of precious metals was Toki's main interest.

"What is it you want?" he asked.

"I want you to take a message to someone on the hill."

"Who?"

"A cook. Her name is Aeldgyth."

We bargained for quite a while. I had to add some more trinkets to the pile but eventually Toki agreed to take the message himself. The next day, Berht was allowed to stay behind while Toki took his cart up the hill. Berht, as dull-witted as ever, did not ask any questions but simply accepted what his father told him to do.

I did not entirely trust Toki not to betray me, so I waited in a narrow alleyway between some houses at the foot of the hill. When I saw that he was making the return journey alone, I went out to meet him.

"Any luck?" I asked.

If he was surprised to see me so soon, he hid it well. He said, "She'll meet you tomorrow. She'll go down to the market early morning. Meet her there."

"Thank you, Toki."

"You can thank me by buggering off," he retorted. "I never want to see you again."

"You won't," I promised.

He scuttled away, leaving me with an afternoon and a night to get through without being found by Beornhaeth's men. Fortunately, the town around Dun Eidyn was large enough for me to lose myself among the jumble of houses and workshops. I spent a cold night sleeping outdoors behind an old shed but I was up before dawn, making my way to the path that led to the hill.

It was a cold, frosty morning, but the early traders were already gathering, setting out their wares in the hope of catching the eye of anyone going to or from Beornhaeth's home. I settled down beneath the bare branches of a tall tree, pulled my cloak up over my head and pretended to be asleep.

I recognised Aeldgyth as soon as she walked out of the gates. She was as fat and heavy as ever, waddling down the path as if every step was an effort. She looked rather tense, but I supposed that was to be expected. I let her pass. I was more interested to see whether a gang of warriors were about to follow her in the hope of catching me when I met her at the market. I waited until she was out of sight then, satisfied that she was alone, I went down the hill after her.

The market takes place on a wide, grassy meadow on the southern side of the rock of Dun Eidyn. As usual, it was a riot of noise, colours and smells. I spotted Aeldgyth almost at once, standing near the edge of the meadow, looking around anxiously. She breathed a huge sigh of relief when she recognised me. Then her face creased into a mask of annoyance.

"The lady Triduana says you are a fool," she informed me. "And I agree with her. You should never have come back."

"Just tell me what she found out and I will be gone," I said.

She looked around, checking that nobody was likely to overhear us. In a hurried whisper, she blurted out Triduana's reply to the message Toki had delivered for me.

"A man came from the north," she said. "The lady does not know his name but he was a small man, stocky with dark hair and he has only one eye. He has been here before, so he is known. He also carries a ring that proves he comes from someone who can be trusted."

"Who?" I asked. "Who sent him?"

Aeldgyth shook her head. "The lady does not know. Whoever it was, the messenger said that a man was coming here with the intention of assassinating the lords Beornhaeth and Wulfric. He told them your name and said that you would likely stay with the innkeeper Thingfrith, or with Toki the brewer."

"He gave those names?"

"Yes."

"What about Triduana? Do they know she is my sister?"

"No. Luckily for her, he did not mention that."

It was my turn to breathe a sigh of relief. "Thank the Lord for the that."

"Amen," said Aeldgyth. "Now, I must go and buy something to explain my visit here and then get back to my duties. You must go too."

"Wait a moment. Did the messenger say anything else?"

"No. Not that I know of, anyway. Now go."

I took hold of her fleshy arm, preventing her from walking away. "What about Triduana? Is she well?"

"She was well before you turned up," the cook retorted. "She will be well again when you have gone." She shook off my grip. "Now please go!"

"Thank you, Aeldgyth," I said. Then I left her, crossing through the market, under the very foot of the looming rock that was Beornhaeth's fortress home. Up there somewhere was my sister. She was my flesh and blood yet I knew I could not speak to her, could not even see her. With a heavy heart, I continued walking, heading out to the open fields to the west.

I was not sure where I was going to go, but I knew I could not stay in Dun Eidyn. Someone had betrayed me. Someone in Fortriu was sending information to Beornhaeth.

That person knew me and, moreover, knew of my associations with Thingfrith and Toki.

While I trudged through the woods and wide lands along the south bank of the Foirthe, I ran through all the people who might have known the names of Thingfrith and Toki. I had told Bleddyn, of course, and Bridei. I had not told anyone else that I could recall, not even Derelei, for there had been no time in our brief meetings. In any case, I knew that none of those three would ever send a message to Beornhaeth. So who else?

I crossed them off in my mind. Not Nechtan. I had told him that I had got information about Beornhaeth's plans, but I had never given him any details.

Medraut? I had barely spoken to him at all. The same for Guret. As for the other two, Uerb was dead and I knew I had not told Donnell.

Which left only Mayota.

Then I remembered those winter evenings at the farm, where Bleddyn and I would sit by the fire, drinking and swapping stories. Mayota had been there all the time, listening to the tales of our escapades. I could not remember everything we had ever said, but I must have mentioned Thingfrith and Toki at least once, if not more often.

She must have guessed where I would go when I left Fortriu. Which meant that Guret must be the traitor because Mayota would have no way of sending trusted messengers to the Northumbrians. She had guessed and she had told Guret who had sent word to Beornhaeth. I was sure of it. No doubt the heartless bitch had hoped I would be seized and executed, leaving her free to marry Guret without waiting for a year and a day.

Mayota and Guret, working together. It was obvious. I had it all worked out but I had no idea what I could do about it.

I struggled with the problem for a long time. Slowly, I made my way north again, crossing through Fib, then following the coast through Circinn. I had no real plan in mind, so I simply kept walking. By the time I reached Dun Foither, I was truly a wandering beggar for I had very little of any value left and I was permanently hungry.

The mighty coastal fortress of Dun Foither was still held by a garrison of Northumbrians. It was their most northerly outpost on the east coast, a place from where they could watch for any army coming down the coastal path across the Mounth, or send word of any fleet that Bridei might send down the eastern sea. Secure behind the massive wall and protected on the other three sides by high cliffs, the men who guarded Dun Foither were the lynchpin of Beornhaeth's eastern defences.

There was a church on the headland, close to where the Dun now stood. People said that Saint Ninian himself had founded it when he first came to spread the word of God among the southern Pecht. There was still a church but the people who worshipped there now were the Northumbrian soldiers and their families. I would find no welcome there.

I knew that there were several farms scattered around the nearby countryside. I wondered whether I should try to find some work at one of these. Spring and Summer were always busy times on a farm, as I knew from personal experience. It would keep me fed until harvest time. After that, I would need to find something else to do if I wanted to eat, because few farmers would keep casual labourers once the harvest was in.

I hesitated, weighing up my options. What I really wanted was to return to Inbhir Nis, to warn Bridei of Guret's treachery, but I knew that was impossible. For one thing, I had no proof and for another, I would be a dead man before I could get close to Bridei. Medraut would make sure of that.

I might be able to reach Bleddyn without being detected but summer was approaching and he would already be on his way to Dun Eidyn to find me. That thought filled me with dread. If Bleddyn arrived in Dun Eidyn and began asking questions about me, he would be in danger himself. I could have sunk to my knees and wept. I could not imagine how things could be any worse.

Fighting off my black mood of depression, I sighed. There was nothing to be gained by feeling sorry for myself. I needed a plan of some sort. I was hungry and dishevelled from spending so many nights sleeping in the open. I needed to find food and shelter, but wherever I stayed, it also had to be somewhere that Bleddyn was likely to pass through.

I decided there was only one place I could go. Hefting my pack, I headed down the hill to the village of Cala na Creige.

Nominally, Bridei viewed this tiny fishing town as part of his kingdom but I knew that the reality was they paid their tithes to the Northumbrians in Dun Foither. Separated from Fortriu by the mountains of the Mounth, the village was both isolated yet also a stopping place for travellers on the coastal roads. There was a chance that Bleddyn would pass this way. I was taking a risk, but it was one worth accepting. All I had to lose was my life.

Chapter 21

The people of Cala na Creige were used to travellers. They did not exactly welcome me with open arms, but I was eventually able to find a fisherman named Ringan who needed an extra hand for his crew because his regular companion had drowned after falling overboard when their boat had been swamped during a storm. That explanation did not fill me with much confidence about Ringan's seamanship but it was the only offer I had, so I took it.

Ringan was short and wiry, his arms dark with tattoos. He was rather taciturn but friendly enough in his own way. He welcomed me into his home where he lived with his wife and eight young children. It was so noisy and crowded that I quickly understood why he spent most of his day at sea.

Cala na Creige is a small place, sitting on the shore of a rock-walled bay, facing the sea to the east and with high ground on the other three sides. The steep cliffs of the bay provide a natural harbour of sheltered water for the score of tiny fishing boats that ply the deep sea to the east, and give the little village an enclosed feeling, as if it is cut off from the rest of the world.

Ringan soon had me at work. We rowed out of the bay in the early light of dawn, with seabirds circling above our heads, riding the winds that swirled around the cliffs. I had been on boats before, during my travels around the lochs and islands of Dal Riata, but this was the first time that I had been involved in handling the vessel. Rowing was easy enough but Ringan alternately laughed and swore at me as he tried to explain the complex rigging that helped adjust the small boat's single sail. The trick, so he informed me, was for me to adjust the sail while he made alterations to the position of the steer-board. If we accomplished these combinations of sail and rudder, the boat would go more or less where Ringan wanted.

Fortunately, I got the hang of things fairly quickly, so Ringan soon contented himself with only swearing at me to keep me on my toes. I think he expected me to be sick, because the sea was choppy, buffeting the tiny vessel constantly, and the stink of fish was ingrained in the wood of the hull, but I never felt a twinge of nausea because I had always loved the feeling of being out on the water.

Once we were far enough from shore, we lowered our nets over the sides, then we waited, bobbing and rolling on the waves. Gulls circled overhead, waiting to pounce on anything that slipped through our nets, and I caught a glimpse of a seal as it poked its head above the water to peer at us before vanishing again.

I sat on a low bench near the prow, my feet sloshing in a shallow pool of sea water that had splashed over the boat in a burst of salty spray. The boat rocked as the swell of the sea surged around us. I loved it. Here, I had that same feeling of splendid isolation that often gripped me when I climbed a high mountain. Ringan and I were alone on the wide sea, yet only an hour or two from home. It was a glorious feeling.

I quickly discovered that these waters were very different to the western sea, where scores of islands, large and small, meant that land was never far away in any direction. Here, while the mainland lay on the horizon to the west, when I looked eastwards I could see nothing except a wide expanse of deep, dark water.

I pointed to the horizon. "They say there are lands across the sea that way," I said.

Ringan shrugged. "So they say."

"You've never tried to get there?"

"What for?" he asked, his brow furrowed in genuine puzzlement. "There are plenty of fish here. There's no need to go any further."

"You've never wanted to just go and see what's across the sea?"

"No."

After that, I confined myself to questions about the boat and the tasks I had to complete. Ringan's lack of curiosity made me realise just how much Bleddyn had shown me. I had walked the land from north to south, from east to west, yet I had still not seen everything and my curiosity nagged at me. But, for the moment, I needed to stay in Cala na Creige, living as one of the ordinary people. I would be a fisherman until I could find a way to warn Bridei about the spy in his home.

Bleddyn was my main hope now. I knew he would keep his promise to go to Dun Eidyn. He would speak to Thingfrith and to Toki who would probably deny all knowledge of me. Even if one or other of them admitted that they knew me, they did not know where I had gone. My fear was that one or other of them might betray him to Beornhaeth. A monk of the Ionian church would be suspect enough in Dun Eidyn but if he was caught, we were both doomed. Even if they did not denounce him, it would still leave Bleddyn with a problem. I hoped that he would pass Cala na Creige on his way home but there was always the chance, indeed the probability, that he would take the more direct, inland route.

I had toyed with the idea of finding somewhere to stay near that route but there were so many paths he could take that it would have been easy to miss him. If he came by the coast, he had little choice except to pass through Cala na Creige, so I warned all of Ringan's children to watch out for a man carrying a heavy staff, who walked with a limp and might be dressed as a monk. I promised them a reward if they saw him and were able to persuade him to stay until I returned from sea with their father.

It was a good plan but, like so many plans, it did not work. Many people passed through the village on their way north or south but there was never a sign of Bleddyn.

The summer saw me help Ringan land his catches of mackerel, cod, skate and shrimp. It was hard work, sometimes dangerous when the sea was rough and we were struggling to haul the heavy nets back onto the boat. Then the fish would flap and jump at our feet as we disentangled them, throwing the smaller ones back. The smell of fish soon became so much a part of my life that it ceased to bother me.

    We were kept busy in winter, too. On the days when it was too stormy to go to sea, we spent our time repairing nets, scraping barnacles from the hull of the boat, then caulking her so that she would be ready for the summer season. We still sailed out when we could, but never too far because the weather is always unpredictable at that time of year. Wind, rain and sea mists were frequent visitors to the east coast during the winter months. Ringan had already lost one friend to a sudden storm, so he was wary of venturing too far from shore unless he was certain that the weather would remain fine.

    At least we were never hungry because the sea provides food all year round. Fish, clams, lobsters and crabs made up a good part of our diet but we often traded some of the catch for grain, vegetables, salted beef, pork or mutton from the farmers who lived inland.

    The Northumbrians in Dun Foither were good customers, too. If we had made a particularly good catch, Ringan would sometimes sail his tiny boat down to the bay on the north side of the Dun's headland where he would beach the boat. The first time he took me there I wondered what he intended because the cliffs were far too steep and high to climb.

    "How do we get up there?" I asked him.

    "Follow me and I'll show you," he chuckled.

    Taking a small sack of freshly caught fish, he led me to a cave near the foot of the cliff. The entrance was narrow but high enough for us to stand upright as we went through. After a little way, the tunnel opened into a larger chamber. Passing through this dark cavern, we followed a narrow path, much of it consisting of rough-hewn steps that led up the side of the cliff to the top of the headland.

It was a dangerous, dizzying climb, but when we emerged on to the headland, we were at the side of the Dun, near a small gate in the wooden palisade.

"Not many people know about that path," Ringan informed me.

"I'm not sure I want to know about it either," I replied. "One slip on those steps and it's a quick fall to the rocks."

Ringan shrugged. Despite the danger of the climb, we made the ascent several times over the following months. At the rear gate, Ringan would sell some of our catch in exchange for meat, wool, leather or metal tools which we then carried back down to the tiny bay.

It was on one of these visits that Ringan learned I could speak English. He had picked up a few words and the Northumbrians had mastered a smattering of our tongue, so basic bartering was done in a local pidgin. Having someone who could speak to the Angles fluently was a revelation to Ringan and to the rest of the villagers who soon elected me as their spokesman in their dealings with the Dun. This role mostly consisted of assisting the negotiations over the tithes and taxes that the villagers were required to pay, but on one occasion it gained me access to the Dun itself.

There was a dispute over the actions of some of the soldiers towards one of the fishermen's daughters. Feelings in the village were running high but the matter was cleared up easily enough once the language ceased to be a barrier. I acted as interpreter and mediator, and managed to obtain some compensation for the girl's family.

In itself, the dispute was not memorable, but while I was inside the Dun, I took the chance to have a look around. I discovered that the thick, stone wall was built only on the side that faced the mainland, with the rest of the perimeter consisting of a ditch and rampart that was topped by a wooden palisade. I supposed that made sense. The only way any enemy could approach was across the neck of the headland, and the defences on that side were formidable. The wall was ten paces thick, the only entrance a double gateway with the gates set back from the front of the wall so that anyone foolhardy enough to launch an assault would be forced into the narrow gap between the ends of the walls on either side of the gates.

Clustered behind this great wall were more than a dozen buildings; the homes and stores for the garrison and their families. I took a mental note of everything I saw, although I had no real reason to. Old habits die hard, I suppose.

Apart from the occasional contact with the Northumbrian soldiers, life went on as normal in Cala na Creige. With no other option, I waited for Bleddyn.

And I waited.

I waited all winter and all through the following summer, and still there was no sign of him.

By this time I was one of the villagers, accepted as one of the leading men in the little community. Ringan's wife mentioned several times that some of the women had been hinting that they had daughters I might be interested in.

"I have no plans to get married," I told her.

She gave me an odd look. My refusal to become involved with any of the few local girls, combined with my constant reminders to watch out for Bleddyn, must have left her with the wrong impression about me because Ringan asked me outright whether I was a boy-lover.

I laughed. "No," I said. "I am already married."

He frowned. "So where is your wife?"

"In Fortriu. There was some trouble, so I cannot be with her just now."

I did not volunteer any more than that and he did not ask. For once, I was glad of his lack of curiosity.

So I waited in vain for Bleddyn to appear, spending much of my time on the sea with Ringan. When we were ashore, we listened to the latest news or rumours that were circulated by travellers or merchant sailors. Cala na Creige was an ideal spot for gathering news because trading ships often visited the harbour, bringing supplies for the fort at Dun Foither or disgorging the more adventurous Northumbrian merchants who were prepared to risk the hazards of the frontier in the hope of making a healthy profit. They brought jet from Streonshal, wine from Gaul, glassware from Italy, and amber from the coasts of the Baltic. They also regaled us with tales of the exotic, distant lands their goods had come from, even though most of the locals had only the vaguest notion of where these foreign places were.

I had met enough merchants to know that it is impossible to prevent them from talking if they think they can make a sale, so I always listened to their sales talk because, amidst the rumour and exaggeration, they also brought news.

I heard little from Fortriu other than tales of fighting against the men of Dal Riata. That was nothing new. I also heard rumours that Mael Duin of Dal Riata had slaughtered many people of the Cenel Loairn, so it was clear that the Scots were still too busy squabbling among themselves to bother Bridei overmuch.

One sailor told me he had heard that the Orcadians had raided the northern coast again but that, too, was normal.

Most of the news came from the south, where Ecgfrith had apparently been involved in yet another war against Mercia. The Northumbrian merchants claimed he had been victorious, but it sounded to me as if he had been defeated or, at best, managed a draw. His younger brother had been killed in a great battle and peace had only been restored when some important bishop had acted as arbiter on behalf of the Church. As part of the agreed settlement, Ecgfrith had lost the kingdom of Lindsey that he had gained only a few years before.

The details did not concern me, but all of this was good news for Bridei because it meant that Ecgfrith's gaze was most firmly on his southern and western borders, not on the north. The longer Ecgfrith ignored the Pecht, the stronger Bridei would become.

I wondered whether Bridei had heard any of this. He certainly had not heard about the spy who was watching him. Two summers had passed now and still I had not been able to get word to him. Then a piece of news reached me that gave me an inspiration. It may have been second or third-hand information, but a Northumbrian sailor swore to me that he had heard there was a new abbot on the island of Iona.

The new man's name was Adomnan.

I cursed myself for not thinking of this before. I may not be able to travel in Fortriu, but the monks of Iona could. If I could reach the island, I could tell them of Bleddyn's new church and what a wondrous thing it was going to be. He had probably finished building it by now. Perhaps they would send some monks to visit it. All I wanted was for them to take a message to him to tell him where I was. It was a simple solution to my problem and I wished I had thought of it sooner.

Ringan was disappointed when I told him I had to go on a long journey but his oldest boy was eleven now and would be able to help him with the boat. With my mind made up, I packed my spare clothes in my bag, took enough food to last me for a few days, then set off for the long hike to the west.

It took me almost five weeks to reach Iona. I knew roughly where it was, but I had been with Bleddyn the time before and we had approached from a different direction, so I strayed off the direct route several times. Not that there is any such thing as a direct route where the mountains, forests, moors and bogs of Dal Riata are concerned, but I could have got there more quickly if I had known my way better.

Having begged passage on a small, hide-covered boat, I stepped onto the little island on a windswept, rainy day. It always seemed to rain when I visited Iona.

My request to see the abbot was greeted by a guarded question.

"Who are you and what do you wish to see him about?" the monk who met me asked.

"My name is Bili mab Mailcon," I replied formally. "I have come on behalf of Brother Bleddyn who has built a fine new church in Fortriu."

It was probably the mention of the new church that gained me admittance, because monks always love evidence of what they deem good works. Whatever the reason, I was soon whisked in to see Adomnan in the same small cell where he had met Bleddyn seven years earlier.

The tiny room did not seem to have changed much and neither had Adomnan. I don't know whether he recognised me, but he certainly gave no sign if he did. He nodded a welcome, gave me his thin smile then asked whether I was a Christian.

"Yes," I replied. I wondered what difference it made. Perhaps he would have thrown me out if I had said no. Or, more likely, have me tossed into the sea as a quick form of baptism. However, my answer must have satisfied him because he permitted me to stay. He even spoke to me in the Scots language, which I could more or less understand.

"You have news of a new church?" he asked.

"That's right." In my halting Gaelic, I explained about Bleddyn's new church, describing where it had been built and what a wonder it was. I praised Bleddyn for building it in stone rather than wood, making it a lasting monument to the glory of God.

Adomnan's thin face appeared to grow even thinner as he peered at me.

"Yes," he said, "Abbot Ronan has written to me about it."

He did not seem overly pleased, but perhaps that was because it was Bleddyn who had built the church. I recalled Bleddyn saying that the two of them did not get on.

Rather impatiently, Adomnan asked, "What is it that you wish me to do?"

It was all or nothing now. "I have vitally important news for King Bridei, but I am not permitted to enter Fortriu."

His thin eyebrows arched at that but I ploughed on, not giving him time to ask any questions.

"I was hoping that you could send a monk to visit Brother Bleddyn, to tell him where I am and to ask him to meet me as soon as possible."

He did not bother smiling this time. "Do you think my holy brothers are messengers for anyone except God? Why should we carry this message for you?"

"Because if you don't, there is a chance that Ecgfrith of Northumbria may soon conquer the whole of Fortriu. If not with his army of soldiers, then with an army of monks. Monks who follow the teachings of the Church of Rome. If that happens, Iona will become the last outpost of a marginalised creed, and you will be abbot of nothing. You can help prevent that. You send letters to Abbot Ronan all the time. I am only asking that you have one of your monks take word to Brother Bleddyn that he will find me in Cala na Creige."

I had shocked him. Actually, I had shocked myself, both at being able to deliver such a speech in the language of the Scots and at addressing an abbot in such strong terms, but I was young and I was desperate, so I held his gaze when he looked at me with a startled expression on his thin, care-worn face.

It took him a moment or two to recover his composure but when he did, he said, "You will wait in the refectory. I will think on this."

I had no choice. I went to the refectory where I found, as I had on my previous visit, plenty of hot food and warming mead. I sat on a long, wooden bench at a long, wooden table with a wooden platter of food and a wooden beaker of mead while I waited for Adomnan to make up his mind.

Outside, the rain had stopped. Shafts of bright sunlight streamed in through the thick glass of the tiny windows, lightening the room and raising my spirits. I was worried that I had gone too far with my outburst, but I needed to contact Bleddyn, and Adomnan was my best hope, my only hope.

While I sat there, picking at the food and sipping the mead, the door opened to admit two men. One of them sat at a table while the other went to fetch some food from the portly monk who was on kitchen duty that day. I recognised this second man. It had been seven years since I had seen him but it was undoubtedly the English servant I had met on my previous visit. That gave me a clue to the identity of the seated man.

I glanced along the length of the table at him. Like Adomnan, he was tall and thin. He wore fine clothes, with intricate designs stitched into the expensive-looking cloth. His long hair was neatly combed while his beard and moustache were expertly trimmed. His eyes were a startling blue, but his thin face was dominated by his prominent, beak-like nose which, together with his manner, reminded me of a bird. He moved slowly and precisely, as if even the smallest action he took was carefully thought out beforehand. Looking at him, it was obvious that he was a scholar. If Bleddyn was correct, this must be Aldfrith, the older brother of King Ecgfrith of Northumbria.

The servant brought back some bowls of fish soup, then sat at a respectful distance from Aldfrith. They exchanged a few words, speaking in English, confirming Aldfrith's identity. From their conversation, I gathered that they had been in Ireland for some time. I recalled Bleddyn saying Aldfrith's mother had been an Irish princess, so I presumed he had relatives there. It seemed that he had returned to Iona because he wanted to study some of the monastery's old books. Studying appeared to be his main interest. A less warlike man it would have been hard to imagine. I am no fighter, but I reckoned that if I had drawn my knife and threatened him, he would have collapsed in terror.

A young monk came in, looking for me, interrupting my study of Aldfrith. The monk said, "The abbot will see you now."

I hurriedly finished off the last drops of the mead and, after taking a last, curious look at the strange, scholarly Northumbrian lord, I followed the monk back to Adomnan's room.

The abbot was perched on a stool, writing at a large, sloping desk, the quill held delicately between his fingers as it scratched out letters on a wide piece of vellum. When the monk who escorted me had left, Adomnan glanced up at me in a disinterested way, then turned his attention back to the parchment as if he was concentrating more on what he was writing than on what he intended to say to me.

With his eyes fixed on his work, he said, "Very well. The next time I write to Abbot Ronan I will have the Brother who delivers it take your message to Brother Bleddyn. If it is as important as you say, then I can do no less."

"Thank you, Father Abbot," I said fervently.

He lifted the quill. Before dipping it in the inkwell he waggled it slightly in my direction. "You may leave me now," he said, still not deigning to look at me.

I had done all I could. I backed out of the cell and left him to his writing.

The long walk across the width of the land from one coast to the other took me another four weeks. All the way, I told myself that Adomnan would get a message to Bleddyn and that my old friend and mentor would come to see me in the Springtime. I did not particularly like Adomnan but he was an abbot, a man of God, so I thought I could trust him.

As it turned out, no message ever got to Bleddyn. I had hoped that my threat of Northumbrian monks spreading through Fortriu might have jolted Adomnan into action. With the benefit of hindsight, I know now that it was a threat that did not really bother him at all. Adomnan may have been a churchman, but he was the sort who was willing to change his convictions in order to be on the winning side. In later years, he spent a lot of time visiting Northumbria. At some point he must have decided that the Ionian Church was doomed, so he decided to change his allegiance. He then spent many years converting the churches throughout Dal Riata and Ireland to the Roman way.

 I may be wrong, but I believe he had already made up his mind when I saw him that autumn. It was either that or he simply forgot to send my message, although I did not believe Adomnan was the sort of man to forget anything.

 Of course, I did not know any of that at the time, as it all lay in the future. For the present, I returned to Cala na Creige believing I had persuaded him to act in the best interests of his church and of Fortriu.

 I arrived at Ringan's home on a dull, mist-shrouded evening to find the family gathered round the fire, with Ringan's wife telling stories to the children, just the way my mother had done when I was young, when I would sit with Triduana and Giric, entranced by tales of heroes and monsters. As I came through the door, I signalled to her to continue, but the children leaped to their feet, rushing to me with their arms waving, all talking at once, babbling that the man had come.

 As I tried to calm them to make sense of what they were yelling, Ringan clapped his hands to silence them. Looking at me over their heads, he said, "Your friend was here. He had to return home, but he said you could go to him whenever you want. He said you are no longer banished."

It was typical of my recent luck that Bleddyn had at last come up the coast road while I was away. Annoyed that I had missed him, I decided that I would go home immediately, without waiting for winter to pass.

 "It's a bad time of year to travel," Ringan cautioned me. "You should wait until the Springtime."

"I cannot wait that long," I told him. "I have waited too long as it is."

"Will you come back?"

I shrugged. "Maybe one day. It depends what happens when I get home."

Ringan clasped my hand in an unusual display of affection. "There will always be a welcome for you here," he told me. "May God watch over you."

"And may your nets always be full," I replied.

The following day, I fastened my cloak around my shoulders, hefted my pack on my back and, after an emotional farewell, set off for the north.

Crossing the mountains, even with a well-trodden path to follow, is never easy and it was late in the year when I began my journey. Snow rarely troubled Cala na Creige, for it lies on low ground, close to the sea. If the villagers wanted snow to pack into clay jars as a way of keeping food fresh for several days, they usually had to climb up the hills for some distance. But I was soon on those upper slopes, and snow began to fall almost as soon as I had reached the high ground.

The path quickly vanished beneath a layer of soggy white. I slipped and slid my way, determined to get home as quickly as I could, whatever the weather. It was an awful journey but I was lucky. The snow soon turned to sleet and gradually to rain, which made the walking just as miserable but not nearly so dangerous. Day by day, chilled to the bone, I plodded northward through Fortriu towards home. At nights, I begged shelter wherever I could, sleeping in barns or cattle sheds, wrapped in my cloak against the bitter winter winds and the heavy frosts that coated the world white each morning. It was, without doubt, the worst journey I had ever undertaken, but I forced myself on, one step at a time, determined to reach home no matter what.

When my weary legs dragged me round the final corner and I turned into the trackway leading to my house, I noticed that there was no cloud of smoke lingering above the roof. Puzzled, I walked up to the door, knocked and went inside.

The main room was in darkness. Everything was neat and tidy, with a fire banked and ready for use, but the house was cold and empty. Checking the bedroom, I found it cold and unused. Frowning, I went back outside. When I looked beyond the yard, I saw the familiar figure of Entifidich striding towards me.

His weathered face cracked into a smile of greeting, which was about as excited as Entifidich ever got. He welcomed me home as if I had been away for only a few days.

"Why aren't you living in the house?" I asked.

"We kept it for you, like we said," he replied in his stolid, imperturbable way. "We knew you'd come back. Especially now everything is sorted. I'll get the fire lit for you."

I waved away his offer. "I need to speak to Bleddyn," I said. "Is he here?"

"Aye, you're just in time," he said. "He's heading off to Inbhir Nis for Christmas. He'll be along this way very shortly."

True enough, I soon saw the cart rumbling up the path from behind the trees, Bleddyn's bulky frame filling most of the driving seat, looking even larger than usual thanks to several layers if furs he had wrapped around himself. When he saw me, he called out my name in delight and urged the horse on, then hauled it to a hurried stop in the yard.

He scrambled down from the cart, arms opened wide to greet me.

"Praise the Lord!" he cried. "I thought I'd never find you and here you are, at home where you should be."

We embraced each other, slapping one another on the back as if to reassure ourselves that we were really together again. Eventually, I released him and took a step back.

"Is it true, Bleddyn? Has Bridei lifted my banishment?"

His face grew suddenly and alarmingly serious. "Yes, lad. It is true enough."

"What's wrong?" I asked. "What has happened?"

He put his large hand on my shoulder, the way he used to when I was younger and he wanted to steer me away from something he thought I should not see.

"Best come inside, lad. Then I can tell you the whole story."

He asked Entifidich to put away the cart and to stable the horse, then led me to the cold house. I could tell that something was wrong, that he was about to give me some bad news, but I could never have guessed just how bad it was going to be. When I heard it, I wished I had stayed in Cala na Creige and never returned.

He stood facing me, his hands on my shoulders, his eyes already misted with tears. In a low, immensely sad voice, he said, "There is no easy way to tell you this, Bili."

"Tell me what?"

"Derelei is dead."

Chapter 22

I did not want to believe him. My legs buckled so that he had to help me to a chair, then I told him he must be wrong, but he shook his head.

"She is dead, lad. I am truly sorry."

"How? How can she be dead?"

"It's a long story, lad. Let us have something to warm us and I will tell you the whole tale."

He found a flint which he used to strike some sparks to light the kindling. The house was bitterly cold but even an inferno would not have warmed me at that moment. I was numb and chilled, and my face was already streaked with tears.

Bleddyn stuck his head outside and called something to Entifidich. He turned back to me, saying, "I'll be back in a moment." Then he left me alone with my cold, empty thoughts in my cold, empty house.

My eyes were red with tears when he returned carrying a small jug of whisky. He poured me a drink which I drained in one go. He poured another, then one for himself which he, too, gulped down before tipping yet another measure into his cup. He sat down, placing the jug on the table between us. Then he began his tale.

I listened, my whole body feeling numb, only the burning fire of the fierce drink telling me that I was alive, while Bleddyn recounted what had happened.

"Derelei had another child," he told me. "That would be about nine months after you left. It was a boy. He was named Nechtan."

I could do nothing except take another drink. Boys were often named after their fathers, so the child's name was not unusual. Except that Bleddyn's words and his expression made it clear that old Nechtan was probably not the father. It seemed I had another son.

Bleddyn continued, "Then, last Christmas, a year and a day after you had left, Guret married Mayota. Bridei allowed him to return to live with his father, thinking that old Nechtan would not live forever and that Guret should be groomed to become the next chieftain."

"So Mayota and Derelei were in the same house?"

"In the same settlement, anyway."

"What happened?"

I was gripping the small beaker so tightly that I thought I might shatter it with my bare hands. The thought of Mayota being close to Derelei filled me with a sense of helpless dread.

Bleddyn shrugged. "Nothing happened. At least, not for a while. Everything settled down. Bridei was down that way a few times, of course, making sure the Scots were being kept well at bay. He told me he had seen Derelei and that she was well. Her sons were strong and healthy. Of course, she was deeply upset at what had happened to you and she kept on at him to lift his banishment but he could not, for the evidence against you was too strong."

He drummed his fingers on the table, thinking about what to say next. Then he said, "Bridei tells me that she explained the truth of that night to him. He knew you were innocent but still he could not say anything because to publicly announce your adultery would have ended his already fragile relationship with Nechtan."

I nodded. I had understood that from the start, but I could only imagine what it must have cost Derelei to tell her father the truth.

Bleddyn had the good grace not to comment on my sinning with Derelei. He said, "It was towards the end of summer that things changed. I was down in Fidach, searching for you, but I heard about it later. Nechtan was killed when he fell down a cliff while walking in the hills around his home."

"An accident?" I asked.

He shrugged. "So they say. He was with Guret. There were no other witnesses."

"Guret!" I suddenly remembered what I needed to tell Bleddyn. The shock of hearing about Derelei had driven it from my mind. "There is something you must know about him. He's a spy for Beornhaeth."

Bleddyn's eyes widened, but he waved a hand at me. "Let me finish. Then you can tell me your tale." He paused, gathering his thoughts, then went on, "Where was I? Oh yes, Nechtan's accident. Whatever happened, he was dead. Naturally, Guret was chosen as the head of the family and local chieftain."

Bleddyn gulped another mouthful of whisky before saying, "Derelei killed herself only a few days later. They say she took poison in her distress at the death of her husband."

I stared at him, incredulous. A brief surge of rage coursed through me but when I spoke, I was deathly calm, absolutely certain of what I knew.

"She would not do that," I said. "Derelei would never do that."

"There is more," Bleddyn said. "A few days earlier, Fincana claimed that she had dreamed she had seen you fighting a black hawk. The bird had picked you up in its talons then dropped you from a great height."

"She said I was dead?"

"Not in so many words, but everyone knows the black hawk is Beornhaeth's symbol, and a rumour had got out that you had gone to kill him."

"Mayota!" I breathed. "You think Derelei heard this story? That is why she killed herself?"

"I don't know," he admitted.

"I do. Even if she thought I was dead, she would never kill herself. She had her sons. Surely Bridei knows she would never abandon them."

Patiently, Bleddyn told me, "She was found alone in her room one morning. She had some fine powder which she had sprinkled on her supper. It could not have been an accident, Bili."

"What sort of powder?"

"I am no herbalist, Bili. I have no idea. Whatever it was, she took her own life. I am sorry."

"No!" I slammed my palm down on the table. "She would not do that! Not Derelei. There must be another explanation."

Remaining calm in the face of my outburst, he said, "Then I will be happy to hear it, but please let me finish. I am almost done. As I say, she took poison. Her body was brought to Inbhir Nis and she was buried near Abbot Ronan's church. Her two sons are now living with Bridei under the care of their nurse. After a while, Bridei made a public announcement that Derelei had explained to him that you could not have killed Uerb because you had been with her at the time. He said that she had assured him that nothing had happened between you, but that she had been afraid to speak up because of what people may think. He told everyone that, while there were rumours that you were dead, he felt it only right to remove the banishment and declare you innocent."

"And people believed that?"

Bleddyn shrugged. "Most people were not concerned either way. They thought you were dead because of Fincana's dream. There was some scurrilous talk, but it soon died down."

"So who do they think killed Uerb?"

"An unknown assailant. Remember, more than a year and a half had passed since his death. Nobody wanted to look into it again."

"Is there anything else?" I asked.

"No, that is the whole, sad story. Now you had better tell me yours."

I was cold with icy fury. I pushed Derelei's death to the back of my mind, something to grieve over later. The tale Bleddyn had told me was one I could not believe, so I tried to change his mind by telling him what I had learned.

I told him of the strange, one-eyed messenger who had visited Beornhaeth and how someone had not only known the names of Thingfrith and Toki, but also knew of my hatred for the Northumbrian lord and his son.

When I was done, Bleddyn rubbed his chin pensively.

He said, "You think Mayota overheard us and told Guret?"

"It's the only explanation that fits," I told him.

"So Guret is placing himself in Beornhaeth's good books. I can see why you think he might want to kill his father, although that is an extreme action even for someone like Guret. And why wait so long?"

"Because he is clever and patient. If Nechtan died just a few days, or even weeks, after Guret went home, it would be too suspicious. But there is more."

"More?"

I nodded. "Mayota visited Fincana frequently. What if she obtained some poison from her and used it to kill Derelei?"

Frowning, Bleddyn said, "I don't understand why she would do that, but I suppose it is possible."

"The why is easy. For revenge. Mayota knows how I feel about Derelei."

Bleddyn was silent for a while before draining his cup. He placed it on the table with the air of a man who had made a decision.

"We need to speak to Bridei," he said. "But his hall will be crowded. It is almost Christmas. Everyone will be there."

"All the more reason to go now," I said. "We can challenge them."

He shook his head. "I think this would be best done quietly." Holding up a hand to stifle my protest, he continued, "Patience, lad. Best not to rush in. Anyway, from the looks of you, you need to rest for a while. And to have a bath and get some fresh clothes." He wrinkled his nose. "You stink of fish."

So we stayed at my farm that Christmas. It was just as well, because I broke down completely the following evening. I had tried to control my emotions but it was no use fighting the hurt. My body was wracked with shivers and the tears would not stop. Hour after hour I thought of Derelei and how I would never see her again. I sobbed and I cried and I knew that, once again, God had deserted me when I needed him.

Bleddyn, of course, did not desert me, nor did he ever lose his faith.

"If wrongs have been done, the Lord shall wreak his vengeance on the wrong-doers," he told me gravely.

When I had cried myself dry and slept for many hours, I woke feeling cold and empty of every emotion except a desire for revenge. The dark road that Bridei had warned me about now stretched ahead of me quite clearly. Until then, I had avoided treading that route, but now I willingly took the first steps.

"If wrongs have been done," I told Bleddyn, "I shall exact my own revenge. An eye for an eye; a tooth for a tooth. Just as it says in the Bible."

"Bili Grim-Hand," he chided. "Beware of that trait, lad. It can lead to the damnation of your soul."

"My soul is already in torment," I told him.

Bleddyn shook his head, but the look in his eyes told me that he understood.

He was concerned for me, although he told me that he was glad I had grieved so much those first days, letting the pain out rather than storing it up. For myself, I did not care. Derelei was dead and I vowed to reveal the truth of her death. Nothing else mattered.

I think my grim sullenness probably spoiled the Christmas celebrations for most folk on the farm. We all went down to Bleddyn's new church on Christmas Day. He was very proud that the work had been completed. The walls of the tiny church were plastered white, the roof was of thick timbers and there was a wooden cross nailed to the wall above the door. Inside, there was room for around forty people to stand, with a small raised platform and an altar at the far end where Bleddyn stood to preach his sermons.

The place was packed that Christmas Day, with families coming from all the nearby farms to celebrate with us. We sang and we prayed. Everyone greeted me, saying how glad they were that I was home and that everything was settled. I smiled and I shook their hands, but I could find no joy in my heart.

Bleddyn and I ate with Entifidich and his family. It was not the regal fare we had enjoyed at Bridei's hall in the past, but Niamh had roasted a fat, young pig and baked a variety of scones and bannocks, so there was plenty for everyone. After the meal, there was some ragged music, singing and even some dancing, although it was the children who enjoyed it most. I sat wishing the time away, waiting for the day we could travel to Inbhir Nis to see Bridei.

There was some snow a few days later, deep enough to block the roads and trap some of the sheep who had to be dug out. That kept me busy for a while. When the snow had melted, Bleddyn at last agreed that it was time.

"Most of Bridei's guests will have returned home by now," he said. "We'll be able to meet him without too many people seeing us."

We travelled the road to Inbhir Nis on another wet, blustery day. On the way, Bleddyn told me that Abbot Ronan was arranging for a junior monk to assist at the new church.

"If he turns up while we are away, the poor lad will have to look after the place on his own for a while," he said. "Ah well, sink or swim."

I could not help smiling. Despite the seriousness of the situation, I think Bleddyn was looking forward to some adventure.

As Bleddyn had predicted, Bridei's hall was free of most guests. The majority of them had returned to their own homes after the Christmas celebrations, so the stockade had an empty feel about it, even though there were still dozens of servants, craftsmen and warriors in evidence.

Bridei met us in his private room where we sat round a small table. He was pleased to see me, but the hurt we shared over Derelei meant that he was rather subdued at first. But as Bleddyn and I outlined our story to him, he grew more and more intense, as if about to burst with anger. He tugged at his beard and his eyes flashed dangerously as he listened to our theories.

When we were finished, he said, "I need proof. I cannot simply accuse Guret of being a spy, or his wife of murdering my daughter, without having some evidence."

"Kings do not require evidence," I said.

Bridei shot me a dark look. "No," he said sharply, "but if I start executing people without any evidence of guilt, I will not remain king for very long. As it is, I am so close to building the army of Fortriu into a force that even Ecgfrith will have cause to fear, but I need the support of all the chieftains and I especially need the men of Dun Nechtan."

I said, "You have lost them already if Guret has turned traitor."

"I still need some proof before I can act against him. If I simply march in and kill him, the other chieftains will begin wondering who might be next to be disposed of."

"There is a simple way," Bleddyn said. "Let me go to Dun Nechtan. I will ask them to swear on the Bible that they had nothing to do with Derelei's death and that they are loyal to you."

"That would not work," I said. "Mayota has already lied once. She would do the same again."

"Guret would not dare," Bleddyn said. "A holy oath is not made lightly."

In a low voice, Bridei said, "If he killed his own father, who is to say what he might not dare? Anyway, if you accuse them we need to be certain that they would confess. All it would do is reveal that we suspect them, but are not able to prove anything. As I said, I need something I can show the other chieftains."

He sat very still, staring down at the floor, thinking deeply. When he looked back at us, he said, "We need to tell Taran. He is still here. I trust him."

"Even with this?" Bleddyn asked.

"Even with this."

A servant was sent to fetch Taran, who arrived a short time later, all dark-eyed and watchful. I had never really spoken to him, although I knew that he was a close friend of Bridei. He had been since the day old Drest had been deposed. I did not want anyone else knowing our secrets but Bridei told Taran almost the whole story. The only detail he missed out was that Derelei and I had been lovers. In that, the king stuck to his official version of events although Taran was not stupid. He shot me several glances while Bridei recounted the tale of what we suspected.

"So you need proof?" Taran asked when Bridei had told him everything. "That should be easy enough."

Bridei looked at him keenly. "Would you care to tell us how?"

Taran regaled us with a self-satisfied smile. "It's simple. All we need to do is find the one-eyed messenger."

Chapter 23

My first reaction was to demand to be allowed to go to Dun Nechtan, but even I knew that would be a bad idea. Guret and Mayota were hardly likely to co-operate with me at all, especially if I started asking questions about their servants and whether any of them happened to have lost an eye.

Bleddyn offered to go, but was forced to concede that Mayota was likely to distrust him almost as much as she hated me. Taran was willing to visit them but in the end, Bridei announced that he would go himself.

"I want to look in their eyes and see the truth for myself," he growled. "If Mayota killed my daughter, eternal damnation will be the least of her worries." He clicked his tongue in disappointment before adding, "The problem is that I can't go until after Easter. I always stay here between Christmas and Easter. If I make a trip like that without good reason, it might make them suspicious."

"Can we afford to wait that long?" I asked. I was eager to see Guret and Mayota punished. There was no doubt in my mind as to their guilt.

"Nothing much is likely to happen," Bridei said. "If Guret is in Dun Nechtan, he is not going to be able to tell Beornhaeth anything that is not common knowledge anyway."

"Assuming that Guret is indeed the spy," Taran pointed out.

"Of course he is," I responded. "Who else could it be?"

Taran fixed me with his dark, clever eyes. "It is always best not to be too hasty in making judgements, young man," he cautioned. "I dare say that Guret is the man we are seeking, but you mentioned Medraut and Donnell. They are close friends of his. I think we should visit their homes as well. I can do that, if only to be satisfied that they are not connected to this affair."

I was not sure that I trusted Taran. He was too sly, too smooth for my liking. I had a suspicion that he might be offering to do this because he had some hidden motive in mind. I tried to think of a reason to prevent him from visiting Medraut or Donnell but the only objection I could think of was to say, "I thought they both stayed here as part of the king's personal household?"

"So they do," Bridei agreed. "Most of the time. But they return home every now and then. It is unfair to keep young men from their families for too long."

Taran asked, "I suppose it is too much to hope that either of them has a one-eyed servant here with them?"

"If they do, he's been remarkably well hidden," Bridei said.

Taran nodded. "It was just a thought." Turning his attention to me once more, he asked, "Do you know which eye is missing? Or whether it is truly gone or merely sightless?"

"I don't know," I admitted. "I never thought to ask."

Taran said, "That is unfortunate. It may be that the man has lost the sight in one eye but that it looks perfectly normal. If that is the case, he may prove hard to find."

"It may be that he wears a patch of some sort over it," said Bleddyn. "In which case he will be easy to find."

Taran acknowledged that with the slightest nod of his head, as if he thought it unwise to rely on our quarry being so obliging. He regarded me with his cold, dark eyes. "Then do you know whether this messenger speaks English?" he asked me.

After a moment's thought I was forced to admit that I did not know. Taran was making me distinctly uncomfortable with his questions, which were making me feel very young and foolish.

"It seems more than likely that he speaks their language," he observed. "Unless Beornhaeth has an interpreter."

"He probably does," Bridei said. "He controls a lot of our people, so he has plenty to choose from."

It seemed to me that Taran was almost amused, as if this were some sort of children's game we were playing. He said, "So we are looking for a short, dark-haired man who may or may not speak English and who has only one eye, although we don't know which eye, nor whether we can tell simply from looking at him that the eye is gone."

"That sums it up neatly," said Bridei.

"Well, it is better than nothing," Taran observed. "You never know, we may find that Guret has a one-eyed servant who also speaks English. Although, of course, he need not necessarily be a servant either. Guret, Medraut and Donnell all come from families who govern large areas with many men owing them loyalty."

I had the distinct impression that Taran was putting up obstacles before we had even begun our search, but Bridei agreed that finding the messenger may not be as simple as we had first thought.

He ended the meeting by saying, "This is what we will do. Taran, you go and visit the homes of Medraut and Donnell. You know their fathers well enough so that it would not be unusual for you to call on them. Give old Drest my regards when you see him."

Taran nodded his agreement.

Bridei went on, "Assuming young Bili is correct and you don't find the man we are looking for, I will go to see Guret after Easter. As for the rest of it, no word of this passes beyond these walls. Only the four of us must know what we suspect. Be in no doubt that I cannot act unless we have proof. If word of our suspicions leaks out, then we may never find that proof."

I don't suppose it was a coincidence that he was looking at me when he said that.

"I don't trust Taran," I said to Bleddyn as we left the king's hall.

He seemed surprised. "Really? Why not?"

"He's too clever by half."

Bleddyn laughed. "Being clever is no sin," he said.

"What if Medraut is involved? What if his father is involved? He has reason to hate Bridei. Taran may be going to warn him."

Bleddyn shook his head. "Bridei trusts Taran, so that is good enough for me. Anyway, old Drest is an honourable man. He may have been deposed, but he would never use that as an excuse to harm Bridei. He is a loyal supporter of the king, whoever that king may be."

"Not like his son, then," I muttered. "He still harbours a grudge about it."

"Perhaps, but we have no real reason to doubt Medraut's loyalty at the moment. Just his involvement in Uerb's murder and his dislike of you."

"Now you sound like Taran," I accused.

"Does that mean you don't trust me either?" he asked with a laugh.

"You are twisting my words, Bleddyn," I protested.

"Well if a friend can do that, just think what an enemy could do if you rush in with accusations you cannot back up. Bridei is right about that. We must take our time over this."

"Until after Easter?"

"If necessary. At least that will give Taran plenty of time to visit Drest and Donnell's father."

"Drest lives up in Cait, doesn't he?"

"That's right."

"How far away?" I asked. "Could Medraut get there easily enough?"

"On horseback it would take him less than a day," Bleddyn said."If he went by sea, it would be even quicker. He could cross the Firth and sail up the coast easily enough."

"Not too far, then," I observed. "It would be easy enough for him to go there, arrange a messenger, then be back the following day."

"I thought you said Guret was the spy," Bleddyn said. "Are you accusing Medraut now?"

"I don't know," I admitted. "I just think they are all in it together. Look at Uerb's murder if you don't believe me."

"Aye, you may be right. Let us hope we can track down this mysterious messenger and discover the truth." He sighed. "But we must be patient, Bili. It will take some time for Taran to see both families."

"Where does Donnell's family stay?" I asked.

"Eilginn. It's off to the east, just a few hours' ride beyond our place."

"Donnell could get there and back in a day at a push," I said thoughtfully.

"Aye, he could," Bleddyn agreed.

I put a hand to my forehead, rubbing at it. "My head is spinning, Bleddyn. I just don't know what to think."

"Then you had best forget it for a while," he advised. "Now, I have to go to speak to Abbot Ronan about the young priest he is supposed to be sending to assist me. Do you want to come with me?"

"No thanks. I have some things I want to do." Seeing the look of concern he was giving me, I assured him, "I will be fine, Bleddyn."

"I'll see you later, then," he said. Leaning on his staff, he limped away, heading down to the Abbot's church.

I waited for a while, wondering where to go. There were three people I wanted to visit, but I could not decide who to go to first. The person I really wanted to see would be the most difficult, so I decided to put that off for a while and went down to the town. Most people I passed on the way paid no attention to me, although I received one or two hesitant looks from some. No doubt they recognised me and were not quite sure how to take me now that I had returned, either from banishment or, as Fincana had suggested, from death.

It was Fincana I wanted to see. I found her, as always, sitting on her little stool in her doorway, her shawl draped over her head. She was grinding some green stalks with a heavy, stone pestle, turning them into a grainy mush. She may have been busy but she always had one eye out for any potential customers and she saw me almost immediately. For an instant, her face registered a look of surprise before her usual, mocking expression quickly re-asserted itself.

"I did not expect to see you, Lord Bili," she croaked as I approached her. "What can I do for you today?"

"You can explain to me why you told everyone I was dead," I said brusquely.

"I did no such thing," she retorted. "I merely announced what I had seen in a dream. It is not up to me to decide how other people interpret such things."

I stood over her, my hands clenched into tight, angry fists. "Somebody put you up to it," I snarled. "Who was it?"

Still seated, she waved her pestle up at me. "Pah! You are talking nonsense, boy. I see what I see, I dream what I dream."

I felt my anger turn to frustration. My attempt to intimidate her had already failed but I persisted. "Was it Mayota? Did she persuade you to say it?"

"Now why should your . . . wife do something like that?" she asked.

Her sharp eyes were challenging me now. I could tell from her deliberate pause before referring to my wife that the old harridan knew something about my turbulent relationship with Mayota, but the only reason my former wife would want such a rumour circulated would be to make Derelei believe that I was dead. I could not admit that to Fincana. She may well have heard rumours, but if I confirmed that I had been Derelei's lover, the whole world would soon know about it. I had talked myself into a trap, just as Bleddyn had warned me I would if I rushed in. I was floundering and I knew it.

Weakly, I snapped, "Because she's an evil, cold-hearted bitch."

Fincana spat on the ground before looking up at me. She said, "Well, I'm glad you are saying that about her, and not about me, although I dare say you are thinking it. Am I right?"

"Don't play games with me, Fincana," I replied. "I want to know why you said what you did. People believed I was dead, but here I am, proving you wrong."

I emphasised the last word, hoping it would rile her into revealing something. Her reputation as a seer depended on her never being wrong.

Again she batted aside my attack. "I never said you were dead. Tell me, did you go to Dun Eidyn, the home of the black hawk?"

"I thought you knew everything?" I shot back at her.

"So you did go there," she chuckled. "And were you cast out? Did you have to flee for your life?"

She may have been guessing. I could not tell, but I knew I was utterly beaten. She was impervious to any accusation I threw at her. I stood there, fists clenching and unclenching in frustration. I did not know what else to do. I was tempted to ask her whether she had ever supplied Mayota with any poison, but that would have given away too much, so I had no option but to content myself with pointing a finger to her face and saying, "Stay out of my life, Fincana. Keep your dreams and your predictions to yourself. I want none of it."

She laughed at me, an evil, triumphant laugh that sent a chill down my spine.

"Such spirit from one so young and fresh-faced!" she said mockingly. Then her expression turned cold and her voice hissed at me. "Begone, boy! I will say what I say and you cannot prevent it. Better and wiser men than you have crossed Fincana in the past. They are all rotting in their graves, but I am still here. If you don't want the same to happen to you, I suggest you watch what you say.

Remember, it is you who has always sought me out, not the other way round. I warned you that there were plots against you, but you did not heed me. Is that my fault?" She waved a hand, ushering me away. "Begone before I curse you."

I had felt my ears and cheeks begin to flush when she had laughed at me but now the blood drained from my face. If she put the evil eye on me, I was doomed. Without another word, I spun on my heel and hurried away. I heard her laughter following me.

I felt like an idiot, a young, silly boy lost in a world of people who all seemed to know more than me and who were more experienced and capable. Bridei, Taran and Bleddyn all regarded me as the weakest member of our group, while Guret and Mayota, with the connivance of Medraut, had outwitted me easily. Now Fincana had brushed aside my attempts to discover whether there was any connection between her revelation about my death and what had happened to Derelei. Worse, I now ran the risk of her cursing me. I felt as if I was cursed already.

Feeling frustrated, lost and alone, I went in search of the one person who might have been able to help me. This was the visit I had put off because I knew how painful it would be. I found her outside the town, on a small, tree-shaded, grassy spot beside the river. She was there because she could not be buried in consecrated ground. She had taken her own life and the Church could not condone that.

It must have hurt Bridei to bring her here to this lonely spot, but it hurt me even more to see the small stone at the head of the grave, the image of a cross carved into it. There were letters on it, too, although I could not read them. Perhaps they spelled out her name. I do not know. I only knew that I loved her and she was gone. My Derelei.

I fell to my knees on the damp turf, knowing she was directly beneath me. Resting my forearms on the headstone, I laid my head on them and cried like a lost child.

I cannot say how long I knelt there. When my tears had run dry, I spoke to her, telling her that I knew she had not killed herself, promising that I would discover the truth. I think at one point I may have told her that I would soon be with her because life had nothing left for me without her. When I took my revenge on my enemies, there would be no more reason for me to live. I may have said that, but perhaps I only thought it, because saying it would have upset her and I did not want to do that. I felt that I had already hurt her enough by not being with her, by leaving her to face my enemies alone. She had died because of me. I was convinced of that.

    The sun was sinking low over the western hills by the time I hauled myself to my feet. I said goodbye to Derelei, promising her that I would come back, then I trudged up the hill to the king's hall. It was time for my final visit.

    I made my way round to the rear of the hall, passing the kitchens where I scrounged a hunk of cheese and a small cup of ale. Then I asked one of the girls to find Sorcha and tell her I wanted to see her.

    A little while later, I was led through the rear door, along the corridor I remembered so well from my last meeting with Derelei, then admitted to a small room furnished with two small beds, low tables and tiny chairs. There was a long, cushioned, but well-worn couch and the floor was scattered with small, wooden toys.

    Sorcha was there, her hair tied back and covered as it always was. She was a grown woman now, eighteen years old and very pretty, but her good looks were marred by her sad and mournful eyes. Behind her, watching me uncertainly were two small boys.

    Something caught in my throat when I looked at them. I had not seen young Bridei since he was a baby, yet now he was three years old, walking around, able to talk. His brother, Nechtan, was standing in the bow-legged way that young children often do, a little unsteady on his feet, gazing up at me with large, blue eyes.

    Sorcha turned to them. She spoke softly, her voice pitched high in a motherly way.

"Boys, this is Bili. He was a friend of your mother. Come and say hello."

She lifted little Nechtan who squirmed in her arms, trying to turn away from me. He began to cry, so I squatted down to my haunches, looking at Bridei who hid behind Sorcha's skirt from where he peered nervously at me. I stood up again, not sure what to do.

Sorcha gave me an apologetic look. "I am sorry. They are wary of strangers, Ever since . . ." She choked on the words, blinking away tears. "I am sorry," she repeated.

"I will come back later," I said. "I would like to talk to you."

She nodded, close to tears. "You can wait in the next room," she managed to say. "I will put them to bed soon."

She put Nechtan down, walked with me out into the narrow corridor and showed me to the next room. It was the bedroom where I had spent those last hours with Derelei.

Sorcha said, "The King allows me to stay here now. He has been very kind." She gestured towards the room's solitary chair. "I will be with you as soon as I can," she said.

I sat and waited. If I listened hard, I thought I could hear her through the wooden wall, speaking to Derelei's sons; to my sons. The sounds were faint but I was sure I could hear her. She spoke to them and she sang to them and although I could not make out her words, I know she was telling them stories to send them off to sleep.

I sat there, listening intently, imagining it was Derelei who was with them, as it should have been.

After a while, everything fell quiet. The only sounds were the usual background chatter of servants scurrying to and from the kitchens. From a distance, the beat of music started up, entertainment for the king's hall. Then the door opened and Sorcha came in.

I stood. To my surprise, she almost ran across the room towards me, her hands raised to her face as tears came in great sobs.

I put my arms around her, held her close, feeling her whole body trembling as she cried. "Oh, Bili," she sobbed. "She is gone."

"I know." I felt my own tears begin again. We stood there for a long time, sharing our loss and our anguish. Sorcha put her arms around me and we held each other in a tight embrace, trying in vain to console one another.

Eventually, the tears subsided. I sat on the chair while Sorcha perched on the side of the low bed. She looked down at the floor, her hands clasped tightly together as if she was fighting to control them.

"I am sorry," she said in a low whisper. "I have just been so alone and so frightened ever since . . ." She wiped another tear away with the back of her hand. ". . . ever since she died. There has been nobody I could talk to, nobody to share what I feel."

"Tell me what happened," I said. "I heard that she killed herself. I can't believe that is true."

She looked at me through red-rimmed eyes. "It is a lie," she said. "I know it is."

Chapter 24

"She was almost inconsolable when you were banished," Sorcha said as she dabbed at her eyes with the ends of her apron. "But you know what she was like. She was determined to find a way to help you. She wanted to tell the King, but she knew that would only cause more trouble. Old Nechtan was already unhappy. She used to tell me that he often talked of how much Bridei needed him and what a state the King would be in if it were not for Nechtan's support."

"I knew she could not say anything," I said. "We both understood what was at stake, although Guret had already guessed."

"I didn't know that," she said with some surprise. "Nechtan didn't know. I am sure of that."

"Guret and Mayota had their own plans," I told her.

Sorcha's eyes widened. "What do you mean?" she asked.

"I'll tell you later. Tell me about Derelei."

She said, "She knew you were innocent, so she began asking people questions, trying to discover what had really happened when Uerb died. She spoke to Medraut. He got very angry with her. He swore that he had told the truth."

"He would."

"Derelei said she believed him. She told me that she thought he was sincere."

"He's sincerely deranged," I commented bitterly. "Did she speak to anyone else?"

"She talked to Donnell. She liked him. He is not like the others at all. I think he is a little afraid of Medraut and Guret."

"I bet he still backed them up, though," I said.

Sorcha shrugged. "He knew nothing about it. He wasn't with Medraut and Guret when they went looking for

Uerb. The first he knew of it was when they carried the body into the hall."

I nodded. I remembered seeing Medraut and Guret outside the hall just after Uerb and I had our argument. Donnell had spoken to me but he had not been with the others when I had last seen them.

Sorcha continued, "She even spoke to Mayota. That did not go well. They argued, so she learned nothing except that Mayota had wanted you dead because she wanted to marry Guret straight away. She was annoyed at having to wait for a year and a day."

"That must have inconvenienced her," I said.

"She was patient enough," Sorcha continued. "Derelei was unable to learn anything else because we returned to Dun Nechtan shortly after Christmas. She never gave up hope, but there was very little she could do. The next year, after Guret married Mayota, they came to live there as well."

"That must have been difficult."

"Actually, it was better than I had expected. A whole year had passed by then. Mayota came to Derelei and apologised for any misunderstanding. She was very pleasant and she always tried to help by looking after little Bridei when Derelei was busy with the baby." She gave me a weak smile when she saw the look on my face. She said, "Yes, Derelei was certain that little Nechtan is your son."

"I didn't even know about him," I told her. "But as for Mayota, I am having trouble imagining her playing with little children."

"Oh, she was always doing that. She said she loved children and was sorry she had not had any of her own."

"That's a lie," I said. "She used to visit Fincana to get some potion or powder that would stop her falling pregnant."

Sorcha looked at me in surprise. "Why would she lie about something like that?" she asked.

I shrugged. "I don't know. Maybe to get close to Derelei? To allay her suspicions?"

"Perhaps. I can't say why, but I know what she said. Then one day Nechtan and Guret went out for a walk. They often did that, just wandering around, speaking to the farmers, looking over the land. Sometimes they took horses, sometimes they went on foot."

"And Nechtan fell?"

She nodded. "Guret came rushing back to the farm. He was very upset. He took some of the men back to bring in the body. He said Nechtan had tripped while they were walking along the top of a steep drop. He only fell about twenty feet, but he hit his head on a rock when he landed and it killed him."

"But only Guret saw it? Nobody else was there?"

"Only Guret was with him," she confirmed.

"So it might not have been an accident? Guret could have pushed him."

Sorcha blinked. Her mouth opened in a silent gasp. She was a trusting soul and I could tell that she had never considered that Nechtan's death might be anything other than an accident. Shocked by the revelation, she put a hand to her mouth. When she spoke, something inside her seemed to have changed, as if a spark had been lit. Her eyes lost their dull sheen and her whole body tensed. Then she hesitated, slumping back slightly and shaking her head.

"I suppose he could have pushed him," she said, "but there is no way to discover the truth. There was nobody else to see it. All I know is that Guret seemed very upset."

Despite the seriousness of the situation, I smiled at Sorcha's innocence. "What about Derelei?" I asked. "Was she upset?"

"No." A hint of the fire inside her reappeared as she became more animated. "She put on a show in public, of course. She was good at that. Well, you know that better than anyone. But privately she was looking forward to returning to Inbhir Nis. She knew that Guret was obliged to look after her, but she was happy to leave Dun Nechtan. She thought if she was here she would be able to persuade her father to recall you. She said it might take some time, but she was sure she could do it."

"Was that when she heard about Fincana's prophecy that I was dead?"

Sorcha nodded. "She heard it. Mayota told her."

"I'll bet she enjoyed doing that."

Sorcha said, "Derelei did not believe it. Well, she did at first, but she persuaded herself that it could not be true. She did not want to believe it."

"So she would not have killed herself over the news?" I asked.

"No," Sorcha replied. "I know that she would never have done that."

"So what happened?"

I thought she was about to burst into more tears, but the spark in her gave her the strength to speak. "I went into her room one morning and she was lying on the floor, beside her table. I knew she was dead. She was so pale and so cold." She gave me an apologetic look. "I screamed. I don't remember much about what happened after that, but the room soon filled with people. They found a small piece of linen on the table, beside her plate. She had asked for a late supper, you see. They said there were some small bits of finely chopped mushroom still on the linen. She must have sprinkled them onto her supper."

"Mushrooms?"

She nodded. "One of the old cooks said it was probably Death Cap or Destroying Angel. It was no accident. She had done it deliberately. She had left the linen to show us."

I closed my eyes for a few moments, trying to visualise the awful scene. When I opened them, I said, "You told me she did not kill herself. How do you know?"

She gave a small shake of her head before fixing me with her large, tear-filled eyes. "I just know. She was too happy. She could not wait to get back here, to get your banishment overturned. She wanted nothing more than to be with you. I know she would not have killed herself. Even if she did believe you were dead, she had her sons. She would never have left them."

"So how do you explain the poison?"

"I can't," Sorcha admitted miserably.

"Did you say anything to the King?"

She gave me a look of alarm. "What could I say? I am just a poor servant. I could not speak to the King."

"I can," I said. I was tempted to drag her off to find Bridei but I took some time to reflect. Taran may have been devious and manipulative, but he had taught me something. I decided to ask Sorcha some more searching questions.

"Did you see the piece of linen?"

"Yes," she replied. "It was right beside her plate."

"Had you ever seen it before?"

"No."

"Had Derelei ever mentioned having poison in her possession?"

She shook her head emphatically. "Never."

I tried another tack. "Who took Derelei's supper to her," I asked.

"I did."

I sagged, putting a hand to my forehead, kneading my brow with my fingertips. I knew Derelei could not have killed herself, and Sorcha had confirmed it, yet neither of us could explain the circumstances of her apparent suicide. I wondered what Taran would have asked next. Leaning forwards, I took Sorcha's hands in mine and looked into her eyes.

"We must find the truth, Sorcha. I want you to think as hard as you can about that night. Did you make the supper yourself?"

If she had said yes, my theory would have been crushed but she answered, "No. One of the cooks did."

"And you collected it from the cook?"

She thought for a moment, then her face went pale. "No," she said in a horrified whisper. "Guret had asked for something too. When I got to the kitchen, Mayota was there. It was her who handed me Derelei's plate."

I took Sorcha to see Bleddyn and made her repeat the story. He agreed that we should tell Bridei, but he gave us a warning. "This is not proof, I'm afraid. All Mayota has to do is deny all knowledge of any poison. It does not explain how the package of poison came to be on Derelei's table."

"It's obvious!" I exclaimed. "Mayota waited until Derelei had eaten her meal, then went into the room and left the package there to make it look like suicide."

"You cannot prove that!" Bleddyn shot back at me. "If we haul Mayota before the King and accuse her of this, she will simply deny it. Even making her swear on the Bible will not help. She has lied before and would do so again. How could Bridei find her guilty if she did that? It would be her word against Sorcha."

Sorcha took my hand, squeezing it gently. "I do not want to stand before the King to accuse that woman," she said nervously. "Do you really think that she and Guret planned all this?"

"Yes," I told her. "It is the only explanation."

"Not necessarily," cautioned Bleddyn. "But it does explain why Guret did not inform his father about you and Derelei. He did not want a rift between Nechtan and Bridei; he just wanted to remove his father and take over without any fuss."

"And Mayota wanted Derelei killed out of spite," I added.

Sorcha gasped, "That's horrible!"

"They are not nice people," I told her.

"What can we do about it?" she asked, still struggling to grasp the immensity of the crimes.

"We will tell Bridei," Bleddyn said. "But I must warn you that there is little he can do. This adds to our suspicions, but that is all."

I was angry, but there was nothing I could do. We went to Bridei to tell him Sorcha's tale, but although his eyes burned with an intensity I had rarely seen, he agreed with Bleddyn.

"We must wait," he decreed.

So we waited.

The next day, I said farewell to Sorcha, promising her I would not give up the search for the truth about Derelei's death. She took my hands, kissing them gently.

"Thank you," she said.

"Take care of my sons," I told her.

"I will."

Bleddyn and I returned to our farm, accompanied by a monk called Aed, the Abbot's choice to assist Bleddyn in his new church. Aed was about my age, although he looked older, his face creased around the eyes by years of straining to read in poor light, and his head already showed signs of balding. He was rather in awe of Bleddyn, so I enjoyed showing off my easy relationship with my old friend.

In turn, Bleddyn acted all grim and serious, so by the time we reached home I was feeling quite sorry for poor Aed. He must have wondered what he had let himself in for.

We settled into a routine again. I lived in the house on my own, although Bleddyn often visited in the evenings. Sometimes he would bring Aed, who would sit, bemused and unsure of himself, listening in silence while Bleddyn and I swapped stories. During the days, the two of them visited all the local settlements, encouraging people to come to their church each Sunday.

Because I was nominally a chieftain, I made a point of attending every service. I was surprised to find that the church was usually crowded. It was also a surprise that many of the people seemed to regard me as the leader of more than just Entifidich and his family; everyone from the nearby farms spoke to me very politely and some came to me with minor grievances or with news of disputes with their neighbours over boundaries or over cattle that had mysteriously wandered onto someone else's land.

At first, I tried to protest that these were not matters for me to decide but they would look at me with stolid, patient expressions and insist that it was my duty to act as their chieftain. I did my best, although I felt far too young to bear the responsibility they were thrusting on me. Bleddyn assured me that I was the only one who was worrying about it.

"They have accepted you, lad," he said.
"But I don't know how to be a chieftain," I protested.
"You'll learn," he chuckled.
"Thanks for your support," I said.

He claimed to be a man of God but sometimes I think that Bleddyn Grim-Hand was still there, trying to get out.

I never did quite get used to playing the part of a chieftain, but my initial introduction to the duties lasted only a few weeks because Taran arrived on my farm, riding a dark horse and accompanied by half a dozen of his warriors. It was a typically wet, blustery winter's day, so I went to welcome him and invited him to join me for a meal.

He waved the invitation away. "You must come to Inbhir Nis," he said. "I have found our man."

As Bleddyn and I rode to Inbhir Nis with Taran, I asked where he had found the one-eyed messenger and what had happened to him. He scowled, hissing at me to keep quiet.

"It can wait until we meet Bridei," he said.

I fell into an embarrassed silence. Once again, he had made me feel young and foolish. The only people who could possibly have heard were his own warriors, but Taran was seemingly determined to heed Bridei's warnings of secrecy.

We hurried to the king's hall. My mind was racing. Taran's discovery meant that either Medraut or Donnell was definitely involved in the plot. I was sure it was Medraut because of his involvement in Uerb's murder, but when we reached Inbhir Nis and met Bridei in his private chamber, Taran immediately said, "It is Donnell."

Even Bridei looked surprised at that. "Donnell? Are you sure?"

"As sure as I can be," Taran replied. "I had no luck at Drest's home, though I stayed for a couple of weeks and even went riding out with him, visiting some of the nearer farms and villages. I saw nobody matching the description of the one-eyed messenger, so I went out to old Enfret's place at Eilginn. I had barely arrived when a short, dark-haired man came to take my horse. His left eye is blind, nothing but milky white."

We all looked at one another. Bursting with excitement, I asked, "What did you do?"

Taran replied, "Nothing. I chatted to Enfret, stayed the night, then came back to find you."

Bridei asked, "Do you think Enfret is involved?"

Taran shrugged one shoulder. "I don't think so, but I could hardly come out and ask him outright. I steered the conversation towards Beornhaeth a couple of times, but he said very little. He didn't seem to know or care much about the Northumbrians."

"Perhaps that was deliberate," Bleddyn suggested. "He may have been trying to conceal his connection to Beornhaeth."

"Maybe," Taran acknowledged, "but I don't think Enfret is that good an actor."

Bridei snorted. "He's a good man, but he's too wrapped up in his cattle and his land to worry much about anything else. I expect he bored you rigid with his talk of crop yields and the number of lambs he expects this year."

Taran's thin lips twitched in what, for him, passed as a smile. "Yes, he did mention those things."

"So what do we do now?" I asked.

Bridei closed his eyes, obviously deep in thought. He stretched his neck and took several deep breaths. Then he sighed.

"I will visit Enfret myself and I will question this one-eyed groom. I will get the truth from him."

"Do you want me to come with you?" asked Taran.

"Aye, that would be a good idea. You too, Bili, if you wish." He looked sharply at Bleddyn. "Not you, though, my friend. You are a man of God, and I doubt that you would wish to be present when I question the man."

Bleddyn shrugged. "I shall pray for his soul," he said. "As long as you get the answers."

Chapter 25

Enfret was a tall, lean man, with greying hair and a bulbous nose. He was nothing like Donnell, either in looks or in manner. Unlike his son, Enfret was voluble and opinionated, although his opinions seemed to be mostly confined to the vagaries of the weather and its impact on his crops and livestock. However. he lost something of his garrulousness when Bridei demanded to speak to him in private. Enfret's small, fussy wife was not happy at being excluded, but when Bridei pointedly asked her to leave, she reluctantly went out, saying she had some flour to be ground.

As soon as she was gone, leaving Enfret alone with Bridei, Taran and me, Bridei ushered me forwards.

"This is Bili," he said to Enfret. "He does important work for me. Gathering information, carrying messages and the like."

Enfret gave me a polite but rather puzzled nod as Bridei continued, "He was in Dun Eidyn for me a while back, but he ran into some trouble."

I kept my face impassive. I had actually been in Dun Eidyn on my own account, but Enfret did not know that.

"I am sorry to hear that," Enfret said. "What sort of trouble?"

"A messenger arrived at Beornhaeth's hall. He took word that Bili was there to kill Beornhaeth. It was a lie but, naturally, it did not go down well with the Angles. Bili was lucky to escape with his life."

Enfret was looking more and more perplexed but it must have dawned on him that something was not right. "Why are you telling me this?" he asked.

Bridei's voice grew hard. "The messenger was a short, dark-haired man with one eye. You have such a man in your service, I believe?"

Enfret paled. He swallowed nervously before answering, "Mochtar. He's a groom. He takes care of our horses."

Bridei stared at him. Enfret was half a head taller than the King, but Bridei seemed to dominate the room like a giant. In a low, hoarse voice he said, "I am going to speak to this Mochtar, but before I do, I will ask you. Do you know anything about this? Have you sent your man to Beornhaeth with messages that were intended to harm me or the people of the Pecht? I advise you to think carefully before you answer."

Enfret shook his head vigorously. "Never! I swear it. On my life."

Bridei nodded. "Then I believe you. Now, let us go and find this Mochtar. Do you have anywhere we can speak to him undisturbed?"

Enfret gestured around the circular house, still puzzled. "I can summon him here."

"Not here. Too many people could overhear."

Taran answered Enfret's confusion by explaining, "We don't want anyone to hear his screams."

Mochtar did scream.

I will never forget the cries of anguish and pain he uttered as Bridei extracted the answers to his questions.

Enfret had taken us down to the stables which stood at some distance from the other buildings. He had dismissed everyone there, telling them to take the horses away until he called them back. Only Mochtar was ordered to stay behind.

He was just as Taran had described him, except that he was older than I had expected, perhaps in his fifties. He wore old, shabby clothes, streaked with straw, and he smelled of horses. After a while, he smelled of blood.

He had denied everything at first, but Bridei had advanced on him, threatening him, and Taran had pinned the man's arms. He was thrown against a wall and Bridei had hit him, hard, several times. Then the King had drawn his dagger. Still Mochtar pleaded innocence.

I was beginning to think that we had the wrong man, but Taran snapped an order to Enfret, asking where Mochtar's belongings were kept. The two of them went off while Bridei stood over Mochtar, telling him what he was about to do to him if he did not tell the truth.

"I am telling the truth, Lord!" the groom wailed miserably. He was on his knees, hands clasped together, blood dripping from his nose where Bridei had punched him.

Bridei said, "If you are, then I will pay redress for what I have done. If you are not, you will beg for death before I am done with you."

I had never seen Bridei in such a determined mood. As our king, he was shrewd, calculating and clever. He could persuade and manipulate people to do what he wanted, he could be generous and kind, firm when necessary, but never cruel. Now, I saw that he could be implacably cruel when the need arose.

"I am not playing games," he told the whimpering Mochtar. "I will do whatever I must to get the truth from you. I suggest you make it easier on yourself by telling me now."

I could see the fear in Mochtar's eyes, but the groom only shook his head, protesting his innocence.

Taran and Enfret returned. Donnell's father was looking paler than ever. Taran walked calmly over to Mochtar then opened his hand to reveal a small purse. He untied the cords, tipping some of the contents into his left palm.

"Is this yours?" he asked.

Mochtar shook his head. "No."

"Then why was it concealed in your bedding?" Taran demanded.

Lowering his eyes, Mochtar said nothing.

Taran showed the contents of the purse to Bridei, who nodded grimly. Then Taran held out his hand for me to see.

There were pieces of silver, chopped from old rings or brooches, mixed with dark pieces of a black stone that I had seen before. I picked one of these from Taran's palm, holding it up to examine it. I said, "This is jet."

Taran nodded. "Which comes from Northumbria." He knelt to empty the contents of the purse onto the ground. He picked up a golden coin.

"That is unusual," he observed.

Bridei took the coin, turning it in his fingers. "It's a Merovingian tremissa. The Franks make them." He turned to Mochtar. "Where did you get this?" he demanded.

Mochtar knelt, blood from his nose dripping to the ground in front of him. He remained silent.

I picked up another coin, a silver one. I had seen its like before. It was a silver penny, sometimes called a sceat. They were minted by the Angles and the Saxons, but sceattas were rare enough in Northumbria, and few among the Pecht would ever have seen them, let alone have a purse full of them.

"He could only have got such riches from one place," I informed Bridei.

We knew we had our man. Bridei exchanged a look with Enfret, who nodded grimly. There was no doubt about Mochtar's guilt.

"Perhaps you should leave," Bridei suggested to Enfret.

"I will stay," Donnell's father replied, his face pale with shock and disappointment.

Mochtar told us the truth eventually. Bridei broke several of his bones and cut away some of his fingers while Taran held him down. I watched, sickened but unable to look away. By the time his ears had been hacked off, the one-eyed groom named Donnell as the person who had sent him to Dun Eidyn several times over the past few years, bearing information to be passed to Beornhaeth.

"Who else is involved?" Bridei demanded.

"Nobody." Mochtar groaned weakly.

"Did Guret of Dun Nechtan ever ask you to take information?"

"No."

"What about Medraut, son of Drest?"

"No. There was nobody else. Only Donnell."

I believed him. He would have told us if Guret or Medraut were involved.

"Very well. Then tell me what Beornhaeth knows," Bridei commanded.

Mochtar screamed and talked, telling us that Beornhaeth knew how many ships Bridei was building, how many men he could raise for war and where his main supplies of food would be stored. It seemed that Mochtar had been carrying messages to the Northumbrian lord for several years.

Taran said, "Donnell must have been quite young when he began sending secrets."

"How was it done?" Bridei asked the blood-spattered groom.

Mochtar moaned feebly, barely able to speak. When Bridei held his knife over another of his fingers, he whimpered, "Master Donnell would give me a ring which would guarantee safe passage."

"You took information to Beornhaeth?"

"Yes."

"And he paid you with a bag of coins or jewellery as a reward?"

Mochtar nodded weakly. "Yes."

"It would also be an incentive for the betrayal to continue," observed Taran.

Bridei nodded. He said, "I presume Donnell gave some of the trinkets to you?" he asked Mochtar. "He was very generous."

Mochtar was silent for a long moment, but he eventually admitted that he had been unable to resist the temptation to help himself to some of the silver coins without

Donnell's knowledge. Once, he had even dared to slip the golden tremissa into his own belt pouch.

"No honour among thieves," Taran said disgustedly.

Mochtar was a bloody mess by this time. I wondered what he thought he could ever do with coins of gold and silver except hide them away in secret. His greed had been his undoing.

Turning away from the bloody mess of Mochtar's ruined body, Bridei turned on Enfret. "Did you suspect nothing?"

Enfret shook his head miserably. "Mochtar taught Donnell to ride when he was just a boy. They have always been close. Sometimes Donnell would ask if Mochtar could join him in Inbhir Nis for a few weeks. I did not know he went any further than that."

"They both went a lot further than that," Bridei growled. "Both in miles and in deeds."

Enfret nodded sadly. For the first time, he walked over to where Mochtar lay sprawled on the ground in a pool of his own blood. Enfret looked down at him.

"You betrayed my trust in you," he said.

Mochtar groaned weakly, blood frothing from his mouth. Enfret held out a hand to Bridei, silently asking for the dagger. When Bridei passed it to him, Enfret knelt beside the mangled body of his groom.

Mochtar would have bled to death soon enough anyway, but Enfret made his passing quick.

The old chieftain stood, handing the dagger back to Bridei. "I will come to Inbhir Nis with you," he said softly. "Donnell is my son. I must see him confess his guilt."

Our return to Inbhir Nis must have caused a stir, because Mochtar's blood still stained Bridei's and Taran's clothing. Bridei, though, was in no mood to be questioned. He stormed into his hall, demanding that it be cleared, scattering the attendants with his angry shouting. Then he sent four of his warriors to find Donnell and to bring him to the hall.

Bleddyn scurried in to join us. He did not ask any questions. He merely looked at Bridei's thunderous expression, saw Enfret, then nodded his head in understanding.

Bridei sat on his chair while the rest of us stood beside him, facing the doors at the far end of the hall.

We did not have long to wait. Donnell walked in quite calmly, the four soldiers in close attendance. Behind them came Medraut. He had not been invited, but Bridei simply stared at him for a moment then ignored him. Medraut moved to one side of the hall while Bridei turned his attention to Donnell.

Donnell looked at Enfret. "Father? What on earth are you doing here?"

Enfret looked to Bridei. The King jabbed an angry finger at the four guards and at Medraut.

"Bear witness!" he barked.

Donnell still appeared remarkably calm, as if he thought we were playing some sort of joke on him.

"What is going on?" he asked.

Bridei leaned forwards, his elbows resting on the arms of his chair.

"I have spoken to Mochtar," he said in a tone as chilly as ice. "We found the silver he had been paid. We also found some coins from the south that he had taken without your knowledge. He told us what he had done at your bidding."

I expected Donnell to panic, to fall on his knees or even try to run. He did none of those things. The iron promise in Bridei's voice was enough to frighten me, yet Donnell merely stood, saying nothing.

Bridei ordered the guards, "Search him. Empty his pouches. He will have a ring hidden somewhere."

Before the guards could move, Donnell held up a hand. He reached into his belt pouch, felt around, then removed a large, silver ring.

"This will be what you are looking for," he said. He handed it to one of the warriors who passed it to Bridei.

Bridei studied the ring, then gave it to Taran who passed it on to Enfret. The old man's face grew pale and stern when he looked at it. He handed it to Bleddyn who, in turn, passed it to me. The ring had a broad band of silver, wide enough to fit a man's finger, and a flat, circular top on which was etched the image of a black hawk's head.

Bridei asked Donnell, "You admit it then? You have passed information to the Northumbrians?"

"There is little point in denying it," Donnell replied calmly. "You have Mochtar's confession and you have the ring."

"Why did you do it?"

Donnell actually smiled as he said, "At first, it was to save my neck. After that, I did it for the money."

"Explain," Bridei snapped impatiently.

Donnell said, "It was after the Battle of the Two Rivers. We were all there." He looked over his shoulder to Medraut. "You remember?"

Medraut's eyes were hard, regarding Donnell with disgust. "I remember," he replied. "We were fifteen years old. It was our first battle."

Donnell nodded. "And our last, I hope. We ran, scattering into the trees, but I did not escape. I was caught. I thought they were going to kill me but they let me live. I think they saw from my clothes that I was the son of a chieftain."

"I searched for you!" Medraut interrupted. "I nearly got caught myself when I went back to look for you."

Donnell ignored him. He went on, "The day after the battle, Beornhaeth came round inspecting all the prisoners. I took a chance. He had someone with him who spoke our language, so when he passed me, I spoke up and offered to help him." Donnell shrugged. "When he heard that I was a friend of the king's son, he accepted. He even gave me the ring so that I could send messages by someone else. Then he let me go."

"You snivelling little bastard!" yelled Medraut. He made for Donnell but Bridei shouted at him to stop. Glaring venomously at his former friend, Medraut snarled. "You said you had been hiding. I remember being so happy when we found you. And all the time you were planning to use me to betray us all!"

Bridei waved Medraut to silence. To Donnell he said, "You did not need to do anything. You could have simply kept the ring and done nothing."

Donnell gave another dismissive shrug. "It was fun. I was young, and it seemed exciting. Besides, I thought the Angles might well come north and conquer us. I didn't want Beornhaeth to come across me if I had disobeyed him. So I sent Mochtar. After the first time, when he came back with a bag of silver, I decided to carry on." With a disdainful look at Medraut, he added, "People are so easy to fool."

"Tell me about Guret," Bridei said suddenly.

"Guret is an ambitious fool," Donnell replied.

"Did he help you?"

"Only unwittingly. Like I say, people are easy to fool. Ask the right questions, make the right prompts and they will tell you whatever you want to know. Not that Guret ever said very much that was sensible, but I knew he would be an important man one day, so I decided to keep in with him."

Then Bridei asked the question I had been waiting for. "What about Uerb's murder?"

Donnell remained quite relaxed. He looked at me calmly, then said, "Uerb annoyed me. The fat idiot was always hanging around me. He was a nobody. Also, he wanted Bili's woman, Mayota, but Guret also had his eye on her." He grinned. "Well, more than his eye, actually. Guret always liked his women well-endowed, and she certainly was. When he discovered she was willing, he wanted a way to get rid of Bili."

Bleddyn placed his meaty hand on my arm, squeezing it to warn me to remain silent.

Bridei asked Donnell, "So who killed Uerb?"

"I did," Donnell admitted casually. "It was easy enough to arrange. Uerb was drunk and needed little encouragement to chase after Mayota. As arranged, she ran to Bili, who had the argument, then I slipped out after Uerb had gone outside. I made sure Bili was out of everyone's sight, then I found Uerb and led him somewhere quiet. All I needed to do after that was wait for Guret to come along as a witness before I stabbed him. I'd already taken Bili's dagger from his house."

Medraut's temper snapped again. "I'll kill you!" he roared.

Again, Bridei bellowed for Medraut to desist. When Medraut had sulkily backed down, Bridei asked Donnell, "So Guret and Mayota were involved in Uerb's murder?"

Donnell gave every impression of being pleased with himself. "Well, they helped me set it up, but I am not sure they believed I would go through with it." He smiled. "But once Uerb was dead, they had no choice except to play along. It meant that I got rid of Uerb and, more importantly, that they owed me a very big favour."

Bridei took a deep breath, his brooding eyes never leaving Donnell's face. His voice dropped to little more than a whisper as he asked, "What about my daughter?"

For the first time, Donnell's expression of calm amusement changed. He frowned. "What about her?" he asked.

"Do you know anything about her death?"

"No. Only what I heard."

I understood how Medraut felt. I wanted to rage at Donnell, to accuse him of lying, but he had answered every other question so coolly that I knew he would not have been able to resist admitting to helping kill Derelei if he had been involved.

Bridei did not pursue the question. Instead, he asked, "So you acted alone in everything except the murder of Uerb?"

"Yes. There are few people I would trust enough to have got them involved."

"And you killed Uerb to place Guret in your debt?"

"And because the fat pig annoyed me," Donnell agreed.

"So why did you warn Beornhaeth that Bili was intending to kill him? How did you get the names of Bili's contacts in Dun Eidyn?"

"I did it because Guret and Mayota wanted Bili dead. Our first attempt had failed and I thought it would be fun to get Beornhaeth to finish our work for us. Mochtar was due to go south anyway. As for the names, I told you, people will tell you whatever you want if you encourage them properly. All I had to do was casually ask Mayota if she knew where Bili would go when he was exiled. She told me everything I needed to know."

We had it all now. At least, we had all that Donnell could tell us. Bridei looked at Enfret who had stood, marble-faced throughout the interrogation. The only sign of emotion was a throbbing vein at his temple.

The King said, "I cannot allow Donnell to remain free. Beornhaeth must not know that we have discovered his spy." After a short pause, he added, "And you know the penalty I must pronounce for the murder of Uerb."

Enfret nodded. "I will take him to Am Broch. He will not betray anyone again. I will make sure of that."

Bridei nodded. He turned to Medraut and the four warriors who still stood watch over Donnell. He said, "You are all sworn to secrecy. If any word of this gets out, I will know who to blame. One whisper of it and all of you will find yourselves chained to the benches of one of my warships for the rest of your lives."

The five men nodded grimly. They could not be in any doubt that Bridei was deadly serious.

He said to them, "Escort Enfret and his son to Am Broch. See that this matter is ended."

Medraut growled, "It will be a pleasure."

Enfret inclined his head to Bridei, then walked stiffly down the hall to the doors. He did not look at his son, nor did Donnell give him any more than a fleeting glance.

The soldiers grabbed Donnell's arms, wheeling him away. He went without protest, still unnaturally calm. Medraut followed, anger radiating from his every move. Like an act of finality, the doors closed behind him, leaving the hall in silence.

When Bridei did not speak, Taran said softly, "I thought we would have to wring it from him. At least he made it easy for us."

Bleddyn said, "Satan must have conquered his soul. I have never seen a man so calm, so unfeeling about what he has done."

"I have," said Bridei, his voice sounding weary. "In times of war, men like that are invaluable. They will kill without a moment's thought. It will never bother their conscience. For them, killing is an act as natural as eating. In times of peace, they are a danger to all around them."

Taran asked, "Do you think Enfret will truly do what needs done?"

"If he doesn't, Medraut will do it," Bridei replied. "One way or another, Donnell will not trouble us again."

Bleddyn sighed, "That will be hard for the old man. Donnell was the only one of his sons to survive infancy."

Bridei's face was hard as he said, "Hard or not, it must be done."

I could not restrain myself any longer. "What about Guret and Mayota? You heard what he said. They helped kill Uerb."

Taran nodded. "Do you want me to bring them here?" he asked Bridei.

Bridei rubbed his chin. After a few moments, he said, "No. We do not have enough."

"They killed Uerb!" I shouted.

Bridei silenced me with an awful stare. "It is not enough!" He snapped at me. "They did not wield the dagger that killed him. They can claim that they did not know he was going to die. They did not help Donnell give information to Beornhaeth, except through speaking out of turn."

Bleddyn stirred. He said, "It is enough for you to pass some sentence on them. Uerb would still be alive if it were not for them. Justice has not yet been done."

Bridei shook his head. "Uerb's killer has been found. Justice will be done. But my daughter is dead. I want the truth of her death to be known. What we have heard is not enough. I still need Guret's support, so I cannot move against them unless we have more. At best, I could sentence them to paying some recompense to Uerb's family. I will not accuse them of involvement in one crime when there is a greater one I need to punish."

"So what do we do next?" I demanded.

Bridei sat back in his chair. For the first time in three days, I saw a faint smile on his lips. Slowly, it developed into a broad grin.

He said, "I think there is a way Donnell and Guret can help us."

"Help us with what?" Bleddyn asked.

Bridei did not answer. "The game begins," he said. "The time is almost right for us to challenge Beornhaeth. Almost, but not quite." He looked at me. "Do you still have that ring?" he asked.

"Yes." I fumbled in my belt pouch, pulling the ring out and offering it to him.

He waved a hand, signalling for me to keep it. He was smiling more broadly now. "Hang onto it, lad. You will need it."

I looked down at the ring, frowning. "For what?" I asked him.

"For when you meet Lord Beornhaeth. I think it is time he received another message from his spy."

Chapter 26

"I can't wear this!" I exclaimed. "I feel like a complete idiot."

"You look like one too," Bleddyn agreed cheerfully. He made some minor adjustment to my cloak then stood back, admiring his handiwork. "You'll do," he assured me.

I was wearing finer clothes than I had ever possessed before, well-tailored shirt, soft leather trousers with elaborate stitching, a thick, padded jerkin and a cloak, dyed green and blue. The cloak was fastened by a large, ornate brooch of what felt like solid silver. My old boots had been replaced by a new pair, soft and supple yet thick-soled and sturdy, lined with lambswool for warmth and comfort.

As if this new splendour was not enough, I had been supplied with spare clothing that was every bit as luxurious.

It had been Bridei's idea, of course.

"We'll dress you like an important man," he said. "I want you to impress Beornhaeth, so you'll need to look the part."

He sent some women to measure and fit me. Four days later they had produced the outfit I was now wearing. They all agreed it was very fine, but I still felt like some child's doll they had dressed up for fun.

I gave Bleddyn a helpless look. "I don't know if I can do this," I said.

"Of course you can," he replied. "You've seen how Bridei and all his chieftains strut around in their fancy clothes at feast times. Just copy them."

I was going to point out that, more often than not, I had seen Bridei in his well-worn riding gear or dressed as if he was ready to go to war, but I knew I had lost this battle, so I held my tongue. Instead, I said to Bleddyn, "I wish you were coming with me."

He gave a sad shake of his head. "Not this time, lad. My old bones are getting too tired for that sort of thing. Don't worry, though, Bridei won't send you off alone. He'll probably give you a troop of warriors to escort you."

It transpired that Bridei was indeed sending someone with me, but his choice did not please me at all. I met the King in his private room once again, just the two of us this time. He admired my new outfit, rubbing some of the material between finger and thumb as if to make sure that the seamstresses had used the best materials.

Apparently satisfied, he said, "So you are ready to go?"

"Yes," I replied warily.

"You should not travel alone, not dressed like that. Medraut will accompany you."

My jaw dropped open. "Medraut?"

Patiently, Bridei explained, "He is the best man for the job. He's as good a warrior as you can hope to find. He's also the son of a former king, so he warrants a position of importance. Unfortunately, he's not really cut out to be a leader of men. He's too brash, too impetuous. Sending him with you will, I hope, teach him the benefits of being more thoughtful and careful. Besides which, he will provide as much protection for you as any three other men could do."

"But he hates me," I said.

Bridei replied in a firm voice, leaving no room for argument. He said, "If it is any consolation, Medraut wasn't too happy about this either, but you will travel together and you will learn to act together, without letting personal feelings obstruct what you need to do. Is that clear?"

Nobody ever disagreed with Bridei when he spoke like that, so I agreed that he had made himself perfectly clear.

It seemed I was stuck with Medraut. He was waiting for me when I left Bridei, leaning against the wooden wall of a hut, his arms folded across his chest, idly chewing on a stalk of grass. He straightened when he saw me, spat out the green stalk and waited for me.

"You've been told?" he asked, his tone less than friendly.

"Yes."

"Let's be sure we understand one another," he said. "You're a little piece of shit who goes around spying on people. I don't like you."

"Thank you for being so honest," I said.

"Don't get smart," he retorted. "Just because you're dressed all fancy doesn't change who you are. Uerb and Donnell are both dead because of you, and Guret's head has been turned by that Orcadian whore you used to call your wife. I have no intention of becoming another one of your victims."

"My victims?" I almost laughed at him. "I think I have been as much a victim as anyone, don't you? I haven't murdered anyone, or betrayed anyone or lied on oath about anyone."

I think he thought that last comment was aimed at him, because he snapped back, "I didn't lie! I told the truth of what I saw. Donnell used me as much as he used you."

"Then we have that in common," I said, making an effort to placate him. "Is Donnell really dead?"

He stared at me, his expression cold. "Yes. He was taken to the cave at Am Broch and his head was cut off. His father did it himself. At least the old man saved his own honour, but I expect the loss will kill him before long."

"I am sorry. I liked Donnell."

"He was a lying piece of shit, just like you," Medraut said fiercely. "You and I have nothing in common except this mission for the King. Don't ever forget that."

I had had enough of him, so I said, "Then I will see you tomorrow."

I stepped past him and made my way to the gates of the stockade. I tried to show that I was not concerned by what he thought of me, but the truth was that he still scared me. My stomach felt queasy at the thought of travelling with him. Once we left Fortriu, there would be nothing to prevent him killing me, then returning to Bridei with the tale of an ambush by bandits.

I cursed Bridei for the thousandth time. He did not appear to appreciate the depth of Medraut's feelings about him having replaced Drest as king. Medraut could not be trusted. I would rather have gone on my own, but the King had insisted that men of rank did not travel alone, so I had to have at least one follower. I wished it had been anyone but Medraut.

Trying to push him from my mind, I spent the rest of the day saying my farewells. I went to Derelei first, standing by her lonely grave, telling her what had happened. I think she would have been pleased to learn the truth of poor Uerb's murder.

I told her what Bridei wanted me to do, but I did not tell her of my concerns over travelling with Medraut because I did not want her to worry about me while I was away. I don't suppose I fooled her.

Leaving Derelei to her peaceful sleep, I went back up to the king's hall where I sought out Sorcha. She was with my sons, as she always was. She clapped her hands in delight when she saw me.

"You look wonderful!" she beamed. "Like a lord!"

"I feel silly," I told her.

"Nonsense, you look very handsome." A momentary shadow flitted across her face as she asked. "Are you getting married to someone?"

"No," I laughed. "I am going away for a while. On the King's business."

"Oh, I'm sorry," she said, looking flustered. "I just thought . . . Well, I've never seen you wearing such fine things, so . . ."

"It's all right," I said. "I just came to say goodbye."

In fact, I stayed for a long time, until the boys were put to bed. They were not so strange around me now, often happy to sit on my knee. Little Bridei would show me his toys, a collection of wooden animals and small, carved soldiers, while Nechtan padded around, giggling because he had recently discovered that he could make Sorcha chase him if he started throwing things around the room.

I often looked at them closely, trying to see whether there was any family resemblance. I could not tell. I thought little Nechtan had Derelei's eyes, and sometimes Bridei reminded me of my father in the way he frowned when he was puzzled about something.

When I mentioned this to Sorcha, she said, "They are themselves. There is something of both of you in them. The main thing is that they are happy here."

I could see that was true. Sorcha was happy too, which helped the boys. Not that she was lenient with them, but she was the only mother they had, and I could not have wished for anyone better.

"Where are you going?" she asked me.

I told her. Bridei had sworn me to secrecy but Sorcha knew more of my secrets than anyone, so I trusted her. I told her all about Donnell and Uerb's murder. She knew some of it, of course, because Bridei had let it be known that Uerb's murderer had been caught and that justice had been done, but nobody outside of those who had been in the hall knew the full story.

Like me, Sorcha was upset that Guret and Mayota were still enjoying an unfettered life together, but she surprised me by agreeing wholeheartedly with Bridei's decision.

"They killed my lady," she said. "They must suffer for that. I don't care about what else they did."

When we parted, I clasped her hands in mine. "Take care of my sons," I told her.

She smiled at that. It had become my usual way of saying goodbye.

As always, she replied, "I will."

She seemed on the verge of saying something else, but then she merely smiled once more and closed the door.

Medraut and I had a pair of fine horses. Their slightly shaggy, grey-brown coats had been brushed and the ornate saddles polished so much that they gleamed.

I examined my mount, a strong mare with powerful, stocky legs, ideal for travelling long distances over rough terrain. She whinnied softly when I patted her neck. I noticed a small patch of dark skin on her forehead, its shape resembling the blade and handle of my knife. I thought that was a good sign.

I said, "We will be good friends, you and I. I will call you Dagger."

"Idiot," Medraut scoffed.

"What's wrong with Dagger?" I asked him.

"The horse already has a name," he said scathingly. "She's called Buttercup."

Shoving my left foot into the foothole, I swung up into the saddle. "She's called Dagger now," I told him. "What's yours called?"

"Avenger," he replied quickly, daring me to argue with him. "I think that's appropriate, don't you?" A wicked smile crossed his face as he added, "Maybe you should call yours Derelei. Then riding her would not be a new experience for you."

"Bastard!" I shot at him.

"Prick!" he responded.

I nudged my mare into motion, turning my back on him. Things had not got off to a good start and Medraut quickly found more fault. As soon as we passed through the gates, I led the way east.

Immediately, he complained, "I thought we were going south."

"We'll go by the coastal route," I replied.

"That's a long way," he argued. "It's quicker if we go directly south."

"South will take us past Dun Nechtan," I said.

He relaxed slightly at that. "I see," he said, taunting me with a laugh. "You don't want to see your woman, is that it?"

"She is not my woman any more," I told him. "Guret is quite welcome to her. But you are partly right. I'll be happy if I never see her again. Mainly, though, it is because I don't trust Guret. This mission is supposed to be a secret and I want it kept that way."

Medraut was silent after that. I was in no mood to speak to him either, so we travelled a long way without saying very much to one another. I was lost in thoughts of how to prove Guret and Mayota guilty, while Medraut obviously had things of his own to occupy him.

He rode with his long, dark hair and his longer cloak streaming behind him, his eyes ever watchful, as if he expected every tree or rock to have someone hidden behind it. From the look of him, he was ready for any threat. He wore a thick, leather jerkin, lined with lambswool, its outer surface liberally dotted with large, round, iron studs. As armour, it may not have been as effective as a coat of mail, but it was lighter and easier to wear.

On his back, he had a circular shield, made from hard wood, curved so as to be slightly convex on its outer side, the surface covered by a layer of thick, toughened leather. It had a heavy iron boss in the centre and a band of iron round the rim. At his side he wore a sword, a long hunting knife and a short dagger.

Sometimes he would draw his sword and sling his shield on his left arm, controlling the horse with his thighs and knees as he charged around, making practice swings and blocks.

"Why do you do that?" I asked him after he had completed one particularly strenuous exercise.

That earned me a scornful look. "You're not a warrior, are you?" he asked.

"No."

"Then you wouldn't understand."

I did not ask him again.

After only three days we crossed the Mounth. I avoided the village of Cala na Creige because I would have felt rather embarrassed if I had met any of the villagers, especially Ringan and his family, while I was wearing such fancy clothes. Medraut did not object to by-passing the village.

"The women probably stink of fish," he said dismissively.

"The whole place stinks of fish," I replied. "What else would you expect?"

I grew more nervous now, knowing that we were in the lands ruled by the Northumbrians and that if Medraut wanted to do away with me, I would not be able to prevent it. I grew worried when I noticed that he, too, was less relaxed than he had been. He was not exactly nervous, but his habit of watchfulness developed a slight tension that was obvious to me now that I had been travelling with him for a few days. I began to imagine that he was looking for a way to dispose of my body somewhere, so I made a point of keeping as much distance between us as possible.

It was only when we stopped at a farmstead at a place called Monadh Feith, on a hill overlooking the broad estuary of the Tatha, that I realised what was troubling him. He was afraid. Or perhaps it would be fairer to say that he was anxious. I almost laughed aloud with relief.

Monadh Feith had once been a small, fortified, hilltop farmstead, but it had been taken over by the Northumbrians and was now home to a band of half a dozen soldiers and their families.

We arrived at the small fort in the late evening, Medraut eyeing the ditches and stockade uneasily. I gave my name as Guret, showed the silver hawk's headed ring and demanded a place to sleep. We were admitted after only the briefest delay. Our horses were led away to be fed, watered and groomed, while we were provided with ample food and drink, then given rough-sewn mattresses that had been hastily stuffed with clean straw.

I enjoyed this unusually lavish reception. I had stopped there because I wanted to see how well my travelling disguise would be accepted and also, I admit, because I wanted to show off to Medraut.

He sat miserably throughout the evening while I chatted amiably to the Northumbrians. I don't think he slept much that night either. He was as nervous and uncomfortable as I had ever seen him. I made a point of laughing at him the next morning when we had set off again.

"What's so funny?" he asked.

"You are. These people are supposed to be our friends, but you acted as if you thought they were going to cut your throat every time one of them moved."

"They are not my friends," he said in a surly tone. "They are my enemies. I don't take well to being amongst them like this."

"Get used to it," I told him. "Until we get back to Fortriu, we are friends of the Angles and must behave accordingly. You'd better be more relaxed when we meet Beornhaeth."

After a few moments' thought, he said, "I don't know how you can sit there, jabbering away with them. You acted as if you were one of them."

"You're not very good at this sort of thing, are you?" I asked. I was not inclined to give him any sympathy. He had made his feelings about me perfectly plain so I was happy to get my own back.

"I'd rather fight the war host of Dal Riata," he muttered in reply. "Give me a sword and point me at the enemy and I'll be happy."

I gained the impression that he was softening slightly, so I said, "Well, I couldn't do anything like that, but you are in my world now. Until we get home, just do as I say and you'll be fine."

Medraut was not done yet. "Why did you say your name was Guret?" he asked.

"Because my own name is known in Dun Eidyn. I thought it would be better to use a different name this time."

"Why Guret?" he persisted.

"Why not? I am supposed to be a treacherous snake who is betraying his own people. It seemed an appropriate name."

"Guret hasn't betrayed anyone," Medraut growled. "He's ambitious and he can be a mean bastard if he's crossed, but he's all right."

"You don't know him very well, do you?" I asked. I was tempted to tell him the full story of what Guret and Mayota were suspected of, but I didn't entirely trust him, so I said nothing.

"You're an obnoxious little turd," he told me with feeling.

"That's more like it," I said encouragingly. He was obviously feeling better. I wondered how he would feel by the time we got to Dun Eidyn.

Chapter 27

Three days later we arrived at Beornhaeth's home. Each night I had deliberately taken Medraut to places that I knew were garrisoned by Northumbrians. I told him this was because he had to grow accustomed to being among them but the main reason was that Beornhaeth's ring assured us of a good welcome and reasonably comfortable beds. The fact that it made Medraut squirm was a bonus.

The ring continued to work its magic at Dun Eidyn, gaining us admittance to the mighty hilltop fortress without question.

Medraut's face was pale and anxious as we were led towards the large, rectangular hall that dominated the fort. My own nerves were on edge because I knew I might meet Triduana or old Aeldgyth the cook. I was fairly sure I would be able to act as if I had never seen them before, but I was not at all certain how they would react if they saw me. I had mentioned this to Bleddyn who had simply told me to act my part and deny all knowledge of anyone called Bili. It was risky, and I knew it, but Bleddyn was confident that I would be able to fool Beornhaeth.

"You are a natural actor," he assured me. " You will be fine as long as you keep your nerve."

I hoped he was right.

We were led into the hall where the ruler of southern Pictavia was sitting at a table, playing dice with a group of half a dozen other men. A serving girl stood near one of the rear doors that I knew led out to the kitchens behind the hall. Other than this handful of people, the hall was eerily empty, the men's voices echoing around the large chamber.

As we crossed towards the gamblers, my nose detected the smell of strong ale. From the noisy shouts of the men as they rolled the dice, I guessed they had been drinking for some time. I could not decide whether that would make my task easier or more difficult, but in one respect things were simplified for me because there was no sign of Triduana.

I recognised Beornhaeth immediately. The years had done little to change his appearance; he was still big and brawny, his shoulders, arms and legs all heavily muscled. As I remembered, he was long-haired and bearded. Only the hints of grey in his hair and beard revealed that he was no longer a young man.

He looked up from his game to cast his eyes over me. I studied him in return. Now that I was close to him, he reminded me of a more confident, more arrogant version of old Nechtan. He gave me a smile that had nothing to do with humour or welcome, revealing two rows of yellowing teeth.

"You have my ring," he said in a deep, throaty rumble that seemed to come from somewhere near his belly. "Where did you get it from?"

"It was given to me by my friend, Donnell, son of Enfret," I replied, desperately trying to appear calm while my heart hammered inside my chest.

"Hah!" he snorted. He turned back to his game, rattling the bone dice in a small, leather shaker, then rolling them across the table. He grunted in disappointment at the result, passed the shaker to the man on his left, then turned back to me. The game went on, the other men listening to our conversation while trying to give the appearance of paying no attention to us.

Beornhaeth asked, "What happened to the other man? The half-blind one?"

"He died," I said casually. "He suffered some sort of accident in the stables."

"So why did Donnell send you? You're no servant."

"I have known him for years," I said. "He knew I am of a similar mind when it comes to our dealings with the kingdom of Northumbria."

"You mean that you are a greedy, money-grabbing bastard, too? You want me to pay you silver to make you rich."

That brought a stifled laugh from the other men at the table.

I knew I had to be careful here. Beornhaeth may have acted like a fat, half-drunken oaf, but I suspected that he was no fool.

I said, "I'd prefer gold, but silver will suffice."

He laughed at that, a rumbling sound from deep in his throat. He slapped the table with one giant hand. "Game over, lads," he said. "I need to talk to this ponced-up little weed."

I knew he was trying to goad me, so I simply smiled while five of the men gathered up their piles of carved, bone tokens from the table before filing past me. Only one man remained seated beside Beornhaeth. I had not been able to see him behind the bulk of the other gamblers but now that they had gone I recognised his fair-haired good looks. It was Wulfric.

The other men were leaving. Beornhaeth signalled to Medraut. "Tell your man to wait outside," he ordered.

"He doesn't speak English," I said, hoping that Medraut would be allowed to stay.

"He waits outside," Beornhaeth repeated slowly, doing nothing to disguise the menace in his voice.

I shrugged, whispering to Medraut to wait for me. "And don't start any trouble," I said to him.

Medraut was not pleased, but he followed the Northumbrians outside, leaving me alone with the two most powerful men in the north, the men who had destroyed my family and who could destroy my entire people. I had a sudden, almost overwhelming urge to kill the two of them, then to walk out, find the horses and ride away before anyone discovered their bodies. I had thought that time would have diminished my thirst for vengeance, but I knew at that moment that it had not. Still, I was not foolish enough to believe I could kill two such powerful and experienced warriors on my own. Even with Medraut's help it would have been difficult.

Thoughts of vengeance continued to run through my mind but I quelled them because I knew that I could do nothing. Not only had I sworn an oath to Triduana, but Bridei had lectured me several times about the need to do nothing that would upset the stability of Beornhaeth's kingdom. The last thing Bridei wanted was for Ecgfrith of Northumbria to turn his attention northwards before Bridei was ready to move.

So I pushed the dreams of revenge aside and walked over to take a seat at the table.

Wulfric pushed a clay mug and a jug of ale towards me. I poured myself a drink.

"You would be Wulfric?" I asked pleasantly.

He nodded. "And you are?"

"My name is Guret."

Wulfric's eyebrows shot up in surprise. Beornhaeth asked, "Guret, son of Nechtan?"

Cursing inwardly, I waved the question away with a polite laugh. "No. Guret son of Bleddyn," I replied as casually as I could.

"So, what message do you bring, Guret, son of Bleddyn?"

"Nothing of great importance," I said. "I just felt that I should introduce myself to you."

"It's a long way to come just for that," Wulfric observed. He was tense, watchful. He reminded me of a fair-haired version of Medraut. If anything, he presented more of a threat to me than Beornhaeth did.

"I thought it necessary," I told him.

"Why?"

I took a drink, wiped my mouth with the back of my hand, then leaned my elbows on the table. "Because Donnell is dead," I whispered to them.

They exchanged a look of surprise but Beornhaeth quickly asked, "How did he die?"

I was growing more confident now. I said, "It seems that Donnell was not the quiet, inoffensive young man we all thought. He got drunk and rather carelessly boasted that he had murdered someone a couple of years back, the son of a minor chieftain, apparently. Donnell thought he was among friends, but someone denounced him. When witnesses swore to what he had admitted, the king sentenced him to death. Before he died, he gave me your ring and confided in me what he had been doing these past few years. As I say, he knew I share his views and he wanted to have the satisfaction of knowing that his work would continue after his death. He said he wanted to get back at Bridei for killing him."

Beornhaeth nodded, apparently accepting my tale, but Wulfric's eyes narrowed in suspicion. He said, "How convenient for you that his messenger also died."

"Convenience had little to do with it," I told him. "I made sure he suffered an accident because I did not want him speaking to anyone he should not have."

"You're a ruthless little bugger, aren't you?" Beornhaeth asked. "I think I could grow to like you."

I smiled. When I looked at their faces I knew I had succeeded. Bridei's gamble had paid off. After some reflection, the king had decided that it would be better to tell them about Donnell's death because there was a chance they might hear of it eventually anyway. What was important was that they accepted me as a suitable replacement.

"In that case, what can you tell us about Fortriu?" Beornhaeth asked.

I gave a slight shrug. "There is little to tell," I said. "Bridei still has the support of most chieftains. Nobody is strong enough to challenge him openly, nor does anyone show any inclination to do so. He has kept the Scots of Dal Riata at bay, so he is popular."

"What about Guret of Dun Nechtan?" Beornhaeth asked. "His father was always grumbling about wanting to be king. Is Guret the same?"

"He is an ambitious man," I agreed. "But he has no support, He is young and inexperienced."

"I heard his wife has more balls than him," Beornhaeth chuckled.

I laughed. "That would be a fair assessment," I agreed.

"So Bridei is secure?" he asked me.

"Yes."

Beornhaeth looked disappointed at that news. He said, "Well, as long as he keeps paying the tribute I won't grumble too much."

"I have heard no suggestion that he will do otherwise."

"Are you close to him?" Wulfric demanded.

"I spend a lot of time in Inbhir Nis. I know what is going on."

"So what is he planning?"

I lowered my voice as if afraid of being overheard. Bridei had told me what to say, of course, but I knew I must make it sound good.

"He has his eyes on Sruighlea," I said. "He may ask you to hand it over to him in exchange for a payment of some sort."

"He can go piss in a stream," Beornhaeth said.

I smiled dutifully. "Well, I will let you tell him that."

"What of his ships?" asked Beornhaeth. "Is he still building?"

"Yes," I said promptly. "The Orcadians continue to raid the north, so he wants to have ships patrolling the seas to drive them away. Nothing for you to worry about."

They asked a few other questions, probing to see how much I knew. None of it was important and I gave them truthful answers, knowing I had to gain their trust. I desperately wanted to ask them what their own plans were, whether Fortriu would remain safe from attack, but I knew that to do so would make them suspicious of me.

After an hour or so, Beornhaeth summoned one of his servants who was sent to bring my reward, a purse filled with small, silver coins. I took it with what I hoped was an avaricious smile, weighing it in my hand.

"It is a pleasure to do business with you," I told him.

He grinned evilly, an expression that chilled me to the bone. He reminded me of nothing so much as a giant bear, red-eyed and hungry for blood. In his harsh, rumbling voice, he said, "There could be a lot more in the future."

I cocked my head to one side. I knew this could be a trap but I could not refuse the bait.

"What would I have to do?" I asked.

He waved a hand airily. "Oh, you know. Speak to people, encourage them to question what Bridei is doing."

"You want me to create some dissent?"

He smiled broadly, though there was still no warmth in his expression.

"I like you, little man. You are quick. Yes, see if you can persuade some of the chieftains to stand behind a rival."

I rubbed my chin thoughtfully. After a while I said, "I don't know any of the older chieftains well enough, but I know some of the younger men. Guret of Dun Nechtan, for example. And I know one of old Drest's sons. They don't have much influence themselves but perhaps they might be willing to consider being less supportive of Bridei. Given the proper incentives, of course."

"Of course," Beornhaeth said.

"But why should they?" I asked. "Material wealth is all very well, but sooner or later such dissent will be crushed. Unless the dissenters attempt something . . ." I paused for effect ". . . drastic. Against a man like Bridei, that would be dangerous."

"Not if they were to appeal to us for help," Beornhaeth said. "We could send several hundred warriors to assist any such revolt."

My insides were as cold as ice now, but I managed to remain outwardly calm. I asked him, "So if I could find someone willing to oppose Bridei, that person could expect to be king? With your support, of course."

"Sub-king," Beornhaeth said. "Just as I am sub-king to Ecgfrith."

Something in the way he said that made me think he was not entirely happy with his status. Still, that was his problem. I acknowledged his words with a conspiratorial smile.

"Sub-king," I agreed.

Wulfric asked, "Do you know anyone who would be prepared to do this?"

"There is nobody I can think of immediately. Guret of Dun Nechtan, perhaps. He is ambitious enough, but we would need a few others."

"Then find them," Beornhaeth suggested.

"I will do that. It may take a considerable time. I do hope you understand that. My connections are limited. Getting information is one thing, but this will require far more delicacy."

"Do what you can," Beornhaeth told me. "I will be ready."

"I will do as you say," I told him.

They both looked at me, their faces unreadable. Neither of them said anything else, so I stood up, pushing my chair back and made my excuses. I offered my hand but Beornhaeth refused to take it. After giving him a slight bow, I turned and left, trying not to appear to be in too much of a hurry to get out of the hall.

Medraut was almost frantic with worry by the time I went outside. The look of relief on his face when he saw me was almost comical.

"Relax," I told him, displaying a calm I did not feel. I showed him the purse, letting him hear the jingle of coins.

"Job done," I told him.

"Then let's get out of here," he replied fervently,

Collecting our horses from the stables, we rode away as quickly as we could.

Chapter 28

Bridei spat in disgust when I told him what Beornhaeth was hoping for.

"Bloody Northumbrian bastard," he grumbled. "I never trusted him."

"What do you want me to do?" I asked.

"Nothing. You certainly don't go talking to Guret. If he finds out that he has a chance to grab the kingship with Northumbrian help, he'd probably jump at it."

"I'll need to tell Beornhaeth something," I said.

"Spin him a yarn," Bridei advised. "Tell him that it may take a couple of years. Tell him Guret may be interested but is too scared to take the plunge without some other support."

"What if Beornhaeth contacts Guret directly?" Taran asked.

Bridei shrugged. "We'll worry about that if it happens. Hopefully Bili will be able to discover anything like that." He sat up, placing his hands on his knees in a decisive gesture. "Now, I suppose I'd better send word to Beornhaeth that I'd like him to hand Sruighlea over to me. That way he will know he can rely on what Bili tells him."

"He won't accept," I told him.

"Of course he won't," Bridei agreed. "But it will keep his attention focussed where I want it."

"On Sruighlea?"

"It's the strongest fortress in the land, and it blocks our only land route south," Bridei replied. "Beornhaeth would think it odd if I didn't want to take it from him."

"It's too strong to take by force," Taran commented.

"It's impregnable," Bridei agreed. "We need to be subtle if we are to have any hope of regaining it."

"Asking to buy it is not particularly subtle," I pointed out.

Giving me a broad smile, Bridei tapped a finger against the side of his nose. "This is merely the first move in a long game, Bili," he said. "A very long game."

I was not sure what he meant by that, but he offered no further explanation. With a wave of his hand, he said, "Be off with you, lad. I will send for you when it is time for you to go south again."

That first visit to Dun Eidyn in the guise of a traitor was the beginning of my relationship with Beornhaeth. I saw him once more that year, when he was at Sruighlea, making sure the garrison was well provisioned and overseeing the defences. It seemed that Bridei's plan, whatever it was, was working.

"You were right," he growled when I met him. "Bridei offered to buy this place back. He must be more of a fool than I thought."

"He wants a cheap success to impress his chieftains," I told him. "He was hoping the lure of silver would persuade you."

"He underestimates me," said Beornhaeth.

"That can only be a good thing," I agreed.

"What about the other chieftains?" he asked. "Have you had any success?"

"I have opened tentative discussions with one or two minor chieftains," I lied, "including Guret of Dun Nechtan. But it is too early to reveal everything. There is always the danger that one of them might denounce me, I must be cautious if I am to be sure of success."

Beornhaeth grunted but did not dispute what I said. He gave me some more silver, telling me that I should continue to persuade men like Guret of the benefits of siding with Northumbria.

"Be assured that I will," I promised, "although it would help if I could give these men some indication of when you might be ready to march north."

He gave me a hard, inquisitive look, as if seeking some sign of a hidden reason for my question. He said, "When King Ecgfrith commands it."

"You require his permission?" I asked.

Beornhaeth's face grew hard, as did his voice. "I require his army," he rasped. "I have sufficient forces to hold what we have, and I can launch small raids, but while the King is fighting the Mercians, he does not want a war in the north."

"That is disappointing," I said, "but at least it gives me time to gather support for when he is ready."

"See that you do," Beornhaeth said darkly.

On the way back north, Medraut and I passed near Dun Nechtan without calling on Guret and Mayota. I gave the excuse that we needed to hurry back to Inbhir Nis, so we could not afford to stop. Medraut laughed at me but did not argue.

I gave the silver sceattas to Bridei. He let me keep a few to share with Medraut, but he had most of the others melted down and re-fashioned into amulets or jewellery, items that were far more valuable among the Pecht than coins.

"It is good of Beornhaeth to keep my treasury filled," he joked.

Other than those visits to Beornhaeth, Medraut and I had little to do with one another. I spent the intervening months on my farm, or I went to Inbhir Nis to speak to Bridei and to see my sons.

Time went by and another year passed uneventfully except for Bleddyn marking his sixtieth birthday. By that time, he was constantly plagued by sore joints and an aching back, causing him to remark that he felt considerably older than he was.

"All those years of working for Bridei and now I am going to be stuck here when things start to happen," he grumbled one night as we sat by the fireside in my little house, drinking mugs of heather ale.

"What is going to happen?" I asked. "Bridei never tells me anything."

Bleddyn wagged a finger. "Just wait and see. But if I know my man, I'd wager that Bridei is ready."

I don't know how he knew, but when the harvest was in, Bleddyn was proved correct. Word reached us that the King wanted men for a campaign. Gartnait, Entifidich's oldest son, went off, spear in hand. I went too, riding to Inbhir Nis to be greeted by Bridei who clapped me on the shoulders and said, "This is it, lad. The time has come. I need you to go and see Beornhaeth again."

I had expected that. "What do I tell him?" I asked.

Bridei grinned mischievously. "You tell him I am gathering an army to attack him, of course."

Medraut fretted that he was going to miss the fighting, despite Bridei's assurances that nothing would happen until we returned. Medraut, as usual, blamed me.

"Look at them all," he said, waving an arm to take in the hundreds of warriors who were camped outside the town. "I should be marching with them, not acting as nursemaid to you."

"What we are doing is important," I told him.

"Well if we miss the fighting, I'll know whose fault it is," he said sullenly.

Personally, I would have been quite happy to miss the fighting. I confess that I struggled to understand the mentality of men like Medraut who revelled in confrontation and violence. He, in turn, could not understand me.

"You are weaker than a woman," he told me in disgust.

Perhaps he was right.

Before we left, I found some time to visit Derelei's grave, to tell her where I was going. I could not hide the fact that it was dangerous, but I promised her I would return. Then I paid a hurried visit to Sorcha and my sons.

The boys hugged me, not really understanding what was happening, although little Bridei said his grandfather had told him he was going to fight the enemies of Fortriu. He asked whether I was going too. I told him I was, which made him frown.

"Don't worry," I told him. "I will be back."

As I left, Sorcha took my hands, raising them to her lips to gently kiss my fingers. Her eyes, always large and expressive, were filled with tears.

"Take care," she said. "There are so many young men going off to fight and some of them will not return. Make sure you do."

"I will," I assured her.

I felt a little awkward with her clutching my hands. I was not sure how to react to her unexpected display of affection. She must have sensed my unease because she released her hold on me, gave me a weak smile and said, "I will take care of your sons."

I left her feeling that the parting had been something more than a farewell. I thought that it was perhaps because the promise of war had heightened everyone's emotions.

Bridei himself was full of energy, issuing orders and constantly checking on whether people were doing what he had instructed. He was gathering a sizeable force, around three thousand men. It was the largest army the Pecht had put in the field since the disastrous Battle of the Two Rivers where my father, along with so many others, had been killed ten years before.

Bridei may have been eager, but he was still cautious in some things. He called me over, told me what to say to Beornhaeth but he refused to tell me what his real plan was.

"Best you don't know, lad," he said. "That way you won't need to lie. Now go and deliver your message."

It took us a while to find Beornhaeth. He had been touring his kingdom, as kings always do, but we eventually learned that he was on his way to Peairt. We galloped off to meet him.

He was travelling with a group of around thirty mounted warriors, all of them heavily armed. His banner, the black hawk's head on a red background, fluttered in the breeze above their heads as they rode along an old Roman road that ran straight as an arrow along the southern side of a low, heavily-wooded ridge.

Beornhaeth raised a hand to halt his troop as we rode towards him.

"Guret?" he said. "What in God's name are you doing here?"

I nudged my horse close to him. "I am glad I found you," I said. "I must get back soon, but I knew I needed to warn you."

"Warn me about what?"

"Bridei is raising an army. I have not been able to discover where he is going to strike, but I know he intends to attack you. I had thought he was marching against Dal Riata, but he has announced that he will no longer pay tribute. He said it is time for him to strike back at you."

"Are you sure?"

Every part of Beornhaeth's massive body tensed angrily. His face, what I could see of it beneath his helmet and above his bushy beard, creased in lines of fury.

I nodded, speaking urgently. "He was gathering men when I left. There were more than three thousand of them. He is probably on the march already."

Beornhaeth's face contorted into a mask of rage. "The treacherous dog! Three thousand men? He must be planning something big." His eyes bored into me. "You don't know where he will attack?"

I shook my head. "There are plenty of rumours, but nobody knows his true plans. He will not tell anyone what he intends to do. I could not afford to wait to find out where he was heading. I would have been too late to warn you. All I know is that he says it will be something that will hurt you."

Beornhaeth clenched a fist angrily. "Sruighlea," he breathed. "He couldn't buy it, so I'll wager he's going after it by force. We'll see about that, by God!" He gave me a curt nod. "You have done well, Guret. I thank you."

I acknowledged his thanks by raising an eyebrow in question.

Beornhaeth grimaced, but reached for his belt pouch. He counted out four silver pennies and half a dozen small pieces of jet.

"That's all I have," he told me. "If this information is correct, you'll get a lot more next time we meet."

I examined the coins and gemstones in my palm, frowning at them. Looking him in the eye, I said, "I am risking my life for you. I think I am worth more than this."

"You're a greedy little bastard," he growled. "That's all I have with me."

"Then I doubt whether we will meet again," I said haughtily. "The next time Bridei tries something, you can discover it for yourself."

I thought he was going to kill me on the spot. His face was dark with anger, livid veins standing out on his cheeks and nose, his eyes blazing like those of a mad dog. I kept my face impassive, staring back at him.

With a cry of rage, he whipped off his leather gloves, then tugged two gold rings from his fingers. He handed them to me, slapping them into my outstretched palm.

"You are trying my patience," he snarled. "If this information is wrong, I will have your guts."

"It is not wrong," I assured him. "I do not know Bridei's plan, but he is definitely marching against you."

Snorting with impatience, he bellowed a command, urging his band of horsemen to turn, then he led them away at a fast canter, heading back the way he had come, west towards the mighty fortress of Sruighlea.

Medraut and I were left alone on the tree-lined, sun-dappled road. The sound of Beornhaeth's riders slowly faded into the distance. I watched them for a long time as they hurried along that impossibly straight road, but eventually they were lost to sight among the distant shadows. Only then did I breathe a sigh of relief and look at Medraut.

"You're bloody mad," he said incredulously. "Did you ask him for more gold?"

"I had to make it believable," I said. I was glad I was on horseback because I could feel my legs trembling now. "He would have got suspicious if I had just accepted that small amount. Anyway, don't complain. You'll get your share, as usual."

"Bugger that," Medraut snarled. "You could have got us both killed. I know I'm good, but there were thirty of them."

"Stop complaining," I told him. "It worked. He's going to Sruighlea and that's what Bridei wanted."

"So where is he really going to attack?"

"I have no idea. Let's go back home and find out."

Chapter 29

We reached Inbhir Nis to discover that the army had already marched. Bridei had led them east, following the coast road, then cutting through the heart of Fortriu before crossing the eastern mountains. He was heading for the coastal fortress at Dun Foither.

Medraut and I pushed our horses hard, chasing after them. The army had a good start on us but many of the war host were on foot, so we caught up with them just as the foot soldiers were streaming down the southern trackway of the Mounth, heading past my former home of Cala na Creige.

We rode along the side of the long column of marching men, our tired horses managing little better than a slow canter. Some of the soldiers cheered as we passed, raising their spears in salute. The welcome may have been because I was still dressed in my chieftain's finery but I thought it was more likely to be because they recognised Medraut. He certainly assumed that was the reason. He waved and called out to the men as we made for the head of the column.

"You didn't think I'd miss this, did you?" he called cheerfully as we passed a group of men from Cait.

Near the front of the war band we found Bridei, sitting astride his tall horse, with Taran riding alongside him. They greeted us with expectant looks.

"Well?" Bridei asked.

"Beornhaeth has gone to Sruighlea," I said, unable to keep the smile from my face.

That was the first time I ever saw Taran actually smile. His broad grin matched the one on Bridei's face.

The King said, "By God, you have done well, lad. Now we must hurry. Thanks to you, we have gained at least six days. It will take that long for word to reach him and for him to march against us. We have even longer if he wants to bring foot soldiers. But we need to have this done by the time he gets here."

The army climbed the steep hill to the south of Cala na Creige. Bridei had already sent his cavalry racing ahead to block the exit from Dun Foither, pinning the Northumbrian garrison inside. Scrambling up the rugged slope, the foot soldiers circled round to join them before the Angles could make a sally to drive the horsemen away.

Late in the afternoon, we made camp at the end of the headland and the siege of Dun Foither began.

Bridei had travelled light, bringing no wagons, only a string of pack mules to carry the army's provisions. Everyone, including Bridei himself, would have to sleep in the open or under crude, hastily constructed woodland shelters. Still, the mood of the men was good. They knew that they outnumbered the fort's garrison and expected the Northumbrians to surrender soon.

As we settled down to watch Dun Foither, Bridei roamed the camp, making sure that everyone was in their allotted place. He had said we had at least six days, but he was never one to take chances, so mounted warriors were sent to watch the western approaches, ready to bring word of any Northumbrians coming to the aid of the fort. On the side of our camp that faced Dun Foither, a cordon of spearmen was set to watch the fort in case the Angles decided to charge out at us. Only then did Bridei rest.

I sat with him at his camp fire, telling him what had passed between me and Beornhaeth. He chuckled when he heard how I had asked for more in payment.

"You're a cool one, Bili," he said. "Bleddyn always said you were a natural at that sort of thing."

I said nothing. I had not felt cool at the time, but I had known it had been necessary. It had only been after Beornhaeth had ridden away that I had felt the true fear taking hold of me. I was ashamed of that reminder of my innate cowardice, but I was determined to conceal it, so when

Bridei complimented me, I simply shrugged as if it had been nothing.

Taran absently poked at the fire with a long stick. "It was well done," he agreed, "but the real work begins tomorrow."

Bridei clucked his tongue. "Aye, it will be bloody work. That wall is a real bugger. I dare say we will lose a lot of good men taking it."

"You could ask the garrison to surrender," suggested Taran.

"Oh, I'll do that right enough, but I doubt whether they will agree. They'll know we have to be quick about it, so they'll trust in their ditches and their walls to keep us out until help arrives."

"It's a pity we can't get round the sides," Taran said. "They don't have enough men to hold the entire perimeter."

"They don't have to," Bridei grumbled. "We can only attack from one direction." He sighed. "Aye, it will be hard fighting, that's for sure."

"There is a way round the side," I said.

They both stared at me. Bridei said, "Tell me about it."

I explained about the cave and the path that led up to the small gate at the side of the fort.

"The path will be guarded," Taran said.

"I don't think so," I replied. "We could not get many men up there anyway, and it doesn't get you inside the fort, only to the gate."

"Then it's not much use to us," said Bridei.

"Yes it is," I said. I told him what I thought could be done.

He considered my plan, told me I was out of my mind, but agreed anyway.

"You are insane!" Medraut exclaimed when he heard what I planned to do.

"You don't need to come," I said. "I'm sure Bridei can find some men who are brave enough."

He glared at me. "You're an annoying little toad, do you know that?"

"So you'll come, then?"

I felt quite pleased. He may have thought I was a toad, but that was a step up from his previous verdict that I was a piece of shit.

"Of course I'll bloody come," he grumbled. "And I'll find two other lads to come with us."

"Could you find me a change of clothes as well?" I asked. I gestured down at my elaborate chieftain's costume. "This isn't really suitable."

"You think the lads travel with a spare wardrobe?" he asked.

Muttering under his breath, he wandered off in search of the men from his father's estates, promising to find two who would accompany us.

With a sigh, I unfastened my silver brooch, folded my cloak and took off my expensive jerkin, leaving me in my shirt, trousers and boots. I wandered back to Bridei's fire where I left my cloak and jerkin in Taran's care.

"Do you want a sword?" Bridei asked.

I tapped the hilt of my dagger. "This will do. I'm not much use with a sword."

Bridei stood facing me. He held out his hand. "Good luck to you, lad."

"Just be ready," I said.

"I'm always ready," he assured me.

Medraut arrived with two burly warriors, each armed with spear, sword and shield. "This is Wid and Domnach," he announced. "They're good lads."

I looked at the two shadowy figures, each of them as large as Medraut himself, both of them long-haired and bearded.

I said, "Has Medraut told you what we are going to do? It will be dangerous."

The one called Wid laughed, "There would be no fun if it wasn't."

"Then leave your spears and your shields," I ordered. "They will hamper us."

The two men looked to Medraut for confirmation. He nodded. "He may be an arse, but he knows what he's doing. Usually."

The two men dutifully laid down their spears and shields while I tried to work out whether Medraut considered an arse to be a step up from a toad.

We said farewell to Bridei and Taran, then rode back down the winding hillside path to Cala na Creige. It was fully dark by the time we arrived, the moon flitting among streaks of grey cloud to cast its pale light on the sea, illuminating the cluster of fishing boats that had been hauled up on to the pebbled shore of the bay.

Medraut glanced up at the night sky, where the stars were concealed behind gathering clouds. "It feels like it's going to rain," he observed.

"So much the better," I replied. "It will help to hide us."

The houses in the village were unnaturally quiet, devoid of the sounds of laughter or music that I remembered so well. I guessed the villagers had seen the army marching past and were nervous, wondering whether they would be safe from whatever was about to happen.

I led the three warriors to Ringan's house. I heard the sound of voices coming from inside but they stopped when our horses drew near. Dismounting, I crossed to the door and called Ringan's name.

"It's me. Bili."

The door was cautiously opened to reveal Ringan's familiar face peering out into the night.

"Bili?" he asked uncertainly.

"Hello Ringan. I came with the king's army. I need your help."

A whisper of curious voices came from behind him but Ringan had seen Medraut and the others, so he ducked back inside, hissing at his children to stay where they were. Then he stepped out to stand in front of me. As incurious as ever as to what had happened to me in the two years since I had last seen him, he asked, "What is it that you want?"

When I told him, he shook his head, assuring me it was madness.

"Madness or not," I said. "We must try it."

He gave in eventually and led us down to the shoreline. It was raining by the time we got there, a fine drizzle that seemed to hang in the air rather than to fall, yet was relentless enough to soak everything and everyone. Wearing only my shirt and trousers, I was soon cold and shivering. I am sure it was the rain that made me tremble, not fear.

Ringan took us down to a group of currachs that lay upturned on the shore. They were small, oval vessels with lightweight, wooden frames covered by waterproofed animal hide. They were normally used for gathering lobster pots in the shallow waters of the coast. We selected two which we pushed out into the gentle swell of the bay where they bobbed gently on the waves that lapped against the stones on the beach.

Ringan nodded to the sea, saying, "It's slack water. The tide is just beginning to turn."

"That should help us, then," I said.

Ringan looked doubtful, but it was not the tide he was concerned about. He gestured towards the two currachs.

"Those aren't mine," he said.

"Don't worry," I told him. "In the morning you can walk over to the next bay and fetch them back."

He scratched his head uncertainly, clearly not pleased about this theft of village property, but I told him again that it was on the king's business and that Bridei would pay some compensation, so he let the matter drop and ran over what we would need to do, reminding me to pay attention to the wind and the tides.

"You'll probably end up crashing onto the cliffs'" he observed morosely.

"You should go back home now, Ringan," I told him. I clambered into one of the currachs, sitting on the single bench that spanned the tiny craft. Medraut splashed into the shallow water, then climbed in to join me while Wid and Domnach awkwardly boarded the second. With a final wave of farewell to Ringan, we gripped the paddles and splashed our way out of the bay.

The other three men were used to the sea because they had grown up near the eastern coast of Cait but even so, paddling a currach is no easy task. Fortunately, we were able to clear the rocky arms of the bay before the tide turned. Once out beyond the protective cliffs, the swell of the ocean caught us, making our progress slow and difficult. The drizzle gradually transformed into genuine rain, heavy droplets soaking us and hissing as they struck the surface of the sea around us.

Medraut began swearing at me in low whispers, cursing me for a fool and insisting we would all drown. I was too cold and wet to bother arguing with him. I kept paddling, my numb fingers clenched tightly around the coarse wood of the large, flat-bladed oar as I drove it into the inky darkness of the water, driving us on.

I don't know how long it took us. The distance we had to cover was not great; a mere trip round one headland and into the next small cove to the south. I knew that from my time on Ringan's fishing boat but that night it seemed to go on forever. Even with the tide turning, helping to push us back towards shore, I felt as if we had been on the sea for hours.

The moon was hardly visible now, masked by a curtain of dark clouds. The wind, which had been so light on the shore, was considerably more fierce out on the sea. The swell, although it had appeared relatively calm, still surged beneath the flimsy currachs, causing them to rise and fall alarmingly.

From somewhere ahead of us I heard the splash of waves hitting against the foot of the cliffs. I peered into the darkness, blinking the water from my eyes. With a start, I realised that the darkness in front of me was not just the black of night but was the sheer wall of the cliff. I gasped a warning to Medraut, then dug my paddle into the waves and turned the currach, frantically battling to drive us away from the rock wall while the tide and the wind forced us inexorably closer to the towering cliff face.

I called a warning to Wid and Domnach but I had no time to watch for them. I could not even tell whether they were still with is.

On the bench beside me, Medraut gasped, his massive muscles straining to power our flimsy vessel away from danger and into the comparative shelter of the bay.

I could hardly see a thing but I could sense the looming height of the cliff to my left as we struggled to keep ourselves from being wrecked. My world was confined to the currach and my paddle as I fought to stay alive. Then, with no hint of warning, there was a transition from desperate struggling to an easy calm. The cliff fell away, the waves diminished and in only a few strokes we had crunched gently onto the shore. Medraut immediately leaped from the boat, splashing into the shallows to drag the currach further up the gentle, curving shelf of sand and pebbles. I jumped out to help him, then turned to look for Wid and Domnach. They beached beside us, both of them offering prayers of thanks for their survival.

Medraut turned on me. "I told you that was a stupid idea!" he hissed.

"We're still alive, aren't we?"

"No thanks to you. Now find this bloody cave and let's get going."

Under a dark, cloud-enveloped sky, with the high cliff of the Dun's headland rearing above me, I floundered around the edge of the cove, desperately looking for the cave. With my arms outstretched in front of me, I stumbled along like a blind man, slipping and splashing into the sea, scraping my hands on what felt like sharp, jagged rocks. Medraut, Wid and Domnach followed me, whispering curses all the way.

At one point I lost my footing completely and fell headlong into the shallow water. I came up, spluttering to rid myself of the salty taste of the sea, water cascading from me as Medraut grabbed my shirt and hauled me upright.

"Idiot!" he hissed.

I could not argue with him. Drenched and smelling of the sea, I pushed my hair back from my face and blundered on. I soon felt the faint tingle of panic, convinced that I had missed the entrance. Then, after what seemed an age of fruitless searching, I remembered that it was set a little way above the shoreline, so I scrambled up the embankment, still groping blindly for the cave. Almost immediately, we stumbled into the relative shelter of the entrance tunnel.

I ignored Medraut's bitter complaints about how long it had taken me to find my way. I was so cold and wet that I needed to keep moving, so I felt my way along until I found the narrow opening that led up to the fort. Almost on all fours, I crept up towards the top of the headland.

Again, my memory failed me. The narrow, uneven steps seemed to go on forever, climbing up the side of the exposed cliff face. We scrambled higher and higher, the rain blinding us. The path was wet and slippery, exposing us to the constant danger of sliding out into the emptiness of open air and a plunge to the bay far below. I was as terrified as I have ever been in my life, but I crawled on because Medraut was behind me and I could not face telling him that I was too afraid to go any further.

At last, I reached the top where I sprawled onto the wet grass of the headland. Medraut immediately clawed at me, hauling me back out of sight.

"They will have sentries," he warned me. This time, he did not bother to waste his breath telling me I was an idiot.

We lay at the top of the path, peering into the wet night towards the fort. All I could make out was a slightly darker line against the dark of the sky. It was around twenty paces away, with no cover whatsoever except the rain and the darkness. If there were any sentries there, I could not see them.

"We have to get to the side gate," I whispered to Medraut.

He said nothing. He just lay there, his eyes scanning the side and rear of the fort. I nudged him. "We can't stay here," I said.

He gave me a scornful look. "There is only one man I can see. We can make a run for it when he turns his back."

"What if he hears us?" I asked.

"Pray he doesn't. But he's wearing a helmet, so all he'll be hearing is the rain hitting that."

I swallowed nervously, wishing I could be as calm as Medraut and the other two appeared to be. I said, "You give the word, then."

We squatted at the top of the path, poised to run. I still could not make out where the sentry was, but Medraut touched my elbow, then rose to a crouch, running for the wall. I ran after him, praying I would not trip or fall. I heard the faint swish of wet grass as Wid and Domnach followed close behind.

Medraut grabbed at my arm, steering me away from the ditch, guiding me towards the gate. Then we were there. Somehow, we had made the crossing with no shouts of alarm greeting us. We pressed ourselves against the wet wood at either side of the gate, balancing precariously on the slippery turf at the top of the fort's wide ditch.

Medraut drew his dagger then nodded to me, indicating that it was my turn now.

I pulled my shirt off, tugging the sodden cloth over my head. Then I hauled off my boots before unbuckling my belt and removing my trousers. I stood there in only my undergarments which were already so wet from my fall into the sea that the rain could not have soaked them any more. Pushing my clothes to one side, I moved to the gate.

Speaking in English, I called out, "Help me! Open the gate!" I banged a fist against the thick, rounded beams of the gateway. I had been worried that I might not be able to sound frightened enough, but I did not need to act in order to sound terrified.

There was no reply. I called again, thumping on the damp wood. This time I heard someone coming to the gate from above me, obviously walking along the rampart behind the fence. I stepped back so that the sentry would not need to lean out too far to see me. If he looked straight down, he could not fail to see the huddled shapes of my three companions.

"Please! Let me in!" I called up to him in a hoarse whisper.

"Who is there?" came a gruff, anxious reply.

"My name is Thingfrith," I replied, using the first name I could think of. "I'm a merchant from Dun Eidyn. Please let me in, for pity's sake. The Picts ambushed me a few miles down the road. They chased me. I had to dive into the sea to escape and I've swum all the way to get here."

I heard another voice, demanding to know what was going on. Then I saw the silhouettes of two helmeted men looking down at me from above the gate. One of them laughed, "I don't think he's much threat. Open the gate."

"Thank you!" I called up.

As I stepped towards the gate, I gave Medraut a nod of warning. "At least two," I whispered.

He nodded, holding his long knife ready.

I heard the sound of the great locking bar being lifted off, then the gate swung open. I darted forwards, into the narrow gap, whispering my thanks.

As soon as I entered the fort, I knew I had made a mistake. I had expected to find only two guards but there were three men there, two with spears ready, the third holding the gate open for me. I pretended to slip, falling face down in the mud, blocking the gate so that it could not be closed. The Northumbrians laughed, reaching to haul me to my feet.

Like an owl swooping through the night to grab its prey in its talons, Medraut exploded silently into the fort. He vaulted over me, stabbing his dagger into the throat of one spearman, then slashing at the second, taking him across the face. The third man barely had time to react when Wid followed Medraut, knife in hand. There was a brief flurry of grunts, a strangled cry, then all three Northumbrians were lying dead on the ground.

The fight had sounded incredibly noisy but there were no other sounds except the steady drumming of the rain.

Medraut wasted no time.

"Shut the gate!" he snapped at me.

Medraut, Wid and Domnach each took a helmet, spear and shield from the fallen guards and hurried away through the fort towards the front gate, leaving me alone and almost naked. I slipped my way back outside, retrieved my clothes, then returned to the fort, closing the gate behind me. Then I made for the relative shelter of a nearby building, where I stood under the eaves as I struggled to dress.

My body was wet, the clothes soaked and clammy, but I did not want to be found undressed in the middle of an enemy fortress, so I pulled them on. As an afterthought, I dashed back to the three bodies and pulled their knives from their belts. Holding one dagger in my right hand and clutching the other two in my left, I followed Medraut and the others, making my way through the buildings towards the main gate.

I had got to within a stone's throw of the front wall when shouts, screams and the ringing clash of weapons broke the calm. Instinctively, I ducked to one side, circling to my right, moving round the outside of the buildings until I was close to the northern perimeter wall. From somewhere ahead of me I could hear a voice bellowing in English, calling men to arms, telling them the fort was under attack. Movement stirred inside the buildings as men and women woke to the sounds of desperate fighting.

With my heart thumping in my chest, I crept close to the corner of a long, low building, gaining some shelter from the rain thanks to the overhanging thatch of the roof which I hoped would also offer some concealment in the dark shadows. Cautiously, I peered round the corner of the building. What I saw was a scene of chaos.

It was still dark, the rain having extinguished all fires and torches, but I could see that the gates had been opened. Bodies lay on the muddy earth and a whirling, shouting tangle of men stood inside the gateway, battling furiously. More men were streaming from the various buildings within the fort, all of them carrying spears, axes or swords as they hurried towards the melee, drawn to the sounds of battle.

Medraut's voice rose over the tumult, screaming defiance. I caught a glimpse of him hacking down a Northumbrian, then parrying a blow from another swordsman before slicing his sword across a third man's face. Beside him, I saw Domnach struggling furiously to keep the Angles from closing the gates. There was no sign of Wid, but the mass of bodies and the darkness made any details difficult to see.

One thing was plain. The three of them could not hold for long. More than a dozen Northumbrians were now crowding round, trying to cut them down, while yet more men were rushing to join the struggle. Only the narrow confines of the gateway and their own ferocious resistance had kept Medraut and the others alive this long.

I wanted to help. I knew I must help. But it was like watching Beornhaeth and Wulfric as their men killed Giric and raped my mother and sister. I was frozen, unable to move because I knew that if I went into that gateway I would die.

I stared, fighting my fear. Then I thought of Derelei and I knew that she would be waiting for me if I died. Gripping my knives, I stepped out into the open.

The Northumbrians had their backs to me. When I got to within twenty paces I saw that some of them had hurried to the fight without donning their armour. I selected one of these, flipped the knife in my right hand so that I could hold the blade, drew back my arm and threw.

The dagger was lighter than my own, but the throw was good. The Northumbrian stiffened as the blade thudded into his back. He staggered, one hand clutching backwards as he sank to the ground.

My second knife was already in the air. It took down another soldier, catching him in the side, just below his armpit. He lurched sideways, slipping and falling to the wet mud of the gateway.

I was preparing my third throw when one of the Angles turned to see why his companions were falling. He cried out in rage when he saw me, and ran towards me, raising a huge axe over his shoulder as he charged.

His head was bare but he was wearing a coat of mail that protected his entire torso and covered the upper parts of his legs. A thrown knife would simply bounce off, or embed itself in the armour without penetrating any deeper than the thick leather and padded wool beneath the rings of iron. He knew it and so did I.

I whipped the third dagger into my right hand, waiting until he was almost on me, then I hurled it at his face. Still running, he ducked aside, allowing the knife to sail past his head. I had no time to watch what happened to it because his axe was already swinging down in a blow that was powerful enough to drive it through me, cleaving me from my shoulder to my crotch.

The only thing that saved me was that the thrown dagger had forced my attacker to twist slightly so the strike of his axe was less accurate than it could have been. I leaped backwards, yelling in fright as the heavy blade skimmed past in front of me, missing my face and chest by barely a finger's breadth, so close that I felt the rush of air as it fell past me.

I dived to one side to avoid the Northumbrian who had continued his charge, intent on bowling me over. I landed in a muddy puddle, slipping and splashing as I rolled to my feet. I whipped out my own dagger, holding it low as he came for me again.

He did not run this time. With a savage yell, he whirled the long haft of the axe, swinging another ferocious blow at my head. Again I dived away, flinging myself to my right in a desperate attempt to escape the curved axehead.

Rolling his wrists expertly, the Northumbrian sent the blade twisting after me. The upper tip of the sharp metal caught my left forearm, scoring across the flesh and drawing blood from a deep gash. It was a glancing blow but it was still powerful enough to jar my arm to numbness.

I screamed, although it was as much with fear as with pain. The axe flashed down to thud into the ground. I turned, scrabbling on my knees, to see that the power of the Angle's swing had driven the head of the axe deep into the cloying mud. He was tugging at it, trying to haul it back up for another attack. I had only one chance. I flipped my dagger in my hand and threw.

He was only three paces from me. I could not miss at that range and he had no time to dodge out of the way. The knife took him in the left eye, driving into his skull and killing him stone dead. He toppled backwards, crashing to the muddy ground with a dull, wet thump.

Desperately, I scrambled over to him to retrieve my dagger. It was stuck fast, the handle wet and slippery. I eventually resorted to putting my foot against the dead man's head so that I could wrench the blade free. It came loose with a horrible sucking sound.

I lurched upright, blood streaming from the gash in my arm. It seemed like an age had passed but my battle against the axeman must have lasted for only a few heartbeats. I looked towards the gateway. Medraut was still standing, streaked with mud and blood, his dark hair and beard plastered by the rain, but he was alone now, facing a horde of furious Northumbrian warriors. Already, some of them were circling behind him, trying to close the gates. I knew what I had to do. Gripping my bloodied knife, I ran towards him.

I had barely taken two steps when I heard a loud cheer from outside, the sound of hundreds of voices. The Northumbrians at the gates heaved frantically on the huge wooden doors, knowing they had very little time left before our warriors reached the gateway. Medraut hacked one of the Northumbrians down with a wild sweep of his sword, while blocking the savage thrust of a spear with his shield. Again the Northumbrians heaved, more intent on closing the gates than on killing Medraut, who still fought like a demon. But the entrance was clogged with bodies, preventing the huge doors from swinging shut, then the path between the walls was filled with charging men and sharp swords as Bridei led his army into the fort.

I watched, entranced, as Medraut swayed backwards, blood spraying from a wound in his shoulder, then he disappeared from sight behind a black tide of warriors as Bridei's men surged through the narrow gateway.

The Northumbrians fought desperately but were overwhelmed, swamped by the masses of men who were pouring through the open gates. Some of the Angles, seeing they were outnumbered, turned to run. They did not get far before they were mercilessly cut down.

After everything that had happened that night, that was the most dangerous moment for me. I could easily have died then. I was standing in the open ground, my feet sinking into the mud, my dagger in my hand, as the army of Fortriu flooded towards me, intent on killing any man they found. I gawped at them, unable to move.

Just then, Bridei saw me. His voice cut across the clamour as he ran towards me.

"Leave him be!" he bellowed at his warriors as he dashed towards me. "He's one of us! Leave him!"

I stared in dumb amazement as the men ran past me, going in search of other victims.

I stood there, bleeding, soaked to my skin and exhausted. Bridei faced me, sword in hand, rain lashing at his face. Above the roar of his victory he said, "You did it, lad. Dun Foither is ours."

Chapter 30

Medraut took most of the credit. He was still alive, wounded in his shoulder, his leg and his side, but exultant at his victory.

Wid and Domnach had not been so lucky. They were both dead, although everyone agreed they had died the way a warrior should, so they were buried with honour while the Northumbrian dead were simply piled into a deep, mass grave.

Medraut's wounds and my injured arm were cleaned and bandaged by a monk who had been found hiding in the Dun. He was the only man who was allowed to live. The rest were put to death while the women and children were taken as slaves. I watched, sitting miserably inside the Dun, leaning my back against the stone wall as the women were dragged out, wailing and sobbing. Some of them were Pecht, women who had become the wives of the Northumbrian garrison, either voluntarily or by force. That made no difference to their fate; they were led north along with all the others.

The rain had stopped by mid-morning. I was desperately tired and I could not summon the energy to move from my spot beside the wall, despite the chill and discomfort from my saturated clothing. Medraut, much more seriously injured than I was, still managed to strut around, regaling the warriors with the story of how he had held the gate. He claimed to have killed seven Angles in that desperate struggle and I supposed he might not be boasting. He deserved his moment of glory.

Eventually, Taran found me sitting there. He took my hand and pulled me up, then led me to a building near the rear of the fort. Inside were the kitchens. Some of the women who had accompanied our army had taken this place over and were busy ensuring that the warriors would be fed.

Taran said to me, "I've brought your cloak and jerkin. You'd better strip off those wet things and hang them near the fire. Wrap yourself in your cloak and get some rest."

I did as he said, curling up in a corner to sleep.

I was young and fit, so I recovered fairly quickly after that first day. My arm was sore for a while but the wound healed without becoming infected, which was always the greatest worry with any wound. I would be left with a scar, but that was no hardship.

Bridei presented me with some new clothes to replace the ones that had been ruined by the sea water. I have no idea where he got them, but he added a small purse, filled with scraps of copper and silver.

"It's not enough, lad," he said. "I know that. When we get home, I'll see you are rewarded properly."

"When are we going home?" I asked.

"Not for a while yet," he replied. "We have to see what Beornhaeth is going to do. I suspect he'll not be too happy."

I thought for a moment that he was going to ask me to go to Beornhaeth, but instead he gave orders that Medraut and I were to stay within the Dun and were not to leave under any circumstances.

"That is not fair!" Medraut protested. Against the evidence of his many bandages, he complained, "I am fine now."

"I dare say you are," Bridei replied, "but I want you to stay out of sight. Understand?"

The two of us were given a small section of one of the long barrack rooms where we could sleep. We were allowed free range inside the fort but Bridei insisted that we stay well clear of the front wall and the gates.

"I can't afford for Beornhaeth to see you," he told us, which explained everything and nothing.

Medraut, of course, chafed at this enforced confinement. Even the solicitous attentions of several of the women, who seemed to be queuing up to share his bed, did nothing to quell his eagerness for a fight. He had revelled in the adulation he had received as the hero of the storming of the Dun. When Bridei took the bulk of the army west to meet Beornhaeth, Medraut was left with only the men of the garrison to boast to.

Several times I was tempted to tell him of the part I had played in the defence of the gate. I had killed three men, even if two of them had died with my knives in their backs, but I had tackled an armoured axeman, armed with only my dagger. I felt that I had acquitted myself well, but I decided to keep quiet about what I had done because I knew I could never have stood in the gateway with Medraut. All the same, his arrogance annoyed me.

Typically where Medraut was concerned, he surprised me one evening by asking, "Why don't you brag about your part in taking the fort?"

"What do you mean?" I asked.

He rolled his eyes. "You were there. It was your plan and you got us in. But you never tell anyone what you did, you just sit there all quiet as if it was nothing."

"I didn't do all that much," I said. "Not as much as you."

"You did more than enough. Mind you, I thought you'd be killed when you started chucking knives at them."

"You saw that?"

"I caught a glimpse," he said with a knowing smile. "I was a bit busy at the time, but I saw you get one of them."

"I got three of them," I said, delighted that I had a chance to impress him at last.

"So why don't you tell anyone?" he asked.

I shrugged, trying to appear casual about my exploits. "I don't feel I need to prove anything to anyone." Except myself, of course, but I wasn't about to tell him that.

Medraut shook his head. "You're a strange one," he said. "All calm and cool whatever happens. You should make more of things. Instead of sleeping alone, you could get a woman in there with you if you impressed her enough. They all love a hero."

"Yes," I said. "I'd noticed. Have you left any for anyone else?"

"Only the ugly ones," he grinned. "But I'm sure you could talk one of the pretty ones into bed if you didn't act so secretive all the time."

"I'm happy the way I am," I told him. "I'll let you do all the talking."

"You've spent so long being a spy you don't know how to relax and enjoy yourself," he said accusingly.

Perhaps he was right. My life was certainly full of secrets, but whether I was quiet and secretive because I had learned how to become a spy, or whether I was a good spy because I was naturally quiet and secretive, was a question I could not answer, not even to myself. Either way, I continued to let Medraut take the glory. He seemed quite happy about that, and so did the women.

Beornhaeth arrived ten days after we had taken the fort, riding at the head of his thirty warriors. I don't know what was said, but Bridei went to meet him and spoke to him for a long time. When they were done, Beornhaeth rode away without a fight. All Bridei would say was that Beornhaeth was not a happy man but that he was no fool and knew he had lost Dun Foither.

Bridei rubbed his hands together gleefully. "Now I can bring some ships to Cala na Creige to safeguard this coast," he said.

"What happens now?" I asked.

Bridei said, "Now Beornhaeth goes back to Dun Eidyn and waits for Ecgfrith to come north with an army. I doubt they will come north in the winter, but we'll watch for them anyway. I expect Ecgfrith will march against us in the Spring. Now that the coastal route is secure, they'll probably come up through Peairt or Sruighlea. We'll be ready."

My nerves were tingling again. "Do you believe we can defeat them?" I asked. I remembered how the Northumbrians had destroyed our army at the Battle of the Two Rivers when I was a boy. Ecgfrith had spent the intervening years battling against Mercia and would be able to bring a huge force of highly experienced warriors against us.

Bridei tapped a finger to the side of his nose. "I wouldn't have started a war if I didn't think I could win," he told me.

"What do you want me to do?" I asked.

He said, "Rest. Come the Spring, when Ecgfrith marches north, that's when I'll need you. In the meantime, go home and work on your farm." He turned to Medraut. "You go home too, lad. I'll need you in the Springtime as well."

So the army split up, a few of Bridei's best men riding west to watch for the Northumbrians in case Ecgfrith tried to attack us in winter. We all knew that only a madman would do that but Bridei, as always, was not one to leave anything to chance.   Dun Foither was left with a strong garrison who had orders to seal the rear entrance of the cave and destroy the cliff stairway. That was an unenviable, dangerous task, but Bridei wanted no repetition of our stealthy attack. Now that he had reclaimed Dun Foither, he had no intentions of losing it again.

With everything settled, the rest of the army was allowed to return home to wait for the following year's campaign. Before we left, I went to Cala na Creige to visit Ringan. I gave him a handful of the silver that Bridei had given to me. That left the taciturn fisherman even more speechless than usual, but his wife was overjoyed and insisted on hugging and kissing me so that I had to wrestle myself clear of her clutches.

I rode north feeling relieved and happy, but that happiness was to be short-lived. We had barely crossed the Mounth when a rider came galloping in search of Bridei. The news he brought spread through the army like a forest fire.

"The Orcadians have raided Fortriu again!" Taran informed me. "They have destroyed dozens of farms and small settlements."

"Bloody Orcadians," muttered Bridei. "You can't trust them." He looked at me with a grim expression. "You'd better hurry home, lad," he told me. "Your farm was one of the ones they attacked."

I found young Gartnait among the spearmen, then I begged a spare horse from Bridei and the two of us galloped home as fast as we could. It was a miserable journey because we were both worried about what might have happened. Gartnait had left home thinking that he would be the one in danger, but he had seen no fighting at all because the fort had been taken by the time he had reached the gates. Now he was worried that the family he had left behind could all have been killed. He kept asking me if I thought they were safe but there was nothing I could tell him to reassure him.

That evening, he asked me to pray with him, which I did, although I thought it was a bit late if the Orcadians had already done whatever it was they had come to do.

My fears seemed about to become true when we arrived at the farmstead. My house was a burned-out ruin and the fields were strewn with the bodies of cattle and sheep.

"God preserve us," Gartnait whispered when he saw the horrific scene of devastation.

Then we shouted for joy when we saw Entifidich. He was busy butchering the carcasses of our slaughtered livestock, piling cuts of meat into bags of salt to preserve them. He looked up when he heard us, then hurried to meet us as we rode into the yard.

"Praise the Lord!" he cried. "You are safe!" He clasped Gartnait's forearm, welcoming his son with undisguised joy.

I leaped down from Dagger's back. "What about you?" I asked. "Is everyone safe?"

"Aye, we all still live. We were lucky. I saw them coming, so we all ran for the church." He gestured towards the dead animals. "But they made a right mess of the place. Killed anything they couldn't take away on their ships. All the cattle are dead and they herded away quite a few of the sheep."

"Never mind that," I said. "As long as nobody was harmed."

Entifidich frowned. "Your friend the priest was hurt," he said. "Hurt bad, but he's still alive."

"Bleddyn? Where is he?"

"At the church, along with a lot of other folk."

I climbed back onto my horse. I barely gave my house a second look as I rode past it. There was not much to see anyway. The stone walls stood like a skeleton, the interior charred and piled with the ashes that were all that remained of the timber roof beams and the thatching. All my belongings had been burned to cinders, yet that did not concern me as much as the news that Bleddyn had been injured.

Jabbing my heel's to Dagger's flanks, I set off for the church at a gallop.

The barn, granary, roundhouses and huts had all been burnt to the ground, Bleddyn's home included, but his stone church stood, unscathed by the devastation surrounding it. Leaving my horse to crop the grass, I hurried inside.

The church had been turned into a temporary home until new houses could be built. It was crowded with people from neighbouring farms who had come there seeking refuge and were too afraid to return home in case the Orcadians returned.

Bleddyn was lying on a pallet, his face pale, wrapped in bandages which covered his chest and belly. He grinned weakly when he saw me.

"Hello, Bili. We had some trouble while you were away."

"What happened to you?" I asked as I dropped to kneel beside him.

"I'll live," he wheezed, brushing my hands away to stop me fussing over him.

Brother Aed, standing beside me, was unusually outspoken. He said sharply, "Only if you rest, Brother Bleddyn. You have lost a great deal of blood."

"You fuss too much," Bleddyn told him.

I sensed an ongoing argument between the two of them but as far as I was concerned, that could wait.

"Tell me what happened," I said urgently.

Between them, they pieced the story together for me. They had been remarkably lucky because Entifidich had seen the smoke rising from a neighbouring farm. He had caught sight of a band of raiders, some ten or twelve of them, streaming towards him. Realising their intent, he had sent his young daughters running to warn the rest of his family. They had all hurried to the church, reaching it just in time, with the Orcadians hard on their heels.

Bleddyn had stood in the church's narrow doorway, his great staff in his hand, defying the raiders to enter a house of God. The raiders had laughed at him and had tried to get past him. Of course, they did not know Bleddyn. Whirling his staff, he smashed the skull of one and downed three others by breaking their arms or legs.

"That only served to infuriate the rest of them," he admitted with a wry smile.

The raiders had attacked Bleddyn even more ferociously. He clubbed another one to death but a spear caught him in the chest and only the intervention of Brother Aed had saved him. The little monk had hurled a heavy stone at the nearest raider, catching him in the face. Then he had grabbed at Bleddyn's robe and somehow hauled him inside the church, allowing Entifidich to slam the door shut.

"That was well done," I said to Aed.

"God gave me the strength to do it," he said modestly before continuing his story. "We barricaded ourselves inside the church while the Orcadians battered at the door and tried to set the building alight. When they realised that they could not get in, they gave up and went in search of easier plunder."

"I am surprised they dared attack a church at all," I said.

Aed shrugged. "They are heathens. The word of God has not yet reached the Orcades. They see churches as easy targets."

Bleddyn laughed, "They would have been disappointed it they had got inside here. They think all churches are filled with gold and jewels but they have not seen how poor we are." His laugh turned into a cough, forcing him to lie back and close his eyes. After a short while he opened them again to look at me. "Your farm is ruined, Bili," he said. "Apart from a few jars of grain that Entifidich had buried, the food we had stored for winter is all gone. What the raiders could not carry, they burned."

"The Lord will provide," Aed intoned gravely.

I said, "Bridei will provide. He will not let us starve."

Bridei did provide. That was a hard winter for all of us, but the king sent men out to help rebuild homes and barns, he gathered crops and fodder from other parts of Fortriu and Cait that had not been raided, and he distributed supplies to those who had lost everything.

My own farm was reasonably lucky because nobody had died, but other places along the coast had not been so fortunate. We learned that several women had been carried off to the raiders' ships, leaving their men lying dead on the ground.

Entifidich, Gartnait and I worked all the hours of daylight, rebuilding homes and doing what we could to keep some semblance of normality on the farm. I would have liked a big, stone-built house but I settled instead for a large roundhouse with two storeys because it was much quicker to build a traditional, wooden home. Instead of reserving the lower floor for somewhere to keep the livestock, I kept it as a living and cooking area and I divided the upper part into sections so that many people could sleep there in some privacy. It was a grandiose thing because I had no family to share it with, but Bleddyn and Aed moved in with me as soon as the house was completed, so it did not feel too large and empty.

Bleddyn was pleased. "It's a home fit for a chieftain," he said.

I still did not consider myself much of a chieftain, but I rode around the neighbouring farms to see what the people needed and I made sure that everyone received a fair share of the grain Bridei had distributed.

We built another home for Entifidich and his family. He refused anything grand, insisting they would all live together as they had always done. He was more concerned with rebuilding the barn, granary and shelters for the animals, and he worked tirelessly so that we had more or less completed everything by the time the first signs of Spring began to show.

It is easy to look back on that winter now and laugh about the hardships, but it was a difficult time, and not one I would care to repeat. Without Bridei's help, things would have been much worse. He even sent me some more cows and sheep to replace the livestock I had lost, so although it was a difficult winter, we did not starve.

Best of all, Bleddyn survived his wound and although he was often tired, he was soon spreading the word of God once more.

Because we were so busy, the months seemed to fly past and it was Spring before I knew it. One day in early March, Bridei himself came out to visit me. He wandered the farm, admired my new home, visited Bleddyn's church and took an interest in everyone he met, making a point of speaking to as many people as he could. He was relaxed, but concerned to ensure that everyone's welfare was being taken care of. That day, as he walked around my farm, he was as much a king as I ever saw, but I should have known that there was more to his visit. He spent some time talking privately to Bleddyn then, when he was done, he sought me out.

"I need you to come back to Inbhir Nis with me," he said. "It is time."

Chapter 31

I think that was the only time I ever saw Bridei really worried. Over the winter he had been readying his ships, determined to take revenge on the Orcadians and prevent them repeating the raid. His problem, of course, was Ecgfrith.

Bridei could not afford to attack the Orcades because he needed every man to face the Northumbrian king when he came north.

"There has been no sign of any movement from Beornhaeth," he said to me. "I've got men watching every route, ready to bring me word at the first sign of a Northumbrian army coming for us, but there has been nothing, so I'd like you to go and see if you can learn what they are up to. I don't trust the bastards."

I took a deep breath. I knew how dangerous this would be. My warning to Beornhaeth had tricked him into rushing to Sruighlea when Bridei had attacked Dun Foither. I doubted very much whether the Northumbrian lord would be in a forgiving mood when he saw me. But I owed my allegiance to Bridei. He had allowed me my few days with Derelei, a gift that placed me in his debt more than I could ever repay.

"I will leave in the morning," I told him.

He said, "We are committed now, Bili. There is no turning back."

"I understand."

"War is never easy, you know."

He seemed to have something on his mind. I wondered what he was trying to say. It was not like Bridei to be so unsure of himself. I waited for him to gather his thoughts.

He cleared his throat. "You are an important man, now," he said.

"Only thanks to you."

"Don't try flattery on me, lad," he said with a half-smile.

"Is there something else you want me to do?" I asked.

Again he hesitated. "It's not so much that I want you to do anything, but that I think you should do something."

"What might that be?"

"I think you should take a wife."

That caught me off guard. I recovered as quickly as I could. "I take it you have someone in mind?"

He nodded.

I said, "Perhaps I should remind you of what happened the last time you wanted me to get married."

"I know that well enough. But sooner or later you are going to have chieftains' wives coming to you, bringing their daughters and offering dowries."

"I'll worry about that when it happens. I have no thoughts of getting married just now."

He could see that I was slightly annoyed at his interference in my life. Lifting his hands in a placatory gesture, he said, "I understand. Look, this is not easy for me either, lad. Damn me, but I knew I should have got Bleddyn to speak to you about this."

"It's none of his business either," I said firmly.

"No, but it is my business," Bridei said sharply.

"What do you mean?"

"I mean that my grandsons need a father." His eyes bored into me, daring me to say anything. When I remained silent, he went on, "You are probably too blind to see it, but there is a certain nurse who has been mooning over you for the past few years."

I blinked. "Sorcha?"

"You should talk to her, lad. Before you make another mistake."

"Sorcha?" I repeated.

"Just talk to her. I won't force you into anything, but the girl needs a husband. She's well past the usual age for getting married. Not that she's had no offers, because she's a bonny lass, but she has refused them all. Besides, the boys need a proper father. Just think about it."

I needed to think, so I went to see Derelei. I had not visited her for several months because I had been so busy repairing the damage to my farm. I had intended to go to her anyway, but Bridei's words had thrown me into confusion and I knew I would find peace at her graveside.

    To my surprise, Sorcha was sitting on the grassy bank beside the grave, enjoying the sunshine while she watched the boys who were running up and down the riverbank. When my sons saw me, they came running, arms waving excitedly. I grabbed at each of them, lifting them high in the air. They squealed with delight.

    "Come and catch us," little Bridei challenged as he dashed off again.

    Laughing, I waved him away. "I need to speak to Sorcha first," I said.

    Young Bridei pulled a face, but he and his brother charged off, chasing one another round in circles. I walked over to where Sorcha was sitting.

    She smiled at me, an expression that was all too rare for her, and one that lit up her face. For once, she had removed her headscarf, allowing her long, auburn hair to fall in lustrous curls around her shoulders. She had unfastened her apron, placing it on the grass so that she could sit on it. Whether it was her happy, relaxed appearance or whether it was Bridei's revelation, she looked so lovely that she almost took my breath away.

    "I thought you would come here," she said.

    I was not sure how to respond. I had known Sorcha for a long time. I considered her a friend, perhaps my closest friend apart from Bleddyn, but when I saw her then, I was all too aware that she was a woman.

    "Is something wrong?" she asked.

    "No. I am just surprised to find you here."

"Oh, we often come here. I enjoy the quiet and there is room for the boys to play."

I sat down beside her, but not too close.

There was an awkward silence. I wondered whether Bridei had spoken to her. I doubted it, but there was definitely a tension between us that had not been there before. Perhaps that was my fault.

"I am going away tomorrow," I said, trying to fill the silence.

She was quiet. She did not look at me. "When will you be back?"

"I don't know. Perhaps a few weeks."

"I suppose it will be dangerous?"

I shrugged. "It is always dangerous."

"Then you had better spend some time with the boys. They have missed you these past months and now you are going away again."

"I have missed them, too." I reached out with my left hand, resting it on her right arm. This time she turned to face me. "And I have missed you," I said.

Her eyes were bright, her lips slightly parted. I saw then that Bridei had been correct. I leaned towards her to kiss her. Our lips met, then she was turning towards me, her arm moving to encircle my neck, pulling me close to her. I put my arm around her waist, gently urging her towards me. For the first time since Derelei had died, I felt the stirrings of true desire.

Then Sorcha suddenly stiffened. "No!" she gasped. Hurriedly, she pulled away from me, rolling clear. She sat up, re-arranging her dress, then folding her arms across her chest. She sat rigidly, hugging herself.

"What's wrong?" I asked. "The boys? We could take them home. Then we could be alone."

"No." She shook her head. "No, it is not that."

"Then what? I thought . . ." I stopped. What had I thought?

Sorcha checked that the boys were still playing safely, then she turned her large eyes on me again. She said, "I love you, Bili. I think I always have. I used to listen to you making love to my lady and I would imagine that it was me who was lying with you, that it was my name you were whispering."

"Sorcha. I did not know."

She said, "If things were different, I would give myself to you in a moment. But I cannot. Not the way things are."

"What do you mean?"

I reached for her but she shrugged me off.

"Please don't make this any harder than it already is," she said.

"I don't understand. Why should we not be together?"

She brushed a hand to the corner of her eye, wiping away a solitary tear.

"There are lots of reasons," she said.

"Then tell me what they are."

She breathed deeply. "I am twenty years old," she said. "I know it will be difficult for me to find a husband at my age, but I need a man who will always be here, who will not go away for weeks at a time and perhaps not come back."

"But lots of men go away. We are at war."

"You go away in times of peace as well, Bili. I saw what that did to Derelei. She was stronger than me in so many ways, but still it hurt her when she did not know what had happened to you or whether you would ever come back. I do not want that to happen to me. Can you understand that?"

"Yes, but surely we should not deny our feelings because of fear of what might happen. You cannot live your life like that."

She shrugged. "Perhaps not. I know I will suffer whenever you go away, but there are other reasons. You are a great lord and I am just a nursemaid. I do not want to be someone who keeps your bed warm only to be discarded if some rich chieftain's daughter comes along."

I laughed at that. "Sorcha! Do you think I would do that to you? You are much more than a nursemaid, and I am much less than a great lord. We can be married as soon as you like."

She looked at me then and I saw that her eyes were full of tears.

"You have barely looked at me in all the time we have known each other. Now you talk of marriage. How can you decide so quickly?"

This time I rolled to my knees, facing her. I gripped her shoulders, forcing her to look at me.

"Sorcha, listen to me. You have been my friend for a long time. You have been a mother to my sons and you have shared in all my secrets. Perhaps I have never noticed just how beautiful you are, but I have seen it now, and you are very beautiful. These reasons you are giving me are just excuses. You do not need to be afraid. Believe me."

"I am afraid," she said. "I am afraid of many things. I am afraid of being left a widow, perhaps with an unborn child in my belly. All I want is a man who will stay with me always, and a family of my own. You would not stay with me, Bili. You would go off whenever the king called you."

"Only for a few weeks each year," I protested. "You should not deny yourself some happiness, Sorcha. Please."

She shook her head. "There is another reason we cannot be together," she said softly.

"What reason is that?"

"You love somebody else."

I frowned. "What do you mean?"

She gave me a sad, lost look as she said, "You are still in love with Derelei."

Medraut was waiting for me at the stables the following morning. He was busy fastening some bags of provisions to the saddle of his horse when I arrived. He acknowledged me with his usual grunt, but then took another look at me.

"What's wrong with you?" he asked.

"Nothing," I replied as I lifted my own saddle onto Dagger's back.

"It must be a woman," Medraut commented. "Only a woman could make you look that miserable. What was it? One of the kitchen maids turn you down? Or did you let her down?" He moved his hand in a drooping gesture.

"Shut up, Medraut," I snapped.

"I knew it was a woman," he chuckled.

I tightened the girth strap then climbed up into the saddle. "Are you ready to go?" I asked him.

He swung himself up onto his horse. "Lead on," he said with a mocking wave of his hand.

His mood had altered by the time we crossed the hills to the south of Inbhir Nis. He asked, "How do you think Beornhaeth will react when he sees us?"

"I don't expect him to welcome us with open arms," I said.

"He's likely to kill us."

"Probably. You can turn back if you like."

That sort of comment always riled him. He snorted angrily. "I'm not frightened."

"I never said you were."

"By God, she's really messed you up, whoever she is," he said.

"Mind your own business. Why don't you just go home and let me do this by myself?"

"Don't think I'm not tempted," he growled. "You're still a little piece of shit. But the king says you need looking after, so I have to stay with you."

His opinion did not matter to me. I was more preoccupied with what Sorcha had said to me. I had not been able to argue with her because what she had said was true. I was still in love with Derelei, which was why I had never been with another woman in the three years since her death. Whatever excuses Sorcha gave, the one fact I could not dispute was that she could not replace Derelei.

Sorcha had been in tears when we parted, but she had refused to change her mind.

"How can you say you love me when you cannot let her go?" she had cried.

I had no answer for her.

I was in a sombre mood as Medraut and I rode south, but I was forced to shake off my melancholy thoughts as evening approached and we drew near to Dun Nechtan.

"Are we going to see Guret?" Medraut asked.

"Yes."

"You usually avoid this place."

"Not this time."

"Is there any particular reason we are stopping there this time?"

"No," I lied.

The truth was that I had no real wish to see Guret or Mayota, but I had no choice this time. Bridei had told me to stop here.

We rode along the pass, descending to the low valley. Ahead of us, the loch shimmered in the evening sun, tiny sparks of sunlight dancing on the smooth surface of the water, almost dazzling me. On either side of us loomed the high hills, their tops still white with winter's snow. By the shore of the loch, surrounded by an irregular maze of tree-covered hillocks, was the familiar farmstead of Dun Nechtan.

In one way this visit did me some good because it forced me to think of something other than Sorcha. For Medraut's benefit, I put on a show of being relaxed, although the truth was that I was nervous about going to Dun Nechtan.

As we drew near to the gates, I turned to Medraut and said, "I suggest you don't eat anything while we are here."

He frowned. "What are you talking about?"

Of course, I could not tell him. All I had done was make a fool of myself. Again.

Guret met me with an expression of mixed surprise and hostility, to which an element of trepidation was added when he saw Medraut. Still, he invited us in to his home, because the laws of hospitality left him with no option, especially when I told him that we were travelling on the king's business. He led us to the main room of the house where Mayota greeted us coldly.

We sat at the table I remembered so well, Guret and Mayota at one side, Medraut and I at the other. Guret called for some supper to be brought for his guests while we all sat stiffly, regarding each other with suspicion.

Guret had put on some weight since I had last seen him, hinting that he may soon grow to match his father's bulk. Mayota, though, had not changed at all except that she was wearing a finer dress and had more jewellery than she ever wore when she was my wife. Her blonde hair was immaculate and the short sleeves and low-cut front of her dress displayed her flawless skin. She was undeniably beautiful, but her green-brown eyes studied me coldly, her hatred plain to see.

An awkward tension filled the room but I did nothing to ease it. Guret was our host, so it was up to him to make us welcome. Besides, my own nervousness had vanished when I had seen their reaction to our arrival. They were afraid of me, of what I might say. I let them stew for a while.

"You are on the king's business, you say?" Guret asked when the silence had gone on too long.

He had directed the question at Medraut, but I answered, "Yes. We are going to Dun Eidyn to see Beornhaeth. We are hoping to agree a peace settlement."

Guret did not want to talk to me, but he had no choice. This was a matter that affected him more than most.

"Do you think he will agree?" he asked.

I shrugged. "Who can say? Medraut thinks he will kill us."

He did not know what to say to that. He probably hoped it would come true, although he could hardly admit it to our faces.

Medraut said, "If anyone can do this, Bili can. He has a talent for things like that."

His tone was slightly scornful, as if he despised such talents, but even his half-hearted support was a pleasant surprise. Then I remembered that he had been fooled by Donnell and Guret when Uerb had been murdered, so I supposed he had reason to despise the pair opposite us almost as much as I did.

I said, "A lot will depend on whether Ecgfrith is there. If he is, and if he is determined to fight, Bridei wants me to assure you that he is ready. He will bring the entire army of Fortriu to face any invasion. He is counting on your support."

"Of course," said Guret, looking unnecessarily flustered.

"That is good," I commented. "You may have heard some rumours that Beornhaeth has been trying to persuade some chieftains to oppose Bridei, or at least not to support him."

No," Guret replied. "I had not heard that."

"Well, I can't name names," I said, "but I am pleased that the king can rely on your loyalty."

"Of course he can."

I watched him closely, noticing that his face had gone rather pale. Mayota's expression, in contrast, was growing more flushed as she struggled to remain calm. Unable to restrain herself, she blurted, "You have done well for yourself since we last saw you, Bili."

I clenched my jaws tight to prevent myself from laughing. It was such an inane comment considering the way we had parted that I knew she had only said it to switch the subject away from the question of Guret's loyalty. That told me a lot.

I smiled pleasantly at her. Guret may have been ambitious, but Mayota was the driving force in their relationship.

I managed to say, "Yes, the king learned the truth of Uerb's murder. It was Donnell who did it."

Guret was tense. I knew he was waiting for me to accuse him of complicity, so I looked at him, still smiling.

Mayota, who seemed to have recovered her composure slightly, said, "Then justice has been done."

"Indeed." I left that word hanging.

The ambiguity of my reply did not escape them. I looked at Mayota and I knew that she understood my unspoken accusation. But she had settled now and she was good. I almost felt like applauding her performance.

She turned to Medraut, leaning forwards on the table to expose a good portion of her cleavage. Smiling sweetly, she asked, "And what about you, Medraut? We heard the story of your bravery at Dun Foither."

I expected Medraut to launch into his boasts but he merely replied, "It was a good fight, but I lost two good friends."

I said, "Medraut is too modest. He took the fort almost single-handed. I am glad he is on my side. I would hate to have him for an enemy."

Guret was positively squirming by now, refusing to even look at Medraut, but Mayota was made of stronger stuff. She said, "I am sure you were very brave, Medraut. Guret always said you were the greatest warrior he had ever seen."

Guret coughed. "Yes. Yes, that's right. I knew you were destined for great things."

He was rescued by the arrival of a pot of steaming food. Serving girls brought bowls and mugs, then Mayota began serving the broth into the bowls while one of the girls poured ale into the mugs.

I watched closely, making sure that Guret and Mayota were served the same food as she presented to me.

"Are there mushrooms in it?" I asked Mayota as I took my bowl.

She froze, just for an instant, before saying, "I don't think so."

"It's just that I have developed an aversion to mushrooms," I told her.

She knew then that I knew. She hid it well, but I had known her the way a man knows his wife, and I could tell that she understood my meaning.

I watched her, pointedly waiting until she had supped from her own bowl before I tasted the broth. It was actually very good.

Medraut and I set off early the next morning. We had a long ride ahead of us because we wanted to get to Dun Eidyn within a few days. It was a good excuse to leave Dun Nechtan as soon as the sun peered over the snow-capped mountains.

I had gone to the kitchens and fetched our breakfast myself, so I was sure it had not been tampered with. I did not think that Mayota would have done anything so obvious as poisoning us, but I had learned from Bridei not to take anything for granted, so we had eaten and were ready to depart before she was out of her bed. We rode away just after sunrise, with Guret watching us go, his face sullen.

"What in God's name was that all about last night?" Medraut asked as we rode along the reed-lined shore of the loch.

"I was just delivering a message."

"Bloody strange message, then. They didn't seem to appreciate it, whatever it was."

"No, but I quite enjoyed it. I learned quite a lot."

Medraut shot me a dark look. I knew he was not as slow-witted as he sometimes made out, but he did not know what I knew about our hosts of the previous evening. He still believed that Nechtan had died in an accident and that Derelei had taken her own life. I could not tell him what I suspected, but that did not stop him probing for answers.

"What did you learn?" he asked.

"I learned that Guret would be happy to abandon Bridei if he thought he could gain favour with Ecgfrith and Beornhaeth."

"I could have told you that," Medraut said.

"Yes, but now they know that I know and, more importantly, that Bridei knows."

"So why doesn't Bridei just execute the pair of them?" he asked. "That's what I would do."

"They will get what they deserve in time," I said.

Medraut scoffed, "I suppose you are going to tell me that God will strike them down for their sins."

"Amen to that," I agreed, refusing to rise to his goading. As I said it, I learned something else. Or rather, I recognised it. Mayota did not fear God's wrath. She had lied on oath after Uerb had been murdered and nobody had understood why she had dared to do that. But I suddenly recalled what Brother Aed had said about the raiders who had tried to burn Bleddyn's church. The word of God had not yet reached the Orcades, Aed had told me.

Mayota was an Orcadian. Eternal damnation held no fears for her. She had married me and she had married Guret, never letting slip that she did not recognise holy matrimony. She was a pagan, a follower of heathen ways and a worshipper of false gods.

When that realisation came to me, I thought that I understood her at last, but I had no idea just how clever, how ambitious, she truly was. Perhaps I should have been able to guess at the scale of her designs, but I had other things to worry about because Medraut and I were about to enter the lions' den.

Chapter 32

We reached Dun Eidyn without incident, the hawk's head ring working its wonders as usual. It was near evening as we entered the town, which seemed to have grown larger since our last visit. At first I was worried that this was because Ecgfrith had brought his army north, but a closer look showed me that the sprawling houses and workshops were simply spreading out along the southern side of the great plug of rock that was Dun Eidyn. It seemed that more and more Northumbrians were making their homes here.

It was growing dark as we rode up the steep slope to the gate, the sky fading from blue to dull grey and gradually to black, with the merest hint of orange just visible on the western horizon. Torches flared on the ramparts and around the gates, lighting the entrance and illuminating the warriors who stood on watch. I showed them the ring, telling them I needed to see Beornhaeth. No questions were asked and they quickly swung the massive wooden doors open to admit us.

As we rode into the Dun, I noticed that Medraut crossed himself.

"Stay calm," I told him.

He looked at me apprehensively. "This is a bad idea," he said. "Are you not nervous at all?"

"Of course I am," I told him. "But we cannot let them see that."

He took a deep breath. "Just get us out alive," he said fervently.

"I will do my best."

Stablehands ran to meet us as we passed through the gates. Our horses were taken to be fed and watered while we were escorted to the main hall.

The sound of music and many voices greeted us as we walked through the tall doors which were hurriedly closed behind us, sealing us inside. Torches were blazing around the walls, providing a baleful, flickering light, illuminating dozens of men, and even a few women, who were seated at long tables which filled the hall. Serving girls scurried along the tables, carrying plates of steaming food and huge pitchers of ale.

In a corner to our right sat three musicians, playing harp, flute and drums, but struggling to make themselves heard over the clamour of voices. The hall was hot, and filled with the smells of food, beer and human sweat.

It was clear that a feast was in progress, even though we had arrived during Lent, when everyone was supposed to fast in the days leading up to Easter.

Beornhaeth was sitting at the head table, facing the doors. On his left sat a large, fat man dressed in a priest's robes, with a jewelled crucifix hanging from a gold chain around his thick, fleshy neck. The torchlight flickered from the many rings he wore on his chubby fingers as he lifted a hunk of roasted meat to his fat lips. Whoever he was, his enormous bulk showed that fasting was clearly not a duty that he observed rigorously, if at all.

I quickly scanned the rest of the people at the top table. To Beornhaeth's right sat Wulfric, his long, blond hair distinctive as soon as we entered the hall. To Wulfric's right, her hair elegantly pinned high on her head, a gold necklace hanging round her bare throat, sat Triduana.

The sight of her made my steps falter. I could not look at her. Inwardly, I cursed my bad luck. Among the Angles, women were accorded lower status than men, and they rarely attended great feasts like the one in progress around us.

If this had been a gathering of the Pecht, it would have been different, for we honour our womenfolk and accord them similar rights to men, but I had not expected to see Triduana here. I hesitated, unsure what to do.

Fortunately, Medraut gave me a gentle nudge.

"Don't fail me now," he whispered as he urged me to keep walking.

With Medraut a pace behind me, I held my head high and crossed the hall towards Beornhaeth. Willing myself to remain outwardly confident, I kept my gaze from going anywhere near Triduana. I knew I would be forced to acknowledge her at some point, but I needed time to steel myself. I hoped that she would do the same. If she revealed my true identity, all was lost. We were in the Lion's Den and she could set the beasts loose on us with a single word.

My heart was pounding as I approached the long table at the head of the hall. Conversations died away as we walked between the tables. Heads turned to watch us and whispers followed in our wake. Even the musicians stopped playing.

I kept walking, looking neither to left nor right.

Beornhaeth greeted me with a growl as I stood before him. "Well, it's my old friend, Guret," he said. "I haven't seen you for a while. Not since you tricked me out of Dun Foither last autumn."

The hall had fallen silent. The only sound was the crackle of the flaming torches. The menace in Beornhaeth's voice was unmistakeable, but compared to the threat that Triduana posed, it was nothing to me.

I spread my arms in a gesture of helplessness. "My lord Beornhaeth," I said. "I did not trick you out of anything. If you recall, I warned you that you were about to be attacked but that I did not know where Bridei was heading. Do you think I would risk coming here if I had betrayed you in any way?"

Never taking his eyes from me, Beornhaeth raised his beaker and downed a mouthful of ale. Old Toki's ale, I guessed. Some of it dribbled from the corners of his mouth, staining his beard. He belched noisily, then wiped his sleeve across his mouth.

He continued to regard me suspiciously. After some thought, he nudged the fat priest who sat beside him.

"Abbot Trumwine," he said. "Perhaps you could ask this messenger to swear an oath that he is telling the truth."

Trumwine licked his fingers clean. "Of course, my lord," he said. He looked at me through small, porcine eyes. Slowly, he lifted the large, jewelled cross from around his neck and placed it on the table in front of him. "Put your right hand on that and swear before God," he instructed me.

I stepped closer. I could sense Medraut's tension but I did not so much as glance at him. Keeping my eyes on Beornhaeth's craggy face, I placed my right hand on top of the crucifix.

I said, "I swear on this holy cross that what I told you last year was the truth as I believed it to be. When I saw you, I did not know that Bridei intended to storm Dun Foither."

I lifted the crucifix, handing it back to Abbot Trumwine who took it with an expression that suggested he had rather hoped I would have been struck down by divine wrath. With a shrug, he said to Beornhaeth, "He is speaking the truth."

Beornhaeth nodded. Only then did I look at Wulfric and incline my head to him. He gazed back at me with an expression of distrust.

At last, I summoned the courage to look at Triduana. I bowed my head and said, "My lady."

She looked horrified, but she said nothing, merely acknowledging me with a slight nod of her head.

"Some chairs for my guests," Beornhaeth boomed. "Make room."

We were seated beside Abbot Trumwine, which did not please him greatly. Medraut, who still spoke no English, sat in stony silence, picking at the food that was brought to us while the hall filled with a buzz of conversation now that the entertainment was over. At Beornhaeth's signal, the musicians began playing again.

Beornhaeth asked me, "So, what news from the north? What is that treacherous dog Bridei planning now?"

"He is planning to raid the Orcades," I replied as I chewed on a piece of delicious beef. "But he is worried because he cannot afford to do that and still keep enough men ready to face King Ecgfrith."

That brought a bark of laughter from Beornhaeth. Beside me, Trumwine's enormous body wobbled as he chuckled.

Beornhaeth said, "He's in for a long wait, then."

Trumwine saw my puzzled expression and explained, "King Ecgfrith is not coming north. He has other worries on his mind at present. The cessation of tribute from the Picts is a minor concern for him."

It took all of my willpower not to betray my excitement at that news.

"Other worries?" I asked.

Trumwine was obviously one of those people who like to gossip, to show that they are close to men of importance and are in possession of privileged information. He needed no encouragement to tell what he knew.

"Mercia is always a threat, of course," he said. "But the king has also rather fallen out with some of the kings of Ireland. Between those two foes, he has more than enough to occupy him. Added to which, he has his ongoing argument with Wilfrid, the former Archbishop of York."

I did not know the details of Ecgfrith's relationship with Archbishop Wilfrid, although I knew they had been at loggerheads for years. I was aware that Ecgfrith had expelled Wilfrid from Northumbria some years earlier, and I had heard that the Pope had decreed that Wilfrid should be reinstated but that Ecgfrith had responded by throwing Wilfrid into prison. He had reluctantly released him, but now the Pope was unhappy with the Northumbrian king. This feud was the source of much gossip, but what mattered to me was that Ecgfrith was not going to be bringing his army north. I had to concentrate so as not to show my relief.

I said, "It seems King Ecgfrith does not have to look far to find enemies."

"Sadly, that is true," Trumwine agreed.

Beornhaeth leaned forwards to look at me past the Abbot's impressive girth. "So what about the other matter we discussed?" he asked. "Is Bridei's support still strong?"

I looked around, as if trying to make sure that nobody could overhear, then I made a slight gesture with my head towards the Abbot.

"Perhaps we should discuss that later," I suggested.

Beornhaeth dismissed that. "You can speak freely. Trumwine is now Abbot of Pictavia. He is building an abbey at Obar Chuirnidh, just a few miles out by the river. Isn't that so, Trumwine?"

Trumwine nodded. "I have been charged by the Archbishop of Canterbury with ensuring that the people of these lands observe the proper calculation for reckoning the date of Easter and that they follow the edicts of the Church of Rome," he said.

It sounded as if he was reciting his remit from a text he had memorised. His little eyes narrowed as he looked at me. "You follow the Ionian tradition, I presume?"

"I do," I said. "Not that there is much choice among the Picts."

"That will change soon," Trumwine assured me. "When King Ecgfrith turns his attention to the north, this fellow Bridei will be crushed, and all churches will be compelled to follow the true religion."

"If King Ecgfrith comes north," Beornhaeth observed sourly.

"He will come eventually," Trumwine asserted.

In response to that, Beornhaeth merely grunted. He repeated his question to me. "What about Bridei's support?"

"I spoke with Guret of Dun Nechtan only a few days ago," I told him. "He is not quite ready to openly defy Bridei, but if King Ecgfrith is not coming this year, it will give me more time to work on him. I think I will be able to persuade him to switch sides at the appropriate time." I paused before adding, "Although it would help if I could offer him some tangible reward."

"Another greedy Pict," Beornhaeth grumbled.

"It would be worth it if he joins our cause," I said. "It would make King Ecgfrith's victory so much simpler. When he does come north, of course."

Beornhaeth asked, "So tell me, how many men will Bridei send to the Orcades, and when will they sail?"

"I would guess that he could only spare a dozen ships," I replied. "As for when they will go, I think he will send them soon, whenever the weather is good enough for such a voyage. He wants to strike the Orcadians, then have his men back as quickly as possible in case you attack him."

Beornhaeth grunted. "So I'll need to move quickly if I want to get Dun Foither back."

"Very quickly," I agreed. "Even then, it will be difficult. Bridei has left a strong garrison there. He will not strip his defences for the assault on the Orcades."

"Bastard," Beornhaeth muttered. Despite his grumbling, I could tell that he was pleased at my news. We had entered his hall not knowing whether we would survive, but my oath had pacified Beornhaeth's temper and he entertained us lavishly. Not only were we fed, but he gave me another heavy pouch containing silver and gold which he said was to be used to persuade Guret and others to switch sides. I promised that I would do my utmost to bring Guret over to King Ecgfrith's side.

That night, when the feast was over, Beornhaeth allowed us to sleep in the hall. He had so many guests who had arrived to celebrate Easter with him that the floor was covered with sleeping bodies, but we found some space near the side wall where we wrapped ourselves in our cloaks. Speaking softly, I told Medraut what I had learned.

"That is good news," he whispered. "We will need to tell Bridei as soon as we can."

"We will leave at first light," I assured him.

So Medraut and I spent the night in the Lions' Den, safe in the knowledge that Ecgfrith would not be coming north.

My only regret was that I could not speak to Triduana. I had stolen a few glances at her. I thought she looked very pretty with her curled hair and her gold jewellery, but she seemed nervous and refused to look in my direction. The only time our eyes met was when she held my gaze for a brief time as she left the hall. But she stayed close to Wulfric and did not come over to speak to me.

I suppose she was wise not to. It was sensible to avoid one another but, looking back now, I regret it even more because I never saw her again after that night and I was never able to learn what became of her and her children. That still hurts.

Medraut and I returned to Inbhir Nis unscathed. We did not stop at Dun Nechtan on our way back. In fact, we made as few stops as possible, riding hard to give Bridei the news that Ecgfrith was not coming north and the Pecht were safe for at least one more year.

"By God, that helps," he said, clapping me on the shoulder when I told him the good news.

I said, "I think Beornhaeth will make an attempt on Dun Foither, even without Ecgfrith's support. I have convinced him that he must do it soon."

"Then let him try," said Bridei. "At best, he will be able to muster no more than a thousand men. If he comes soon, I can more than match that. Then I will still have time to send a strong fleet to the Orcades." He thumped my shoulder again. "By God, you have done well, lad."

I gave him the money that Beornhaeth had paid me. "Some of this is supposed to be used to bribe Guret into betraying you," I told him.

"I can put it to better use," Bridei said. He took half, telling me to split the other half with Medraut. Then he asked, "Did you speak to Sorcha?"

"Yes."

"And?"

I shrugged. "And nothing. I will speak to her again."

After I left Bridei, I went down to the river to visit Derelei's grave and to tell her I was back. I went to see Sorcha later that evening, when the boys were asleep.

She smiled when she saw me, but she would not let me kiss her.

"Are you back for good?" she asked.

"No. The king will need me again."

"Then nothing has changed," she said sadly.

We sat and talked for a while, but there was now a distance between us that had not been there before. I asked her, "Will you not re-consider?"

I could see that her decision tormented her, but she remained determined. "We both loved Derelei," she said. "I want to see her murderers brought to justice, but that desire does not consume me as it does you."

"They must pay," I said.

"It has been three years," she pointed out. "Who knows when you will ever get the proof you need?" She paused to lay her hand on mine. "I am not asking you to forget her, Bili. Neither of us will ever do that. But she is gone. Do not let the desire for vengeance consume you."

I could feel my anger rising, as it always did when I thought of Derelei and what had happened to her, but Sorcha's words struck a chord in my memory. Bridei had warned me of the dangers of walking the dark road. I had trodden that path for years now. Had I gone too far to turn back?

Sorcha drew her hand away. She said, "You want her back, don't you?"

"Of course I do," I said sharply.

Sorcha sighed. She was close to tears again. I could see that my words had upset her but I could not help myself. I wanted Derelei more than I wanted anything else.

Sorcha said, "That is why I will not marry you, Bili. Can you not see? I will wait for you for as long as it takes, but I will not give myself to you until you can tell me that you are home for good and that you are at peace with

Derelei. Until then, I would always be second in your life. I do not want that."

I hung my head. I knew she spoke the truth.

I felt the soft kiss of her lips on my cheek. "I will wait for you," she whispered. "I will wait until you are ready. But I think you should go now."

Having lost what I had thought would be a new love, I threw myself into working on the farm and acting the part of a chieftain. Bleddyn saw through me, of course, but I told him it was nothing more than trouble over a girl, so he did not pry. Knowing Bleddyn, he probably knew the truth of the matter anyway. Bridei would have told him.

In every other way it was a good summer, with a fine harvest. Our sheep produced many new lambs and our cows bore three calves. One of these was a strong young bullock who would, in time, make a fine stud and would increase the size of our small herd even further.

Our family increased as well, because young Gartnait married a girl from a nearby farm. Bleddyn conducted the ceremony in his church, which was crowded with people who came from miles around to witness the occasion. Then I laid on a feast which we held in the open, with great bonfires and roasted meat, supplemented by fish from the river and copious amounts of ale and whisky.

There was music, dancing and laughter. Old Entifidich was so delighted at his son's marriage that he became uproariously drunk and insisted on telling everyone that he would be a grandfather before next summer. By the end of the evening, he could hardly stand, so Aed had to help me carry him home. As we laid him in his bed, I could not shake off the feeling that if Ecgfrith came against us, none of us might live to see the following summer.

While I tried to push Sorcha to the back of my mind, and to settle back into the rural life, things beyond the confines of my estate continued to boil. Beornhaeth sent raiding parties into the southern hills and, as I had predicted, he gathered an army of several hundred men in an effort to re-take Dun Foither. Of course, the wall was too strong and there was no longer any cliffside access, so he was forced to return home when Bridei hurried across the Mounth at the head of a relief force. There was no great battle, merely a few skirmishes as Bridei chased Beornhaeth's army south.

Once Beornhaeth had been driven back, Bridei sent a fleet of thirty ships to the Orcades, each vessel crammed with warriors. They devastated the islands, sinking or burning every boat they encountered, destroying farms and villages, killing the men and bringing away a host of women and children as slaves.

Medraut, who had managed to find a place on one of the boats, told me about it afterwards.

"There are nearly seventy islands in the Orcades," he informed me proudly. "We did not leave a single one unscathed. They won't be able to raid us again for many years."

I suppose the Orcadians had brought Bridei's revenge on themselves, but a part of me could not help wondering whether our actions were any better than those of the Northumbrians. Even Bleddyn could not answer that for me.

Bridei, as full of energy as ever despite being more than fifty years old, also dealt with the usual raids from Dal Riata, although most of the Scots had other things on their minds that year. Mael Duin, their manic king, decided to launch an attack against Elfin of Alt Clud. The raid was a disaster. Mael Duin was repulsed, leaving one of his sons among the many dead.

I heard about these far-off events, but they did not trouble me. Bridei kept his word to leave me in peace all through that year and into the next. Then, just as the new lambs were being born, he called for me again. I said farewell to my friends, especially to Bleddyn, then I rode to Inbhir Nis.

My first stop was a visit to Sorcha, but it was an awkward meeting. Neither of us was able to relax or speak as freely as we had once done. She cried when I told her I was going away again, but she would not let me hold her or comfort her. Not knowing what to do, I went to see my sons, who were growing at an alarming rate, terrorising the king's hall as only young boys can. I could not bring myself to tell them I was leaving, so I laughed and joked with them, chasing them around the room until Sorcha came in to restore order. She gave me a weak smile as I brushed myself down before going to see Bridei. It was, I thought, a sad way for us to part.

As usual, Bridei called me to his private room. He said, "Ecgfrith is preparing to attack the Irish. He won't come north this year."

"That is good news," I said.

He shook his head. "No, it isn't. I want him to bring his army here. All these raids and small skirmishes with Beornhaeth are no good to anyone. If we are ever to regain the southern lands, we need to destroy the Northumbrian army. I can't do that if it won't march north."

That was the first inkling I had of the scale of what Bridei was planning.

"What is it you want me to do?" I asked him.

"I need to provoke Ecgfrith. Something that will worry him about us expanding our power, but that won't cost a lot of lives."

"You'll never take Sruighlea," I said, thinking that was what he intended. "Beornhaeth has strengthened the defences. It is far too strong."

"I know that, lad. The only way we'll take that place is if we drive the Angles out of the rest of our lands and leave them isolated."

"Then what is it you want?"

His mouth twisted in a grimace as if he had tasted something bitter. He said, "I need to take Dundurn back from the Scots. It's a thorn in my side and I want it plucked out. I want you to find me a way to do that."

I remembered the hillfort at Dundurn. It sat on the borders of Dal Riata, guarding a narrow, loch-filled valley. I recalled how Mael Duin had seized it when the garrison had abandoned the fort because they were afraid of being left exposed to attack from both the Scots and the Northumbrians. That was the only way Mael Duin could have taken it because although Dundurn was smaller than Sruighlea, it was just as impregnable. There were no secret passages or hidden ways to get in.

Bridei raised an eyebrow. "Well?"

"It can't be done," I told him. "It's impossible."

"You'll think of something," he said confidently.

Chapter 33

I went home to speak to Bleddyn. I had been little more than a boy when we had visited Dundurn, and it had been held by our own warriors at the time, so there had been no real need to investigate it. I hoped that Bleddyn would remember more about the place than I did. He did, but none of what he remembered was of any help to me.

"The wall is high and thick," he said. "There is only one entrance and it is easy to defend. The hill is not that big, but it is very steep, and the path leading to the gate leaves attackers exposed on their sword side."

I nodded. That was common with hillforts. The path would climb across the slope at an angle so that anyone making for the gates would have their right sides exposed to the walls as they approached the entrance. Most men are right-handed, so they carry their shields on their left. It was a simple, but highly effective defence.

If any attackers did manage to reach the walls or the gate, they still had the problem of how to get in. Alone and unhindered, a man could climb the wall, for the massive stones always had gaps and cracks that would provide finger-holds, but to attempt such a climb while carrying a spear and shield, with the defenders hurling filthy garbage, rocks and stones down at you, was something only the bravest or most foolhardy would contemplate.

Bleddyn agreed that, as I had told Bridei, it was impossible. Looking pensive, he rubbed at his cheek, saying, "I suppose Bridei wants to take Dundurn to keep the Scots from interfering when we face Ecgfrith. Mael Duin has been weakened by his battles with Elfin of Alt Clud, so now would be a good time to take advantage."

"He's also trying to provoke Ecgfrith," I informed him.

"Aye, it would give us a good base to launch attacks against the Angles."

"That's all very well," I said. "But the place can't be taken without a full-scale siege."

"Why do you think he has asked you to do it?" Bleddyn said. "He knows that he cannot take it by storm, not unless he is prepared to lose hundreds of men, and he can't afford that with the threat of the Northumbrians still to be faced."

"I am no magician!" I exclaimed. "What does he expect me to do? Conjure the defenders away or make them all fall asleep so that he can simply walk in?"

"That would be a good trick if you could do it," agreed Bleddyn.

A trick. That was what we needed. The first vague glimmerings of an idea came to me. I sat for a moment, thinking about it, then, with mounting excitement, I told Bleddyn how it might be possible to take Dundurn.

"I would need your help," I told him.

His brow creased as he threw questions at me, challenging the plan. Between us, we spent the evening teasing out the details. Then Bleddyn sat back, smiled and said, "You know, I think that might work."

We set off for Inbhir Nis the following day. When we arrived, I left Bleddyn at the hall while I went down to the town in search of Fincana the seer. My plan depended on her co-operation, which I knew was not likely to be offered willingly. She had baffled and deceived me before, but this time I was sure I had the upper hand.

Almost sure, anyway.

She was sitting in her usual spot at the doorway to her roundhouse, using the daylight to help her as she mixed her potions and powders. Her wrinkled face broke into a malevolent grin when she saw me.

I walked right up to her. "I need something from you," I said.

"Everyone comes to Fincana when they need something," she replied. "What is it you want, I wonder? Something to kill an unborn child you have planted in a young girl's belly?"

I gave her my best stare. "No. I need something that will cause sickness. I want to put something in someone's water that will make them so ill that they will be incapable of doing anything, but not so serious that they won't recover. I do not want to kill anyone. Can you provide something that will do that?"

"Perhaps," she said, returning her attention to the fine powder in the bowl that lay on her lap. "But why should I give this to you? What can you give me in return?"

I squatted down so that my face was on a level with hers. Reluctantly, she lifted her gaze from the bowl as I said, "I can pay. But if you still refuse to help me, I will bring Bleddyn Grim-Hand here and I will tell him you wish to be baptised as a Christian."

"You would not dare!" she snapped.

"Would I not? Did you know that the Christians must confess their sins, Fincana? What will you confess? That you supplied the poison that killed Bridei's daughter? That you gave it to Mayota so that she could sprinkle it on Derelei's supper?"

"You cannot prove that!" she said coldly.

I had her now. For once, I had her. I could see the spark of fear in her eyes. I said, "Bleddyn will drag you to the river and he will push you under the water to wash away your sins so that you will be protected by God. Whether you wish it or not, the old gods will be unable to help you after that. You can say farewell to Epona, to Taranis, to Grannos and all the other false gods. The Lord will forgive your sins as long as you confess them, but everyone will know what you have done. And you know that Bridei is not as forgiving as God."

I was exaggerating, of course, but I doubted whether Fincana had ever witnessed a baptism. I was not convinced that a symbolic ducking in the cold waters of the Nis would be sufficient to prevent Fincana believing what she had always believed, although Bleddyn had assured me that it would, if only because Fincana knew the power of symbols. He had joked, "If all else fails, I'll just hold her head under the water until she drowns."

At least, I think he had been joking.

Whether it was fear of confessing her involvement in Derelei's death, which I had only guessed at but which she had more or less admitted, or whether it was the thought of being baptised as a Christian, something scared Fincana enough for her to say, "I have something that will do what you need."

"I need a lot of it," I said. "Enough to affect at least a hundred people."

"Then come back in four days and I will have it for you," she barked. Her eyes flashed darkly at me, but she knew I had the power over her now.

"Thank you," I said as I stood up once more. I took one of Beornhaeth's gold rings from my belt pouch and handed it to her. "That should be more than enough," I said. As I made to turn away, I stopped and added, "Oh, and I will be testing your potion on someone first, so it had better do what it is supposed to. Nothing more, nothing less. If not, I can soon fetch Bleddyn."

"You have become a hard man, Bili," she said. "It is not wise to make an enemy of Fincana."

I said, "I am not your enemy, Fincana. In fact, I can help you. If you do this thing for me, then wait for five days after Bridei rides away and then have another dream. You can predict another victory for him."

Fincana gave me two clay phials, each one sealed with a plug of cloth and moss. She handed them over grudgingly, but she swore that they would do what I needed.

I tested them anyway, tipping a tiny drop into a bowl of water which I gave to one of Bridei's dogs. The poor beast fell ill within a few hours, vomiting and defecating everywhere. Eventually, it lay down, whimpering and shivering.

I thought I might have given it too much because it seemed close to death, but by the following day it had recovered enough to eat and drink again. Satisfied, I wrapped the two phials in my pack.

"That will do," I said.

Bridei grinned. "I knew you'd come up with something," he said.

We left the following day. Bridei took two hundred mounted men and gathered more foot soldiers as we drew near to Dundurn. Bleddyn and I rode with him.

It was a difficult ride for Bleddyn, whose various wounds, allied to the aches in his joints, made every hour of the journey an agony for him. I could see the strain in his face but he persisted without complaint.

"Bleddyn Grim-Hand rides once more," he joked. "Just like old times." Yet he needed assistance to dismount from his horse and each morning his joints had stiffened so that I had to help him to his feet and support him while he took faltering steps to ease his bones into motion.

"I doubt that I'll be much good if it comes to a fight," he told me.

"You won't need to do any fighting," I assured him.

He winced as he took another painful step. "I pray you are right, lad," he said fervently. "Every time I take a man's life. the Lord punishes me with an injury. He has shown me that I have strayed from the path I was intended to follow. I will not kill again."

"Nobody will be killed," I said.

"Amen to that."

I wished I had not asked him to do this, but he bore the pain stoically and somehow dragged himself all the way to the old realm of Fidach. That part of the country is a warren of hills and forests. It is a wonderfully majestic place, a land that inspires awe through its beauty. The old people, our ancestors from a long-forgotten past, must have thought so too, because they had built many grave barrows and circles of large stones, and they had piled cairns on many of the hilltops, all monument so ancient that nobody could tell how long they had been there.

There are many places to hide in such a varied landscape. Bridei and his men were able to find a sheltered spot well out of sight of the hillfort but close enough that they could get there quickly. They settled down to wait while Bleddyn and I continued on our difficult journey.

Leaving Bridei and his warriors in their hidden camp, we climbed the hills that lined the long glen, heading west, then picking a slow route down through the forests to the lochside before doubling back along its pebbled, tree-lined shore to approach Dundurn from the west. It was desperately hard on Bleddyn, but this detour had been his idea.

"Best to approach them from the direction of Dal Rata," he had said. "That way they will not be suspicious of us."

I agreed with him, but the discomfort he suffered was painful enough to see, let alone suffer.

The Scots were suspicious enough anyway, only grudgingly admitting us after a long discussion. Once they were satisfied that Bleddyn was a genuine monk and that I was his simpleton servant, a role I took up with an ease that rather worried me, they opened the massively thick wooden gates to let us in.

Bleddyn blessed them and begged for beds for the night. He did not need to act to portray someone who was tired and in considerable pain.

We were fed and told that we could sleep in one of the larger roundhouses. These, as Bleddyn had reminded me when we were discussing the fort, were communal dwellings, shared by several families who all crowded in, living, eating and sleeping together. There would be little chance of sneaking out of such a place undetected, even during the night, so we had only one chance if our plan was to succeed.

Bleddyn shrugged off his weariness and asked whether he could preach to the garrison and their families. The commander, a burly, scar-cheeked man named Bresal, agreed willingly.

"We don't often get monks passing this way," he said.

Bleddyn beamed at him. "Excellent. Then gather your people and we shall sing and pray together." As an afterthought he turned to me. "See to the horses, boy. Make sure they are fed and watered."

I bobbed my head obediently and led the two horses away from the main buildings to the great, stone-lined cistern that was used for gathering rain water. Here, I busied myself, checking all the time to see whether anyone was watching me. I need not have been worried. I could hear Bleddyn's booming voice, haranguing the assembled men and women. Even the warriors patrolling the walls were paying more attention to him than to anything else. They did not get many monks passing that way, Bresal had said. They certainly did not get any like Bleddyn.

He was in his element, giving a spellbinding performance with his tales of the miracles of Jesus Christ, interspersed with dire warnings of eternal punishment for any sinners. It was, as he had said, just like old times. He held the people entranced while I went about my less noble business.

At the side of the enormous cistern I found three wooden buckets which were attached to long ropes. I lowered two into the cistern, scooped up water and placed the buckets down for the horses to drink. Then I used the third bucket to fill our waterskins. Checking again that nobody was watching me, I moved to stand between the two horses. Satisfied that I was hidden from view, I reached for my pack which was slung on Dagger's back. I pulled out the two phials that Fincana had given me.

Moving carefully, I waited until the horses had finished drinking, then emptied the thick liquid out of the phials, pouring it into the buckets. I hurriedly stuffed the phials back in my pack then lowered the buckets into the cistern, sloshing them around, swirling them in the water as if I was playing some sort of game. One at a time, I hauled them back up, checking to see that no traces of Fincana's potion remained. They were clear.

I left the buckets beside the cistern then took the horses to one side of the fort where I found some hay. After removing the saddles from the horses' backs, I pulled a brush from my pack and groomed the beasts, whistling tunelessly while I worked.

From the far side of the fort I could still hear Bleddyn preaching. I laughed when I heard him tell a tale of Saint Columba scaring away a fearsome beast that lurked in the depths of Loch Nis. He had waited several years to steal Adomnan's story.

It was growing dark by the time Bleddyn came to find me, cursing me for a half-witted fool as he limped his way across the fort. He did not ask any questions, merely raising his eyebrows as he drew near.

I nodded. "It is done."

He gave the slightest nod of his head then cuffed me round the ear, calling me a careless dolt, raising his voice so that the nearest sentries stopped to watch and laugh.

I clutched a hand to the side of my head. "That hurt!" I hissed at him under my breath.

"I have to make it look genuine," he whispered back.

"You don't have to hit me at all," I protested.

He grinned and hit me again. "Come, boy!" he ordered loudly, "We shall have some supper before retiring for the night."

Sitting on our lumpy pallets in a smoke-filled, noisy and desperately crowded roundhouse, we drank only ale that night. We were given some bread and cheese but we refused everything else. Not that we expected them to have drawn water so soon, but it was better to be safe.

The following day we left early, anxious to be away. We rode down the steep path to the foot of the hill, then crossed the shallow river, the same Eireann that ran all the way to my father's old farm before joining the Tatha on its way to the sea.

Once on the other side, we turned east, along the foot of the towering, wooded slopes, then climbed again, seeking Bridei. We found him before mid-day, sitting with his small war band in a corrie high above the valley floor.

He grinned broadly when we told him what we had done. Raising his arms, he called out, "Right, lads. Time to go to war!"

Bleddyn and I tagged along, but we stayed well to the rear, hoping to keep out of sight of anyone in the hillfort. While we watched from the shelter of a stand of leafy birch trees, Bridei and his men took up positions at the foot of the path that led up to the fort. Dismounting and going on alone, Bridei walked up to the gates to demand that the garrison surrender.

Bresal laughed in his face and told him where he could stick his puny war host. Bridei turned back and settled down for a siege.

Sieges are strange things. There are a few different ways they can end. If the attacking force is large enough, they are occasionally able to storm the walls, clambering up the slopes and overwhelming the defenders by sheer force of numbers. That is not a good way to take a hillfort because the attackers will almost certainly lose hundreds of men. If they succeed, of course, the defenders are put to the sword. Nobody can expect mercy from men who have stormed a fort.

More often, a siege is a long, largely tedious affair which ends when the men inside the fort run out of food and water, or when help arrives to drive off the besiegers. Bresal and his men probably expected help to arrive long before they ran out of food, but the siege of Dundurn was over far more quickly than anyone could have guessed.

By late afternoon, it was evident that there were fewer and fewer men guarding the ramparts. Bridei walked back up to the gate and demanded to speak to Bresal, but was told the commander was busy. Once more, Bridei offered them the chance to surrender but once more he was refused.

He waited until evening, then made the offer a third time. This time, he pointed out that if his warriors stormed the walls, they would kill every man inside. He asked what chance they thought they had of preventing his soldiers from scaling the walls. A short time after that, the gates were opened.

Bridei and his men took Dundurn without a fight. Bresal and his followers were disarmed, then sent packing. Most of them were too unwell to walk far, but they hobbled their way along the loch, heading for Dal Riata.

The cistern was emptied, the water being thrown away. That took a lot of time and effort but it was not as arduous as filling buckets, jars and waterskins from the river and carrying them up the steep slope to the fort to re-fill the great tank. Bleddyn and I did not wait to see that work finished. We rode home.

"You should be pleased with yourself, Bili," Bleddyn told me. "Bridei now has his eastern flank secured by Dun Foither and his western flank by Dundurn, and both are thanks to you."

I suppose I should have been pleased, but I knew that the main threat was to the south. Taking Dundurn would surely provoke some reaction from Ecgfrith, just as Bridei had intended. I knew that a storm was coming. What I did not know was that, when it came, I would be standing in the very centre of it.

Chapter 34

I entered my twenty-eighth year as a man of some wealth and fame. I believed that I had considerable influence with Bridei so, after we had taken Dundurn, I mentioned to him that I thought it was time we forced Guret and Mayota to confess their crimes.

"Fincana would speak against them if you put enough pressure on her," I told him.

He was strangely apathetic. "Leave them, lad," he told me. "Their time will come. For the moment, they can be useful to us. We have greater things to tackle first."

"They killed Derelei," I reminded him.

He looked at me with a grim expression. "I told you once before that it is sometimes necessary to make difficult decisions, to put the good of the people above personal desires. This is one of those times. We have more important things to worry about." He wagged a finger at me. "And don't go doing anything on your own. Leave Guret and Mayota to me."

I complained to Bleddyn, but he assured me that Bridei would have his reasons. "He is right about us having greater problems, though," he said.

And he was. In the early Spring of the year Six Hundred and Eighty Five, came the news we had expected and feared for so long. In the three years since we had taken Dun Foither, Ecgfrith of Northumbria had been too busy to do anything about Bridei's growing power, but he had not been idle. His armies had sailed across the sea to Ireland, where they had wrought havoc, returning with a great many slaves and with their ships low in the water, weighed down by the huge quantities of plunder they had taken. With that great venture completed, and having established an uneasy peace with Mercia, Ecgfrith came north at last.

There was no need of spies to learn of his coming. Word of his approach spread like a forest fire. In April, we heard that he had arrived in Dun Eidyn, bringing an army of nearly eight thousand men with him. It was a huge force, the largest army to march north since the Romans had left our shores nearly three hundred years before, and it was coming to destroy the Pecht.

I will not claim that I was not afraid. I could still recall the dreadful sight of the Northumbrian horsemen charging across the river to smash our army while I stood on the hilltop, watching in terror. Now, after thirteen years, they had returned. The prospect scared me more than I would ever admit to anyone, and yet there was also a sense of relief, a feeling that, at last, the interminable waiting was over.

Everyone was anxious; everyone except Bridei. This was the moment he had been waiting for. He summoned me again. When I arrived at his chamber, Taran was with him, the two of them playing a game of King's Stone. Bridei was obviously winning, his counters of blue glass having captured most of Taran's white ones. I was not very good at the game, but I could tell that Bridei would soon capture control of the small, white bead that was the King's Stone, the piece that both sides set out to capture.

I watched patiently while they finished the game. Bridei persisted in picking off Taran's counters until there were only two left. To my surprise, he passed up several chances to finish the game by taking the King's Stone itself. Eventually, Taran leaned back.

"You win again," he conceded.

"You still have some men left," Bridei said.

Taran swept his two counters from the rectangular board. "You win," he repeated. "As usual."

Bridei gave a throaty chuckle as he looked up at me. "Do you play, lad?"

"Not very well."

Taran grunted, "Then don't play him. He doesn't just want to win, he wants to destroy his opponent."

"Which is what we will do to Ecgfrith," Bridei said, his expression more sombre now. "Victory is no good to us on its own. We must destroy him." He waved me to a seat beside him. "Sit down, Bili, and I will tell you how we are going to do that."

I sat down, eager to hear what he intended to do. Of course, this was Bridei, and I should have known better than to think he would confide in me unless there was a great need.

He said, "Bili, I must ask you to do something for me. It is something that only you can do, but it is more dangerous than anything you have done before. I will not blame you if you refuse me."

I felt the tension of fear crawling through my limbs and eating at my belly, but I had pledged myself to him the first time I met him. I could not refuse him now.

"What is it you want me to do?" I asked.

That was when he told me his plan and revealed the part that he wanted me to play in it. It was bold, it was dangerous and, for me, it was almost certainly a death sentence.

When he had explained the details, he said, "If we succeed, we will destroy Ecgfrith's army. We will reclaim the lands of Circinn, Fidach and Fib. We will drive the Angles back across the Foirthe. Will you help me accomplish these things, Bili? Will you do this for me?"

I felt a dull emptiness engulf me, but I could not deny him. He had given me so much that I was forever in his debt. Yet what he wanted from me frightened me to my very core. It was almost as if I was not in control of my body as I heard myself say, "I will do it."

"Thank you," he said. "Medraut will go with you. I pray that he will find a way to keep you alive."

"Does he know what you are planning?"

"No. Only Taran knows. Nobody else must know. Medraut does not need to be told."

"If you are sending him to his death, I think he deserves to know why," I said.

Bridei shook his head. "Medraut is a warrior. He will do what he is told to do. You will leave in the morning."

I nodded bleakly.

Taran clasped my forearm in a rare gesture of respect. He said, "I am leaving this evening. I wish you luck."

I replied, "I think I will probably need it."

I went to see Sorcha, to say farewell. She recognised instantly that something was wrong. Placing a concerned hand on my cheek, she asked, "What has happened?"

"I am going away again. One way or another, this will be the last time."

"Oh, Bili." She took my hands in hers.

Bridei had sworn me to secrecy, but I could not help telling her what he wanted me to do. I told her because she was my friend and I trusted her. I told her because I wanted her to be more than a friend and I knew I might never see her again.

Little Bridei, now eight years old, came into the room, with his brother, Nechtan, trailing after him. Their faces were dark with patches of mud and dirt, but they greeted me excitedly when they saw me. Then Bridei looked up at Sorcha and asked, "Why are you crying, Sorcha?"

That only made her cry all the more.

I told him, "Sorcha is sad because I am going away. So is your grandfather and so are a lot of other men. The Northumbrians are coming, and we must fight them."

He looked at me gravely. "Will you kill them all?" he asked.

"Not by myself," I laughed. "But with your grandfather's help, I hope that we will drive them away."

I made him and little Nechtan promise to be good for Sorcha, then I went to say goodbye to Derelei.

Her lonely grave was as peaceful as ever. I stood by the headstone for a long time, saying nothing, just remembering.

It was late in the evening when I heard a rustle of movement, a mere whisper over the gentle murmur of the river. I turned to see Sorcha walking towards me.

Her face, framed by its habitual headscarf, was immeasurably sad. Wordlessly, she took my hand and squeezed it gently. Together, we stood there in silence as we remembered Derelei.

As the evening faded to night, Sorcha said, "If you die, you will not see her avenged."

"I know. But the future of the Pecht is at stake. Those who are living are more in need of my help."

Sorcha turned to me. She paused, then reached up, putting her arms around me, pulling my face towards hers. She kissed me. It was a lover's kiss, gentle yet passionate.

I could feel the longing in her. I pulled her close, kissing her soft lips. Then I stopped.

"Have you changed your mind?" I asked, not daring to hope too much.

"No. You have changed yours. I wish it had not taken you so long. Now we have only this one night."

"I want you," I said. "But only if you are sure."

"I am sure," she smiled. "You came to see me before you came here, and you have realised that the living are more important than the dead."

"I cannot forget her."

"Neither can I. She will always be in our hearts, but it is long past the time for you to move on."

She gripped my hand, turning to lead me away.

"Where are we going?" I asked.

She replied, "If this is our only night together, I want to make it one I will never forget."

She led me back up to the king's stockade, hurrying past the guards at the gate who laughed knowingly as we passed them. By the time we closed the door of her bedroom behind us, we were both more than ready.

We kissed hungrily. She lifted her head, letting me kiss her neck while she raised her hands to unfasten her headscarf and let her hair fall loose. Her eyes were closed.

My fingers fumbled awkwardly for the ties at the front of her dress. Laughing, she pushed my hands away, then unfastened the cords, letting her dress slide down. She wriggled her hips to let it fall to the floor. I thought she was very beautiful.

I bent to kiss her breasts and she held me close, moaning softly at the touch of my lips and tongue.

I had not been with a woman since that fateful night with Derelei, and my desire took over. I lifted Sorcha, carrying her to the bed. She was tugging at my clothes, helping me to pull them off, then we were together on the bed.

She rolled on top of me, letting her long hair hang down over my face as she kissed me. My hands roamed over her body. I wanted to feel every part of her.

She held her self above me, whispering soft encouragement, letting me touch her. Then she gasped as she lowered her hips onto me and our bodies began to move to the rhythm of our primal need.

I forgot everything. I forgot Derelei, I forgot Bridei, and I forgot the fate that awaited me in the morning. I knew only Sorcha and I lost myself in her.

We made love again early the following morning, before dawn. It was slower, less desperate, but just as passionate. It was, as she had promised, a night I would never forget.

With a sigh, she slipped from the bed, scrabbling in the dark to light a candle. By its dim light, I watched her as she dressed.

"Come back to bed," I said.

"I must see to the boys soon," she said. "And you must go to do the king's bidding."

"I'd rather stay here with you."

"You are such a fool, Bili. It is too late now."

"I know. I am sorry."

"I am sorry, too." She brushed her tangled hair, then tied it back and fastened her headscarf once more. "Now we have no more time together," she said sadly.

"When I get back, we can be married," I told her.

She gave me a weak smile. We both knew that there was little chance of me returning this time, but she said, "I will be waiting for you."

"I wish . . ." I stopped. I wished a lot of things.

"I know." She took a deep breath. "I will fetch some warm water for you to wash and shave," she said. She left the room, heading towards the kitchens.

I lay back on the bed, the moss and straw filling of the mattress now crushed and flattened beneath me. I had been such a fool. I knew it now. I briefly thought of Derelei but, for once, the memory did not hurt. I knew she would have understood. Above all, I thought of Sorcha.

She returned with a clay bowl of warm water, a small piece of fatty soap and a towel. She sat beside me while I washed and shaved. I still struggled to grow a decent beard, so I always kept my razor sharp. The soap was dark and rough, made from tallow and ashes. It felt raw on my skin but it helped to refresh me. All the time, Sorcha sat close to me, watching me. That felt good. If it had not been for the fact that I had to leave, that morning would have been truly wonderful.

I had left my change of clothing in the guest house that Bridei had set aside for me. In the first misty light of dawn, Sorcha walked there with me, hand in hand. She helped me dress, fastening my thick cloak with the heavy, silver brooch. She kissed me again, then we held one another tightly, neither of us wanting to let the other go.

From outside, we heard the sounds of people moving around, the stamp of many feet, the snorting of horses and men's voices. Reluctantly, we drew apart.

"Come back to me," Sorcha said softly.

"I will, God willing."

"Promise?"

Only the day before, I would have hesitated before responding to that special word, but today I smiled and replied, "Promise."

Then I went to do Bridei's bidding.

Chapter 35

Chieftains were gathering from all across Fortriu, bringing their warriors with them. They came on foot and they came on horseback. They came with spears and shields, with swords and axes. Some even came with scythes or billhooks. They all knew that the coming weeks would decide the fate of the Pecht. This was a fight for the survival of our people, so they marched with grim, determined faces as Bridei sent them south.

He sent supplies with them. Large, heavy wagons, small carts and even strings of pack mules, all laden with food for the army he was gathering. It was early May, so these stores must have been held in reserve for months, waiting for this moment. It was as Bridei said; he was always ready.

The king waved to me as I fetched my horse from the stables. He smiled and winked at me. I think he had noticed Sorcha walking with me to the roundhouse.

Medraut had noticed something, too. "You're in a good mood," he observed. "Did the kitchen maid say yes this time?"

"Shut up, Medraut."

He laughed. "I see she must have done."

"Mind your own business," I told him. "I don't ask you about your love life."

"Just as well. You'd only get jealous. I spent last night with two of the most beautiful girls you could ever hope to meet."

"Liar."

"They both wanted to—"

I threw a clod of earth at him. "Shut up, Medraut. Come on, we have a long way to go."

We were also riding south. Medraut did not ask many questions but he was no fool, so I think he guessed what we were going to do. All he said was that he hoped he would get an opportunity to fight the enemy properly instead of acting as nursemaid to a spy.

"I'm sure you'll get your chance," I assured him.

We made a brief stop at Dun Nechtan, where Guret was gathering his own war band. Hundreds of warriors were already encamped near the loch, and more were arriving by the day.

"The king is on his way," I told Guret.

"What about you?" he asked. "Where are you going?"

"To find out what Ecgfrith is doing," I replied.

"That will be dangerous," he said. Then he looked at Medraut and said, "I hope you come back alive."

"I intend to," Medraut replied.

I said nothing. I had a sense that something had passed between them, a coded message of some sort. Perhaps it was simply an easing of Medraut's hostility in response to Guret's good wishes. Perhaps it was nothing more than the fact that men often forget their quarrels when danger approaches. For myself, I could never forget or forgive what Guret had done.

I noticed Mayota watching me, her lips curled in anticipation of seeing me ride off to my death. I could not resist making one last parting shot. I said, "I intend to come back, too. I have unfinished business to attend to."

I don't think my words scared them at all, but I felt better for saying it.

Ecgfrith had reached Sruighlea when we found him. His army was camped on the wide, flat plain by the river, hundreds of cooking fires sending thin plumes of smoke into the evening sky. The warriors looked every bit as formidable as I had feared. These were not farmers who turned to war when called by their chieftains; these were men who practised the art of fighting, who lived for battle. They wore armour of leather or chainmail, they had helmets and shields, sharp swords and heavy battle-axes. These were men who had defeated every foe they had ever faced.

Horses grazed in the meadows by the camp, cropping the lush, Spring grass. I tried to count their number as we passed them, but there were so many that I did not have time. Several hundred at least, I guessed.

When I showed the hawk's head ring to the picquets, they sent us up to the great fortress itself. It was an impressive stronghold. The great rock of Sruighlea, with its sheer, towering sides, dominated the river plain below it. In the distant past it had been an outpost of the ancient kingdom of Gododdin, but it had been in Northumbrian hands for many generations, a bastion that guarded their northern frontier.

Various kings of the Pecht had tried to wrest Sruighlea from the Angles, but no army on earth could storm this place if it was held by determined men.

I could see that Medraut was thinking the same thing. His eyes flickered from side to side as we rode up to the gates, taking everything in, judging it. Medraut was in his prime now, an impressive bulk of a man, strong and powerful. Our relationship was still uneasy at best, but as we rode into the midst of our enemies, I knew that Bridei had been correct and that Medraut was the best protector I could have had. Whatever he thought of me, he would fight to the end to protect me. I was sure that he would get that chance soon enough.

We clattered through the wide gates into the fortress. Our horses were led away and we were shown to a large, single-storey building with foundations and lower walls of stone, topped by wooden upper walls and a roof of turf and reeds.

Four warriors stood outside the low doorway. They demanded that we hand over our weapons before we would be allowed to enter. Medraut grumbled menacingly but unbuckled his sword belt, reluctantly handing it over.

"Knives, too," one of the soldiers growled.

I protested that we would need the knives if we were to eat, but the four of them squared up, ready to remove our daggers by force, so we handed them over.

"Bastards!" muttered Medraut.

They could not understand him, but they grasped his meaning from the tone of his voice. They positively bristled, ready to teach us some manners.

I hurriedly waved the ring in their faces. "I must see Beornhaeth," I said insistently. "Now!"

"Tell your man to watch his lip," one of the guards snarled.

I said to Medraut. "Keep your mouth shut. This will be difficult enough without you provoking a fight."

Medraut was never one for acting contrite, but he closed his lips tightly and nodded his head. I gestured to the guards, indicating that I wanted them to open the door. Staring hard at us, they stood aside, although they made no other move. I opened the door myself.

Inside, the building's solitary room was dark and filled with writhing tendrils of smoke from a great hearth fire that sent a blast of heat across the room to greet us. As my eyes adjusted to the gloom, I saw that around a dozen men were gathered near the fire, seated on wooden chairs or low stools. All of them were richly dressed and wearing more gold than I had ever seen in one place. Finger rings, neck rings, arm rings, all glistened in the firelight.

Beornhaeth was there, as bulky and hairy as ever. So too was Wulfric. I wondered whether Triduana would have accompanied them, but I doubted it. This was a war, and the Northumbrians usually left their women at home when they went to war. There were certainly no women in evidence apart from a handful of slaves who were serving food and ale to the men. There was, though, a priest. I recognised the huge bulk of Abbot Trumwine sitting near the fire, beads of sweat shining on his fleshy face. I briefly wondered what he was doing among these warriors, but it was the man sitting next to him who caught my attention.

He was tall, his light brown hair held back by a thin band of gold that circled his head. As soon as I saw him, he reminded me of Aldfrith, the scholar I had seen on Iona years before. This, I knew, must be Aldfrith's younger brother, Ecgfrith.

The family resemblance was uncanny. He had the same bright eyes, the same beak-like nose, but the man seated by the fire was very different from his brother. Where Aldfrith was slow, delicate and methodical, Ecgfrith was alert and well-muscled. My over-riding impression was that he seemed alive and impatient, bursting with impetuous energy. His brother, Aldfrith, had reminded me of a bird, but Aldfrith was a dove, while Ecgfrith was most definitely a hawk.

He was younger than I had expected, perhaps around forty years old, beardless but with long hair and a fashionable, drooping moustache. His keen eyes studied me as I approached the fire.

Beornhaeth waved a large mug in my direction. "Well, well," he boomed. "I thought I had seen the last of you. What brings you here this time, Guret?"

I gave Ecgfrith what I hoped was a polite but not too grovelling bow. Addressing both the king and Beornhaeth, I said, "I heard that you were coming north at last. I thought I would assist you."

"Who is this little man?" Ecgfrith demanded in a clipped, precise but authoritative voice. Impatient was definitely the word to describe him.

Beornhaeth said, "This is the fellow I mentioned to you. His name is Guret. He has supplied me with information several times in the past. He can be trusted."

Ecgfrith turned a steely gaze on me, as if trying to read my very soul. "And how can you assist me?" he asked. "I have eight thousand men who are perfectly capable of completing what I need done."

There was a ripple of obsequious laughter from the other men. I waited for that to die down, then said, "Guret of

Dun Nechtan is ready to betray Bridei, thanks to me. Also, I can tell you what Bridei's plans are. I was present at the gathering of his chieftains."

Ecgfrith's look of wary scepticism was replaced by one of keen interest. He leaned forwards. "Tell me more," he commanded.

He did not offer me a seat, so I stood in the centre of the room, beside the crackling fire, with the eyes of every man studying me. I ignored everyone except Ecgfrith. He was the most powerful king in the whole of Britain, a man who ruled half the island and was paid tribute by the kings of the other half. His reputation as a warlord was unrivalled, but I knew that I could not afford to be cowed by him. I told myself that he was just a man, with the same failings as other men. He may have been a king, a ruler who could command thousands to do his bidding, but as I stood in the light of that smoking fire, I saw him as just another Northumbrian who could be tricked in the same way that I had fooled Beornhaeth for so long.

The time for vengeance had come.

An eye for an eye.

I said, "Bridei is afraid of you. He is gathering his army at Inbhir Nis, intent on guarding his home. He is fortifying the hills to the south, setting traps along the banks of Loch Nis. But he does not want to do battle with you. He hopes that you will return home when you see how strong his position is. Then he will harass you when you are forced to retreat due to lack of provisions."

"He is just going to sit and wait for me?" Ecgfrith asked.

"Yes. He has sent some men south, a small force. Their task is to harry you, to maintain contact and to draw you onto his fortified defences. But he will not face you in the open."

"He thinks he can win a war by sitting on his backside," Ecgfrith commented.

His men laughed, but I could see Ecgfrith's mind already working. His fingers were drumming a tattoo on his knee as he sought a way to gain a quick victory. Fourteen years before, when he had newly come to the throne, he had dashed north with an army that was a fraction of the size of the one he commanded now. He had slaughtered our men at the Two Rivers. Ever since then, he had conducted fast-moving campaigns against his enemies, always intent on striking a quick, decisive blow. Where Bridei was careful and methodical, Ecgfrith would rush in, determined to overwhelm his opponents with the power and ferocity of his assault. It was a tactic that had served him well for fourteen years, but Ecgfrith was no fool. I could see that he was wary of charging against well-fortified positions.

"How strong are his defences?" he asked.

"Formidable," I replied. "He has dug several ditches, placed sharpened stakes at the foot of each one, and built walls of stone on the hilltops. He has warships on Loch Nis, ready to sail men down to strike at your rear if you pass that way. The path along the shore is strewn with pits and massive walls of timber. Your army may be strong but it would need ten times their number to storm what Bridei is building."

"I presume you know a way to overcome these defences," Ecgfrith commented.

I smiled as I said, "Indeed. Bridei's position is strong, but it is not invulnerable. His plan depends on you doing what he wants. You can defeat him if you attack from a direction he does not expect."

"What direction might that be?" Ecgfrith asked, tempted by the bait I had offered.

There was no sound in that dim, smoke-filled room except the soft rustle of the fire and my voice. Every man was still, watching me intently.

I said, "Guret of Dun Nechtan is prepared to help you. Bridei's plan leaves his lands exposed to you. Guret is unhappy about that. If you march to Dun Nechtan, he will join with you."

"In exchange for what?" Ecgfrith asked sharply.

"In exchange for being acknowledged King of the Pecht when Bridei is dead. A king who owes his loyalty to you, of course."

"Of course. But a few hundred extra men will make little difference if we cannot lure Bridei out of his fortress."

"There is more," I told him.

He gestured with his hand in a signal of encouragement. "Go on."

"From Dun Nechtan there are several passes through the hills. The main one leads north, directly to Inbhir Nis. That is where Bridei wants you to go. But there is another that leads further to the east. I can lead you there. Guret's men are supposed to be guarding that path, blocking it to force you to go north, but they will let you through. You can cross the mountains into the very heart of Fortriu. From there, you can strike north to the coast and approach Bridei from behind. He will be forced to either let you seize his home or come to face you in the open."

Ecgfrith sucked in his cheeks. I saw that he had clenched his hands together, as if to prevent them from shaking. He was trying to appear calm but the excitement in him was palpable. I recognised it because I, too, was struggling to maintain a calm expression. I had revealed what Bridei wanted me to reveal, but his plan depended on me not betraying that every word I had spoken was a lie.

Everyone waited for the king to speak. He was silent for what seemed an age. At last, he turned to Beornhaeth. "You say this man can be trusted?" he asked.

Beornhaeth replied, "He has always told me the truth before now. But this is a dangerous plan. It means marching a long way through hostile territory."

Ecgfrith snapped, "You would rather I allowed Bridei to mock me? He has not paid tribute for the past three years. He has stolen one of my forts from me and now he thumbs his nose at me from behind a defensive wall, daring me to attack him!"

The king's voice rose to a shout as he recounted the list of Bridei's crimes. Even Beornhaeth blanched in the face of Ecgfrith's temper.

"I am sorry, lord king," Beornhaeth said.

It must have taken a lot for such a powerful lord to be humble in front of so many witnesses, but Beornhaeth had made a mistake and he knew it, so he did his best to regain the king's favour.

"I was merely trying to point out the difficulties of such a campaign, lord king. You are, as always, correct. Bridei must be punished."

Ecgfrith continued to stare at Beornhaeth for a few moments before saying, "It is Spring. We can live off the land easily for the next few months if need be, although I expect a victory within a few weeks."

He turned his fiery gaze on me once more. Jabbing a finger at me, he said, "You will march with us. You will be our guide. Beornhaeth says you can be trusted. If that is true, you will be well rewarded." Staring into my eyes, he added, "But if you are false with me, I will see your head on a spike. Do I make myself clear?"

"Perfectly," I replied.

"Excellent," said Ecgfrith. He stood up. "We leave tomorrow," he announced.

"What in God's name was that all about?" Medraut asked me later.

We were walking along the high rampart of Sruighlea which afforded us a magnificent view of the river and of Ecgfrith's army camped far below us. Off to the west was the vast expanse of the Great Moss, miles and miles of treacherous bog, a maze of pools and tall reeds that forced anyone travelling between north and south to pass under the eyes of the great fortress.

Casually, I turned as if to take in the panorama. There was nobody within earshot. I doubted whether any of the Northumbrians spoke our language but I could not afford to take any risks. Satisfied that we could not be overheard, I told Medraut what Bridei wanted us to do and what I had told Ecgfrith.

He was remarkably calm. When I had revealed the plan, he took a deep breath, before exhaling slowly. Then he said, "Bridei has sacrificed us."

He did not sound particularly annoyed, or even disappointed. It was merely a statement of fact.

"It is necessary," I said. "But that is why you are with me. My task is to take Ecgfrith where Bridei wants him. Your job is to get us out of the trap alive if you can."

Medraut was staring out over the high wall, gazing towards the horizon. He said, "That should be easy enough. There are only eight thousand of them. You can escape while I hold them off." He turned to face me. "You could have told me earlier," he accused.

"I could not take that chance. I did not know how good you would be at acting. Bridei didn't want you to know at all, but I think you deserve to be told the truth. Just don't give us away. Say as little as possible and look sullen. You're good at that. If anyone asks you questions, which I doubt they will, tell them that all you know is that I have met Guret several times and that Bridei is building defences near Inbhir Nis."

"Is he?"

"Of course not. But that is the story we must stick to."

"You think you're smart," he growled. "But you're still an obnoxious little turd. Do you know that?"

"That has been said before. Mostly by you."

"It must be true, then." His face was like stone, unreadable. He said, "All right. You do what you need to do and I'll try to think of a way of getting us out of it alive. We'll need to think of some signal or other so that we can warn each other when to be ready."

"You'll have around ten days to think of something," I said. "This lot won't cover much more than ten miles in a day."

He gave me a curious look, his head tilted slightly to one side. "You don't care, do you?" he asked.

"About what?"

"About whether we live or die."

I shrugged. "Yes, I care. I'd much rather live. But I have no great hopes of it."

"Bugger that," he said with feeling. "If there is a way, I will find it."

He said it with such passion that I almost believed him.

"Ten days," I told him. "That's all the time we have left."

Chapter 36

Abbot Trumwine blessed the army before we set off. We gathered on the plain below the Dun, the soldiers standing with heads bowed while Trumwine, seated on a horse so that he could be seen by everyone, assured us that God was on our side and that we would soon destroy the rebellious Picts.

I noticed that, while some of the soldiers crossed themselves, others made the sign of the hammer, Thor's sign. Trumwine must have seen these pagan gestures, but he pretended not to have noticed.

The Abbot exhorted the warriors to fight for their king and for God, and he promised that any man who fell in battle would find a glorious reward in Heaven. Then he said a prayer in Latin, blessed the men and made a hasty retreat, explaining that he must return to Obar Chuirnidh to oversee the completion of his new abbey. With almost indecent haste, he rode away with a train of monks and servants trailing after him.

I saw Wulfric shake his head in amusement as he watched the abbot's cavalcade head eastwards.

"You'd think the abbot of Pictavia would want to come with us," he muttered scornfully. "He could preach to his people."

Beornhaeth replied, "Most of his new flock are wolves, not lambs. They'd probably rip him to pieces, and for a man who preaches about the glories of the afterlife, I don't think our friend Trumwine is in too much of a hurry to get there himself."

Ecgfrith stopped their banter with a peremptory command to set the army in motion. The king sat on a richly caparisoned horse, wearing a coat of mail and with a polished, iron helmet on his head. His armour, helmet and belt were all decorated with finely worked gold, covered with intricate designs of boars, snakes and dragons. He drew a long sword, its hilt also embossed with ornately patterned gold, holding it aloft for his army to see. Then he pointed to the north.

"To victory and glory!" he shouted.

The soldiers cheered, raising their own swords and axes to the heavens. Most of them were more interested in plunder than in glory, but they knew that Ecgfrith would give them opportunities to gain both. Anticipating another easy victory, the horsemen set off at a slow trot and the foot soldiers filed behind them as the army of Northumbria marched north to destroy the Pecht.

I glanced at Medraut, whose face was set hard. I did not need to speak to him to know that he was thinking the same as me. The Northumbrians marched in the confident knowledge that no power on earth was strong enough to oppose them.

Bridei had told me what he wanted me to do, but I doubted whether he had any idea of what was coming against him. We were committed now, but as I watched Ecgfrith's war host, I felt an almost overwhelming sense of despair. I could not imagine how Bridei could possibly hope to defeat them.

Ten days. That was all it would take for Ecgfrith to reach Dun Nechtan. In ten days, the Pecht could be destroyed forever.

To my horror, Ecgfrith's army marched more quickly than I had expected. The bulk of his men were on foot, but despite the terrain growing increasingly hilly as we went north, they managed to cover at least twelve miles each day, sometimes as many as fifteen. This was partly due to the fact that they had no supply wagons to slow them down. The warriors refilled their waterskins at every river or stream, while Ecgfrith sent his cavalry scouting ahead with orders to raid farms and to herd sheep, pigs, goats and cattle to provide his army's food. He did not care that the people of Fotla would starve.

He instructed his men to take what they wanted and to kill anyone who protested.

    The Northumbrian cavalry roamed far and wide ahead of the army's march, but they found little food because Taran had anticipated what Ecgfrith would do. Most of the farms had been abandoned, the livestock herded ever further north or taken high into the hills until Ecgfrith's soldiers had passed. Undaunted, Ecgfrith used the meagre rations to spur his men on even faster, telling them of the vast granaries and storehouses they would be able to plunder when they reached Inbhir Nis. So the army raced north and the ten days I had anticipated shrank to eight.

    Ecgfrith was delighted with his progress. There had been little opposition to his advance. Small groups of Pecht launched raids, ambushing unwary cavalry scouts or darting into the camp at nights to kill a sentry before vanishing into the hills and forests, but these were pinpricks.

    I knew that these raiders were commanded by Taran, that Bridei had ordered them to keep watch on the Northumbrian advance, to pester them and pick them off when possible, but above all to ensure that Ecgfrith led his army ever further into the hills.

    Taran did his work well. Every day, Ecgfrith's scouts brought reports of small groups of Pecht who were always tantalisingly close but constantly retreating. The Angles were never able to catch them.

    These tactics helped convince Ecgfrith that I had told him the truth. As the days wore on, I was increasingly accepted as one of the king's companions so that, by the time we drew near Dun Nechtan, I was able to ride just behind the king, with Medraut at my right side. Behind us came Beornhaeth and Wulfric, followed by several hundred mounted warriors, with the foot soldiers bringing up the rear in a long, snaking column that stretched behind us for more than a mile.

    Banners and pennons fluttered above the army, Beornhaeth's black hawk's head among them. I looked at that red and black flag and I remembered. It was almost time. Whatever happened, I was determined to take my revenge on Beornhaeth.

In the evenings, Ecgfrith would often ask me questions about Bridei. The two kings may have been cousins, but they had never met, and Ecgfrith was curious about what type of man he was facing.

"What is he like?" he asked me.

"Cautious," I replied, knowing it was an answer that would please him.

"That will be his undoing," Ecgfrith declared. "Being cautious never won a battle. Boldness is what is required. Seize whatever opportunity presents itself and seize it quickly." He slapped his hands together, as if crushing some invisible foe between them.

I knew that some of his nobles, including Beornhaeth, were growing anxious about how far north they had travelled, but Ecgfrith would not listen to any advice except his own. Bridei had refused to pay tribute and must pay the price. That was all that mattered to Ecgfrith. I assured him that, with my help and Guret's betrayal, he could not fail to achieve another rapid victory.

Ecgfrith was too impetuous to see through me. Beornhaeth had known me for a few years and believed me to be trustworthy, despite his misgivings about the current campaign. I was confident that I was playing my part well, but Wulfric had always been suspicious of me. As we settled down for the night, only a few hours' march from Dun Nechtan, he walked up to me, just as I was wrapping my cloak around my shoulders, ready to bed down.

Medraut hissed a warning and I saw him reach for his sword. I waved at him to remain seated. Wulfric appeared friendly enough as he drew near, but Medraut continued to watch him carefully.

Wulfric squatted down on his haunches to look at me.

"What is your game?" he asked.

I propped myself up on one elbow. "What do you mean?"

"Why are you helping us? What do you get out of this?"

I replied, "I hope to be a rich man when this is done. The king will need loyal chieftains once he has dealt with Bridei. I expect to receive a large parcel of land as a reward. A very large parcel."

Wulfric's blue eyes did not blink. He said, "Simple greed? I don't believe you. A man like you does not betray his people just for money."

My heart was racing. I had always regarded Wulfric as little more than his father's henchman, but I realised now that he was more perceptive, and posed a greater threat, than I had thought.

Medraut must have realised the danger, even though he could not understand what Wulfric was saying. From the corner of my eye I saw him watching Wulfric like a cat about to pounce on its prey. Medraut had his cloak wrapped around his body against the chill of the night but I guessed that, beneath its folds, he had his dagger drawn. I had to think quickly. We were so close to Dun Nechtan that we could not afford to fail now.

Dropping my gaze from Wulfric's face, I sighed. "Well, there is a bit more to it," I admitted.

"Like what?" he wanted to know.

I pushed myself up so that I was sitting facing him. Keeping my voice low, as if afraid of being overheard, I said, "Some years ago, I was in love with Bridei's daughter. I wanted to marry her, but he did not think I was worthy. He gave her to another man. I have hated him ever since."

Wulfric sneered, "You are betraying your king over a woman?"

"Can you think of a better reason?" I shot back at him. "Have you never been in love?"

He shook his head. "I can't say that I have."

For a moment I was tempted to let Medraut kill him. Triduana had extracted a promise from me because she believed Wulfric was a good man at heart. I wondered whether she knew that he thought so little of her.

I hated him even more at that moment, but I had sworn an oath to my sister, so I hid my feelings and said, "Then you cannot know how much it means to have someone you love taken from you. Believe me, it hurts. Bridei ruined my life. Can you understand why I hate him?"

"Perhaps I can," he said softly.

I looked into his eyes and said, "Believe me, Wulfric, you have nothing to fear from me. I swear by all the saints that I would never harm you."

He considered that for a moment then stood up. Looking down at me, he said, "You are a strange man, Guret. I think there is more to you than you are telling us, but I will reserve my judgement until we see what happens when we meet Bridei."

"You will see sooner than that," I said. "We will reach Dun Nechtan tomorrow. You can judge me then."

"I will. Have no fear about that."

Leaving me to think about his threat, he wandered off into the night. When he had gone, I lay down, staring up into a star-filled sky, feeling drained. I had kept my promise to Triduana, but what would I have done if Wulfric had denounced me? I did not know.

I glanced over to Medraut who lay on his side, watching me. I did not have the energy to speak to him. Fortunately, he did not ask any questions. We both knew that a moment of danger had passed. We also knew that the morning would place us in even greater peril.

I gazed up at the sparkling stars, wondering whether Derelei was looking down on me and wondering, too, whether this was to be the last night I would ever spend on this earth.

We came within sight of Dun Nechtan in the late morning of Saturday, the twentieth day of May, the ninth day since we had left Sruighlea. It was a wonderful Spring morning with bright, warm sunshine reflecting from the white snowcaps on the hills that surrounded us. Ahead of us, the loch, fed by the mountain streams, lay blue and calm, nestled among reeds and trees.

To my heightened senses, the land seemed alive and beautiful, vibrant with an almost sentient energy. I could have wept at the thought of never seeing such glory again. Medraut had accused me of not caring whether I lived or died, but that morning was so wonderful that it awoke the fear in me, the fear that had first taken hold of me on the day my family had been destroyed by Beornhaeth and Wulfric. I had spent years fighting that paralysing terror, pretending that I had conquered it, but I knew deep inside me that it had never truly left me.

I felt its malevolent grip as we approached Dun Nechtan. It gnawed at my belly, left my arms and legs useless and uncontrollable, and threatened to engulf me. Desperately, I sought for a way to control it before someone noticed how afraid I was.

I wondered whether Wulfric was watching me. If he saw how terrified I was, he would know that I had lied. Panic threatened to grip me, but I clung to the thought of Wulfric and how he had stolen Triduana. How he had raped her as if she was of no importance and how he still had no regard for her, even though she had borne him two children.

The desire for vengeance welled up inside me, forcing my terror down. I held to the thought that the time had come at last, when all of the Northumbrians would pay.

Then I worried that Bridei had under-estimated the size of Ecgfrith's army and that we were all doomed. I told myself that it was too late to turn back now. I remembered how, only a few hundred paces from this very spot, I had once faced Medraut and his gang, and had beaten them. I needed the same determination now. I gritted my teeth, dug deep into my resolve, and the fear slowly faded until it was a mere tingle in the pit of my stomach.

It was time.

As we rode down to the narrow strip of low land that lay between the loch and the hills to our left, I moved up beside the King. I pointed.

"There is Dun Nechtan," I said. "Beyond the lake."

Ecgfrith reined in his horse, forcing the following column to jostle to a halt. He called to the horsemen of his vanguard to ride ahead.

"Where is Guret of Dun Nechtan?" he asked me.

"He is supposed to be guarding the pass away to the right, beyond the lake."

"Then who are the men inside the Dun?" he demanded.

"Perhaps Bridei has sent some men to hold it," I suggested. I was genuinely puzzled by that but there was no doubt that the gates of Dun Nechtan were firmly shut and that there were armed men lining the wooden walls. Even from this distance, I could see the tips of their spears glinting in the morning sun.

"We'll soon get them out of there," Ecgfrith declared. He signalled for the advance to resume.

My heart was racing now. I had mastered my fear, but the blood was pumping in my veins and all my senses were on edge. I kept looking from side to side, scanning the hills and forests, but there was no sign of anyone except Ecgfrith's army and the men in Dun Nechtan.

An eagle soared high above us, circling lazily on the air, its outstretched wings barely moving as it rode the wind. I checked the valley again but there was no other sign of life. The cattle and sheep had gone, herded away to safety, leaving Dun Nechtan's valley devoid of life.

I turned to Medraut. "It will be nice to see home again," I said.

He nodded, acknowledging my signal. This was where Bridei had said he would launch his attack. This was where he had wanted me to bring Ecgfrith. I was ready, but there was no sign of any threat, no hint of danger. I began to wonder whether Bridei had deliberately misled me for some reason, whether his true plan was not the one he had told me. The valley was as empty as on that day when I had first sat alone on the hillside looking down on Dun Nechtan.

We had almost reached the far end of the loch. The vanguard were already cantering round Dun Nechtan, seeking to surround it. Ecgfrith had called up some of his foot soldiers who were jogging forwards, preparing to attack the farmstead.

I was breathing hard now, feeling slightly light-headed. I had done what Bridei had asked of me and now I had to make a decision.

Medraut nudged his horse alongside mine, giving me a quizzical look. He seemed impossibly relaxed.

"Wait," I said softly. I knew that if we moved too soon, we might jeopardise everything. Yet if Bridei had tricked me, we might miss our opportunity to escape.

A cry of delight from Ecgfrith snapped me back to the present. The king was pointing beyond the Dun, to a stand of trees where a group of horsemen had appeared. They burst from the woods, galloping towards the Dun with swords drawn. Yelling wildly, their long hair streaming out behind them, they charged at the thin cordon of Northumbrians who had surrounded the farmstead, sending them fleeing for their lives. They were unable to catch Ecgfrith's vanguard but, having driven them off, the Pecht horsemen swerved towards the advancing Northumbrian infantry, hoping to catch them unprepared.

Ecgfrith raised a hand, waving it to summon his cavalry. There were fewer than two hundred Pecht, while Ecgfrith commanded a thousand horsemen. For eight days they had been unable to close with their elusive enemy, but now Ecgfrith saw a chance to catch some of Bridei's men at last. He had told me that boldness would win battles. He saw the opportunity and he seized it.

"After them!" he screamed. He drew his sword, jabbed his heels to his warhorse, and led the charge.

The king's sudden decision caught most of his followers by surprise. There was a brief instant before anyone could react. In that moment I made my own decision.

I drew my dagger from its scabbard at my waist, sliding my hand down the blade in readiness for a throw. Then I twisted round in my saddle and shouted, "Beornhaeth!"

Medraut was already hauling his horse around, drawing his sword. Beornhaeth, sitting on his horse barely five paces behind me, was preparing to gallop after Ecgfrith, but he pulled back on the reins when he heard me call his name, He looked straight at me, wondering why I had shouted to him.

I hurled my dagger.

He was wearing a coat of mail and had a heavy, iron helmet on his head. I did not have much to aim at if I wanted to be sure of killing him, but I had made this throw before and I knew where to send the knife. It flashed across the short distance between us, taking him in the right eye. I waited only long enough to see him topple backwards before I yelled at Dagger, clapping my legs to her flanks, setting off to my right, intending to cut between the Dun and the loch.

Crouching low over Dagger's neck, I glanced back to look for Medraut. He was wheeling his horse away from Wulfric, who was tumbling lifelessly from his saddle, his face a mask of blood. I was not sorry. I had kept my promise to Triduana because I had never spoken to Medraut about what Wulfric had done, but I was glad he was dead. Now Medraut was charging after me, whooping with delight, his face alive with pleasure as a dozen Northumbrians turned to chase us.

The air filled with the noise of thundering horses and screaming men. Most of the Northumbrian horsemen had charged after Ecgfrith. I could see the Pecht cavalry turning away, scattering as the king led hundreds of his own riders after them, galloping beyond the left side of Dun Nechtan while Medraut and I led our pursuers to the right, arcing round to follow the loch, heading towards the river. My sole aim was to reach the far side, hoping that the Angles might give up the chase or perhaps that Medraut would somehow be able to fend them off if we were able to get across to the far bank.

We galloped past the trees that lined the northern edge of the loch. I could see the river now, broad and fast-flowing but easily forded on horseback. I leaned low over my mare's neck, urging her on.

It was as we passed the trees that I heard the signal. It was the unmistakeable sound of a carnyx, a great war-horn. It echoed across the valley, the notes rising and falling in an eery, ululating cry that called men to battle and promised death to the enemies of the Pecht.

I yelled in delight, screaming at Dagger to gallop on, that help was close at hand.

I had not realised how close. Released by the sound of the carnyx, the valley exploded.

Hundreds of men suddenly charged out from my right, where they had lain hidden in the narrow strip of woodland by the shore of the loch. I swerved away in fright, but Medraut galloped alongside me, yelling at me that they were our men. Then, from beyond the Dun, behind and to my left, a vast cheer echoed round the hillsides like a thunderclap as Bridei unleashed his trap.

Chapter 37

I wanted to ride on, to reach what I imagined would be the safety of the river, but Medraut stretched across, grabbing at Dagger's reins to guide me to a halt. We turned to see that the Northumbrians who had been chasing us were either dead or riding back to join their main force. Pursuing them was a mass of spearmen.

More Pecht warriors were streaming from near the riverbank, running past us as they hurried to close the gap between the Dun and the loch. From the Dun itself, hundreds more warriors were charging out to hurl themselves at the Northumbrian infantry, while the hillsides, which had seemed so empty, were alive with thousands more men who had risen from their hiding places to run, screaming like devils, to smash down into the exposed flank of the Northumbrian army, most of which was penned between the hills and the water, still strung out in a long, marching column.

The scale of the ambush was stunning. Bridei had gathered thousands upon thousands of men, and had somehow managed to keep them hidden until the Northumbrians had walked right into his trap.

I could not see what had happened to Ecgfrith. He had rushed ahead with his horsemen galloping after him, but the area they had charged into was narrow, uneven ground, a mass of hillocks that were covered by rocks and trees. Horses could not operate properly there. I could not see it, but I could hear the furious noise and I could see great clouds of dust swirling into the air above the Dun as men piled into the fray.

I sat watching, only a few hundred paces from the nearest part of the struggle, yet somehow isolated from it.

"I can't believe we are still alive," I said to Medraut.

"Lucky for us the king charged off like that," he said.

"I think Bridei had more to do with it than luck."

He shrugged. "Maybe. Come on, let's get into the trees. I'd rather keep you out of sight until it's over."

"Don't you want to join in?" I asked.

"Maybe later."

That was not like him, but I did not care, I was alive. This day had hung over me like a sentence of death and I could scarcely believe I had survived. Beornhaeth was dead, Wulfric too. I had escaped and Bridei had caught Ecgfrith in a deadly trap, just as he had promised. Life was sweet at that moment, sweeter than it had been for many years.

Medraut led me into the trees. We dismounted, allowing our horses to crop the grass. I wanted to watch the battle, but Medraut pulled me further back towards the water, deeper into the wood.

"Someone is coming," he said.

He held his sword ready.

I could not tell how he had heard anyone approaching over the fearful noise of the battle that was raging only a few hundred paces from our hiding place, but he was right. A lone rider trotted up, dismounted and led his horse through the trees to join us. He was wearing a long coat of chainmail and he held a shining sword in his hand. He stopped when he saw us, smiling broadly at Medraut.

"Welcome back," he said.

It was Guret.

My mind was reeling. I could not understand why Guret was here, but I could tell from his stance that something was very wrong.

"Shouldn't you be leading your men?" I asked him.

"Oh, they can manage well enough without me," he replied. "I have other business."

I felt suddenly very cold. For several years, I had been dreaming of confronting Guret, but not like this. I was standing with a tree at my back. Behind that was marshy ground, filled with tall reeds, and beyond that lay the deep waters of the loch. In front of me, blocking my way out of the narrow strip of woodland, were Guret and Medraut, both with swords drawn and both grinning like wolves about to bring down their prey.

"What is going on?" I asked.

"What is going on is that I am about to rid myself of an annoying problem," Guret told me.

I looked at Medraut. "Are you just going to let him do this?"

"Oh, no," said Medraut cheerfully. "But I might help him do it. In fact, I might just do it myself. You nearly got me killed you little shit."

It was like the worst horrors of my boyhood again, except that this time they had swords and I did not even have my knife which was still embedded in Beornhaeth's brain.

In desperation, I asked Medraut, "But why? I thought you hated him? He helped kill Uerb."

Medraut took a step towards me. He said, "Because Guret is going to be a very important man soon and I intend to be on the winning side."

"I don't understand," I said, looking from one to the other.

Medraut said, "One way or another, Bridei will not live much longer."

My eyes darted to Guret. "And you think you will be king of the Pecht?" I asked him.

Medraut let out a mocking laugh while Guret shook his head. "Do you think I am that stupid?" he asked me. "The chieftains would not elect me. Not yet, anyway."

"Then who?"

Medraut snapped, "My father. Guret will support him and others will agree. They know he is an honourable man. He should still be king. He would have been king if it were not for you and your meddling friends."

"But that was years ago!" I exclaimed, scarcely able to believe that Medraut had harboured that old grudge for so long.

Guret clucked his tongue in disappointment. "Do you really think that we have not learned to be patient? We have bided our time, waiting for the right moment. It has arrived. Let Bridei destroy the Angles. Then we will take charge. Medraut will once again be the son of the king and I will be one of the foremost chieftains. Sadly, old Drest will not live forever. In a few years, perhaps sooner, he will die, and then Medraut, who will be an important chieftain in his own right by then, will propose a new king."

"King Guret," said Medraut.

I gaped in astonishment at the enormity of their plot. Their ambition was breathtaking, but they had forgotten the most important obstacle.

"Bridei will stop you," I said defiantly.

Guret waved a hand impatiently, making as if to step forwards. "I have had enough of this," he said. "Let's kill him now."

Medraut lifted his sword, gesturing for Guret to hold his ground. He said, "No, I want him to know everything. He's dragged me up and down the country for years now, showing off how clever he is, sucking up to Bridei. I want him to know what is going to happen after he is dead. He can die knowing that there is nothing he can do to stop it."

"We have no time for this, Medraut." said Guret impatiently.

Medraut stood his ground, preventing Guret from passing. All the time, his eyes were on me, his face hard. I was in no doubt that he would kill me as soon as he had finished his gloating.

"Tell him," he said. "Tell him why Bridei will not live beyond this day."

Guret snorted. "Very well." He looked at me coldly. "With any luck, Bridei will be killed in the fighting. If he survives and manages to defeat Ecgfrith, he will have a victory feast when he returns to Inbhir Nis. Something in that meal will disagree with him. We will make sure of that."

"Mayota?" I asked. "With poison supplied by Fincana?"

"Very clever of you to work it out," Guret said, his voice heavy with sarcasm.

"The way she killed Derelei," I said.

"You can't prove that."

"No, but I know it all the same. Why did you do that? Why did you kill Derelei?"

Guret shrugged as if Derelei's death was of no importance to him. "It was part of the bargain," he said. "Mayota wants power. I want to be king. Together, we have been able to help one another. As for Derelei, the bitch deserved it for the way she betrayed my father. You kept that very quiet, but Mayota guessed the truth of what you had done. I think she was rather jealous. She knew how much you loved Derelei and I think she felt slighted. Mayota is used to getting her own way and she is a passionate woman. She takes such things personally."

Medraut's eyes were wide with surprise. "Mayota poisoned Derelei?" he asked.

"Why so shocked?" Guret asked. "She will do the same to Bridei."

"And Fincana supplied the poison?"

"Of course she did. She wants to see the old gods return. So does Mayota." Guret saw Medraut frown but he gave the big warrior no time to protest. He snapped, "Enough of this. He knows it all now, so let's kill the little bugger. If we hurry, we should be in time to join in the final destruction of Ecgfrith's army."

"You're right," agreed Medraut. "It is time to finish this." He hefted his sword as he took another pace towards me. "Time to die, you treacherous worm," he snarled.

I opened my mouth, desperately seeking something to say, anything to save my life, but no words would come. I backed away, pressing myself against the gnarled trunk of the tree behind me, almost falling as I waved my arms in front of me, as if I could fend off the blow with my bare hands.

Medraut took another step towards me. The sword rose over his left shoulder, then he spun on his heel, his arm sweeping round to ram the edge of the blade through Guret's neck.

Blood sprayed in the air. Medraut's sword hacked through flesh, muscle and bone, the blow so powerful that it almost removed Guret's head. Medraut stood poised as the partially decapitated body collapsed at his feet in a welter of blood. He took a careful step back to avoid staining his boots, then hacked down several times until Guret's head tumbled clear, rolling across the grass until it came to rest against the trunk of a tree.

I could not move. I blinked, unable to comprehend what I had just witnessed.

Medraut knelt to wipe his sword clean on the coarse grass then stood to face me.

"Come on," he said coolly, "We'd better go and see how Bridei is doing."

"But . . ." I waved a hand helplessly in the direction of Guret's head. "I thought . . . You said . . ."

He sheathed his sword with a flourish. "Do you think you are the only one who can put on an act?" he asked.

I took several deep breaths, trying to force my brain to begin working again.

"What about all that stuff you said about your father and Guret becoming king?"

"Oh, Guret thought I was up for that," he said. "But my father would never have considered it, so when Guret mentioned it to me, I played along, then my father and I went to tell Bridei."

"And you hatched this plan?"

"Well, it was mostly Bridei's idea, to be fair," he admitted. "You know I'm not a great one for thinking."

My shock was wearing off now. "You could have told me," I complained.

"I wasn't sure how good an actor you were," he said, his face devoid of expression as he threw my own accusation back at me. "Anyway, you never told me about the plan to lure Ecgfrith here."

"You knew already," I said accusingly. "Bridei told you, didn't he?"

He shrugged. "He may have mentioned it."

I pointed an accusing finger at him. "You're a real bastard, do you know that?"

"Yes, and you're a little—"

"I know," I interrupted.

"I don't know why you are complaining," he said. "You have your proof now. Guret admitted his and Mayota's guilt in front of a reliable witness."

"That would be you, I suppose?"

"Naturally. The chieftains are more likely to believe me than a little turd like you. I am the son of a king, after all."

"A former king," I corrected.

I had recovered my wits by then, so I managed to dodge away before he could hit me.

Chapter 38

The battle was still rampaging along the valley when we rode out of the trees. I was carrying Guret's sword in my right hand. I had little idea of how to use it properly, but I did not want to be caught up in a battle without some sort of weapon.

Medraut reined in to check what was happening. The Northumbrians were penned between the hills and the loch, under attack from all sides. We learned afterwards that hundreds of our men had hidden in the loch itself, standing naked with only their heads above water, huddling among the reeds. They must have been bitterly cold, yet they had remained concealed even when the leading part of the Northumbrian column had ridden past them. Then, when the blare of the carnyx had released the attack and the Angles had turned to face the charging warriors who hurtled down the hillside, the men in the loch had hauled themselves to the shore, spears in hand, to strike at the Northumbrians from the rear.

I could only marvel at the bravery of men who would go into battle stark naked, facing armoured foes with no protection except their own skill and courage. But they did. They stabbed and they slashed and they killed. Caught between the two arms of Bridei's trap, the Angles died in their hundreds.

But Bridei had not won yet. The Northumbrians were fierce warriors and they fought like demons, locking their shields together and wielding swords or axes while the Pecht swarmed around them, baying for blood. Both sides called on God to grant them victory as they slashed and cut at one another.

I saw a phalanx of our spearmen advancing, standing shoulder to shoulder, their spearpoints forming a bristling hedge in front of them. Most people think that a spear is a simple weapon, nothing more than a long stick with a sharp point, but I knew how difficult it could be to master its use. The long poles of ash or beechwood were used to strike at an enemy while keeping him at a distance, but any long piece of wood becomes difficult to control when its weight is all in front of you. The solution was to attach a heavy sphere of metal to the butt end of the shaft to act as a counter-weight. Our warriors could grasp the ends of their spears without the weapons becoming unbalanced, and so they could jab at the faces and legs of the Northumbrians whose own spears did not have the same reach.

The Angles fought bravely, but Bridei had drilled his men for years in preparation for this day and the Angles died as the deadly spears drove at them.

The Northumbrian foot soldiers were in chaos, divided into small clumps of men, each group surrounded by hordes of our warriors. Some of the Angles were forced, step by inexorable step, towards the waters of the loch. Floundering as they stepped into the water, most of them were cut down. A few, mad with desperation, tried to escape by swimming, only for their heavy armour to drag them beneath the surface. Whether by spear, sword or drowning, Ecgfrith's army was being destroyed.

I was mesmerised by the awful scene, but Medraut took one look along the shore of the loch and dismissed that fight. There was nothing he could do to influence the outcome, so he hauled on his reins, turning to gallop in the opposite direction, circling round the farmstead of Dun Nechtan towards the spot where Ecgfrith and the remnants of his cavalry were still fighting. Feeling useless, I dragged Dagger round and sent her galloping after him.

Beyond the Dun was a tumult of horror. The land was so broken by hillocks and ruts, trees and rocks, that all sense of order had broken down. The carnyx still wailed and roared its encouragement from somewhere away to my right, but ahead of me, small groups of men were battling ferociously, screaming and shouting, weapons ringing as they clashed. Dead and wounded men and horses lay on the ground while others fought around them, sending clouds of dust rising into the air.

Some Northumbrians had dismounted, or perhaps had their mounts killed. They gathered together in small clumps, standing back to back to fight off their attackers, but the unearthly sound of the carnyx echoed around the valley, calling more and more Pecht to the fight. Charging out from their hiding places, our men hurried to obey the summons.

Northumbrian horsemen charged around, singly or in small groups, wheeling and turning, slashing with their swords, but horses were hampered in this broken ground and Bridei had unleashed so many foot soldiers that there was no escape for the mounted men. They could not break through the walls of spears and swords that penned them in.

Medraut leaped down from his horse. He turned back to me.

"Stay here!" he yelled. "Watch the horses."

"Where are you going?" I shouted back.

He pointed with his sword. Some hundred paces from where we had stopped, clustered at the foot of a tree-topped mound, was a group of around forty Northumbrians who were battling a horde of our warriors. The fighting seemed particularly vicious around this spot and I saw a pennon still proudly held aloft above the heads of the Northumbrians. It was Ecgfrith's banner.

"Stay Here!" Medraut repeated.

"Wait! You can't go. If you die, I have no witness to what Guret said."

Medraut grinned at me. "If we don't win this fight, it won't matter a damn anyway." He turned and ran towards the fight.

I sat on Dagger's back, holding the reins of Medraut's horse. Both beasts were nervous, frightened by the sounds and smells of the fight, but I could not move. I watched as Medraut dashed into the fray, dodging and weaving as he picked a way round the side of the struggle. He vanished from my sight behind a screaming horde of warriors who were pressing in on Ecgfrith's men.

I caught a glimpse of Bridei, still on horseback, sword and shield in hand, guiding his horse with his thighs and knees. He smashed his heavy sword down on the head of a fleeing Angle, then yelled and pointed, sending a group of mounted men in pursuit of some fleeing Northumbrians who were trying to break out towards the hills.

Men screamed. Men died. Blood flowed and limbs were crushed or hacked off, but still the fight continued. Ecgfrith's banner still flew and the Pecht surrounding his small group of warriors could not break them down.

Ecgfrith's men had formed a wall of shields. They swung their swords, trying to drive off our warriors. The long, heavy spears were picking them off one by one, stabbing into their unprotected legs or driving into their faces, but still they fought on. I could see the tall figure of Ecgfrith, hacking with his long sword, refusing to surrender. I wondered why they did not throw down their weapons and beg for mercy, but then I saw Bridei again, urging his warriors to finish off the king. It was like the game he had played with Taran. Victory was not enough for Bridei. He wanted his enemy utterly destroyed. Ecgfrith knew that no quarter would be given, so he continued to fight, even though he must have known it was hopeless.

I heard a roar from a little way to the south. A troop of over a hundred Northumbrian horsemen had rallied and were charging across the broken ground, trying to reach their king. Bridei had seen them. He screamed at his men to block the path, sending hundreds of spearmen to form a barrier of sharp points that the horses would not charge. The Northumbrians were halted by the hastily arranged barrier of flesh and spears, but only just. So many men had run to block them that the pressure was lifted from Ecgfrith's men who, rallying to their king's call, now dared to push away from the side of the tree-covered hummock that protected their rear.

Ecgfrith had seen his chance and he led his warriors in a desperate attempt to join with their would-be rescuers.

Bridei was almost hoarse with screaming as he jabbed his sword, directing men to surround the Angles, but the Northumbrian shield wall surged forwards, knocking men aside. Ecgfrith, who must have thought he was trapped, was now barely thirty paces from safety. He had fewer than forty men with him, but ahead of him scarcely sixty of our spearmen were left to block his path. If the heavily armoured Northumbrians could brush our warriors aside, they could launch themselves at the rear of the hastily-gathered phalanx of spearmen who were battling to hold back the Northumbrian cavalry.

Then I saw a shadow move among the trees behind and above Ecgfrith's position. Medraut was there. He had circled round, climbed the mound, and was behind the Northumbrians. He leaped down, sword already swinging. He dropped behind them, vanishing from my sight, but I saw the pennon fall and I heard the cries of panic. Ecgfrith's men turned in confusion, trying to see what this new threat was, then Bridei jabbed his heels to his horse's flanks and charged at them, dealing death.

Screams of delight burst from the throats of our warriors as the Northumbrian shield wall collapsed and the spears of the Pecht pressed in for the kill.

The frantic, bloody melee degenerated into a score of small, deadly struggles as the Northumbrians were cut down. Then I heard a victory yell as Medraut staggered from the morass of bodies, his sword in his right hand, his left arm raised to present a head to the screaming warriors around him.

It was Ecgfrith's head.

Medraut ran to show his grisly trophy to the Angles who had been trying to reach the king. When they saw it, they lost heart and fled.

Bridei galloped over, raising his blood-stained sword in salute to Medraut, then he shouted more orders, sending our jubilant, victorious warriors charging after the fleeing Angles.

It was over quickly after Ecgfrith died. Medraut hurried back to me. He vaulted into the saddle, grinned maniacally at me, then rode off down the side of the loch, guiding his horse with his legs, holding Ecgfrith's head aloft for all to see.

The sight dismayed the few Northumbrians who remained alive. They could not escape, but the fight went out of them and our men hacked them down mercilessly.

Bridei still refused to take prisoners. He rode the length of the valley screaming at his warriors to kill every Northumbrian they could find.

The tide of the battle swept past me, running south along the side of the loch. Not knowing what to do, I rode slowly round Dun Nechtan until I reached the open gates. I went inside and waited. Glancing up at the sun, I was astonished to see that it was barely half way to its zenith. Ecgfrith's invincible army had been destroyed in less than an hour.

Bridei and Taran found me a short time later. They came riding at the head of a gaggle of horsemen, including Medraut, who still carried Ecgfrith's severed head like a symbol of victory.

Bridei rode up to me. He was covered in dust and grime but he smiled when he saw me. "You did it, Bili. You did well. I am glad you escaped."

I nodded, unable to say anything.

Bridei dismounted wearily. He signalled for Taran, Medraut and me to join him, then ordered his men to see to the horses. He walked towards the gates to stand in the entrance, gazing out across the battlefield.

Medraut ran to the palisade where he rammed Ecgfrith's head onto one of the sharpened stakes of the wooden wall. Spattered with blood but grinning hugely, he swaggered back to join us.

Bridei accepted a mug of water from one of his warriors. he gulped it down noisily.

"Is it over?" I asked him.

"Aye, lad, it is. We have won a great victory."

And we had. A few hundred Northumbrians, mostly those who had been at the rear of the long column, furthest from the ambush, had managed to escape. They were running south, pursued by our cavalry. The vast majority of their army was dead. Demoralised, trapped between the hills and the loch, most of them had fallen where they stood. A few of the mounted men had broken free and ridden for the mountain passes but they, too, were being hunted. It had been more a massacre than a battle.

Bridei seemed tired but quietly satisfied. He had worked towards this for years and I had thought that he would have displayed more emotion, but he remained composed, as if what he had achieved was no more than he expected.

Medraut, on the other hand, was exultant, which I supposed was understandable. Bridei calmed him down a little when he asked, "What about Guret?"

"He is dead," Medraut replied. "He confessed his guilt and Mayota's. I will bear witness that your daughter was poisoned."

Bridei closed his eyes. He stood very still for a long time. When he looked at us again he said, "I am grateful to you both. I am in your debt. Now justice can be done."

"Where is Mayota?" I asked.

"Inbhir Nis," said Bridei. "We sent all the womenfolk there."

"What will happen to her?"

"I have not decided yet. In some ways it would be better if she was quietly disposed of. I will think on it."

"So what happens now?" I asked, gesturing towards the piled corpses. Our warriors were moving among them, rifling through the bodies in search of any valuables and finishing off any wounded Northumbrians. The stench of death hung in the air, bringing back old memories. A raucous call from overhead made me look to the sky. The crows were already gathering.

Bridei said, "Now, we will reclaim the lands of the south. You never know, even the garrison at Sruighlea might surrender when they learn what has happened here. But first I will take back Circinn, Fidach and Fib. Who knows? We may even get as far as Dun Eidyn. It depends on what the new king of Northumbria does."

"Who will be king now?" Medraut asked.

Bridei shrugged. "I don't know. Ecgfrith has sons, but they are young."

"He has a brother," I said.

"Aldfrith? By God, yes. He would do nicely. A more ineffectual king you could not hope to find. If he was on the throne, we wouldn't need to worry about Northumbria for years to come."

"He's on Iona," I said. "With Adomnan."

"Is he indeed?"

"Well, he was. If he is not there now, Adomnan will know where he is."

Bridei glanced at Taran, who said, "I could be there in a week."

Bridei gave a low chuckle. "I am sure Adomnan would love to see his friend take his rightful place as King of Northumbria. Tell him that he would have my thanks and enough silver to build a new monastery if he can persuade the Northumbrians to accept Aldfrith."

Taran actually smiled as he asked, "What do I tell Aldfrith?"

"Tell him Northumbria ends at the Foirthe. Everything north of that belongs to the Pecht. Including Sruighlea if you can get it."

"I'll get it," Taran said confidently. He added, "I suspect he would concede more if you asked."

"I am not greedy," Bridei said. "Let us take back what was ours. Aldfrith can keep the rest." He turned back to me and Medraut. "What about you two?"

"I will accompany you," Medraut said instantly. "I'd like to see the Angles thrown out of our lands."

"You are more than welcome," said Bridei. "What about you, Bili? You are no fighter, I know. Perhaps you would like to return to Inbhir Nis. There is some business there you could take care of for me."

He did not need to tell me what that business was. It was time for justice to be done.

Chapter 39

I was one of the first to reach Inbhir Nis with news of the victory. Other men were making their slow way back up the well-worn trackway; the wounded who were able to walk and wagons bearing those who could not. I overtook a few of them, although I did not push my horse too hard. It was still a wonderful day to be alive and I wanted to remember every moment of it, to imprint it on my memory so that I would never forget.

I had delayed my departure only long enough to search for Beornhaeth's body in the hope of retrieving my dagger. It took me a while to find him among the tangled masses of dead men and horses. When I did, my dagger was gone and so, too, were his sword, his coat of chainmail, his iron helmet and all his gold and silver rings.

Wulfric lay nearby, his face smashed by Medraut's sword, his mangled, sightless eyes staring skywards. I wondered what Triduana would think when she heard of his death. Would she blame me? I hoped not. I may have led him into a trap but I had kept my promise to her. I had not harmed him, nor had I asked anyone else to harm him. That is what I told myself. It was a fine line, perhaps, but I had not crossed it.

I had no need of Guret's sword, so I rode north with no weapon, armed only with the knowledge that the Pecht had been saved and that I had played my part in that victory. It had taken many years, but I had gained my revenge and I was satisfied.

I knew that there was still a great deal to be done, for there were still Northumbrians in many settlements throughout the southern lands, but I would leave that problem to Bridei and to Medraut. There were only two more things I needed to do.

The sun was sinking over the western hills when I arrived at the king's stockade. With most of the warriors having followed the King to war, only a handful of men had been left there to safeguard Bridei's home. They called anxious challenges as I rode up to the gates. I shouted back that Bridei had been victorious, that Ecgfrith and all his nobles were dead. That was met with a loud cheer which rippled through the fort as men dashed off to spread the news.

I went to the stables, repeating my story to the stablehands as I passed Dagger into their keeping. They grinned and laughed, clapping each other on the back. One of them danced around, waving his hands so much that he frightened the horses. I left them to their celebrations and went to find Sorcha.

She was in her room, sitting alone with a solitary candle for company. When I went in, she leaped to her feet and ran to me. Neither of us spoke for a while, we simply held each other. I wiped a tear from her cheek.

"It is almost over," I told her. "Guret is dead. We have our proof. Now I need to find Mayota."

"She is in one of the guest houses," Sorcha said.

"Wait for me."

"I will."

I made my way outside, going in search of Mayota. Bleddyn found me first, intercepting me as I crossed the open yard in front of the roundhouses where I knew the guests were quartered. Staff in hand, he hobbled to me as quickly as he could, calling my name.

"Praise the Lord!" he cried. "You are safe and well."

He threw his arms around me, crushing me in his massive embrace and whirling me around so that my feet lifted from the ground and he almost fell.

"Enough, Bleddyn!" I said. "One of these days you will kill me with your welcomes."

"Tell me all about it," he demanded. "Is it true? Ecgfrith is dead?"

"It is true. Medraut cut his head off." He had put me down now so I picked up his staff and handed it back to him. "What are you doing here?" I asked him.

"Waiting for news of the battle, of course. Tell me what happened."

I said, "I will tell you the whole story later. First, I need to find Mayota."

Dozens of people were now milling around, talking excitedly, some swigging from cups of whisky to celebrate, others asking repeatedly whether the news was true. I called over two of the guards. They came with a bounce in their step, still elated over Bridei's victory. I asked them to take me to Mayota.

"You'd better come, too," I said to Bleddyn.

We found her in one of the larger houses. She was alone, sitting at the dresser, brushing her long, blonde hair. She was wearing a dress of blue-dyed wool, decorated with threads of silver and gold that swirled in intricate patterns from her shoulders to her ankles. I knew she was still very beautiful, but when I looked at her, I saw only ugliness.

She looked up in alarm when the four of us burst into the house. For a moment, she held the hairbrush quite still, frozen on the point of running it through her hair, then she calmly laid it on the wooden dresser and turned on the stool to face me.

"What do you want?" she asked. She was trying to sound like somebody important, as if we had no right to interrupt her, but I think she must have known why we were there.

"The Northumbrians have been defeated," I said. "Bridei has won."

"Yes, I heard people shouting that," she said. "That is good news." She spoke quite calmly, as if it was nothing to get excited about.

"But there will be no victory feast."

She stiffened slightly. "Perhaps that will happen later," she said.

"Perhaps. But you will not be there."

"What do you mean?"

She was nervous now. She hid it well, but I could tell. I said, "Your husband is dead."

Did she smile? I could not be sure. There was only one small, tallow candle burning smokily on the dresser and it was behind her. It may have been my imagination.

With no trace of emotion in her voice, she said, "Then I will need to find another one."

"Not this time," I told her. "Before he died, Guret confessed. To everything."

She was definitely not smiling now, but Mayota was a cool one. "I don't know what you are talking about," she said dismissively.

"Yes you do. I was there. I heard every word of his confession. So did Medraut. He has already informed the king, and will swear to what he heard. You poisoned Derelei. You planned to poison Bridei and to install Drest as king. After a suitable time, you would poison him as well, allowing Guret to replace him."

I could hear Bleddyn and the two soldiers stirring when I said this. Bleddyn muttered under his breath; something about the Whore of Babylon. I paid no attention to them. My gaze was fixed on Mayota.

She remained astonishingly calm. If I had hoped to see her break down and confess, I was disappointed.

"Guret said that?" she asked, her tone full of incredulity. "What nonsense! It is all lies."

"Medraut will swear to it. He only pretended to go along with your plan in order to get Guret to confess. Drest also knew of it. He informed Bridei of your plot."

Haughtily, she retorted, "Medraut is a brutish oaf, and his father is an old fool. They can say what they like. I will swear that it is not true."

"You will swear before God and with your hand on a holy cross?"

"Of course."

She was definitely smiling when she said that. I took a step towards her. "Just as you swore once before that I killed Uerb? Nobody would believe you this time. Do you know why?"

She did not answer.

I said, "Your oath means nothing, because you are not a Christian."

"She will still burn in eternal hellfire," whispered Bleddyn. He sounded as angry as I had ever heard him.

I turned to the guards. "Bring her. If she resists, kill her. The king has declared her a murderer."

They hesitated for a moment, then they saw the look in my eye and crossed the house to Mayota. Taking an arm each, they hauled her to her feet.

Only then did her composure desert her. "Bili!" she cried, "You cannot do this! Please!"

"Bring her!" I ordered the soldiers.

We went to the rear of the hall, past the kitchens and on to the servants' door. I led the way along the corridor to a door that I knew was a small storeroom. I opened it to look inside. There were mops, buckets, brooms, spare pots and pans and an assortment of boxes. It would do. Grabbing Mayota's arm, I ordered the two guards to clear it all out.

"Put everything outside," I told them.

Bleddyn went into the tiny room. Propping his staff against a wall, he began passing the contents out to the soldiers, who carried them along the corridor then dumped them outside.

Mayota leaned in to me, half turning to face me, pressing herself against me.

"Bili," she whispered. "There must be something I can do to change your mind."

I looked at her. She had been born with a face and a body that would let her get her own way, but I was immune to her now.

"No," I said flatly. "There is nothing you could ever do."

Her face contorted into a mask of rage. She tried to slap me, but I caught her arm. She struggled, but I spun her round, wrapped my arms around her and held her tightly, pinning her arms to her sides. When the room was empty apart from a solitary bucket I had told Bleddyn to leave, I threw her inside. She staggered, squealing in outrage. By the time she had regained her balance, I had slammed the door shut. Bleddyn quickly dropped the locking bar into place, sealing her inside.

I said to the two soldiers, "You stay here. Nobody is to speak to her. She is not to be allowed out and she is not to be given any food or water. Nothing. No matter what happens, the door stays shut unless I say so. Is that clear?"

"Yes, lord," they chimed.

"Good. Now, can one of you lend me a knife?"

"What happened to yours?" Bleddyn asked as one of the guards handed me a dark-handled dagger with a double-edged blade.

"Beornhaeth took it," I replied. I put a finger to my eye. "Right here."

"May God have mercy on his soul," Bleddyn said. He sounded sincere but he smiled as he said it.

I gave the guards a final warning that Mayota was to remain in the room. She must have heard me because she banged her fists on the door, shouting, "Bili! Let me out! Do you hear? Let me out!"

I walked away.

The leather hide that covered the door to Fincana's roundhouse was pegged shut. I rapped my hand on the wooden lintel.

"Let me in, Fincana," I called.

"Go away!" came the rasping reply.

I was carrying a small jug of potent heather ale, the top covered by a cloth that was tied around the neck of the jug by a thin string of twisted sinew. I placed the jug on the ground so that I had both hands free, then shoved my fingers into the gap of the doorway. I grabbed the edge of the leather hide and pulled. It was stiff, thick leather, but after I had yanked at it a few times, it began to yield as the pegs came loose. From inside, I heard Fincana screeching at me, threatening to curse me.

Retrieving my jug, I shoved my way through the door. Inside, I saw Fincana standing at the far side of the house, keeping the hearth fire between herself and the door. For once, her head was bare, her hair hanging in long, greasy strands around her shoulders. In her hands, she held a long, sharp knife. It wavered slightly when she recognised me.

"What are you doing here?" she demanded angrily. "Go away."

"I came to see how you were," I told her. "To bring you news of Bridei's victory."

"I have already heard that," she snapped irritably.

"Ah, but you have not heard everything," I said amiably. "Or have you seen it all in a dream?"

"Don't mock me, boy," she warned. She waggled the knife at me.

"Well, I won't tell you if you don't want to know, but I think you will be interested."

"Interested in what?" She still held the knife in front of her, clasped in both hands, but the blade had dipped slightly now.

"In what will happen next," I said. I moved to the dresser. I kept my back to her, letting her see that I was not afraid of her knife. Finding two empty beakers, I poured some of the amber ale into each. The floral-scented, peaty aroma of the ale filled the house. Taking a beaker in each hand, I turned back to face her.

"Let's discuss it over a drink. We have a lot to celebrate."

"Are you drunk?" she asked.

I gave a careless shrug. "I've had a few," I lied. "Here, try some." I held out a mug for her. "From Bridei's own stock," I told her.

I took a swig from my own beaker.

She did not move. "What do you have to tell me?" she asked.

"I'll not tell you anything unless you put that knife down. Come and toast Bridei's success with me, then I will tell you everything."

Slowly, she laid the knife down. I held out the beaker again and this time she took it, although she did not drink.

"It's good stuff," I told her. I took another sip of my own. It was very good.

"So?" she asked. "What news do you have for me?"

I leaned back against the dresser, moving rather unsteadily, as if I was more than a little drunk. I told her what had happened at Dun Nechtan, how Ecgfrith had charged into Bridei's trap and how his army had been slaughtered. Then I told her that she might want to predict that Aldfrith would soon become King of Northumbria. That caught her interest.

"Are you sure of that?" she asked.

"Pretty sure," I replied, tapping a finger to the side of my nose.

"That is information worth knowing," she admitted warily. She took a drink from her beaker.

I had finished my own drink, so I poured some more. Fincana shook her head when I offered her what was left in the jug. She drank again, as people usually do when they refuse an offer of a re-fill.

Putting my mug down, I fished inside my belt pouch. "There is more to tell you," I said. "Guret of Dun Nechtan is dead. But before he died, he admitted that he and his wife were planning to kill Bridei."

Fincana peered at me over the rim of her beaker, holding it still to conceal her reaction while she watched me. She said nothing.

I waited until she had drunk some more, then I passed her the small piece of folded cloth I had taken from my pouch.

"What is that?" she asked.

"I was hoping you would tell me," I said. "I found it hidden among Mayota's things."

Fincana laid down her mug, placed the cloth on her knees and slowly unfolded the edges to reveal a fine, pale powder.

"Well?" I asked.

She sniffed at it, placed the tip of one finger on it and put it to her tongue. She promptly spat it out.

"Not nice, then?" I asked.

"It is a concoction of various poisons," she said.

"I thought so. Would it kill someone?"

"Yes," she nodded. "There is enough here to kill several people if it is mixed with their food."

"She must have been planning to use it to kill Bridei," I said. "I wonder where she got it from?"

Fincana gave me a hard stare. "I would not know," she said coldly.

"Would you know whether it is effective if it is placed in someone's drink?"

"It would kill just as easily, but they would taste it in water."

"But not in heather ale," I said.

Her eyes went to the cup she had drained. "What have you done?" she asked in a horrified whisper.

"Guret confessed everything, Fincana, including where Mayota obtained her poisons."

"No!" She reached for the cup, sniffing at it. She looked at me, hope flaring in her expression. "You drank it, too," she said.

I shook my head. "I took some of the powder out earlier. I tipped it into your cup when I was pouring the drinks. Mine is fine. In fact, it's rather good." I took another drink to prove it to her. Then I said, "Bridei knows everything. You supplied Mayota with the poison that killed Derelei. You supplied her with this mixture, knowing what she intended to do with it. Bridei would not let you live, Fincana. He would drag you out and have you executed in front of the whole town. Your head would be kicked from one end of the town to the other. This way will save you that."

Her voice was little more than a hoarse, throaty whisper. "You have killed me," she wheezed.

"You helped them kill Derelei," I said coldly.

I thought she might try something. I was ready for her to lunge for her knife or to fling herself at me. Instead, she just sat there. I think the poison was already working inside her. I had not known how powerful it was, so I had emptied half of it into her cup. Still, I was careful. I drew my borrowed dagger and I sat watching her closely. I did not want her making herself sick to bring the poison back up or mixing some antidote. I did not know whether either of those things would have worked, but I was not prepared to take the chance, so I sat and watched her until her eyes went wide and she clutched feebly at her chest.

Slowly, she toppled from the stool, crashing to the floor where she lay in a crumpled heap, her breath coming in faint wheezes. I think she tried to say something else, but whatever it was I could not make it out. After a while she stopped breathing.

I waited until it was well after midnight, until I was absolutely certain that she was dead. Then I took the empty jug and walked back up to the king's hall.

Bleddyn was waiting for me at the gates, his face illuminated by the guttering flames of burning torches set on brackets at either side of the entrance. Two sentries were on watch but they were warming themselves by a peat-filled brazier and were more than half-drunk. As I drew near, the pungent smell of whisky reached my nostrils.

Bleddyn looked at me, his eyebrows raised in question.

"It is done," I said softly. "Fincana is dead."

His expression altered to one of concern. "You have taken much on yourself, Bili," he said. "This is the dark road that Bridei warned you of."

"I did what was necessary," I told him.

Bleddyn, of all people, could not argue with that. He led me to one of the guest homes where a small fire was burning low. He fed the dying flames with a fresh block of peat, then we each sat on a three-legged stool beside the stone hearth and I told him everything that had happened since I had last seen him.

I told him how Bridei had concealed Medraut's true role from me, and how Guret had been tricked into confessing his guilt, then I recounted what I could of Bridei's great victory and Ecgfrith's death. His eyes grew misty as he listened, but he laughed when I explained what was likely to happen to Aldfrith.

"Well, lad," he said. "It has taken a long time but, with your help, Bridei has done everything that he said he would do."

"You must be very proud of him," I said.

"Of course I am," he agreed. "And of you, too. I could not have done what you achieved."

I said, "You could have done more if you had wanted, Bleddyn."

"What do you mean?"

"You could have been a warlord, or even a king if you had wanted."

He frowned. "Someone has been talking to you about me, haven't they?"

I smiled at him. "I have known for years, Bleddyn. You are Bridei's older brother."

"Half-brother," he corrected.

"You are a son of Bili of Alt Clud, a grandson of a former king of the Pecht. You could have claimed your birthright. Why did you not do that?"

He gave a slight shake of his head, the way he used to when he was trying to teach me something and I had not grasped the point.

"Well, for one thing, my mother was only a slave. But mainly it was because I was never meant for that life, lad. You know that. Bleddyn Grim-Hand scared me more than he scared any of my foes." He held up a hand, his thumb and forefinger extended, almost touching. "I was this close to becoming a monster, to becoming a person I despised. And that was only in war. I always knew what had to be done, and I did it, without hesitation. But it hurt my soul." He shrugged. "Those decisions were bad enough, but if I had become a chieftain or a king, I would have had to make far more difficult decisions. I would know what needed to be done and I would have ordered it done, but I knew that such decisions would cost other men their lives. I don't think I could have borne that responsibility. Not the way Bridei can."

Echoing Bridei's words, I said, "Sometimes, those who lead must make difficult decisions. They must put the good of the people above their personal desires."

Bleddyn nodded. "I knew as soon as I met Bridei that he was the sort of man who could take those difficult decisions. He may be younger than me, but he is much better suited to achieving greatness."

"Perhaps he is," I said. "But I think you are a great man, too."

"As are you, Bili. But when we are both long dead, it will be Bridei's name that is remembered, not yours or mine. Men will carve stones to commemorate his victory, and monks will write about him in their annals, but only Bridei will be remembered."

"Does that bother you?"

"Not in the slightest," he grinned. "Let men like Bridei and Medraut have the glory. You and I must be content with knowing that we have done what we could to help. And when we face Saint Peter at the Gates of Heaven, we will be able to show some good deeds to offset whatever sins we may have committed."

"I am not sure that I have ever done any good deeds," I said.

"Then tomorrow would be a good time to start. What do you intend to do with the rest of your life?"

"I will get married and raise a family," I told him.

"Really? Do you have any particular woman in mind?"

I laughed. "Don't pretend you don't know, Bleddyn. You can marry us in your church."

"That would be an honour," he said. "I must say that I think your choice is rather better than the last wife you picked."

"She is," I assured him. "But now that you mention my last wife, I must do one more thing."

Bleddyn looked at me gravely. "You do not need to do anything, Bili," he said softly.

"Yes, I do, Bleddyn. An eye for an eye."

As the first rosy fingers of dawn were climbing into the eastern sky, I left Bleddyn and made my way to the kitchens. The cooks and maids were already hard at work, preparing breakfast for the king's household. Cooking fires had been lit, corn was being poured into the quern stones for the daily grind to produce flour for baking. The first hot loaves were already being pulled from the large ovens, filling the long room with the wonderful aroma of fresh baking.

The kitchens were always busy. Even without the king and most of his warriors, there were still plenty of mouths to be fed, although I suspected that, after the celebrations of the previous evening, more than a few people might oversleep that morning.

I ordered salted porridge for the prisoner. One of the cooks served it up into a small, wooden bowl, adding a small spoon before handing it to me. I turned away. While the cook returned to stirring the pot, I poured the rest of Fincana's powder into the bowl, mixing it in with the spoon. I hoped that the salt would disguise the taste.

Sorcha was waiting for me in the hallway. She held out her hands.

"Let me take it," she said.

"Are you sure?"

The expression on her face was more determined than I had ever seen before.

"Very sure," she said.

I gave her the bowl, then I signalled to the guards to open the door. When they pulled it open, I watched Sorcha take the bowl inside. I heard her tell Mayota that this would be her only meal until evening, then she came back outside. The guards quickly closed the door and replaced the locking bar.

Sorcha and I went to her room where we sat side by side on the bed, holding hands. I told her everything that had happened since I had ridden south to find Ecgfrith. When I had finished the tale, including what I had done to Fincana, she squeezed my hand. Then we sat in silence for a long time, taking comfort from each other.

After an hour had passed, I went back to the small room.

"Open the door," I said to the guards. "I want to speak to her."

They pulled the door open.

Mayota was lying on her side, stretched out on the floor, her eyes blank, one arm clutched to her chest, the other extended towards the door. The bowl lay beside her. It was empty.

"What happened?" one of the soldiers asked.

I picked up the bowl, sniffing at it. "Poison," I said. "She must have had some hidden away. We should have searched her."

"Damn shame," the soldier said. "Fine looking woman like that taking her own life."

"She was a cold-hearted murderer," I said. "Perhaps it is better this way. It will save a lot of trouble."

His eyes moved from Mayota to the bowl, then to my face. If he suspected anything, he had the sense to keep his thoughts to himself.

Taking one final look at Mayota, I walked out of the room. I left her there, the last of my enemies. I could not find it in my heart to feel any remorse for killing her. Bleddyn had taught me how to do what needed to be done. I had learned the lesson well.

Sorcha stood in the hallway, dressed as usual in her long dress, her apron and headscarf. I went to her and took her hands.

"It is over," I said. "I am ready to stay at home now. Will you come with me?"

"What about the boys?" she asked.

"They can come too. I have already asked the king."

Her eyes were sparkling with happiness as she said, "Then I will gladly go with you."

She reached up to kiss me but I held up a hand.

"There is one condition," I said.

She blinked in surprise. "What condition?"

I pointed to her headscarf. "You must wear your hair down from now on."

Laughing, she reached up to pull the scarf from her head, letting her hair fall free.

Author's Note and Acknowledgements

The Battle of Nechtansmere, also known as the Battle of Dunnichen, was fought in the year 685 A.D. In terms of its importance in securing the independence of the nation that was eventually to become Scotland, it ranks alongside Bannockburn, yet very few people have ever heard of it. This may have something to do with the fact that the Picts ultimately lost the struggle for dominance of northern Britain and were gradually absorbed by the Scots. Nechtansmere was a Pictish victory and therefore it was perhaps of less importance to the later ruling classes of Scotland. However, if it had not been for Bridei III's stunning victory over Ecgfrith, the northward expansion of the Anglo-Saxon kingdom of Northumbria may well have continued unchecked and the nation of Scotland may never have come into existence.

    The battle has been traditionally associated with the village of Dunnichen, near Forfar in Angus but, with apologies to my friends at the truly excellent Pictavia Centre, I have followed a more recent and very persuasive theory which places the battle much further north, at Dunachton, near Loch Insh in Badenoch. This theory also places the Pictish kingdom of Fortriu in Moray and Aberdeenshire rather than Strathearn and Angus. No doubt the debate over the true locations will continue.

    Wherever the battle was fought, it was a tactical masterpiece by Bridei. There is no suggestion that any spies, or what we would term double-agents, were involved but there was certainly a feigned withdrawal which lured Ecgfrith into a trap where his army was destroyed and he himself killed. The details, though, are very scanty and, for the avoidance of any doubt, the account of the battle as related in this story is entirely fictional.

A consequence of placing the battle and the kingdom of Fortriu further north is that I have extended Northumbrian influence throughout the southern half of Scotland, as far as the southern fringes of the Highlands. There is no doubt that the Angles reached the Forth-Clyde line, but whether they did, in fact, extend their rule further north is open to debate. It would, however, make some sense of the northerly site of the Battle of Nechtansmere if the Angles had taken control of most of Lowland Scotland.

As for the series of events mentioned in the story, Ecgfrith did destroy a Pictish army at a Battle of Two Rivers. The site has yet to be identified but I opted for the Earn and the Tay as being in keeping with Northumbrian expansion up the eastern coast.

Bridei III became king of the Picts the following year, after Drest had been deposed, with Bridei's reign seeing a gradual resurgence of Pictish power.

There are records of sieges at Dunnottar and Dundurn in the years preceding the Battle of Nechtansmere. While the details of who was besieging whom, and whether the sieges were successful, are not known, they are often associated with Bridei. If he was involved, then strong candidates for his opponents at Dunnottar would be the Angles of Northumbria.

At this point, I should mention that my description of the fort at Dunnottar is entirely imaginary. Although the remains of at least one Pictish wall have been found on the site, the present Dunnottar Castle dates from much later. There is a cave on the north-west side of the headland and I am told that there are rumours of a secret access route from there to the castle, although it has never been found.

As for Dundurn hill, near Loch Earn, it is still strewn with massive rocks which once formed part of the immense stone fortifications of this strategically important hillfort.

Bridei's unexpected victory at Nechtansmere saw the beginnings of a rise in the fortunes of the Picts who, over the following century, became the dominant power in northern Britain. This dominance was to last until the Viking onslaughts of the 9th century which changed the whole political balance of the British Isles.

Bridei continued to rule the Picts until 694 A.D. when he was succeeded by a man named Taran who reigned for only four years, being followed by a man whose name is recorded as Bridei, son of Derelei. In 709 A.D., this Bridei was in turn succeeded by Nechtan, son of Derelei, who was presumably his brother.

Here, I must make some comment on the widespread belief that the Picts had a matrilinear succession, where sons inherited from their mothers rather than their fathers. This is a convention I followed in my previous novel, "In the Shadow of the Wall", but the evidence for it is not as clear-cut as it is often portrayed. The monk Bede mentions it in his "History of the English-Speaking People" but Bede never ventured from his monastery at Jarrow and must have heard this second-hand at best. Certainly the often contradictory Pictish King Lists never show a son succeeding a father, but there may be other reasons for this. It has been suggested that some of the names detailed on the King Lists - of which Derelei is one - may be the names of the kings' mothers rather than their fathers, thus adding weight to Bede's statement. However, it is not entirely impossible that the Picts elected their kings, which view could be supported by the fact that Drest was deposed rather than killed in 672 A.D.

In my story I have combined these two theories to explain the strange succession pattern recorded in the earliest King List. The truth may be that Derelei was a male name rather than female as I have used it in this story, but we will probably never know for certain. My only excuse for manipulating the few known facts in this way is that it fitted the story I wanted to tell.

Another aspect that was of major importance in the seventh century was religion. Saint Columba and Saint Ninian are credited with being the driving forces in the conversion of the Scots and the Picts, but whether that conversion was wholesale remains a matter of debate.

Equally, the motives of those who were converted can perhaps be called into question. Certainly the new religion did nothing to prevent the various peoples of Britain from attempting to slaughter one another on a regular basis. This even extended to the monks themselves. For example, Saint Columba left Ireland to begin his missionary work in Scotland as a voluntary exile following his involvement as an instigator of (and presumably a participant in) the Battle of Cul Dreimhne. The fictional character of Bleddyn may not be too much of an exaggeration after all.

Another convention regarding the Picts is that the name derives from the Latin, "Picti", meaning, "The Painted Ones". Again, I have followed this traditional view in an earlier story, but for this book I wanted to show that the Picts were not savage barbarians and I therefore followed a more recent suggestion that the name Picti derives from a Roman misunderstanding or misinterpretation of the name the Picts called themselves, which may have been something like, "The Pecht". Again, we will probably never know which theory is correct, but I wanted to show that Pictish society could have been every bit as sophisticated as the Anglo-Saxons of the south.

Pictish carved stones show details of kings and warriors wearing armour and riding horses. The people represented in this way could not have done this without a society that was capable of producing metalwork, of breeding horses, of clothing, feeding and housing every member of that society. We also know that they had the skills to build sea-faring ships, as evidenced by the record stating that Bridei "destroyed" the Orkneys. This, combined with the magnificently detailed carved stones and the exquisite jewellery they have left behind, prove that, whatever else they were, the Picts of the 7th Century were not merely blue-painted savages.

Finally, some ardent Scots may think that I have been unkind in my portrayal of their ancestors. I can only plead guilty. However, the Annals of Ulster, and other ancient texts, do record almost constant strife among the various clans of Ireland and what was then known as Dal Riata, so perhaps my interpretation is not too far from the truth. What is true is that I wanted to tell a story from the Pictish perspective because the Picts have, rather unfairly in my view, been relegated to a minor role in the history of Scotland. I hope that this story will go some small way to help redress the balance.

There are few records available that document events in northern Britain during the 7th Century. Those that do exist are often vague. In my research for this story, I have therefore relied heavily on the books of modern historians. In particular, the various works of Stuart McHardy, Alistair Moffat and Alex Woolf. I must also thank Jenny Sharp of the Pictavia Centre for her invaluable help and support.

    I also owe thanks to Moira Anthony for reviewing the various manuscript drafts and for providing the photograph for the book cover. Thanks also to Stuart Anthony and Moira Gee for providing feedback and comment on the initial draft. Stuart also provided invaluable topographical information thanks to his extensive walking trips. Maintaining the family connection, the book cover design is due to the graphic editing skills of my son, Philip.

GA
January, 2012

Other Books by Gordon Anthony

All titles are available in e-book format. Titles marked with an asterisk are also available in paperback.

In the Shadow of the Wall*

Hunting Icarus*
Home Fires*

The Calgacus Series:
World's End*
The Centurions*
Queen of Victory*
Druids' Gold*
Blood Ties*
The High King*
The Ghost War*
Last Of The Free*

The Constantine Investigates Series:
The Man in the Ironic Mask
The Lady of Shall Not
Gawain and the Green Nightshirt
A Tale of One City

A Walk in the Dark (Charity booklet)

ABOUT THE AUTHOR

Born in Watford, Hertfordshire, in 1957, Gordon's family moved to Broughty Ferry in the early 1960s. Gordon attended Grove Academy, leaving in 1974 to work for Bank of Scotland. After a long but undistinguished career, he retired on medical grounds in 2008 without having received any huge bankers' bonuses.

Registered blind, Gordon had more time on his hands after retiring so, with the aid of special computer software, he returned to his hobby of writing and had his debut novel, "In the Shadow of the Wall" published in 2010. Gordon's books are now being read by a world-wide audience. As well as his historical adventure stories, he has ventured into crime fiction with some spoof murder mysteries in the "Constantine Investigates" series. He is also kept busy with speaking engagements, visiting libraries, schools and community groups to talk about his books.

In addition to his novels, Gordon devotes some of his time to raising funds for the RNIB. As well as visiting schools and social clubs to talk about his sight loss, he has self-published a charity booklet titled, "A Walk in the Dark", a humorous account of his experiences since losing his eyesight. The booklet is available free from Gordon's website www.gordonanthony.net All Gordon asks is that readers make a donation to RNIB. This booklet can also be purchased from the Amazon Kindle Store. Gordon will donate all author royalties to RNIB.

Now completely blind, Gordon continues to write stories and, in his spare time, attempts to play the guitar and keyboard with varying degrees of success.

Gordon is married to Alaine. They have three children and one grandchild. The family lives in Livingston, West Lothian.

You can contact Gordon via his website or by sending an email to ga.author@sky.com

Printed in Great Britain
by Amazon